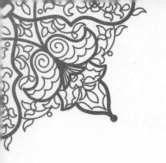

THE SKY WEAVER

KRISTEN CICCARELLI

HARPER TEEN

An Imprint of HarperCollinsPublishers

Also by Kristen Ciccarelli
The Last Namsara
The Caged Queen

HarperTeen is an imprint of HarperCollins Publishers.

The Sky Weaver

Copyright © 2019 by Kristen Ciccarelli

All rights reserved. Printed in Germany.

No part of this book may be used or reproduced in any manner whatsoever without
written permission except in the case of brief quotations embodied in critical articles
and reviews. For information address HarperCollins Children's Books, a division of
HarperCollins Publishers, 195 Broadway, New York, NY 10007.

www.epicreads.com

ISBN 978-0-06-256805-2

Typography by Michelle Taormina

20 21 22 23 24   CPIG   10 9 8 7 6 5 4 3 2 1

❖

First paperback edition, 2020

For Jordan Dejonge: no matter how far apart we are, I take heart knowing our roots are forever planted in the same soil.

Eighteen Years Previous

Skye was only a child the first time she watched them put a traitor on trial. She saw them take the man's hands. Saw the blood run swift and dark over the stone altar as the soldier wiped his blade clean, like a storm sweeping over a sapphire sea.

Skye remembers the way the severed hands twitched like crushed spiders dying on their backs, thin legs curling inward. Remembers the way the enemy stared at the stumps of his arms as the blood ran down to his elbows.

Remembers how he screamed.

That was a lifetime ago. Tonight, they'll put another traitor on trial. Skye is waiting in her cell. Because it won't be an enemy's hands they take this time—it will be Skye's hands. And she has only herself to blame.

Be a good girl. Keep your head down. Remember your place.

These were the words she lived by once. The lessons instilled in her since birth.

That was before she met Crow. A boy from the shadows undid all her lessons. He undid everything.

Crow. Like a swallowed thorn, the name stings her lips and tongue and throat.

How could she be so naïve?

Skye will tell you how. She will weave you a tapestry while there's still time. It will be her last weaving. Because once the moon rises and they come for her, Skye will weave no more.

You can't weave without hands.

One

Eris had never met a lock she couldn't pick.

Lifting the oil lamp, she peered into the keyhole, her wheat-gold hair hidden beneath a stolen morion. Its steel brim kept slipping forward, impeding her vision, and Eris had to shove it back in order to see what she was doing.

The wards inside the lock were old, and from the look of them, made by a locksmith who had cut all possible corners. Any other night, Eris would have craved the challenge of a more complicated lock. Tonight, though, she thanked the stars. Any heartbeat now, a soldat would round the corner. When they did, Eris needed to be on the *other* side of this door.

The lock clicked open. Eris didn't let out her breath. Just slid her pin back into her hair, rose to her feet, and wrapped her slender fingers around the brass knob, turning slowly so as not to make a sound.

She glanced back over her shoulder. The hall lay empty. So Eris pushed open the door and stepped inside.

Holding up the lamp, its orange glow alighted on a simple desk made of dark, scuffed wood. An inkwell, a stack of white parchment, and a knife for breaking wax seals were neatly arranged on top.

Eris shut the door gently behind her. Her gaze lifted from the desk to the object hanging on the wall: a tapestry woven of blue and purple threads. The very thing she'd come for.

Eris knew this tapestry by heart. It depicted a faceless woman sitting at her loom. In one hand, she held a silver knife curved like the moon. In the other, she held a spindle. And on her head sat a crown of stars.

Skyweaver.

The god of souls.

But it wasn't just the image that was familiar. It was the threads themselves—the particular shade of blue. The thickness of the wool and how tightly it was spun. The signature way it was woven.

The moment Eris glimpsed it from the hall two days ago, she nearly stumbled. Every morning for years, this tapestry stared down at her from stone walls flanked on either side by the sacred looms of the scrin—a temple devoted to the Skyweaver.

What was it doing here, in the dragon king's palace, all the way across the sea?

Someone must have stolen it, she thought.

So Eris decided to steal it back.

She had some time, after all. Her captain—a heartless man named Jemsin—was currently meeting with the empress of the Star Isles. It was why he sent Eris here, to steal a jewel from the dragon king's treasury. Not because he needed the money. No. He needed Eris out of sight while the empress and her Hounds came aboard his ship—for his sake as much as hers. If it was ever found out that Jemsin harbored the very criminal the empress had been hunting these seven long years, it would mean death for both Eris and her captain.

But Eris had already stolen the king's jewel. And she still had a day before needing to report to Jemsin's protégé. She had some time to waste.

So here she was, wasting it.

Eris pushed herself away from the closed door and set the oil lamp down on the dark wood of the desk. The moment her gaze lifted to Skyweaver, there was that sharp shock she'd felt two days ago. Memories of warmth, friendship, and belonging flooded her . . . quickly followed by feelings of terror, grief, and betrayal.

She narrowed her eyes.

"I'm not doing this for you," she told the god as she reached to untie the tapestry from where it hung on the wall. "As far as I'm concerned, you're a traitor and a fraud." She kept her voice low, knowing the security had been doubled since the king's jewel went missing two nights ago. "I'm doing this for the ones you betrayed."

Eris no longer believed in Skyweaver, god of souls. But the one who'd woven this tapestry believed in her—and he'd died for that belief. So, lifting it down from the wall, Eris rolled it up tight, then tucked it carefully under her arm. As she did, she plucked the gray, spiny scarp thistle from the pocket of her stolen uniform. Careful not to prick herself on its thorns—which were poisonous—she set it down on the desk.

In some ways, the signature was more for Eris than the ones she stole from. A way of proving to herself that she did, in fact, exist. She might live an invisible life, but she was still *here*. Still alive.

The scarp thistle was proof.

With the tapestry still under her arm, and her signature there on the commandant's desk, Eris reached for her spindle. It was time to go. She would take this tapestry and put it with the rest of her loot. Then she'd head for the *Sea Mistress* and wait for her summons.

But before she could pull the spindle free of its pouch, a voice behind her broke the quiet.

"Who let you in here?"

The voice was low and gruff and it made Eris freeze—except for her right hand. Her fingers tightened around the smooth, worn wood of her spindle, slowly drawing it out.

"I asked a simple question, soldier."

Soldier.

Eris had forgotten she was in disguise tonight. With the heightened security, it was easier moving through the palace dressed like a guard.

So Eris turned. A soldat stood in the doorway. He hadn't quite stepped into the room, clearly startled by the sight of her, but he wore the same uniform she did: a steel morion on his head and the dragon king's crest across his shirt. The only difference was that a saber hung from his hip, while a woven pouch hung from hers.

Eris hated soldiers.

"I was sent to remove this ratty old thing," she lied, nodding her chin toward the tapestry of the god of souls, rolled up beneath her arm. She winked as she said, "Apparently our commandant isn't exactly the pious type."

Her wink had the desired effect. The soldat relaxed. He smiled then, leaning against the door, seemingly about to remark on the commandant's piety or lack thereof, when something on the desk caught his eye.

Eris watched his face go blank, then light up with recognition. Looking where he looked, she silently cursed herself.

The scarp thistle.

"You . . . you're the Death Dancer."

He didn't wait for her to confirm it. Just drew his weapon.

Time to go.

Eris gripped the spindle hard in her hand as she crouched down. As the soldat stumbled into the room, she pressed the spindle's edge to the mosaicked floor and drew a straight line.

The line glowed silver. The mist rose.

The soldat lurched toward her, calling for help and alerting the other soldats nearby.

But by the time he rounded the desk, Eris was already stepping into the mist, and beyond it.

By the time he reached for her, Eris was already gone.

When the mists receded heartbeats later, Eris was not where she should be.

Instead of being *Across*—surrounded by stars and darkness—she was surrounded by walls. A dark hallway spread before her, lit every few paces by flickering torchlight. Beneath her feet lay that same mosaicked pattern as the room she'd just left. And it smelled like mint and lime.

She was still in the palace.

Eris gritted her teeth in annoyance.

It happened sometimes. If she was concentrating harder on the place she was trying to leave rather than the place she was trying to get to, the spindle would get confused and blunder up the crossing.

Eris was just about to curse the godsforsaken splinter of wood when something slammed into her from behind, hurtling her forward and causing her to drop the spindle altogether.

"Kozu's balls!" She spun, watching the spindle roll toward two black leather boots with silver buckles polished to a shine. A hand reached down, picking it up, and as the newcomer rose, so did Eris's gaze.

The young woman before her was dressed like a palace guard. Only instead of the king's crest, a flame-like flower blazed across her shirt. She wore no morion, and tucked into her belt were five throwing knives.

"Apologies, soldier." The young woman's voice was hard and commanding. The voice of someone used to giving orders—and used to her orders being obeyed. "I didn't see you there."

Eris's gaze snapped to eyes as cold and blue as sapphires. The torchlight made it impossible not to notice the girl's strong cheekbones or ink-black hair braided away from her face.

Eris knew who this was.

The commandant.

This young woman before her was not only cousin to the king—and therefore royalty—she held that same king's army in her fist.

A dark memory flickered in Eris's mind of another cold commander. Fear pooled in her belly. She shook the memory off, stepping back. But the sharp sliver of it lodged in her chest, reminding Eris of who she was. That she needed to leave this place.

Now.

Except her spindle was currently in the commandant's hand.

The young woman's gaze moved over Eris quickly and dismissively. It made Eris stiffen. She should have been glad the commandant found nothing of interest in the girl standing before her. Eris wanted—no, *needed*—to be invisible.

For some reason, though, that indifferent glance rankled her.

The commandant's lips parted, as if she were about to say something, when a shout echoed from down the hall, interrupting. Making them both turn.

More and more voices joined the first. The soldat Eris had just left was alerting the entire palace to the thief in their midst.

It was an alarm.

Eris waited for the truth to dawn on the commandant's face the way it had with the soldat. But the commandant was no longer looking at Eris, only frowning in the direction of the alarm.

"That Death Dancer." Her eyes were sharp with ire. "If he thinks he can steal from the king without consequence, he has no idea who he's dealing with."

Eris should have kept her mouth shut. This commandant had her spindle, after all. Her only escape.

But Eris couldn't help herself.

"How do you know it's a *he*?"

The commandant looked straight at her then. Eris shivered under that cold gaze. *Stupid,* she thought, even as she stared into the girl's eyes. *What a stupid thing to say.*

The commandant studied her as the alarm grew louder in the distance. On her face Eris could clearly see the need to respond to the alarm warring with . . . what? Wariness? Suspicion?

Any moment now, she's going to figure it out, draw her weapon, and arrest me.

But the commandant did none of those things. Instead, she held out the spindle, her eyes seeing Eris now, taking all of her in. "You dropped this," she said.

Eris swallowed, staring at the elegantly carved spindle lying on that callused palm.

Is this a trick?

When Eris reached to take it, though, the commandant's hand fell away. She turned on her heel. "Come on. Let's see what that cocky bastard has done this time. . . ."

Concentrating on the alarm now, the commandant failed to notice that Eris didn't follow.

The moment she strode away, Eris crouched down to draw a silver line across the floor.

Cocky? she thought, working quickly.

It felt like a challenge.

She shook her head. She couldn't let herself get distracted this time. She needed to pour all of her focus into her destination.

As Eris finished drawing the line, the air grew thick and damp. The mist billowed up. But the sound of those diminishing footsteps drew her attention back. Eris paused, watching the commandant turn the corner. Watching her disappear from view.

Eris rose to her feet. Before putting Firgaard and the palace and that girl out of her mind, she thought: *I'll show her just how cocky I can be.*

And then she stepped across.

Two

Ever since the door to the king's treasury was found open and a bright red ruby missing, Safire hadn't been able to sleep.

Someone had walked the halls of *her* palace, slipped past every single one of *her* guards, entered a locked door, and stolen the very ruby King Dax intended to give the scrublands tomorrow. One that would be sold and the profits divided to help remedy the starvation caused by the blight—one known as the White Harvest. Years ago, it had spread like wildfire through the scrublands, destroying all their crops, cutting off their main sources of food. Every season, farmers would try again, but the blight would only infect the new harvests, driving the people further and further to the brink of starvation.

Safire knew things were getting worse, but it wasn't until Queen Roa returned from her last visit home that Safire realized how dire the situation really was. Roa's father was now bedridden. Unbeknownst to her family, he'd been going without food for some time now, so that those less fortunate than him could eat. But it wasn't only Roa's father who was at risk of starvation—her best friend, Lirabel, was also chronically malnourished due to her pregnancy. The physician told Roa if they couldn't get access to substantially more food, and quickly, Lirabel would lose the baby.

When Roa returned to Firgaard, even Safire had seen the change in her. She looked exhausted and frail. At meals, Dax cast worried glances her way whenever she refused to eat— because how could she, when her loved ones were starving to death?

They needed a permanent solution, and quickly.

Dax planned to sell the ruby in the royal treasury—a jewel that once belonged to their great-grandmother—and use the profits to buy meat and vegetables and grain to supplement the weekly rations Firgaard was already sending, in hopes of keeping starvation at bay.

The fact that someone had stolen the jewel without a second thought? It was intolerable. Unforgivable.

It made Safire tremble with fury.

There was only one clue left behind: an ugly gray thistle. Safire had never seen anything like it, with its stem littered with thorns, some as long as her smallest finger and nearly half as thick. So she showed it to the palace physician.

A scarp thistle, he told her. *It grows on the scarps of the Star Isles. A single thorn carries enough poison to make a person sleep for days.*

More than both of these things, though, it was the mark of a criminal. A thief known as the Death Dancer because he walked through walls, was uncatchable, and constantly eluded death. He'd been haunting the halls (and treasuries) of barons and kings for years.

Well, thought Safire that day, *he won't elude me.*

So she'd doubled the guards and started patrolling the palace herself.

Now, two days later, she stood staring down at a *second* scarp thistle. Only this one lay on her own desk, behind her own locked door.

As the soldats in the room around her whispered to themselves, all of them watching their commandant, Safire's eyes lifted to the wall beyond it.

This morning, a tapestry hung on that wall. It had been a gift from Asha, her cousin. The tapestry was gone now. The plaster wall stripped bare.

The thistle on her desk told her the thief had taken it.

Why?

Safire's eyes narrowed. She understood the king's ruby. It was worth more money than most people saw in a lifetime. But a ratty old tapestry? What could possibly be the value in that?

Unless, thought Safire, *he's trying to taunt me.*

And then, suddenly, that young soldat's lilting voice rang through her mind.

How do you know it's a he?

Safire's stomach twisted.

She'd been in such a hurry, she'd thought nothing of the girl's morion—which, now that she was thinking about it, was far too big for her and shielded half her face.

But there were other things, too.

The soldat carried no weapon, and she spoke with an unfamiliar accent. Safire had never heard a lilting voice quite like hers. It was almost . . . lyrical.

Not to mention that rolled-up bundle tucked beneath her arm.

Safire froze, thinking back to that bundle. The old, fraying threads. The considerable size.

It was a tapestry.

Her tapestry.

The one Asha had given her.

Safire sank down in her chair. "That thieving bastard."

Safire tripled the guards. She stopped leaving the palace and remained on patrol through the night. The next day, despite her vigilance, the king's seal went missing from Safire's drawer. The day after that, Safire left her rooms only to return and find every single one of her uniforms gone. And in their place? Scarp thistles.

It was enough to make a person lose her mind.

Safire now had a collection of the gray thistles sitting in a glass jar on the windowsill of her bedroom. When she was feeling particularly broody, she would lock herself in and glare at them for hours, trying to think of a solution to this infuriating problem.

"I don't think she's a threat," said Asha as she picked out a rock lodged in Kozu's claw. The First Dragon stood over her like a shadow while Safire lay in the warm grass beside them, staring up at the indigo sky.

Where they sat, the former hunting paths ended in a scrubby field surrounded by forest. To the north, a huge round tent was pitched, and between them and the tent several dragons prowled, all of them being trained by hopeful riders. Safire could hear the clicked commands from where she stood.

These were the dragon fields. Asha hoped to build a school here—one that would simultaneously preserve the old stories while repairing the damaged relationship between draksors and dragons.

"A thief who can walk through the palace halls completely undetected doesn't sound like a threat to you?" Safire asked, her hands cradling her head.

Asha set Kozu's foot down, thought about it, then shook her head. "This one doesn't."

Safire sat up and crossed her legs. "Please explain."

Kozu—an enormous black dragon with a scar through one eye—nudged Asha's hip with his snout, as if to tell her something. But whatever passed between them was a mystery to Safire.

"She sounds . . . bored," said Asha, rubbing the First Dragon's scaly neck. "Like she's tired of being the cleverest person in the room. What if she's *provoking* you because she needs a challenge?"

Safire frowned at this. "Do you think I should give her one?"

Asha left Kozu and came to sit in the grass. Her black gaze held Safire's. "*Can* you? Right now she seems three steps ahead of you."

Safire bristled at this.

Seeing it, Asha leaned forward. "All you need is to get *one* step ahead."

Propping her elbow on her knee, Safire rested her chin on her fist. "And how do you propose I do that?"

In the rising heat, Asha began undoing the brass buttons of her scarlet flight jacket. Dax had it sewn especially for Asha, to mark her as his Namsara. As Asha shrugged it off, the buttons flashed in the sun and Safire leaned in, squinting, to find that each brass orb was impressed with the image of a flame-like seven-petaled flower—the namsara, Asha's namesake.

"These are the things you know about her," Asha said, laying her new jacket down beside her, then ticking fingers off her burned hand as she spoke. "She's brash—there's no room in the palace she won't break into. She steals things that have monetary value—the ruby, Dax's seal. And she steals things that are valuable only to *you*—like the tapestry I gave you and your uniforms."

Asha leaned back, planting her palms on the red-brown earth beneath her. "So," she said thoughtfully, looking out over the dragon fields, "what is the brashest, most valuable thing she could possibly steal from the king's commandant?"

They both fell silent, thinking.

Safire didn't have any valuables—other than maybe her throwing knives, which were a gift from Asha. She might have royal blood running through her veins, but there had been nothing royal about her upbringing. Safire didn't like to think about the time before the revolt, when she was kept out of sight, forbidden to touch or even stand near her cousins, taunted and abused while the palace staff looked the other way.

Just as she was shaking off the memories, a sound issued from across the field.

It was a series of quiet, nervous clicks familiar to both Safire and Asha, who looked up. Across the grassy plain, away from the commotion of the dragons and their riders, a tall, thin boy with coppery hair and freckled skin made his way toward them.

Torwin.

Several paces behind Torwin walked an ivory-scaled dragon with one broken horn. He stepped warily, casting his gaze ahead and behind, looking like he would bolt at the slightest irregular movement. Safire knew this dragon. His name was Sorrow.

Several weeks ago, while Asha and Torwin were collecting old stories in Firefall—a city west of Darmoor—they'd found this half-starved creature chained in the courtyard of a wealthy home, with an iron muzzle locked around his jaws. He'd been severely abused by the children of the house, who were keeping him as a pet.

As a result, Sorrow let very few people get close. He stayed deep in the Rift mountains and never came near the city. Asha didn't think he'd ever pair with a rider, because he was so mistrustful of humans. A few had tried, but the bond that normally formed in first flight never took.

As Torwin stepped toward the two cousins, then sat down in the dirt next to them, Sorrow crept toward Kozu, whose hulking black form was curled in the sun, soaking up the warmth. Sorrow's ivory scales were a sharp contrast to Kozu's obsidian.

"Everything's packed," said Torwin. He held a large knife in his hands, its silver sheath embossed with intricate star patterns. "If we leave at dawn, we should arrive before sundown."

Despite having just returned from Firefall, Asha and Torwin were flying to the Star Isles tomorrow. The reason for their trip was currently gripped in Torwin's hands: the Skyweaver's knife.

The weapon had saved Roa's sister a few weeks previous, and Roa now wanted it returned to where it came from. She believed it was too dangerous an artifact to keep here in Firgaard. So Asha and Torwin had gone through the accounts of the last man who'd bought it—one of Firgaard's wealthiest barons—and tracked down its history to a place called the scrin.

"If Roa wasn't so insistent, I'd drop this thing to the bottom of the sea and be done with it," said Torwin, sliding the blade out of the sheath just enough to reveal the silver-blue blade concealed within. He shivered. Looking up, he squinted through the sunlight. "Are you sure you don't want to come with us, Safire?"

"Come? To an archipelago known for its monsters, tempests, and ship wreckers?" Safire wrinkled her nose, thinking of the treacherous waters of the Silver Sea. "I think I'll pass. Besides, Roa and Dax will be joining you in a few days."

The empress of the Isles—a fearsome woman named Leandra who was rumored to be deathless—wanted to present the new dragon king and queen with a gift. One that Leandra hoped would help the dire situation in the scrublands. As Dax's Namsara, Asha had been invited to the empress's citadel, too, but she'd turned down the invitation.

I don't have the time or the interest in rubbing shoulders with foreign monarchs, Asha told Safire when the invite came. *That's Dax's role.*

"Someone has to be the responsible one," Safire said. "Someone has to stay behind to ensure this city doesn't fall apart."

Those were her official reasons for remaining in the capital. But as she spoke them, she thought of the criminal prowling through the palace like it was her own personal playground.

Safire would never leave Firgaard at the Death Dancer's mercy.

Torwin, as if sensing her thoughts, said, "Caught that thief of yours yet?"

Sighing, Safire fell back into the grass. "No."

That was why she was here on the dragon fields. The king's commandant was running from her own failure. She'd hoped to have the Death Dancer locked in a cell by now. Instead, the criminal continued to elude her.

Sometimes she felt a . . . presence. In the middle of the day or the night. In the palace or in the street. Watching her. Trailing her. But when she turned, knife in hand, all she found was shadows. Sometimes, when she entered a room, she couldn't shake the sense that her thief had been there just a heartbeat before. It felt as though they were playing a game of cat and mouse.

Only Safire wasn't sure who was the cat and who was the mouse.

She needed to catch this Death Dancer. She wanted to see the look in the thief's eyes when she locked her up for good.

Once she did, she could go back to sleeping through the night.

"Saf's beginning to believe the rumors are true," said Asha.

Torwin shot her a look. "Rumors?"

"They say the Death Dancer is uncatchable," Asha explained. "That she's half god, half shadow."

Safire closed her eyes, letting the sun warm her face as she thought of Asha's idea. One step ahead . . . a trap was what she needed. But with what could she bait it?

"Well," Torwin said, "if anyone can catch her . . ."

His voice trailed off. Safire waited for him to finish, but the silence continued. And then, even with her eyes closed, Safire felt it: a cold darkness sliding across her face. It smelled like musk and smoke.

She opened her eyes.

The dragon called Sorrow stood over her. Ivory scales. Broken horn. Black eyes staring down into hers.

It amazed Safire how much sadness she always found in the depths of those eyes.

Normally, her first instinct would be to reach for her knife. But Safire knew what it was like to be at the mercy of brutes. She knew the horrible things that had been done to this creature and how little it took to frighten Sorrow.

So she lay still, forcing herself to relax.

Beside her, Torwin and Asha were tense and silent.

What they didn't know was that when Safire couldn't sleep, she liked to walk the hunting paths up into the Rift. Most often, they took her here—to the dragon fields. The fields were always bare beneath the stars, the riders gone, the dragons sleeping somewhere in the hilly terrain. All except one: Sorrow.

With no one else around, Safire told the dragon stories. Not old stories, though. Not the myths of gods and heroes Asha was so good at, the ones the dragons liked best. Safire didn't know many of those. Instead, she told Sorrow the stories that kept her up at night.

She told him about being the daughter of an unlawful union and, as such, growing up forbidden to be touched. She told him about the revolt she helped lead—a revolt that put her cousin Dax on the throne. She told him about the day that same cousin made her his commandant.

And then, whenever she finished telling a story, they played a game. It involved Safire stepping as close as possible, and Sorrow standing as still as he dared.

Sorrow always bolted before Safire came close enough to touch.

That was why, when Safire reached her hand slowly toward the dragon's ivory snout now, she expected Sorrow to flinch and run.

Except Safire hadn't flinched when she'd opened her eyes. Hadn't reached for her knife. And Sorrow sensed it—Safire's instinct, as well as the suppression of it. Sorrow was doing the same now.

The dragon trembled with the fear of being touched, but he didn't run.

When Safire's fingertips touched the warm scales of Sorrow's snout, her skin prickled. She felt the effort it took the dragon to keep himself still. Safire held her breath as more and more of her skin came in contact with the dragon's scales. Soon, Safire cupped Sorrow's snout and the dragon's warm breath was moist on her palm.

Sweet boy, she thought. *How could anyone want to hurt you?*

And then, like the wind changing, Sorrow jerked away. Safire froze, but the dragon only lifted his head, turning into the wind. Sensing or smelling or hearing something Safire herself couldn't. She sat up, looking where Sorrow did.

Safire felt it then—that same feeling that haunted her footsteps through the palace: that tingling sense of being watched.

Sunlight flickered through the dark green boughs of the forest's edge, the trees bending in the wind.

"What is it?" Asha whispered.

Safire rose, striding toward the cedars, thinking of the Death Dancer. She was about to plunge into the pines when the strange pitch of her cousin's voice stopped her.

"Saf . . ."

Safire turned to find both Torwin and Asha watching her with worried eyes. Only Sorrow still scanned the trees.

"What?"

"Some time away from Firgaard might be good," Asha suggested. "It would only be for a few weeks. Surely your soldats are too well trained to let Firgaard fall to pieces in so little time."

Safire was about to point out that they themselves had led a revolt in less time, breaching Firgaard's walls and dethroning the former king. But Torwin interrupted.

"Come on, Saf," he said, stepping toward her. "You haven't been able to rest since Dax promoted you."

Safire hadn't rested since long before that. She couldn't afford to rest.

"Come with us," urged Torwin, throwing an arm over her shoulder as he smiled that half smile of his. "Have a little faith in your soldats. Let *them* catch this Death Dancer while we're in the Star Isles. I'm sure when we return, she'll be waiting for you in a cell."

Not likely, thought Safire as her fingertips tapped each hilt of her throwing knives. The feel of them, there at her hip, calmed her a little. And as she did, Asha's question echoed through her mind.

What is the cockiest, most valuable thing she could possibly steal from you?

Suddenly, Safire knew the perfect thing to bait a trap for the Death Dancer.

"I should get back," said Safire, already thinking of a plan. Sighing loudly, Torwin dropped his arm. Safire looked from him to her cousin. "Be safe, all right? No flying in bad weather."

Asha nodded, then pulled her into a hug. Safire squeezed her back.

When Asha let go, Safire turned to Sorrow.

"And you be good," she told the dragon.

Sorrow only tilted his head, watching Safire back away through sad, silent eyes.

"Good luck with that thief of yours!" Torwin called after her.

Safire nodded, waving. The dried pine needles crunched

beneath her feet as she headed for the hunting path. But as she made her way down through the Rift and toward Firgaard's gates, she couldn't shake the sense that someone was dogging her, keeping just out of sight.

Whenever Safire turned to look, as ever, she found nothing but shadows.

Three

Go to Firgaard. Steal the king's jewel. Report to Kor in three days.

Those were Eris's orders. The job was long since done now. And yet she hadn't reported to Jemsin's protégé: a pirate named Kor who who was in charge of Eris while Jemsin met with the empress.

It was foolish. Way too risky. But after four days of playing games with the commandant, Eris wasn't quite ready to give up. A raven had followed her through Firgaard's streets earlier. Eris panicked at the sight of it until she realized its eyes were black, not red. That it wasn't Jemsin's summoner; it was just a boring old bird.

Still, its presence was enough to scare Eris. And her fear was a reminder: it was time to go.

She had one last thing to do before she left. Because the commandant was right: Eris *was* a cocky bastard. And more than the triumph of eluding Safire was the pleasure that came with knowing just how furious Eris made her.

The anger showed every time Safire spoke about her.

Every time she *thought* about her.

The knowledge of that brought Eris a rush of irrational pleasure.

Eris smiled to herself now as she stood behind the terrace curtains of the commandant's bedroom, keeping herself hidden. She knew the commandant's routine by now. You didn't creep through the palace without memorizing the movements of the person in charge of its security first. Eris knew when Safire retired for the evening. So she waited.

But as she fingered the stem of the scarp thistle in her hand, tracing the thorns, she started to have second thoughts. Why *was* she still here? She should have headed straight for the sea after stealing that ruby. She should be heading for it now.

She was four days late reporting to Kor's ship, the *Sea Mistress.* She couldn't stay here much longer. To do so was to tempt the captain's wrath.

Forget the knife, said a voice inside her. *Step across now and head for the* Sea Mistress.

But something else—something stronger than her fear of Jemsin—rooted Eris to that spot behind the commandant's curtain. Maybe it was nothing more than recklessness, but Eris wasn't leaving until she got what she'd come for.

There was a time when, tired of his abuse, she had tried to escape her captain. That was before she knew better. The first time Eris ran, she got as far as Firefall—a city on the south shore of the Silver Sea—before Jemsin's summoner found her and dragged her back to his ship, the *Hyacinth*—where several lashes and a week without food or sunlight awaited her.

She tried twice more. Both times, she was caught. Both times, her punishment was more severe than the last. She carried the scars still—on her wrists and ankles, and across her back.

Eventually, Eris stopped trying.

After all, things could be much worse.

Jemsin was a monster, but if not for him, she wouldn't be alive. He'd kept her safe from the empress before, and would do it again. That counted for something.

Suddenly, the door clicked but didn't open all the way.

Eris held her breath, listening, as two voices issued into the room. One belonged to the commandant; the other she didn't recognize. Eris glanced out the window, to the starry sky above Firgaard. It was well past midnight.

Who would she be bringing back to her room?

A sweetheart? Eris wondered. Her stomach turned over at the thought.

But when the door opened wider and the commandant stepped inside, Safire stepped in alone.

The moment she did, her strong posture softened. Her shoulders folded in. And just like that, she wasn't the commandant. Wasn't the proud cousin to the king.

She was just a tired girl.

Through the lace edge of the curtain, Eris watched Safire light the lamps, then move through the room. She disarmed herself first—unbuckling the saber at her hip, then the belt holding her throwing knives. She set both of these down on a tabletop near an arching window, then slid off her boots and undressed, donning a pale blue tunic that fell almost to her knees. The last thing Safire did before getting into bed was slide a slender, decorative throwing knife out of the knot of hair at the back of her head. This she hid under her pillow before blowing out the lamp flame.

That was the knife Eris had come for.

The sheets rustled. The wood creaked. And then: silence bled through the room.

Eris remained still as a shadow while her sight adjusted to the darkness, waiting for the right time to strike. It wasn't long before the commandant's breathing changed: deepening and evening out.

As soon as Eris was certain Safire was asleep, she stepped out from behind the curtains.

This bedroom was far simpler than the king's and queen's rooms—which Eris had crept through simply to slake her curiosity. After the king and his sister, Safire was next in line for the throne. Eris expected lavish furnishings and fine silks. But Safire's room was small, her bed even smaller—not big enough for even a bedfellow.

Eris cloaked herself in shadow as she slunk across the room, awash in the silvery-blue night. Her footsteps made no sound as she stepped up to the bedframe. She should have reached immediately for the knife beneath the pillow. It could have been quick and easy. Over in an instant. But as she stood over Safire's sleeping form, Eris . . . hesitated.

The commandant looked so different asleep. Her black hair spilled like ink across the pillows. Her skin was much fairer than her two cousins' and her pale brown fingers curled gently against her cheek. She looked not at all like the fearsome soldier who snapped and snarled and doled out orders. She seemed . . . young. Too young. Like a sapling that hadn't quite taken root.

Eris stared, drinking in the sight of her.

It was only when the girl stirred that Eris remembered why she'd come. She set the scarp thistle down on the bedside table, and then—gently, slowly—slid her hand beneath the pillow.

Soon, her fingertips brushed the cool steel of the commandant's favorite throwing knife. Eris knew it was Safire's favorite, because she'd spent the past few weeks trailing her like a shadow.

When you watched someone as closely as Eris watched Safire, you couldn't help but notice things.

Carefully, Eris pulled the knife out from beneath the pillow. She stood there for several heartbeats, running her fingers over the decorative hilt, smiling a little as she did.

The moment Eris turned to leave, however, something tightened around her ankle.

Eris looked down. It took several heartbeats before she could make out what it was.

A loop of slip-knotted rope. One made of twisted silken sheets that appeared to snake beneath the bed.

Shock made Eris go still. Had it been there all along? Before Safire even entered the room?

Had Safire *anticipated* her coming here tonight?

"Who are you?" came that voice from behind Eris. The cold

tip of a blade pressed into the back of her neck, digging into the skin.

Eris felt a tug on the silk rope and knew the other end was gripped firmly in the commandant's hand.

This was a trap. One set for *her*.

A torrent of conflicting emotions washed through Eris. If she wasn't already late reporting to Jemsin, she might have been flattered.

But she *was* late. And while the raven following her through Firgaard's streets today might not have been Jemsin's summoner, it wouldn't be long before his summoner *did* arrive.

A low and steady panic hummed within her. She needed to get out of here.

"Who am I?" Eris said without turning, lifting her hands to show she meant no harm . . . all the while trying to determine just how far away Safire was. "I'm just a petty thief."

Safire's voice was low and dangerous as she said, "How did you get in?"

If Eris reached for her spindle, would the movement provoke Safire? She swallowed, casting her gaze through the moonlit room, trying to think of how to put space between her and this girl long enough to open the way across.

She stalled for time.

"How did I get into the palace? Or into your *bedroom*?" Eris asked the second question a little huskily, just to irritate Safire.

The pressure on her ankle tightened as the blade against the back of her neck dug in hard, drawing warm, wet blood. Eris bit her lip at the prick of pain.

"*Both*," Safire growled. Clearly sick of Eris's games, her voice rung with authority now. "Drop the knife. Then turn around slowly and answer my question."

Eris chewed her lip. Safire hadn't looked upon her face since the day they'd run into each other in the hall—right after Eris stole the tapestry from the commandant's office. Remembering the dismissive look in those blue eyes, Eris steeled herself. She dropped the knife, which clattered against the tiles at her feet, then slowly turned.

Safire stood in nothing but a tunic. Eris's gaze trailed up the girl, whose dark hair was loose around her lean shoulders. In one hand was a knife, held to Eris's throat now. Her other gripped the end of the makeshift rope.

When Eris met her gaze, she was surprised to find a sliver of admiration in Safire's eyes—hidden beneath loathing and disgust, of course, but admiration nonetheless.

It made Eris want to do something drastic.

Something *reckless*.

"Answer my question." Safire repeated herself, narrowing her eyes. "How did you get in?"

Eris smiled, thinking of the rumors she'd heard about herself. Lowering her voice to a whisper, she leaned in, as if to tell Safire a secret. "Didn't you know the Death Dancer can walk through walls?"

Safire took a careful step toward Eris, like a predator warily approaching prey. "You think you're clever?" she said without breaking her gaze. "You think you impress me?"

Eris's smile fell away.

"I deal with criminals like you by the *barrelful*. Every day." Those blue eyes narrowed. "Trust me, Death Dancer. You're just another delinquent with nothing better to do than bring chaos to people's lives."

Safire took another step, moving in so close Eris could almost feel the heat of her body next to her own. "Do you know where people like you end up?" she said, drawing the steel of her knife gently across Eris's skin, softly tracing her collarbones. Suddenly, her voice went flat. "You end up alone and forgotten in the belly of a dungeon. Which is exactly where I'm putting you."

Maybe it was the assumption beneath Safire's words—that she was used to having the upper hand and thought she had it now. Or maybe it was the threat of her locking Eris up and forgetting about her—forever. Like she was nothing.

Either way, it would not do.

"I'd rather rot in a cell full of honest criminals than walk free among you and your ilk," said Eris, her knuckles bunching.

Safire stared as if Eris were mad. "You consider thieves and murderers *honest*?" She shook her head. "You're delusional."

But Eris wasn't finished. "You helped King Dax *steal* a throne. Isn't that why he made you his commandant?" She sneered at the thought. "And that cousin of yours—the *Namsara*—didn't she kill a man to make her brother king? Sounds a lot like thieving and murdering to me. And yet here you all are, sleeping in silken beds, eating off silver platters, doling out judgments on everyone but yourselves."

That steel was back against her throat, pressing hard. It

brought Eris out of herself—out of her fury—and back to reason.

The longer you stay here bickering with this girl, the worse your punishment from Jemsin will be.

At the thought of Jemsin, one of his lessons rose to Eris's mind. From the early days when he'd first made her part of his crew. When she was yet too young to realize the monster he really was.

The bent elbow forms a point, you see? He'd shown her using his own arm. *It fits perfectly below the enemy's ribs.*

"The former king was a tyrant," Safire was saying, her voice sharp with warning. As if speaking against the commandant and her cousins was a felony in itself.

Never fight fair, the captain's voice rang through her mind. *You understand? That's not how you stay alive.*

"I'm not judging you for killing him, princess. I'm just wondering. . . ." Eris kept her gaze locked with Safire's as she clenched her small fist. "Can it truly be justice when those who enforce the laws are the only ones exempt from them?"

Safire's nostrils flared.

Before she could lash out, Eris punched—right where Jemsin showed her, all those years ago. Into the soft place beneath the girl's ribs.

The air whooshed out of Safire as her eyes went wide. She doubled over in shock, her knife falling away from Eris's throat, gasping for a breath that wouldn't come.

Eris wasted no time. She took several steps away from the bed, then ran, diving beneath it and alongside Safire's makeshift rope, grabbing the dropped knife as she did. Her slight frame slid swiftly and easily to the other side, putting half the room between her and Safire within heartbeats.

Only half recovered from Eris's punch, the commandant yanked on the rope, but there was too much slack now. Nothing happened.

Eris bent down and slashed the silk with Safire's knife.

It severed easily.

Fingers trembling, Eris withdrew her spindle from its pouch and immediately drew it across the floor tiles. The night seemed to deepen. A bright line—pale as starlight—flared to life. It quickly formed a threshold over which silver mist poured and rolled. The air turned damp, cold, and with it came the gentle pull of *Across*.

It was then, with the door to another place yawning open before her, that Eris hesitated a second time.

Rising to her feet, she looked across the room to where Safire stood in her nightdress: her nostrils flaring, her mouth pinched with fury. Fully recovered.

I'm going to miss playing this game with you, Eris thought. The commandant had proven to be a formidable opponent.

"It's been fun, princess. But I have to go."

Safire moved, coming around the bed now. Coming straight for Eris. "The only place you're going is into a prison cell, thief. . . ."

The mist swirled, concealing her now.

"Good-bye," Eris said softly, stepping into the gray. Leaving the commandant behind. Trading the palace of Firgaard for a path of mist and starlight.

She heard Safire begin to say something else, but the words were lost. Which was how Eris knew she was already a world away.

When the mist receded and Eris opened her eyes, she was alone.

But that was all right. Eris was used to being alone.

Loneliness was a small price to pay for staying alive.

The Shadow and the Fisherman's Daughter

Once there lived a boy with eyes as black as the sea, hands as swift as the wind, and footsteps as silent as death. He was a creature of the shadows who walked through the world alone and unheard and unseen.

But the fisherman's daughter saw him.

Whenever he passed by her father's wharf, Skye shivered. Each time she looked up, she saw the shadow moving through the meadow. Curious, she stepped away from the women of the cove and the codfish drying on the salt flakes, and followed him.

The first time, she followed the lonely shape of him for three days. By the time he turned around and saw her, Skye was weak with hunger.

The shadow recoiled at the sight of her.

Skye knew what she looked like. Her body was too small, too slight, too bony. Her eyes were set too wide apart and one of them always looked in the wrong direction.

She'd been born too early. No one had expected her to live. Skye looked down at her knobby hands, studying them as if for the first time. Seeing what he saw.

The shadow scowled. Before he could tell her to go away, though, she looked up at him with her one good eye.

For such a frail thing, she had a fierce gaze.

"What's your name?" her small voice asked.

He shook his head, annoyed by her presence. He didn't have time to indulge the whims of mortal creatures. They were nothing more than soon to be ghosts; their finite little lives beginning and ending in the span of a sunrise.

"I don't have a name," he told her.

"Then I'll call you Crow."

"Call me whatever you like," he said, turning away. It wouldn't matter. He would never see her again. He would make a point of walking more silently past her father's wharf next time.

"Crow," she said, and her voice pinned the word to him like a spell. "Where are you going?"

"Somewhere you can never come." And with that, he slipped into the shadows, into nothing, leaving the fisherman's daughter alone.

A month later, as he was walking at dusk, Crow heard familiar footsteps behind him. Turning to look, he found the crooked-eyed Skye trailing after him through the cliff-top meadow.

"What are you doing?" he growled at her, his pace quickening.

"Coming along."

He spun. "No!" This time, he spoke with the voice of the sea—thunderous and terrifying. After all, Crow had only to breathe on her and she'd crumple like a pile of sticks.

Skye took a step back, quivering.

But she did not stop.

Again and again, when he walked past her father's wharf, or through her cove, or up the cliffs looming above her house, Skye saw and followed him.

He bellowed at her. Threatened her. Chased her back.

Just when he thought he was rid of her, there she was. Again and again and again. Always a little older than she was the time before.

Finally, he gave up. Gave in. Stopped trying to lose her in the shadows. Instead, when he heard those familiar fragile footsteps, he slowed and let her catch up.

In the beginning, he ignored her endless nattering as she spoke about everything under the sky. But days turned to weeks, and though he wasn't sure how or when it happened, he found himself lulled back from dark thoughts by the sound of her voice. Again and again, he found himself drawn to her knowledge of the winds and the tides and the skill of her small hands—rowing her dory through an angry sea; pulling nets full of shimmering fish into her father's boat; and, most especially, weaving rough spools of wool into beautiful webs of color. Tapestries, she called them.

More than anything else in the world, he learned, Skye loved to weave.

But things from the shadows did not make friends with mortal girls. And fishermen's daughters grew into women. Women who fell in love with mortals just like them. Mortals who bore children and grew old and eventually stepped through Death's cold, dark gate.

And yet, Crow waited for her.

Worse still, he began to seek her out.

Four

The *Sea Mistress* was moored just north of the Rif Mountains, about a day's sail from the port city of Darmoor. The moment she stepped aboard, Eris went to report to the pirate Kor, as per Jemsin's orders. Kor's cabin door was closed and she could hear the faint sound of muffled voices within. Not wanting to risk his temper by walking in on something, Eris handed over her spindle to Rain, the first mate—something Kor insisted on. She told Rain to inform Kor that he could find her belowdecks when he finished.

Kor was Jemsin's precious protégé. A year after the scrin burned, Jemsin found Kor beaten half to death by a dockhand in Axis's port. Kor was thirteen at the time, and the dockhand was his father. Jemsin killed the man and took Kor, raising him like his own son and turning him into a formidable pirate. Jemsin's crew grumbled about the favor he bestowed on Kor. Thirteen-year-old boys were half-grown men and less moldable than children, they said. He should have been more careful.

They were right. When Kor turned eighteen, he started showing signs of dissatisfaction. It wasn't enough to be part of Jemsin's crew, obeying Jemsin's orders. He wanted his own crew. He wanted to *give* orders.

Kor was an investment Jemsin couldn't afford to let spoil. So he gave Kor his own ship—with the understanding that Kor would continue to do his bidding. He would patrol the waters Jemsin wanted him to patrol. He would attack the ships Jemsin wanted him to attack. He would come to Jemsin's aid when requested. In order to ensure Kor's obedience, Jemsin gave him a crew full of spies. That way he could keep an eye on Kor from a distance, enabling him to get word if Kor ever planned to stab him in the back.

Fully aware of the spies in his ranks, Kor bided his time, sniffing them out and slowly winning them over, making promises better than the ones Jemsin made. Now, two years later, his crew was fully his own—a fact Jemsin knew, and one that made him nervous.

But other than outright killing Kor, there was nothing Jemsin could do. Kor hadn't done anything to provoke such an action. Not yet, anyway.

It was only a matter of time, though. Because the more power Kor tasted, the more he wanted. One day, Kor would break free of Jemsin. Eris knew this. So did Jemsin. But before Kor made his final move, he wanted one more thing. Something Jemsin would never give him.

Kor wanted Eris.

As she lay in her borrowed bunk, Eris listened to the wind

howl and the hull of the *Sea Mistress* groan. The single lantern in this cabin swayed, casting light back and forth across the dark room as she studied the slender throwing knife in her hands.

She'd been gripping it in her fist when she stepped across.

It was different from the other knives the commandant kept sheathed in her belt. The blade was thinner and more delicate. The hilt was more ornate.

As Eris ran her fingers over it, she thought of the commandant alone in her room—her trap dismantled, her criminal gone.

Strangely, it brought Eris no pleasure this time.

The sudden sound of heavy boots clomping down the stairs made Eris go still. She'd barely sat up when the cabin door swung open, and the glow of her lantern illuminated the young man standing there.

He had a square face and deep-set eyes. Long dark hair was pulled back from his shoulders and the pale cotton shirt he wore was wrinkled, the cuffs undone. His left ear was missing, cut off by his father in a rage when Kor was only five. In one hand was the neck of a bottle. In the other, two copper cups.

Her stomach turned over at the sight of him.

"Kor," she said, forcing a smile as she lowered the knife in her lap.

"Would you look who it is. Jemsin's little pirate thief. Four days late." Kor grinned thinly as he stepped into the cabin, kicking the door shut behind him. He set the bottle and cups down on the overturned supply box in the corner. "I'm assuming you have it?"

"Have it?" asked Eris, watching him uncork the wine.

He stopped and looked back over his shoulder, shooting her a puzzled look. "The loot Jemsin told you to steal."

Right. Eris shook her head. She'd stolen the king's ruby so long ago now—was it a week already?—she'd forgotten it was the thing Jemsin sent her to Firgaard for. "Of course I have it."

That strange look didn't leave his face as he turned back to the wine and started to pour. "Well, what took you so long?"

I got distracted, she thought as she slowly traced her thumb along the hilt of Safire's knife. "I took my time," she said instead. "Didn't want another run-in with the empress. Or her dogs."

When Kor turned and offered her a full cup of wine, Eris was tempted to refuse. She didn't like taking things from Kor. Didn't like owing him anything. Kor had a mean spirit and a temper. But Eris was under strict orders from Jemsin to do what was needed to keep Kor on his quickly fraying leash.

Kor wanted Eris—for more than just thieving. Therefore, so long as Eris remained with Jemsin, Kor would remain with Jemsin too. It was one of the reasons the captain made her report to Kor so often. Made her stay aboard Kor's ship—where her spindle was locked away, keeping her bound and defenseless until Jemsin summoned her for her next assignment.

Please him, Jemsin told Eris in no uncertain terms. *Keep him close.*

So she took the wine Kor offered her.

But she didn't drink it.

For a heartbeat, she wondered if she might be able to slip a pinch of scarp thorn powder into Kor's cup without him noticing. It was how she'd drugged the guards in Firgaard's palace, enabling her to walk undetected into the king's treasury.

"You know, I've been thinking." Kor sat down on the bunk across from her. Eris's fingers tightened around the cold copper, mentally measuring the space between them. "Thinking about how the captain always seems to send you away whenever he's meeting Leandra."

This time, Eris did drink—just a sip—if only to have somewhere to look other than Kor's eyes. Which were staring hard at her now. No one but Jemsin knew who Eris really was: the fugitive the empress had been hunting for years now.

Eris and Jemsin had a deal: he would never reveal her or hand her over to the empress so long as she did his bidding. She had to steal whatever he wanted her to steal. And, more recently, she had to keep Kor biddable, too.

But the presence of the empress's army—soldiers called *Lumina* because they "illuminated" her law—had increased on the Silver Sea these past few years. Eris feared Jemsin wouldn't be able to keep her hidden forever.

If she could have run, she would have. She'd get as far as the southern isles, or maybe farther, just to be out of Leandra's reach. To be free and safe.

But the three times she'd tried it, Jemsin's summoner always found her. It always brought her back.

"It's almost as if Jemsin doesn't want you and Leandra to cross paths," said Kor thoughtfully. "As if he's afraid she'll know who you are and take you away from him."

Eris froze, looking up into his hard eyes. *Has he figured out who I am?*

He laughed then. "Can you imagine it? Jemsin losing his precious Death Dancer to the woman he despises? I would pay to see that."

Eris tried to relax. Kor didn't know who she *really* was. He thought of her only as the Death Dancer—a thief.

"I'd rather be owned by a pirate than a monster," she said.

"Is there a difference?" Kor lifted his cup.

Eris forced herself to lift her own, clinking it against his.

They both drank.

Eris wiped the wine from her lips and then set the cup down on the floor. Thinking of his closed door, she asked, "Who was in your cabin tonight?"

He raised one dark brow. "Why? Are you jealous?"

Ugh. No. Not in a thousand years.

Kor took another sip. "Kadenze was there."

Fear rippled through her as Eris thought of the creature who did all of Jemsin's summoning. Red eyes. Black talons. A voice as old as the sea.

It was Kadenze who'd located her all three times she tried to escape.

According to the cook on the *Hyacinth*, who liked to tell Eris stories when she helped him wash up after dinner, Jemsin killed Kadenze's former master and took the bird for himself. Kadenze was an ancient creature, sung about in old sailor's ballads, said to be capable of tracking down three things: treasure, enemies, and the blood of immortals.

"Jemsin wants us in Darmoor," Kor said. "Both of us."

Another assignment? That was good. It would keep Eris away from the sea—and those hunting her on it.

It would also keep her out of Kor's reach. He tended not to toy with her when there was a mission occupying him.

"What does he want us for this time?" she asked, picking up Safire's stolen knife and running her hands over it again. The cool steel had a calming effect.

"Didn't say. Just that he expects us there by tomorrow."

Kor talked on, but Eris was no longer paying attention. Because this time as she traced the knife, her fingers found something new. When she raised the blade, trying to catch the lantern light, she found something embossed in the steel: a pattern of fiery-looking flowers.

"Tides, Eris. Would you *listen* to me?"

She had just leaned in to examine the pattern when suddenly, the knife was gone. Snatched out of her hands by Kor.

"What are you fidgeting with?" He squinted at the knife.

Annoyance broke like a wave through Eris. She reached for it. He jerked it out of the way.

"Give it back, Kor," she said through gritted teeth.

"Gilt handle," he murmured, ignoring her as he studied the weapon. "The owner must have a good deal of coin—or at least connections. And the flower pattern is very pretty. Delicate, you might even say. A girl's knife?" He looked up to see if he was correct.

Inexplicably, Eris felt her cheeks heat.

"Whose is it?"

"It's mine now, you sandeater."

She lunged for it. Kor pulled away, getting up off the bed.

"Give it back!" she said, rising with him. But that's where she paused.

Kor was twice her size and twice as strong. Eris was faster, lighter, trickier. But the cabin was too small to move well in, and the ship rocked over the waves, making it difficult to stay steady.

"I'll give it back . . ." Kor smiled too calmly, his gaze taking in too much. "*If* you give me something first."

Eris's stomach twisted. Her body hummed with hate. She knew what he wanted.

She also knew she would never give it to him.

Seeing her answer on her face, his own darkened.

"There's no chance it took the legendary Death Dancer seven days to steal that ruby. What were you doing the rest of the time, Eris? Meeting with a sweetheart?"

A sweetheart? She would have laughed, but he took that moment to lunge for her. With the bed to one side and the cabin wall to the other, she had nowhere to move.

He grabbed her shirt, pulling her toward him.

Before he could do worse, Eris kneed him in the groin.

The ship lurched. Kor stumbled back, dropping Safire's blade and wincing hard.

"Bitch." He spat the word as Eris snatched up the knife before it slid across the floor. Her hand shook as she gripped the hilt, pointing it at him. She was no good with weapons, and Kor knew it. He also knew that without her spindle—which was currently locked in a box somewhere aboard the ship—she couldn't step across.

With Kor blocking the cabin door, there was no escape.

But the scariest thing? Eris didn't think about all the ways she might possibly get out of this unscathed. Instead she thought about what Jemsin would say.

Kor was cunning and cruel and power hungry. He'd be a dangerous enemy if he ever turned against Jemsin. It was Eris's job to keep Kor cooperative and loyal and close.

Kor might hurt her if he got his hands on her, but the captain would hurt her worse if he lost his dominance over Kor.

"You're not so formidable now, are you Death Dancer?" Kor gripped the door handle, still weak from the blow she'd dealt him.

Eris kept the knife steady. Her heart pounded in her temples. Her breath came quick and fast.

"Without that spindle, you're nothing. Just a helpless . . ." His words trailed off. He smiled, his eyes lighting up with a sudden thought. "That spindle. What would happen if I accidently used it for kindling, I wonder?"

Eris went cold. "You wouldn't," she said, even though the look in his eyes said the opposite. "Jemsin would kill you."

"Or, useless as you'd be to him, he'd kill *you*."

He turned the doorknob. Eris moved then, throwing herself at him. But he'd already opened the door. Her shoulder collided hard with wood as he shut it on her. She heard the sound of clinking keys. She grabbed the handle, trying to wrench it open.

The door was locked.

"I'll come back for you when it's over," he said through the wood.

Eris's rage grew within her like a tempest's screaming winds.

And that's when she remembered . . .

She still had the pin in her hair.

✦ ✦ ✦

Eris didn't think about Jemsin this time or what the conse-
quences would be. She just took the eight steps up to the deck,
Safire's stolen knife gripped in her hand.

The crisp cold turned her breath to fog. The wind caressed
her face. The stars shone down, lighting her path across the
wooden planks.

Eris followed Kor into the galley. An oil lamp glowed on the
table while he pushed aside pots and pans, then pulled something down from the shelf next to the hatch.

It was a crude pewter box. Big enough to hold her spindle.

Eris crept toward him, silent as a shadow. As he turned the
key in its lock, she readied her knife. When he lifted the lid,
Eris struck, stabbing him in the back, just below the ribs. She
shoved the blade in and twisted. *Hard.*

Kor screamed.

The box fell, taking the spindle with it. Eris pulled out the
knife just as Kor turned to face her. He touched the wound,
then stared down at the blood coating his fingers as he stumbled
back against the shelf.

"How did you . . . ?"

Eris didn't hear him as she picked up her spindle. She turned
to leave, but at the sight of the oil lamp burning on the table,
she stopped, considering it.

Behind her, Kor was screaming again. Screaming at her this
time. She felt the heat of his rage. Heard him push away from
the shelf, coming toward her.

Before he got within reach, Eris swung out her arm,

knocking the oil lamp to the floor.

The glass broke.

The oil spilled out.

The galley floor went up in flames.

At the sight of it, a memory flickered within her. Of another time and place. Of flames that raged, eating away at a place she'd once called home.

Kor stumbled back, away from the fire, and the movement pulled Eris out of the memory. He stared—first in bewilderment, then in fear.

Eris left him there. She stepped out onto the deck gripping the bloody blade in one hand, her spindle in the other. She could have crossed right then. She probably should have. But there was another lamp burning just above the galley. And there was something so soothing about chaos. Something almost beautiful.

Alerted by Kor's screams, the crew began to stagger up out of their cabins.

But not before Eris unhooked the lantern and threw it across the deck.

It shattered. Fire spluttered up, released from its confinement. As if in a rage, it devoured the wooden planks, moving toward the sails.

But Eris still didn't step across.

Instead, as the crew panicked around her, she stepped up to the side of the ship, cut the only rowboat free of its ropes, then pushed it into the waters below. From across the deck, her gaze caught Rain's. The first mate's hair was a red, tangled mess as she screamed for everyone to get topside and put out flames. At

the sight of Eris escaping, Rain's eyes went black. *You are dead,*
she mouthed.

Not tonight, thought Eris as she swung herself over the side
and dropped, landing on one of the rowboat's benches. Sitting
down, she secured the oars in the oarlocks, then started to row,
taking the only means of escape with her.

And there she watched the *Sea Mistress* burn.

The red flames gorged themselves. The smoke curled
through the sky, leaving a trail that blotted out the stars above.
And all the while, Eris rowed.

She would make her way to Darmoor. And if Jemsin wanted
to kill her when she got there . . . well, it wouldn't be the first
time.

Five

Three days later, in the darkest corner of a rowdy inn called the Thirsty Craw, Safire sat at a table alone. Her ink-black hair was hidden beneath a sandscarf, she wore no uniform, and her weapons were concealed beneath her clothes. She frowned at the scarp thistle pinched between her fingers, careful not to prick herself on its poisonous thorns as she thought about her last encounter with the one who'd left it beside her bed.

One moment, the thief was right there in her room, caught in Safire's trap. The next moment, she was . . . gone.

Safire had tugged on the rope—fastened out of her own bedsheets—to find it cut. She reached into the space where the thief had disappeared, but there was nothing there.

She'd considered afterward whether her thief was a ghost. But a ghost couldn't steal a knife. And there was that strange scent, just before she disappeared. Like the salt sea in a storm. Powerful. Charged.

Ever since that night, the palace had been quiet. There were no more thefts. No more scarp thistles. It was as though the Death Dancer had well and truly gotten bored and moved on to more interesting heists. As if Safire had failed to meet her expectations. Had failed to *challenge* her.

Safire set down the thistle. She needed to let it go—as Dax had told her numerous times in the past three days. She needed to turn her mind to other things—like the fact that the deadliest pirate on the Silver Sea was rumored to be in Darmoor.

It was why Safire was here, instead of back in Firgaard.

She'd heard stories about Jemsin and the unspeakable things he did to his enemies (and sometimes his allies, too). Things like torturing prisoners until their minds broke and carrying out kidnappings where—once the ransom was paid—the kidnapped came back with one less hand. Or eye. Or lung.

If the pirate was in Darmoor, there had to be a reason. She needed to find out what that reason was, and if it had anything to do with Dax and Roa setting sail for the Star Isles tomorrow. Once the king and queen were out on the water, they'd be less easy prey, since there were several dragons flying with them.

It was the time they spent in port that Safire worried about.

So she passed the day trawling the slick cobbled streets of the port city studying the ships in the harbor, eavesdropping on gossiping dockhands, and—after coming up with nothing—planted herself in the seediest inn she could find, watching and listening for any hint of pirates in the harbor.

But she heard not a word of Jemsin, his crew, or his ship—the *Hyacinth*. So perhaps her source had gotten the details wrong. Or perhaps it was a rumor.

Safire tipped back her now-cold tea, swallowed, then rose to her feet.

She was stepping out the door and onto the street when she bumped shoulders with someone on their way in.

A familiar scent enveloped her. Sea salt and lightning. It was the same smell that filled her room the night her thief escaped for good.

Safire's footsteps slowed.

The Death Dancer? Here?

Safire recalled the two times she'd come face-to-face with the thief. She had piercing green eyes, a small stature, and kept her wheat-blond hair knotted at the nape of her neck. The first time, she'd been dressed like a soldat. But the night in Safire's bedroom, she'd been dressed all in black. Like a shadow.

"Tell Jemsin his *dog* is here to report, will you?"

Safire knew that voice. It was the same voice that mockingly called her *princess*. Her pulse sped up.

A gruff voice replied, "Tell him yourself, Eris."

The door swung open and shut.

Eris? thought Safire. *Is that her name?*

Turning slowly, she found the stoop of the Thirsty Craw empty. Her heart pounded in her chest. Not only was the Death Dancer inside the inn, but Jemsin was in there, too?

She nearly smiled at her good luck.

To keep from being seen by the thief—*Eris*—she waited outside. Then waited some more. Finally, Safire retraced her steps back to the door. She would find out exactly where they were meeting in this inn and what their plans were. Once she did, she would return with her soldats and catch two notorious criminals in one night.

Breathing in deep, Safire pushed the door open and followed the Death Dancer in.

Six

When the truth of what she'd done set in, Eris thought of running. She'd stabbed Kor in the ribs without caring that wound might kill him. She'd set fire to the *Sea Mistress* and taken the only rowboat without considering that some of the crew might not know how to swim. The smart thing to do was to run. But if she ran, Jemsin would send every pirate on the Silver Sea after her—not to mention his summoner. So here she was, crawling back to port like a dog to her master. Wanting to bite, but knowing it would only earn her a swift kick in the ribs.

Eris moved like a thundercloud through Darmoor's rain-soaked streets. It had been nearly three days since she'd left the *Sea Mistress* burning on the Silver Sea. Which was plenty of time for Jemsin to get wind of the news. When Eris closed her eyes, she could still see the sails going up in flames. Could still feel the acrid sting of smoke in her lungs.

That memory flickered again, of the last time she'd watched something burn.

She shoved the image away.

Whatever punishment Jemsin had in store for her, it was better to get it over with.

Eris made her way past the sprawl of shop fronts and public houses and oil lamps lining the streets. She bared her teeth when the Thirsty Craw came into view. Karsen was out front, easily identified by his barrel-like beer gut and the beard that was probably growing at least three types of mold. After he growled a gruff hello, he pushed the door open. Eris stepped onto a floor sticky with gods knew what, bumping shoulders with someone on their way out. Probably a sailor who'd just spent the last of their wages on food, drink, and women. Eris shook her head, pityingly. She knew the type well.

Behind the bar, Kiya caught her eye and gave a subtle nod, letting Eris know in one small gesture everything she needed to: Jemsin and the rest of the crew were upstairs, in their usual room.

Eris smiled her thanks, then headed for the stairs. But someone was already coming down, blocking her way. The moment Eris saw their face, her heart lurched and she stepped behind Karsen. A girl with a rat nest of red hair and a sandpiper tattoo on her pale inner arm headed straight for the bar.

Rain.

At the sight of her, Eris's chest constricted. She ducked into the shadows beneath the stairs, crouching low next to stacked boxes full of whisky, watching Rain talk to Kiya behind the bar.

Had the *Sea Mistress*'s crew survived the blaze? The notion brought a rush of relief. Despite her rage at Kor, Eris didn't want his blood on her hands, nor his crew's. But how had Rain gotten to Darmoor in the same amount of time as Eris? It wasn't possible. Unless another ship had seen the *Sea Mistress* burning and come to its aid.

Hells, thought Eris.

She heard Rain utter the words, "Death Dancer."

Kiya shrugged nonchalantly as she wiped down a mug of ale and set it back on the shelf. "Haven't seen her."

"You sure about that?"

Kiya glanced up, arching one black brow in a move Eris knew from personal experience was two parts pretty, one part peril. Kiya smiled that devilishly sweet smile of hers. "She's often at Moll's place when she's in town. You could try there."

Rain studied Kiya hard for a long moment. Then glanced out over the dining room, grunted her thanks, and left.

Eris swung herself out from under the steps. She saluted Kiya, who winked, then took the stairs two at a time. Jemsin's regular room was at the end of the hall on the top floor. As Eris approached, she stretched, rolling her neck and shoulders, trying to rid herself of the tension building all the way here.

Finally, she sucked in a breath and rapped on the door the way Jemsin taught her all those years ago. When it swung in, the orange glow of a lantern made her squint.

"Evening, comrades," Eris drawled, forcing a lazy grin as she lifted her arm to block the light.

When they grabbed her shirt, Eris knew better than to fight back.

They yanked her inside and slammed the door behind her.

Seven

It took three hard pulls before the door came open and dust flew into Safire's face. She sneezed, then froze, listening hard.

But no sound came from the hall behind her.

Safire let out a breath, then stepped into the room. Holding up the lamp, she found it full of dusty crates. She sniffed and the smell of old wine engulfed her. A storage room of some kind, then.

Looking upward, she scanned the ceiling until her gaze caught on the square crawl space door.

After she'd heard a red-haired girl at the bar say the words "Death Dancer," Safire ordered a drink, found the drunkest looking man in the room, and asked the right questions. He happily told her all about his *golden days*, as he coined them. Days when he used the crawl space above the second floor of the inn to watch the patrons undress in the rooms below.

Safire forced herself to listen to his disgusting escapades, but as she stood beneath the crawl space now, she silently thanked the foul man for giving her precisely what she needed. (And vowed that if she ever found herself the occupant of an inn, she would thoroughly check the ceiling, and maybe the walls, before undressing.)

Safire began stacking boxes. When they were high enough, she climbed up to the crawl space door and unlatched it. More dust fell. She turned her face in to her elbow to stop the sneeze this time, then pulled her sandskarf up over her nose and mouth. When the particles settled, she lifted the lamp, set it inside the crawl space above, then climbed up after it.

The space was long and narrow, dark and crowded, and her palms were soon coated in dust. She swiped preemptively at cobwebs while testing each and every board before putting her full weight on it to avoid creaking.

Half crouching, she made her way toward the far end of the crawl space, pausing every once in a while to listen to the sounds below. When she heard two voices arguing, she stopped just above and set down the lamp.

Safire slid the sleeve of her shirt across the boards beneath her, wiping away dust and dirt before laying her cheek against the rough wood.

"I warned you *not* to wreck things with Kor," growled a man's voice, partially muffled by the wood between Safire and the room below.

Silently, she turned down her lamp, listening.

"I didn't wreck it," came the familiar voice. The one, she was sure, belonged to the Death Dancer. "I set it on fire."

Safire found a crack in the boards wide enough to look through and peered into the room below. The surface of a worn table lay directly beneath her. On it a slender wooden object spun around and around, nudged by long fingers.

That was her thief.

"I told you to stay on his good side," said the man through gritted teeth. "Trying to burn him alive is the opposite of his good side."

Safire tried to make out just how many people were in the room, but the lighting made it difficult. As she listened, she slid out one of the throwing knives from her belt and began to move the blade back and forth between her knuckles—a trick she'd taught herself while sitting through too many of Dax's tedious council meetings.

"He wanted something I couldn't give him."

That wooden object kept spinning.

"That's not how this works, Eris," growled the man. "I don't care what he wants. Next time, you give it to him."

"I may be in your debt, *Captain*, but I'm not your whore."

A chair scraped the wooden floorboards. With the hilt of her knife back in her palm, Safire watched the man's gray head lean over the table.

The pirate Jemsin? she wondered.

He slammed his hand down on the spinning object, halting its rotation. A silver ring glinted on his smallest finger. "You are whatever I say you are."

And then he lunged for her. Safire flinched as he flipped the girl on her back, pinning her to the table with one meaty hand wrapped around her throat.

"I can't afford to carry dead weight around."

Safire's stomach twisted as he squeezed. She watched the girl kick and thrash, trying to push him off. Safire's whole body coiled, ready to go down there and stop this . . . before she

remembered the girl was the *Death Dancer*. A criminal who—
she realized now—clearly worked for Jemsin.

Not to mention the room below could be full of deadly
pirates. And Safire was here alone.

"I'll give you one chance," said Jemsin as the Death Dancer
writhed beneath him, trying to dig her nails into his hands.
"You got that?"

Finally, he let go. The Death Dancer moved like wind,
scrambling out from under him and landing on the other side
of the table, keeping it between them. She gulped down air,
hands cupping her neck. Her pale blond hair was a mess and her
eyes were wild.

"I've got a new job for you," said Jemsin. "You get it done,
and your debt is paid."

The Death Dancer frowned. Her hands fell away from her
throat.

"Paid?" she whispered. "What do you mean, *paid*?"

He tossed her the spindle. Eagerly, she caught it.

"You do this job, and you'll go free. You can run to the ends
of the world, and I won't follow you. I won't even care. In fact,
I'll be glad to be rid of you."

Safire leaned closer to the crack in the boards, listening hard.

"But fail me again—sabotage me in any way—and I'll hand
you over to the ones you're running from. Got it?"

The Death Dancer watched him in silence for a moment, as
if trying to find the loopholes. Finally she said, a little warily,
"What's the job?"

Jemsin sank back into the chair. "Catch the one they call the
Namsara," he said. "And bring her to me."

Safire went stone-still, her whole body attuned to that title. The Namsara.

Asha.

What did the deadliest pirate on the Silver Sea want with Safire's cousin?

The Death Dancer was saying something else but so softly, Safire couldn't hear it. She shifted, trying to listen. But as she did, the board beneath her creaked.

The air turned immediately cold as the room below plunged into silence.

Safire froze as a soft thud echoed—the sound of two chair legs lowered to the floor. A heartbeat later, between the crack in the boards, two watery brown eyes peered into hers.

Safire rolled back just as a knife surged up between the boards, narrowly missing her face. When she turned to look, the blade was so close, her breath fogged the steel.

"Come out, little spy," Jemsin called up to her.

Safire jumped to her feet as a loud *thump!* resounded, followed by the crack of breaking wood. The board between her boots splintered and lifted, letting light shine through the slit and into the crawl space.

The man barked an order. But Safire didn't hear what it was—she was already running.

Through cobwebs, kicking up dust, tripping over things in the dark, Safire did not care that her racket could likely be heard throughout the entire inn. Quickly, she lowered herself into the storage room and jumped down from the stacked crates.

The moment her boots hit the floor, she swung open the door . . .

And ran straight into the person standing beyond it.

"*Oof.*"

Nimble hands grabbed her arms. Safire flinched, glancing up into two green eyes flecked with gold.

The air shifted around her.

Illuminated by the glow of the lamps was a small, slender girl. Her pale, messy hair was knotted at her neck and she smelled like the sea.

"Now where are you running off to?" The Death Dancer smiled as her fingers reached to pull down the sandskarf hiding Safire's face. Before she could, Safire flicked out the hidden folding knife in the toe of her boot and kicked her in the shin, embedding the sharpened metal point deep into her flesh.

That smile vanished as the girl cursed, reaching for her leg.

Safire rammed into her shoulder, knocking her off balance. The girl stumbled backward into the wall. But as Safire whirled and moved for the locked door leading out into the hall, the girl was suddenly before her again, blocking her way.

She moved so fast. It was impossible. . . .

Safire stepped back, drawing two knives.

The girl's green eyes flashed. She stood like a wild cat now: lithe and dangerous. But she carried no weapons. At least none Safire could detect.

Safire's sandskarf obscured her voice as she said, "Get out of my way."

"Show your face and I'll think about it."

Safire threw the first knife. It thunked into the door next to the girl's head.

"That's your first and only warning."

The girl touched her ear, where the blade had grazed the lobe. Her pale brow folded into a bewildered frown.

Safire readied the second knife, keeping her eyes on her opponent.

"You're trapped, sweetheart," the girl said as footsteps rang out down the hall. Jemsin's pirates were on their way. "There's nowhere to go."

Safire spun, looking to the window. It was small, not to mention two stories off the ground. But she'd rather take her chances with the window than the pirates outside the door.

She needed to warn Asha. Needed to get to her before Jemsin did.

As soon as she started for the window, though, the Death Dancer was there. Blocking her way. *Again.*

Safire growled, then aimed the second knife—trying for a blow that would immobilize, but not kill—and threw it.

In a blink, the girl was gone. The steel thunked into the plaster.

She reappeared a heartbeat later, standing once more before Safire.

It was unnatural. No one could move like that.

"*Demon,*" she murmured, stepping back.

Was this why she carried no weapons? Because she could dodge any blow?

"There's no need to be unkind." The Death Dancer's mouth bent up at the side as she moved toward Safire. "Now what's behind that scarf you don't want me to see?"

Safire took another step back, but those quick fingers snagged her sandskarf. The girl tugged it free, revealing Safire's face.

Those green eyes went wide. "*You.*" Her voice became a whisper. "What are you doing here?"

Putting a stop to this, thought Safire. She drew a third knife and pressed its honed tip into the hollow of the girl's throat. Those nimble hands went palm up as Safire backed her into the wall beneath the window, her knee pinned between the girl's legs, ensuring she couldn't escape again.

Safire was just about to rap the hilt hard against her temple and watch her drop when there was a sharp prick of pain in her neck. Like a scorpion sting.

Safire blinked.

She saw the thorn of the scarp thistle dart—gripped in the girl's hand—too late.

A heartbeat later, the room rocked. The Death Dancer's mouth—twisting into a cruel smile now—blurred before her.

Safire's legs started to tremble. Her fingers—suddenly unable to grip—slipped from her knife, which fell to the floor. Before her legs gave out completely, an arm came around her waist, holding her upright.

The room spun. The Death Dancer ducked beneath Safire's arm, looping it around her shoulder.

"You drugged me," Safire realized, the sentence fuzzy in her mouth.

The last words she heard before the world faded were, "Aye, princess."

A Becoming

One morning, Crow found the fisherman's daughter high up the cliffs, far from the footpaths, picking berries. He watched her gather handful after handful of the small dark orbs, dropping them into her basket— except for when she dropped them into her mouth.

Crow had never known hunger. Watching her made him curious.

"What does it taste like?"

Her eyes snapped to him. "You've never eaten one?"

He'd never eaten anything. Why would he need to?

He didn't tell her this.

She picked a plump dark berry and held it up. "Open your mouth."

He did. As she slid the berry in, her fingers brushed his lips. The juice of the berry, the touch of her skin . . . it was like a spell. Changing him. Where he'd once been content, an aching need now gnawed at his insides.

He tried to banish it. But this new feeling persisted, snapping and growling like a wolf cub. Getting louder and fiercer inside him.

Was this hunger?

It unsettled him. He left her there in the cliffs, with her basketful of berries, wanting to escape it. But weeks later—or was it months?—the need drove him back.

He found her in a tiny one room house overlooking the cove. It was hot inside. Crammed with people dressed not for fishing or farming, but for celebrating. Families had gathered here for a binding.

Skye sat on a rotting pine bench at the back of the room. Her spindle and wool were gripped tight in her hands and her gaze was fixed so intently ahead, she didn't feel him sit down.

Crow looked where she looked—to the young couple at the front. The young man had Skye's raven-dark hair and stubborn chin. He reached tenderly for his new wife, sealing their union with a kiss.

He remembered the dark, plump berry.

What would it be like?

He looked to Skye. Saw the same curiosity in her eyes.

What would she be like?

That question scared him most of all.

Here is danger, *he thought. And so he fled.*

Eight

Safire woke on the deck of a ship. Though the world blurred around her, she knew it was a ship because the wood beneath her cheek was damp, she could hear the squawk of gulls, and she felt the gentle rock of what could only be the sea.

A pair of black boots came into sudden focus. At the sight of them, Safire pushed herself to a sitting position and was surprised to find her hands weren't bound.

She immediately reached for her knives—all of which were gone. Even the one she kept hidden inside her shirt, strapped to her torso.

"Well, little spy" came that rough voice from the Thirsty Craw. "Welcome to the *Hyacinth*."

Jemsin.

Safire looked up into the watery brown eyes of a man old enough to be her father. They were the same eyes she'd seen in the crawl space an instant before that knife flew up through the boards. The raised bump of a scar slashed across his forehead above his right eye and on his shoulder perched a huge black raven with bloodred eyes. A silver band encircled its leg, one that matched the silver ring on Jemsin's smallest finger.

The pirate captain looked Safire up and down, taking in her complexion—which was several shades lighter than Dax's and Asha's. "Skral born," he mused.

She bristled, waiting for further indictment of her mixed heritage—an almost daily occurrence in Firgaard. But the captain only shrugged, as if it meant nothing to him. As if the designation hadn't shaped Safire's entire life. "Eris says you're the dragon king's commandant, as well as his cousin. Perhaps you can help me."

I'd sooner throw myself into the sea, she thought.

"What day is it?" she demanded.

"The day after yesterday," he said, making it clear that he had no intention of giving her information until she gave him some first.

Safire held his gaze. "It's true. My cousin is the dragon king, and I'm the commander of his army. Which is precisely why you'll never get away with this."

"With kidnapping you?" Jemsin smiled, gesturing to the empty horizon. "I already have."

Safire shook her head. "My king will come after you the moment he realizes you have me."

He bent over, pressing his hands to his knees, and Safire saw the blood caked in his fingernails. It turned her mouth sour.

"We're half a day's sail from Darmoor, love. We left in the night without a soul knowing. Your precious king will just be waking up, and by the time he tracks you to us—*if* he tracks you to us—there will be very little left of you. Unless you cooperate."

Safire glanced around, needing a plan. The truth was, she very much doubted Dax would be able to track them. Even if he'd discovered Safire's absence by now, how would he know it was Jemsin who'd kidnapped her? And even if he figured it out, how would he begin to look for her?

Safire couldn't depend on her cousin. She needed to get out of this herself.

She checked the sky, but it was cloudy and gray. She couldn't tell where exactly the sun was, nor the direction they were sailing in. And they were so far out at sea, she couldn't tell how far from land they were.

"Tell me where the Namsara is," demanded the pirate captain.

Safire turned back to Jemsin, holding his steely gaze with her own. "Tell me why you want her."

His jaw tightened. Clearly he didn't like being challenged. "I'll give you one chance, skral. Where's the Namsara?"

Safire kept her mouth clamped shut.

"If you're not going to cooperate, I'll let my crew take you down to the brig. And then we'll try again."

If he thought she would endanger Asha so easily, he was deeply mistaken.

When it became clear she wasn't going to talk, Jemsin clenched his fists. He glanced over Safire's shoulder and gestured with his chin. Strong hands grabbed her, hauling her to her feet. They dragged her down damp and rotting steps, through a dim narrow passage, toward what looked like an enormous cage with rusted iron bars on all four sides. Inside there was a small, moldy mattress with a bucket beside it.

Safire wasn't worried about the cell. She still had her picklocks, after all. She could feel the bulge of them hidden in the flap of her boot. It was the fact that this room had no windows. And she was surrounded by men with big, groping hands.

She had been alone with such men before.

Alone where no one could hear her cries.

She would not endure it again.

She nailed the first one in the teeth with her elbow. Then broke the nose of the second. They both let go, cursing and bleeding and staggering back. No longer restricted, Safire managed to grab the daggers from their hips as two more fell in to replace them. She caught the short sword of the first while she stabbed the second with the folding knife in her boot, sending him howling. But everywhere she turned, there were more.

A fist connected with her cheek and Safire fell back, trying to shake off the shock of it. She didn't see the boot until it hit her in the gut, knocking the air out of her lungs as it sent her backward. Her spine slammed into one of the cell's iron bars.

Safire saw stars.

They shoved her, stunned, into the cell.

Safire fell to her knees, trying to stop the world from spinning around her.

She felt rather than saw someone step inside with her. Heard the clang of the door shutting behind them. Suddenly, she wasn't here, in the brig of this ship. She was back in the halls of the palace, cowering before the former commandant—a man named Jarek—and his soldats, waiting for their fists to rain down, for their boots to break her ribs. . . .

"*That's enough.*"

The snarl brought her back. Safire looked up, to the green-eyed girl flying down the steps and into the crowd circling the cell. *The Death Dancer.*

"Get out of there, Remy."

"You ain't my captain," the man called Remy said, cracking his knuckles as he smirked down at Safire.

In the blink of an eye, Eris was through the door and inside the cell, standing between Safire and Remy.

Safire stared, stunned at her swiftness.

Remy staggered back in surprise. "Tides, Eris. What's your problem? The captain said—"

"Change of plan. Captain's orders." Eris's gaze didn't leave Remy, who glared down at her. Without taking her eyes off him, she said to Safire: "Get up, princess."

Safire obliged.

Strange, how this wraith-like girl could command such vicious men.

Stranger still that the captain would change his orders immediately after issuing them.

The Death Dancer led Safire back up to the deck. Safire glanced up to the horizon, searching for landmarks. But there was still nothing but cobalt sea and gray sky.

Before Eris forced her down another set of stairs, Safire caught sight of a small rowboat, tethered to the *Hyacinth*'s starboard side. If she could somehow get free of her captor, perhaps she could use it to escape.

"Keep moving." Eris gave her a shove from behind and Safire stumbled, reaching for the damp clapboard walls of this passage to steady herself. Prickling with anger, she wanted nothing more than to turn and strike. But this was the Death Dancer: a girl who'd dodged Safire's every blow last night as if made of wind and starlight; a girl who'd snuck past the palace guards and into her room, then disappeared before her eyes.

Even if this girl wasn't some kind of demon, even if Safire could overpower her and flee, they were out at sea. There was no way Safire could escape in broad daylight.

More important: she needed to find out why they were hunting Asha.

"Where are you taking me?" asked Safire.

"You would find out sooner if you walked more and talked less," said Eris, nudging her on and nodding toward a door straight ahead. Just before they reached it, Eris reached for her arm, stopping her. Safire flinched, jerking away. That same prickle of memory bubbled up in her: Jarek. His soldiers. All of them hurting her. With the memories came the too-familiar panic.

Safire willed herself to calm. Jarek was dead. She was commandant now.

She could handle this.

"Behave yourself in there, princess."

Safire cringed at that word, thinking of their last conversation in her bedroom three nights past and the things Eris accused her of.

Despite what this girl thought, Safire had no claim on the throne. She wasn't a draksor—not wholly, anyway. Her mother had been a skral. A *slave*. And even though the skral had been freed from their bonds in Firgaard, most draksors still didn't see them as equals. Didn't see *her* as equal.

In no world would Safire ever sit on that throne. Nor did she want to. It was Dax's throne, and she intended to keep him on it.

"It must have been nice, growing up in a palace. Having servants to dress and feed and bathe you. Having guards to protect you." Eris said this with bitterness. Like the thought of it—of Safire—sickened her.

Safire thought of her childhood. Of how she was never allowed near her family at formal events, how she was forbidden to touch her cousins, how she lived every day in constant fear of Jarek and his cruelty.

"Actually," she said softly, "it was a nightmare."

Eris paused, studying her.

Safire stared straight ahead.

Finally, Eris opened the door and pushed her inside.

The room she stumbled into lay at the stern of the *Hyacinth*, full of light that flooded in through the portholes. An ornate desk loomed before her, its sides carved with images of ships and waves and sea monsters. On its surface were a familiar pair of black boots, crossed at the ankles. Just beyond the desk, that same black raven perched in a gold filigree cage, staring at Safire with its eerie eyes.

"Eris." The captain uncrossed his legs and lowered his feet

to the floor, looking from his Death Dancer to Safire and back. "What are you doing?"

"Saving you from a grave error."

Jemsin frowned, leaning over the desk and setting aside the stack of papers he'd been reading. "And what error is that?"

Eris shoved Safire closer. Safire had to plant both palms on the surface of the desk to stop herself from tumbling over it. She scowled over her shoulder.

Eris ignored it. "Your men are brutes. They'll accidently kill her before they get anything useful out of her. I want you to put *me* in charge of her."

Safire shot Eris a look. *Huh?* Hadn't she just told Remy she was taking Safire on the captain's orders?

Jemsin's weathered face showed no hint of emotion or decision as he looked Safire up and down.

"If you give her to me," Eris continued, "I'll find out the Namsara's location before tomorrow morning."

The captain's brows lifted. He leaned back in his chair and crossed his arms. "And if you don't?"

"I will," insisted Eris. But then she shrugged. "If I don't, I'll give her back to the boys."

The captain steepled his fingers, thinking.

"We don't have time for that." He shook his head. "If she doesn't cooperate—if she doesn't give you the Namsara's location before *midnight*—you'll give her to me. And I'll send a very clear message to every corner of the Silver Sea." He fixed his eyes on Safire, speaking directly to her now. "As of midnight, for every hour the Namsara doesn't come for you, I'll take something. Starting with those pretty blue eyes of yours."

Safire held his gaze even as a cold fear spread through her. In that moment, she hated this man even more than Jarek. At least Jarek was loyal to something. Jemsin was less than that. He would use someone's loyalty against them.

Jemsin leaned forward with both hands on the arms of his chair, about to push himself out of it. To Eris, he said, "Bring her back to the brig."

"I don't want her in the brig," Eris said.

The captain paused.

"I want her in my quarters."

Safire nearly choked. She turned, horrified and fists clenching. "I think I'd prefer the brig."

A slow smile curled the captain's lips. But Eris's expression remained neutral.

The captain looked back and forth between them. "Are you sure about this?"

"Trust me," said Eris, her voice quiet. "I can handle her."

Nine

Strong hands plunged Safire's head beneath the icy water of the barrel and held it there. Her fingers gripped the rim, struggling against the strength of those hands. Fighting to lift her head above the surface.

Her lungs were on fire. She was drowning. She needed air.

And then, just like all the times before, her torturers let her up.

Safire gasped, gulping in air, her chest heaving as she clung to the side of the barrel, her wet hair plastered to her face.

Eris paced back and forth in front of her, footsteps agitated.

One of the two men who held Safire in place asked, "Again?"

Eris stopped, staring down at Safire. "I don't know. Are you ready to tell us where your cousin is?"

Looking out of the porthole, Safire could see the sky growing red.

Sunset.

Safire would never tell them where Asha was. But the

thought of going underwater again filled her with dread. And if she didn't give Eris the information she wanted, Eris would hand her over to Jemsin, who would simply kill her.

She needed to buy herself enough time to escape and warn Asha.

"Send them out," said Safire, her breathing ragged as she looked to the two brutes on either side of her. "And I'll discuss terms."

Eris arched a brow. "Terms? You think this is a negotiation?"

Remembering the conversation she'd overheard in the Thirsty Craw, Safire didn't back down. "I think you're more desperate than you let on."

Eris's eyes flashed. She stared down Safire for a long moment, as if deciding her next move, then looked to the pirates holding her captive. "Lock her up. Then leave us."

The brutes secured Safire's wrists in cold shackles attached to an iron ring in the ceiling. When the lock clicked, Safire found the chains weren't long enough to drop her arms. She tugged, but her wrists could only come down as far as her temples.

Eris waved the men off, sending them out of the room. When the door shut and they were alone, Safire said, "You're despicable."

Eris walked over to a large table where a map lay unrolled. Reaching for the pack of matches resting next to an unlit lamp, she said, "The feeling's mutual, princess."

Safire gritted her teeth. "Stop calling me that."

Eris removed the glass chimney of the oil lamp, then turned the thumb wheel to raise the wick. "You'd prefer I call you *commandant?*" She struck the match, lit the wick, then adjusted the flame. After blowing out the match, Eris replaced the glass chimney and turned to Safire. The golden glow illuminated her face as she spoke. "Tell me, then, *commandant*: Do you enjoy making people do what you want? Does it please you when they unthinkingly follow your orders?"

Giving orders was not Safire's job. Her job was keeping the king and queen safe. Keeping Firgaard—her home—safe. And looking out for every single soldat under her care.

"Isn't that what *you* do?" Safire held Eris's gaze, thinking of the conversation she'd overheard in that crawl space. "Unthinkingly follow your captain's orders?"

Eris shot her a withering look.

"My soldats are free to leave at any time," Safire went on. "They stay because they're loyal."

"Loyalty," Eris muttered, her jaw clenched, "is a luxury most of us can't afford."

She said it so matter-of-factly. As if she believed it.

For the merest of heartbeats, Safire wondered what that would be like. To be devoted to no one, and have no one devoted to you.

It made her sad to think about.

Safire quickly changed the subject. "Why do you want my cousin so badly?"

"I don't want her."

"Your captain, then."

Eris opened her mouth to answer, then closed it.

"How about we play a game," she said, clasping her hands.

"For every answer I give you, you give me one in return."

Safire frowned and fell back against the wall of this room, her wrists locked above her.

"I'll tell you why the captain wants your cousin *if* you tell me where she is."

No way was Safire doing that.

It gave her hope, though. If Eris had no idea where the Namsara was, it would be much easier to lead her afield of her target.

"Even if I knew where she was," said Safire, "I wouldn't tell a pirate."

"I'm not a pirate."

Safire narrowed her eyes. "You run with pirates." She looked Eris up and down, taking in her yellowed cotton shirt and dirty trousers. "You look like a pirate. You even smell like a pirate."

Eris stepped back suddenly, then pulled up the collar of her shirt and sniffed. She wrinkled her nose and dropped the shirt collar.

"Come on, princess. It's only a matter of time before Jemsin comes through on his promise. He'll use you—dead or alive—to lure her in."

"And what will he do once she arrives?" Safire said. "Doesn't he know that where Asha goes, so does Kozu? Jemsin and his crew are no match for the oldest and fiercest of dragons."

"A dragon can be taken down," said Eris simply.

"And you'll take Kozu down with . . . what? A net made of sails?"

As if she were suddenly bored with this conversation, Eris

took out a knife—one of *hers*, Safire noticed with hot fury—and started picking her fingernails with it. It was the one Eris had stolen from beneath her pillow.

"There are no less than twelve harpoons aboard this ship," said Eris.

Safire's heart sank. She didn't think Kozu could withstand twelve harpoons. She tucked this information away for later. If she couldn't escape, she would somehow find those harpoons and drop them to the bottom of the sea.

"And the king?" Safire continued. "I'm the commander of his army. You don't think that army will come after me the moment Dax figures out where I am?"

Eris smirked at this. "The king's army is in Firgaard, leagues away from here. It would take them a week to catch up, and that's *if* they have ships, and good weather, and navigational skills." She shot Safire a skeptical look. "I'm willing to bet they have none of those things."

Safire opened her mouth to defend her soldats. But Eris was right: they were an army, not a navy.

"Listen." Eris set down Safire's knife. "That wasn't an empty threat back there. I've seen Jemsin cut up men with my own eyes, piece by piece."

Safire didn't care. All she cared about was that Jemsin never find out where Asha was.

And yet, if she didn't give them *something*, she would be used as bait to lure her cousin into a trap.

"What will he do to her?" she asked.

Eris's eyes brightened, excited that Safire was beginning

to play her game. She leaned back, gripping the table behind her, and pushed herself up onto it, letting her legs swing free. "Jemsin doesn't kidnap people for no reason. So either she did something to provoke him, or she's valuable to someone."

As far as Safire knew, Asha had never had a run-in with a pirate. But if it was the latter, who would she be valuable to? She was no longer a fugitive. After the law against regicide was struck down, Asha was pardoned for killing her father, the former dragon king. There was no longer a bounty on her head.

"If she's valuable to someone, he'll keep her alive," Eris went on. Pulling her feet up onto the table, she rested her arms on her knees and leaned forward. "*You*, however, are in far greater danger. If you don't talk, he won't hesitate to cut you up. And I very much doubt your cousin wants you dead. More important, you'll be no use to her dead."

Why do you care? Safire thought back to the conversation she overheard from the crawl space. Jemsin had offered Eris freedom in exchange for the Namsara. Which didn't make sense to Safire. Eris was the legendary Death Dancer. What kept her—a girl who could walk through walls and disappear at will—tied to the pirate captain?

Safire discarded the question. It didn't matter right now.

"Assuming I do know where she is, what's to stop you from killing me as soon as I tell you?" asked Safire, having no intention of ever doing such a thing.

Eris rolled her eyes. As if she couldn't believe what a novice Safire was. "The only person who'll kill you is Jemsin. And that's if you give him bad information." She gave Safire a hard look of warning. "I don't kill people."

"No," said Safire darkly, remembering the barrels of water. "You only torture them."

Eris raised her hands innocently. "I saved you a bundle of pain today. Jemsin's crew is far less kind in their methods."

Was she suggesting her methods were kind? Unbelievable.

"I answered two of your questions," said Eris, voice hardening. "It's time you answered one of mine. Where's the Namsara?"

Safire looked away, thinking of that barrel of water. Of the building panic and the moment before she was certain her lungs would burst. She couldn't go through that again. She needed to give Eris something. So she said, very softly, "Asha's on her way to Firefall."

Eris went very still, her eyes fixing on Safire's. "I'm not sure I heard you."

There was an edge in her voice. A warning not to lie.

So Safire turned her face and held that green-eyed gaze, ignoring the sweat collecting at the back of her neck. "My cousin is flying to Firefall. It's a city west of Darmoor, ruled by—"

"I know what it is," said Eris. "Are you telling the truth?"

The truth was that Asha returned from Firefall a few weeks ago.

"She's building a school," Safire went on, burying her lie beneath fact. "A school she hopes will preserve the old stories and restore the severed link between draksors and dragons. Firefall's library has one of the oldest and biggest collections of old stories in existence. Asha's gone there to collect them and bring them back."

Except for the fact that this had already happened, it was all true.

Finally, Eris stopped scrutinizing her. Tucking Safire's knife into her belt, the girl rose to her feet.

She moved toward Safire, who immediately tensed and flicked the blade out from the toe of her boot. Eris glanced down, visibly wincing at the memory of its sharpened tip driving into her shin.

"Try it again," said Eris, "and I'll take those boots right off your feet."

Safire went still. Her picklocks were hidden in her left boot. She'd need them if she had any hope of escaping these manacles. So, obediently, she flicked the blade back in and let the girl approach.

Eris studied her. Safire studied her back.

She was startlingly pretty, this girl. Pretty and graceful.

Eris reached for her chin. Safire's skin scorched at her touch and she jerked her face away.

Those green eyes narrowed, but Eris's voice was soft as she said, "Who hurt you?"

"What?" Safire breathed.

"Anyone can see you're afraid to be touched."

This wasn't exactly true. Safire just wasn't used to people touching her. She'd spent most of her life without physical contact on account of her mother's skral blood running through her veins.

Before Dax became king and changed everything—freeing the skral and abolishing the unjust laws that governed them— the only time anyone ever touched Safire was to injure or punish her. So now, something as little as the brush of a hand, if it came from someone she didn't know or wasn't comfortable with, could hit her with the force of a lightning strike.

"Who hurt you?" Eris asked again.

Safire thought of the night of the revolt. Of the knife she put in Jarek's heart. "It doesn't matter," she whispered. "He's dead."

Eris's mouth turned down at those words and she stepped warily back.

"Well then," she said, studying Safire like she was some kind of puzzle. Turning, she headed for the door. Before she opened it and stepped through, she paused and looked back over her shoulder. "Remy is just down this hall. So don't try anything."

The way she said it was less of a threat, more like a genuine warning.

The door shut, locking Safire in with only the lamp, its flame burning low. Safire listened to the lock click into place. Listened to the footsteps disappear down the hall.

Her stomach growled in the silence, making her realize she hadn't eaten since before she'd followed Eris into the Thirsty Craw.

Safire waited several moments more. When she was certain Eris was gone, she pulled her leg up so her bound hands could reach inside her boot. It took her a few tries, but her fingers finally reached the hidden flap between the leather and her calf, freeing the lockpicks there.

With her hands bound, it took longer than usual to get the manacles unlocked. But as soon as they clicked open, Safire moved through the dimly lit room toward the table. Carefully, she reached for the lamp, turning the thumb wheel until the low flame burned brighter, giving her more light to see by. She then began to inspect the room.

First, she searched for her knives, looking in drawers and between folded trousers and shirts. Her fingers meticulously traced the floorboards and clapboard walls, trying to find secret compartments.

When it became clear there were no weapons in this room, she looked for something that could be used as a weapon. But all she found was a rusted directional compass in one of the drawers. She pocketed it.

Where do you keep your secrets? she wondered, thinking of the thief with the moon-pale hair. It seemed unnatural for someone's room to contain no trace of their identity.

Thinking of the night the Death Dancer walked into Safire's own room and stole her throwing knife, she approached the bed, which was little more than a lumpy mattress on a roughly hewn wooden frame. Reaching beneath the pillows, she found a plain wooden spindle there. Drawing it out, she ran her thumb over its smooth curves wonderingly.

Suddenly, footsteps thudded in the hall.

Safire's gaze shot to the door, her heart thundering. Had someone heard her? Seen the light from the lamp?

Before she was caught in the act, Safire put the spindle back, turned down the lamp's flame, and returned to her manacles, closing them around her wrists.

But the footsteps came and went.

The door never opened.

Safire ground her heel against the wall, the chains of her manacles clinking as she did. She closed her eyes, trying to think of what to do.

Asha would surely be at the scrin by now, oblivious to the danger coming for her. Dax and Roa would be fully panicked at Safire's absence. If they tried to pursue Jemsin's ship—as she knew they would—it would delay their arrival in the Star Isles. Not a good start to their alliance with its empress.

She needed to escape, track down Asha, and warn her. She and Asha could then find Dax and together they could inform the empress about the pirates trawling her waters. The empress, Safire was certain, would send her navy after this ship and sink it to the bottom of the sea.

Safire had a compass in her pocket. She knew the Star Isles were northwest of Darmoor.

All she needed was a boat to get her there.

Yearning

The fisherman's daughter was seventeen the next time she saw him. She was down on the shore, scraping barnacles off the hull of her father's boat when she felt a ripple in the air, as if someone had just stepped into this world from another.

What world he came from, she could hardly guess. When he was here, though, he seemed to hover at the edge of things. Sometimes a man, sometimes a shadow.

She set down her scraper and listened.

The wind stung her cheeks. The gulls screamed over the water. The sea spirits had all disappeared from the craggy rocks below the cliffs and gone to calmer waters.

A storm was coming.

Casting her gaze into the junipers, the girl saw no one. Back and forth went her good eye, between the trees. She was just about to turn and quickly finish her task when she saw it—a black shadow—between the jagged gray rocks.

Crow. Dark like the deepest part of the woods and insubstantial as a ghost.

"Are you a ghost?" she asked quietly, putting a voice to her thoughts as she went back to scraping barnacles.

"No" came his voice loud and clear as a bell. Right beside her.

The girl shivered. But not out of fear.

"What, then?" she asked, still focused on her work. "Not a man."

"Are you so sure?"

His response surprised her so much she slipped and cut herself with the scraper.

Blood welled up. She dropped the blade into the sand and stared at the crimson shine blooming across her palm.

He breathed her name. His solid form disappeared as darkness swelled around her, enclosing her in a cocoon of night.

Where a moment ago there was pain, now there was . . . nothing. The sting in her hand extinguished like a snuffed flame.

The wind roared in her ears once more. The gulls and the sea returned.

She stared at her palm. The blood was gone. The skin was split no longer, and in its place was a thin, tidy scar.

Looking up, she found him solid before her. He stood close enough to touch.

"Thank you," she whispered.

A pleased smile tugged at his normally stern mouth. The sight of it made something unfurl within her.

Her pulse quickened. She studied those clear black eyes. Deep as the sea. In all their years of friendship—Was that what this was? Was he her friend?—she'd never touched him.

How she longed to.

But the moment she lifted her fingers to his face, he stepped back. Startled.

She insisted, pushing away from the boat. She touched his cheek, her skin heating at the contact. She stared at him, her good fierce eye searching both of his.

They were so close now. Her fingers slid behind his neck.

His eyes were wild and unsure, his breath unsteady.

She pulled his face gently down to hers, coaxing him to her.

Before their lips touched, her father yelled her name, calling her in from the storm.

Crow jerked away, his voice tight. "We can't do this. You don't realize what I am."

He was melting away from her. Back into shadow. Out of her reach.

Skye took a step toward him. "I don't care."

"You should."

She let out an angry breath. "What are you, then?"

"Nothing good," he whispered.

And then he was gone.

The girl fell against the hull of her father's boat, feeling colder than the sea.

Ten

After using the spindle to draw a shining line, the mists rose up. Eris stepped into them and across.

Her footsteps echoed loudly as she waded through the white fog and down the path beneath the stars. A few moments later, an arching blue door with a silver handle stood before her. Opening it, she stepped into the eerie quiet of the labyrinth. The spindle always brought her to this same place—a place between worlds. A place Day had showed her how to use when she was just a child. *A place to hide,* he'd told her back then.

No sooner had Eris started down its stained-glass halls than she felt the eerie presence of the ghost, following her. Out of habit, she ran her thumb over the familiar curves and grooves of her spindle. When she was younger, she liked to imagine the spindle as a kind of talisman, protecting her from the ghost in the labyrinth. But years of crossing had taught her the thing was harmless. The ghost loved to lurk, which was creepy enough, but it never tried to hurt her.

She started ignoring it, then forgetting it was there.

"Looks like we have a long night of sleuthing ahead of us," she said to the ghost now, making her way toward one of the doors within. She needed to always pay attention to the path she took, otherwise the labyrinth would turn her about, ensnaring her inside itself for hours, or sending her straight back to where she'd started.

The ghost said nothing. But Eris knew it heard her.

At present, there were four doors, each one leading to a different place. The first and most-used door led to the *Sea Mistress*, Kor's now-burned vessel; the second led to the *Hyacinth*; the third and newest door led to Firgaard's palace; and the last stood before her. Painted gold with a brass handle, this one led to Firefall—a wealthy seaside city where Jemsin sent Eris for most of her jobs. A city that just so happened to be crawling with the empress's spies.

She'd nearly destroyed this door after her last visit, months ago now, when she'd been caught mid-heist by four Lumina soldiers. Before she could even draw her spindle, they were on her, locking her hands in stardust steel cuffs—a form of torture the Lumina were best known for. Not only would the corrosive metal eat right through human wrists, but for some reason, it prevented Eris from stepping across.

She discovered this when they threw her into a temporary holding cell before shipping her back to the Star Isles. With her hands bound in the stardust steel cuffs, Eris tried to use the spindle . . . but nothing happened. If Jemsin hadn't found her, hadn't slaughtered them all, she'd be in the empress's hands right now. Or dead.

She shivered at the thought.

But Jemsin wasn't going to stop sending her to Firefall because of a close encounter with some soldiers. If she destroyed the golden door, she'd only have to make a new one. And in order for these doors to open into a place she needed to go, Eris had to fasten them out of something belonging to that particular place. It had taken her months to obtain the material she needed to make *this* door—which lead straight into Firefall's royal archives.

So she'd kept it, and was thankful now for her own foresight. Tapping the stolen knife in her belt, she thought of the information Safire gave her.

"Let's see if she's a liar, shall we?" she said to the ghost.

The ghost said nothing back.

Eris reached for the knob, pulled the door open, and stepped through.

A Place of Her Own

One evening, Crow heard Skye weeping. He tried to unhear it. Tried to stay away. But the sound of her sorrow was a hook caught inside him. It tugged and it pulled until he gave in.

He found her hiding in the rocks, just out of view of the wharf, and he sat down next to her.

Skye lifted her red, chapped hands to show him. "They hurt," she said. "But Papa needs me on the boats and the flakes. And Mama needs me for the washing and the cooking." She stared miserably at her fingers, then looked up at him through eyes full of tears. "What I would give for just one day of quiet and stillness and rest. One day alone at my loom."

Crow could give her more than just one day.

So he set to work, building a place for her. A secret place, between her world and his. Where she could weave, alone, in silence. He made her a loom. He filled baskets brimming with brightly colored skeins so that she would never run out of thread.

He made doors that would help her get from place to place—the wharf, the house, the cliffs, the market—to give her time to rest.

And then he fastened for her a key. One he disguised as a spindle. "You can hide it among your tools," he said.

Skye came to her secret loom often, and it brought Crow joy to watch her weave. To see the look of peace on her face as her fingers worked the threads. To see the way her mouth curved when she finished. He had given her a good gift. And the knowledge of it made a brand-new feeling glow within him.

Happiness.

And though he sometimes saw the hunger in her gaze when she looked at him, sometimes felt his own wanting chewing at his insides, for a time, it was enough.

Eleven

When the door swung open, Safire jolted upright in her chains. Eris stood in the frame. Her face seemed wan and thin, her mouth set in a hard line, and her shoulders drooped with exhaustion. As if she'd walked a hundred leagues in a day.

But they were in the middle of the sea, so that was impossible.

Wasn't it?

In one hand she held a covered platter; in the other, a goblet of wine. She set both on the table, on top of the map, a few feet away from Safire. Rubbing her hand over her face, she lit the lamps, then closed the door.

"Hungry, princess?"

Safire's stomach growled in response, and she cursed her body for giving her away so easily.

Eris studied her. "I'll take that as a yes." Hoisting herself onto the table, she lifted the platter lid to reveal a stale-looking loaf of bread, a lump that looked something like pickled herring, and an apple.

"The captain has your keys." She nodded to the manacles keeping Safire's wrists bound to the ceiling. "So I'll have to feed you."

That sounded terribly humiliating. But Safire's stomach was pinched with hunger. So she said nothing as Eris pushed herself to her feet, ripping the stale bread and dunking it in the wine to moisten it.

Eris stepped up to her, raising an eyebrow.

With her hands locked at her temples, Safire opened her mouth, glaring as she did.

"If you bite me," Eris said as she put the wine-soaked bread between Safire's lips, "you will regret it."

Safire chewed the bread. When she swallowed, Eris did it again. And again.

The wine began to warm her. After going so long without food, Safire's thoughts soon turned fuzzy at the edges.

"Are you trying to get me drunk?" she whispered the next time Eris stepped back to feed her.

Eris smiled a little but said nothing. Just lifted the next wine-drenched piece of bread to Safire's lips.

Safire opened her mouth. Eris pushed it in, her fingers brushing against Safire's lips this time. Her touch was like a spark, and Safire sucked in her lower lip protectively.

"I went to Firefall today."

Safire stopped chewing. *What?* That was impossible. The ship hadn't changed course. As far as Safire could tell, they were still in the middle of the Silver Sea. Nowhere near the coastal city of Firefall.

"You lied," said Eris, her gaze lifting to Safire's. "Your cousin left weeks ago."

Safire swallowed, her appetite suddenly lost. She steeled herself for some kind of blow. A retaliatory lash of frustration.

Instead, Eris asked, "Why would you lie?" She lowered her hands, her gaze searching Safire's. "I told you he'd kill you if you lied."

She seemed actually puzzled about this. As if she couldn't understand why someone would risk her life for someone else.

"If I told you the truth," Safire said, "you'd be hunting her down and dragging her back to that monster you call a captain. Of course I lied."

Eris opened her mouth to respond, then stopped. She was silent a moment, looking to the porthole, which had grown dark.

"I promised Jemsin I'd locate the Namsara by tonight." She returned to the platter and tore off another piece of bread. "You need to tell me where she is. *Now.*"

Safire said nothing.

Eris gritted her teeth. "If you don't give me the information I need, I'll have no choice but to march you straight to the captain's cabin."

Safire looked away—but not out of defiance. Eris sounded genuinely frightened for her. As if she didn't want Safire hurt by Jemsin. As if she *cared.*

Don't be fooled.

Safire remembered the deal Eris made with Jemsin back in the Thirsty Craw. Asha was the key to whatever kept Eris bound to the pirate captain. Her fear for Safire's life was feigned—a ploy to make Safire play into her hands, luring Asha into the clutches of a monster. All so Eris could go free.

"Never," murmured Safire, her hatred for this despicable girl burning bright within her.

Annoyance flashed across Eris's face. "All right, then." She started to pace. "Let's say you don't tell me. Let's say you wait for your chance and manage to escape tonight—which you won't. Where will you go, princess? You're in the middle of the Silver Sea." She started ticking points off her fingers. "You don't know which way land is. You've never sailed a ship. I'm willing to bet you can't even swim."

Safire kept her face carefully neutral. The last two things were true. But she did know where land was, thanks to the compass in her pocket.

"You *really* want me to march you into Jemsin's cabin right now?"

Safire lifted her chin, staring Eris straight in the eye.

"You *really* think I'll put Asha in danger to save myself?" The mere thought of it disgusted Safire. "You are deplorable."

The air grew cold at those words. Eris's expression hardened.

This is it, she thought. The moment Eris unlocked her chains and handed her over to Jemsin.

Instead, Eris kept feeding her—the bread, the fish, the apple. All of it. Only this time, she did it in silence, her eyes stormy, her lips pressed into a hard line.

When the only things left on the platter were herring bones and an apple core, Eris covered it up. "You have until morning to change your mind," she said, as she crossed the room to the bed, taking the lamp with her.

Safire frowned. *Huh?*

"I convinced Jemsin to give you until sunrise to think things over."

"Why?"

"I've been asking myself that same question," she said. "Maybe because I'm too tired to watch him take those eyes of yours tonight."

Unlacing her shirt, Eris tugged it off, giving Safire a full view of her tapered waist, the gentle flare of her hips, and the light dusting of freckles across her shoulders.

Safire suddenly felt very warm.

Too much wine, she thought, looking away as Eris pulled on a loose, oversize shirt.

"Storm's coming," Eris said. "Wake me if you feel sick." Sinking into the bed, she tugged off her boots, then her trousers. "I don't want you puking your guts up all over my floor."

She didn't wait for Safire's answer. Just blew out the flame in the lamp, lay back in the bed, and turned over.

Safire waited for her breathing to deepen, then even out. When it finally did, when she knew the girl was good and truly asleep, she unlocked her manacles and, without looking back, silently slipped from the room.

Pirate thieves weren't the only ones good at picking locks.

Twelve

The boat creaked and groaned as Safire stumbled up the narrow hall. For every step she took, she paused to press her palm to the damp wall, steadying herself as the rocking boat threw her off balance.

The steps were wet. When she emerged onto the deck, she realized why. Rain lashed her face and arms, soaking her clothes and collecting on her eyelashes. Lightning brightened the angry clouds above, giving Safire a momentary view of the deck, which was clear of crew. Only a single man stood watch, facing the sea, his back to her.

Beneath the dim light of the deck lamps, Safire made her way to the starboard side, where the rowboat was kept. Her clothes clung to her. Her teeth clattered with cold. The ship rocked, and a wave rolled over the deck, submerging it completely, soaking Safire up to her knees and nearly knocking her over.

Thinking this was it, that they were going under, she lunged for the side and clung on.

But the ship rose up, unfazed, and soon the deck was clear of water.

When the lightning flashed again, instead of reaching for the rowboat, Safire caught sight of the waves below. Huge and black, they crashed against the hull of the ship, high as the palace walls.

Safire's stomach rolled over itself. She forced the queasy feeling down as her grip on the wet wood tightened.

What am I doing?

Safire couldn't swim. She'd never rowed a boat before in her life, never mind in the middle of a storm. She reached into her pocket, touching the smooth glass face of the compass she'd stolen, trying to find her courage.

I must warn Asha, she thought. *And this might be my only chance.*

She had the compass. She knew the scrin was somewhere in the Star Isles, and the Star Isles were northwest. All she needed was to climb into the rowboat, lower it down . . .

Again, lightning flashed.

Safire stood frozen in fear as she stared into the inky chaos below.

Count to three, she told herself. *On three, you're going to get into the boat, then cut the ropes.*

Safire swiped at her rain-soaked eyes.

One . . .

She sucked in a breath.

Two . . .

She bent her knees, ready to spring over the side.

Three!

Before she could jump, a hand clamped around her arm, fingers digging in hard.

"Are you out of your damned mind?"

Safire's spine straightened.

"Turn around." Eris's voice battled the rain. "Nice and slow."

Safire kept one hand on the wood so that the rocking ship didn't pitch her overboard, then did as she was told.

In the dim light of the oil lamp overhead, Safire found Eris standing before her, pale hair slicked against her face, rain running down her skin. She had the stolen throwing knife in her hand, pointed at Safire's chest.

Safire pressed herself up against the ship's side, waiting for Eris to haul her back into that room.

Instead, Eris let go of her arm. Stepping in close, her gaze bored into Safire's. Something had changed in her. Earlier Eris had been weary and worn, but now she seemed wide awake.

Her green eyes seemed brighter. Her skin luminous as starlight. Her smile dangerous.

She seemed . . . more than human.

Safire should have been thinking of the best way to get that knife out of her hand. Instead, she couldn't look away.

What are you?

Eris glanced over Safire's shoulder, to the rowboat, then the waves beyond it. "That storm will crush you, princess." She looked back at Safire like one would at a child who'd just attempted something utterly foolish.

As if she found the escape attempt *cute.*

Indignation blazed through Safire. She flipped out the blade in her boot, planning to kick, grab her knife, then vault herself into the rowboat.

Before she could do any of those things, a deep and growling voice interrupted.

"How touching."

Eris stiffened.

Safire glanced up, over Eris's shoulder, to find three figures standing on the deck. In the light of the oil lamps, she could just make out a young man and two women.

Other than Eris, Safire hadn't noticed any women on Jemsin's crew. She looked to the man standing on night watch and found him struggling with one of the invading pirates. Before he could alert the crew below, he suddenly dropped to the deck and out of Safire's view—dead or unconscious, she couldn't say which.

"Drop the knife."

Eris's gaze held Safire's, a warning in her eyes as she did as he commanded, letting go of Safire's knife. It clattered to the wooden planks and when the ship surged again, went skittering across the deck.

It was when Eris stepped away, turning to face the three newcomers, that Safire saw the massive black silhouette, looming beyond the deck on the leeward side.

Another ship?

Safire looked from the second ship to the young man now standing directly before her.

"So nice to see you alive, Kor," said Eris. "Where'd you get the ship?"

"From a well-wisher," said the one called Kor. Turning to one of the young women beside him, he said: "Find it." The girl nodded, then disappeared down the steps leading into the darkened galley. She emerged a moment later with what looked like a spindle. The one Safire found earlier under Eris's pillow.

At the sight of it, Eris's whole body went rigid.

Safire suddenly remembered the day of her first encounter with the legendary Death Dancer. Eris had been disguised as a soldat then. The two of them collided, and she'd dropped her spindle. Not knowing who she was then, Safire picked it up and handed it back to her.

Kor cocked his head, studying Safire in the light of the lamps. Safire studied him back. He was missing one ear and his wet hair was pulled back in a braid. His face bore what looked like fresh burn scars, red and blistered, and he held himself rigidly, his mouth a tight grimace, as if every breath caused him pain. It made Safire wonder if there were other wounds hidden beneath his clothes.

The boat rocked suddenly, and Safire nearly slipped. Her knife slid slowly across the deck and out of reach.

"Grab her," said Kor. He turned to Eris. "I'll take care of this fiend."

It was clear Kor hadn't come for Safire; he'd come for Eris. Maybe, if Safire could convince him that Eris was her enemy, too, that she and Kor were on the same side, he would let her go. So when the pirates descended on her, Safire didn't put up a fight. Just let the two girls force her across the deck, to the leeward side, where one of them laid a wooden board down across the gap from this ship to the next. The space between the two vessels was the length of three horses, while the wooden board itself was no wider than Safire's boot.

"You first," said a voice at Safire's ear just before they shoved her forward.

Her hands clutched the damp wood. It was slick beneath her skin.

Safire stared down into the ravenous waves and swallowed hard.

"Nice and easy," said Eris, whose hands were bound in front of her now. Kor had a fistful of her blond hair in one hand, a dagger pressed to her neck with the other. Eris stared at Safire. "One step at a time."

Safire climbed onto the board.

The boat rocked and groaned, and Safire nearly fell backward. She threw her arms out and fought for balance, doing exactly as Eris said: taking one small step at a time. She thought of Asha. How she needed to survive this so she could warn her. How she needed to just get to the other ship.

The rain lashed. The waves roared. The ships rose and fell with the waves. Her foot slipped more than once; and more than once, she thought she was going to fall. But every time, she found her balance. And then the other ship's deck was beneath her, and there were hands grabbing her, and she was so relieved to still be alive, she didn't care that their touch burned like fire. Didn't care when they dragged her belowdecks and threw her to the floor so hard, pain laced through her knees.

Safire counted the pirates in the room, assessed them for

weapons, and found the exits. Then she kept her eyes on her captors. She needed to do everything she could to stay alive. If she wanted to convince these pirates she was on their side, she needed to first be compliant.

So she stayed on her knees, biding her time.

They threw Eris down beside her. The girl's palms hit the floor with a smack and she shook out her hair, sending rain flying.

They were in a long room—half the length of the ship—and on both sides were wide windows streaked with rain. Torches burned every few feet, keeping the room lit.

On the deck above them, someone gave the order to depart.

It seemed odd to Safire that these pirates had boarded Jemsin's ship, stolen only one of his crew—plus a hostage—then left as quickly as they'd come.

Why?

The sound of booted footsteps made Eris flinch beside her. Safire glanced over to find the girl staring at the floor, her gaze boring into the wood beneath her. As if she were trying to think her way out of this.

"Who are they?" Safire whispered.

"Pirates," Eris whispered back.

Helpful, thought Safire. "What do they want?"

And why haven't you escaped already?

She thought of Eris on that last night back in Firgaard: there one moment, gone the next. However she'd eluded Safire that night, surely Eris could elude these pirates the same way?

Eris didn't answer. Because at that moment, the boots

stopped directly before her. Eris's jaw clenched just before she looked up.

"Did you really think I wouldn't come for you?" Kor said. He held the spindle in his hand, squeezing it so hard, Safire was sure he'd snap it in half. "After you torched my ship and ran?"

Safire didn't like the way he looked at Eris. She'd seen that same look before, in another man's eyes. Possessive and ravenous.

"Honestly," said Eris, holding his gaze, "I was thinking you might be dead."

Kor's face darkened. He handed the spindle to one of the pirates beside him, wincing from some hidden pain, then grabbed a fistful of Eris's hair. Looking to Safire, he said, "Is this her? The trollop you were with in Firgaard?"

Safire felt all the gazes in the room turn to her.

With them came a sharp realization.

What? she thought, instantly appalled. "No," she said. "Gods, no." She looked to Eris, her wet shirt clinging to her thin frame, tendrils of wheat-colored hair plastered to her pale skin. "Not in a hundred years."

Eris refused to meet her gaze.

"You two looked awfully cozy on Jemsin's deck. Didn't you think so, Rain? Lila?"

Safire looked to the first girl—tall and muscular with a nest of red hair and a bird tattoo on her forearm.

"Very cozy," said Rain, staring hard.

The girl named Lila crossed her arms and smirked at Safire. "Coziest pair I ever saw."

Safire needed to make it clear she was in no way associated

with the criminal beside her.

"I was trying to escape," she told them, shaking her head in disgust. "She *kidnapped* me. Then tortured me. She would have watched Jemsin kill me tomorrow if you hadn't boarded his ship and taken us hostage."

Rain and Lila exchanged glances.

The boat suddenly dipped and Safire's stomach lurched.

"Come on, Kor," said Eris, kneeling now, her back straight as she stared at him. "You really think I'm the kind of girl who goes in for spoiled princesses?"

A strange silence bled through the room as eyes met.

"Is that true?" Kor demanded, staring Safire down. "You're a princess?"

Safire caught Eris's gaze, which was sharp as a honed blade.

"I'm not—" she said.

"She's the dragon king's cousin," Eris interrupted her.

Safire glared.

Eris ignored it, continuing. "Jemsin found her spying and took her prisoner."

"Really." Kor's gaze slid over Safire, studying her bright blue eyes and tanned skin. He was comparing her, no doubt, to what he knew of the king's line. Of draksor complexions in general. But Safire had never looked like her cousins. Had never looked like anyone in the palace. She didn't *fit* there—a fact she'd spent her life being constantly reminded of. A fact she could clearly see in Kor's eyes.

"I don't care who she is," Kor decided, drawing his dagger. "I think a trade is in order, don't you? You hurt me, Eris. Now

I'm going to hurt your sweetheart."

"I'm not—"

"What should I take from her?" Kor cut Safire off, circling them both. Eris said nothing. "An ear? A hand? Your choice, Eris."

With her first plan going up in flames, Safire glanced at the knife hilt protruding from his boot. If she could seize it . . .

Eris sighed, almost lazily. She shook her head. "*This* is your problem, Kor. You take everything so personally."

Kor's knuckles tightened around his weapon.

"Let's play this out, shall we?" Eris pressed. "Let's say you're right, that I'm out of my damned mind and in love with a Firgaardian princess." She rolled her eyes. "Let's say that's true. So, because you're mad at me, you maim her." Eris paused. "Then what?"

Kor narrowed his eyes, keeping his dagger raised.

"First"—Eris raised one graceful finger, which was when Safire realized her hands were manacled together—"you'll enrage Jemsin. She's his prisoner, and you can be sure he'll give chase once he finds her gone. And second"—Eris raised another finger—"you'll have the entire Firgaardian army—not to mention that cousin of hers, the one with the dragon?—on your tail."

Safire stared at Eris. These were the exact same reasons Safire gave aboard Jemsin's ship. The ones Eris easily refuted.

Is she trying to protect me?

Safire shook off the thought, reminding herself that Eris still needed to find Asha and deliver her to Jemsin. And only Safire knew where Asha was. Nothing had changed. Eris was just a desperate girl protecting her own interests.

"You might be able to outrun them for a day or two," Eris was saying. "But then either the dragon will have reduced you and your ship to a pile of flotsam *or* you'll be spending the rest of your miserable life in the king's prison." She smiled up at Kor, her green eyes sparkling. "It's up to you. But at least *think* before you do something stupid."

Kor's eyes flashed. He grabbed a fistful of Eris's shirt and pressed the edge of the blade to her throat. His hand was steady, but his eyes were feverish.

Eris didn't cry out. Didn't even break his gaze.

But Safire saw the tremble in her shoulders.

She also saw that beneath Kor's steady anger simmered the red craze of desire. It reminded her of Jarek, wanting Asha. Needing to either have her or harm her.

Kor could never have Eris. Safire saw this clear on the girl's face. And if Safire saw it, so did Kor.

In that moment, she knew he wouldn't hesitate to open Eris's throat.

Before he could, Safire burst out: "I knew a man like you once."

The blaze in Kor's eyes flickered. He turned his burned face to Safire, but still kept his blade pressed hard to Eris's skin.

"His name was Jarek and he commanded the king's army. Whatever he said, people did." Safire felt the dark memories creep over her. Only this time, she let them. "He thought he could have whatever he wanted. And what he couldn't have, he tried to destroy."

Kor narrowed his eyes at her. "And why should I care about this man?"

Safire lifted her gaze to his face. "Because I'm the one who buried a knife in his heart."

Into the silence of the room, the ship creaked.

The hunger drained out of Kor. Something far more dangerous rushed in to replace it. He shoved Eris, who fell back. From the corner of her eye, Safire saw the girl touch her throat, then study the blood on her fingertips.

Kor crouched down before Safire now, his face level and so close with hers she could see the open sores of his freshly burned skin. "Let me tell you something about Jemsin's precious Death Dancer. That girl there?" He nodded toward Eris. "She's an enemy of the empress. Seven years ago, she set fire to a temple full of people. Half of them children. Not a single one of them escaped."

Safire drew away from Eris. *What?*

She'd known the Death Dancer was a thief. But a *murderer*?

Eris's voice went taut as rope as she said, "Who told you that?"

Kor rose to his feet. "An eleven-year-old girl burns down a temple, killing dozens, and manages to escape the hordes of Lumina tracking her? Manages to elude them for *seven years*? There's no ordinary girl who could do that." Linking his hands behind his back, he began to walk in circles around Eris. "And then there's the strange matter of Jemsin sending you away whenever he meets with the empress. As if he doesn't want you seen by her." Kor stopped circling and looked down at the top of her head. "I put the rest together myself. I've been putting it together for a while now, in fact. I intended to keep your secret . . . but then you burned down the *Sea Mistress*."

Safire looked to find Eris staring hard at the floor.

"It was Leandra who came to our aid. She's the one who lent me this ship." He waved his hand at the room around them. "If I bring in her fugitive, she'll give me a reward big enough to buy an entire fleet of ships. Do you know what that means for me? *Freedom*, Eris. No more living in Jemsin's shadow. No more coming and going like a dog. Soon I won't just be captain of my own ship, I'll be captain of my own *fleet*. And then *I* will be the fiercest pirate on the Silver Sea." Kor made a fist. "So you better pray to that god of yours tonight. Because tomorrow we reach the Star Isles."

Safire's head snapped up. *The Star Isles.* That was where Asha was. Which meant that once they reached the islands, all she had to do was escape and find her way to the scrin.

A tender spark of hope lit her up.

Eris went very still beside her.

"That's right," Kor smirked. "I'm handing you over to the Lumina."

Safire found a ghost of a girl staring out through Eris's eyes. At Kor's mention of the islands, the color had drained from her face.

The boat rocked. The nausea swept through Safire again and she planted her hands on the deck, trying to shake it.

The girl named Rain hauled her to her feet, then marched her up the steps, out into the storm and across the slick deck, then down a narrow hall. Rain threw her into a room the size of a closet, then tossed Eris in after her.

The moment they locked the door, the ship rocked again. Safire's stomach roiled. She reached for the wall.

"I . . ."

I'm going to be sick.

Eris looked at her sharply. Right before Safire threw up.

Thirteen

Safire spent the night wanting to curl up and die. Eris spent it banging on the door, demanding a bucket. Finally, they gave her one. And now Safire clung to it, vomiting up her dinner—the apple, then the herring, then the wine-soaked bread. She vomited until there was nothing but bile coming up, and all the while, Eris held back her hair in her fist.

Finally the sea settled, and with it, Safire's stomach. It smelled acrid now in this tiny room, lit only by a single lantern high up on the wall. Safire was pretty sure they were both sitting in her vomit. She shook with exhaustion, and her throat felt raw.

Somewhere above her, she heard Eris banging on the door again. This time, demanding water. She heard the creak of the door swinging open, followed by the exchange of barbed words. Then the warmth of Eris returned to Safire's side, pressed up against the wall.

Eris uncorked the jug they gave her and passed it over. "Drink."

Safire took the jug, tipping it back and gulping the cool water down.

"Why did you do that?" Eris asked.

Safire wiped her mouth on her wrist. "Do what?"

Eris stared at the wall straight ahead. "Back there. With Kor. He was going to punish me, and you drew him off. Why would you do that?"

Safire heard the things she didn't say: *Why protect me after I kidnapped you and delivered you to the deadliest pirate on the Silver Sea? After I had you tortured?*

"I don't know," said Safire.

But she did know.

Safire knew what it was like to be at the mercy of cruel men. She and her cousins still bore the marks of their terror. It was why Jarek was dead.

Safire had stopped tolerating abuse a long time ago.

Eris fell quiet beside her. She flicked her wrists, as if agitated, and for the second time Safire noticed the manacles there.

In the growing silence, Safire thought of the things Kor said.

"Is it true that you torched his ship?"

Eris tipped her head back, resting against the boards of the wall. Gone was that luminous otherworldly creature who'd found her on Jemsin's deck. In her place was a bone-weary girl. If she cared that she was covered in Safire's vomit, it didn't show.

"Damn right I torched it." Eris smiled a little as she said it. "I've never been happier to see a thing burn."

But it was one thing to burn down a cruel man's ship. It was another to burn down a temple full of innocents.

"And the burned temple full of children?" asked Safire. "Are you responsible for that too?"

Eris's smile vanished. Her green eyes went dark as she looked away, the shame etched in the hard lines of her face.

"I am," she said quietly.

The horror of it seeped through Safire. Suddenly chilled, she moved to put space between her and the murderer at her side.

If Eris was the empress's fugitive, if she was capable of such an awful thing, then she needed to be delivered to the empress, where she could serve the sentence for her crimes and—more important—never find Asha.

Eris flicked her wrists again, this time gritting her teeth in pain.

Safire glanced down. These were nothing like the manacles Eris had locked Safire's wrists in back on Jemsin's ship. These looked . . . almost elegant. Two thin circles of pale, silvery steel.

Seeing where she looked, Eris plunged her hands into the shadows of her crossed legs—but not before Safire saw the skin around one wrist. Wherever the band touched, the skin was frost white.

"What are those? What's wrong with your wrists?"

"Nothing," said Eris, staring straight ahead.

They clearly weren't nothing; they were hurting her. "Let me see."

"Trust me, princess. There's nothing to be done."

"I told you to stop calling me that."

Reaching across the space now between them, Safire pulled

one of Eris's hands roughly out of the shadows and into the light of the lantern hanging on the wall above them. Surprisingly, Eris let her. With her fingers gripping the girl's forearm—which was eerily cold—Safire held Eris's palm still while inspecting her wrist.

Safire had seen unnaturally white flesh only once before, in the desert back home. At night in the sand sea, the temperature dropped well below freezing, and if you weren't prepared, you froze.

"Frostbite," she murmured.

"Something like that." Eris withdrew her hand and held up both wrists for Safire to see. "It's called stardust steel."

Safire had never heard of such a thing.

"It's a weapon," Eris explained. "Used by the Lumina. Or in this case, Kor. Who's made some kind of deal with them."

Lumina. The name given to the military class of the Star Isles. Safire had heard stories of the empress's fearsome soldiers, who she used to keep order on the islands and to patrol her waters.

But she'd never heard of stardust steel.

"They use stardust steel in all their weapons." Eris's mouth twisted, and there was a haunted look in her eyes again. With her wrists still raised, she stared at the bands. "It's a corrosive metal that . . ." She paused, and Safire saw her skip over whatever she was about to say. "It eats away at whatever it touches. It can take years or . . . days. Depending."

"Depending on what?"

"On the substance. Another metal, for example, will take longer to corrode."

A cold feeling spread through Safire as she studied the frost-white skin beneath the bands. "And human flesh?"

"Three days. At most."

Safire tried to imagine it. What Eris's wrists would look like in three days. First, the flesh would corrode. Then the muscle beneath. Then the bone.

"They'll sever your hands from your wrists," she whispered.

Eris's silence confirmed this.

Safire felt ill—only this time, it wasn't from the tumultuous sea. She tried to tell herself it didn't matter if Eris lost her hands. This girl was beneath her pity. She was the worst kind of criminal. Surely, she deserved this fate.

Still, Safire searched the silvery bands for a clasp or a lock. One that could be picked. But there was nothing. The metal was one smooth circle ensnaring Eris's wrist.

"Where does it open and close?" she asked.

"It doesn't," said Eris.

And then she saw it: a cold-forged pin.

The only person who could get these off was a blacksmith.

A Good-bye

One dark day, the sea changed. Crow felt the powerful, terrible thing moving beneath its waters. Felt something ancient and familiar calling to him.

Hunting for him.

Crow kept his distance from the fisherman's daughter, drawing the thing's attention far away from Skye and her islands. But he was no longer the powerful creature he'd once been. Years walking alongside Skye had changed him.

So, when his pursuer closed in, Crow hid. Deep in the darkness, he forced himself to forget the strength in Skye's rough and callused hands. To forget the gaze of her one good eye and the yearning she awoke in him. In his hiding, Crow forced himself to remember what he truly was: an ancient creature made of darkness.

A god of shadows.

He came out to face his pursuer—a thing as old and wicked as he was. A god of the sea.

"Too long you've wandered," she called to him in dulcet tones. "Come back to me."

When the god of shadows refused, she attacked.

They battled for seven days and nights. They fought with tempests and maelstroms and monsters. And with every strike, the shadow god remembered a little bit more of himself.

Finally, he reared up and dealt her a devastating blow. In shock and defeat, the sea god fell to her knees before him. The shadow god stood over her, lifting a fist to finish her off.

But before he struck, a memory flickered through him: one of Skye in her father's dory, unhooking a spawning fish and throwing it back to the sea.

As he stared down at his enemy, a new and tender feeling unfurled within him.

Pity.

The god of shadows stayed his hand.

Seeing it, his enemy fled.

A long time later, when Crow came back to himself, his first thought was of Skye. Was she safe? But as he went to seek her out, he slowly came to realize that it wasn't seven days which passed while he waged war on the god of the sea, but rather seven years.

Surely, his mortal girl had forgotten him.

"It's better this way," he said.

But he needed to know.

What harm could it do to walk through her cove, past her father's wharf, and up the cliffs, just one last time? To make sure she was safe?

Gathering the darkness around him, Crow set out. He would only look from a distance. He would not seek her out.

But as he neared Skye's home, he heard the sound of music. Felt the joy of dancing. And so, filled with a curiosity he'd tried so hard to extinguish—a curiosity Skye gave to him—he came closer than he should have.

It was the longest day of the year, and her village was celebrating. He found her immediately in the crowd of dancers. She wore a sleeveless white dress that fell just past her knees and a crown of blue forget-me-nots on her head. Her hands were gripped by a man. He smiled as he danced with her, as if she were everything he loved most in the world.

Skye's face was older and her hair longer. It fell around her like autumn leaves as she and the man spun around and around, laughing as they did.

They weren't celebrating the longest day of the year. They were celebrating a wedding.

Skye's wedding.

If Crow had a human heart, it might have broken in his chest.

Suddenly, her eyes met Crow's.

She stopped dancing.

Time seemed to slow as they stared at each other. Her face drained of color as her lips formed his name.

It took all of Crow's strength to turn away from her. From all of them. This had been a mistake. He should never have come here. He did not belong in her world, just as she did not belong in his.

He was already in the trees when he heard familiar footsteps. He closed his eyes, trying not to hear. He gathered the darkness around him, trying to hide himself in it.

But Skye found him. Like always.

"Where are you going?"

The words stopped him, rooting him to the earth the way only hers could. There was a pain in his chest. Like some weighty thing now rested there, beating in time with the waves on the shore.

He didn't turn around. Couldn't bring himself to look at her.

"It's been seven years," she whispered, and he heard the wobble in her voice. "You chose to come back today . . . of all days?"

Suddenly, she was beside him. In front of him.

"And now you're leaving again? Without even saying hello?"

He covered his face with his hands.

"I shouldn't have come," he whispered.

"Then why did you!" Her two small palms collided with his shoulders. Crow stumbled back, hands falling to his sides, shocked by the strength of her. They stared at each other. Her eyes were like hurricanes. He'd never seen her so angry.

No, not angry. Hurt.

He had done that.

"You were never my friend," she said, chin trembling. "I realize that now. You let me believe you were because you pitied me." Her mouth twisted. "Poor, ugly, mortal girl."

That was too much.

He stepped toward her, remembering their last meeting as if it were yesterday. A moment ago. "Don't say that."

Tears trembled on her lashes. He swept them away before they spilled down her cheeks.

"I couldn't come," he said.

But how could he explain it? That seven years were like seven days to him? She wouldn't understand.

Skye reached for him, gathering the shadows around him in her fist. "Take me with you."

"I can't."

"Because I'm mortal."

"Yes."

"Then make me immortal."

He stared at her. She didn't know what she was asking. But he did. And the cost was unbearable.

"I can't. You and I—"

But his words were lost in the softness of her mouth.

For a heartbeat, he remembered the berry she gave him all those years *ago. The way it made him ache for more.*

Her kiss was crueler than that. Because this time what she offered, he knew he shouldn't take.

But he did.

He devoured her, crushing her to him, needing all of her. When she cried out in pain, he realized he'd lost himself. Her kiss had awoken the god in him, and the god would destroy her.

Crow wrenched himself out of her grasp before that happened.

"Skye . . ." Even he could hear his now-human heart—the heart she'd given him—breaking in his words. "You and I can never be."

Before she could stop him, he melted into shadow. Escaping her.

This time for good.

Fourteen

Safire wasn't used to being confined to small spaces. The closet suffocated her. The ship itself was like a cage she couldn't escape. How did Eris bear it, living aboard these things? Safire was used to running the hunting paths through the Rift with Asha. Used to prowling the palace or the city. Used to sparring with her soldats.

All her life, Safire had needed to move and keep herself strong—for her own survival.

Being confined like this was making her fray at the edges.

So, as Eris slept, Safire kept focused by doing sit-ups. As her upper body rose and fell, her muscles burning with the exertion, she devised a plan.

She might feel sorry for Eris, with her hands locked in those corrosive manacles, but the girl was a criminal. Just yesterday, she'd instructed Jemsin's men to torture her for information. The moment Eris knew where the Namsara was, she would hunt Asha down and bring her to Jemsin. Safire couldn't let that happen. The safest place for Eris to be was in the hands of the empress, who would decide what to do with her.

Kor was about to make this happen. It was in Safire's best interest, therefore, to escape at the first opportunity, leaving Eris with the pirates.

But while her purposes might be temporarily aligned with Kor's, Safire had seen the cruel look in his eyes. A cruelty he wouldn't hesitate to dole out on Eris the next time he got her alone. Safire might want Eris locked away, but she didn't want her hurt. And to escape was to leave her completely at Kor's mercy.

And there was the matter of those strange cuffs. What if Kor didn't deliver her in time and they severed her wrists?

It was a dilemma.

In the end, Safire decided to take Eris with her. She'd seen maps of the Star Isles when the empress first invited Dax to visit. Once she oriented herself, she would make her way to the capital, hand Eris over, and *then* find Asha.

All she had to do was stay watchful and alive. She would play along. Be a good, obedient captive. And once the opportunity for escape arose, she would seize it.

Suddenly, Eris woke, jolting upright and breaking Safire's concentration. Safire fell back against the floor, breathing hard now while her muscles relaxed.

"Do you hear that?"

Safire watched Eris from where she lay on the floor, her warm cheek pressed against the wooden planks. "Hear what?"

"Sea spirits. They're singing." Eris rose to her feet and started to pace. "*Hells.*"

Safire sat up, watching her. Trying to hear what Eris heard.

But the only sounds were the shriek of the wind and the croaking of the ship.

With her wrists clasped, Eris banged on the door, shouting for someone to open it. When no one did, she shouted some more. "Listen, you morons! He's sailing us straight into the wrecking grounds! Let me out!"

When they still didn't respond, she began kicking the door hard with the sole of her boot.

Finally, it swung open. Kor himself stood in the frame.

Eris shrank back, cheeks rosy, breathing hard. Safire got to her feet, standing behind her.

"That landmass straight ahead? It's Shadow Isle," she told him. "Shadow Isle is known for its wrecking grounds. This *seems* like a shortcut to Axis, but it's actually a—"

"You're a thief, not a sailor," he growled. "Leave the navigating to me."

"There are spirits ahead, waiting for idiots like you!"

His eyes narrowed into slits. "Sea spirits don't exist, Eris. They're tales made up by delirious scurvy-ridden sailors. And who says I'm taking you to Axis, anyway?"

Eris frowned, going suddenly quiet.

"If I have to come down here again," he said, stepping in close, "you will regret it. The empress may want you alive, but she never said in what condition."

Eris backed up, straight into Safire.

Kor stared Eris down until she looked away. For a moment, Safire thought he might come through on his threat right then. But when he remembered the girl standing behind Eris, his eyes met Safire's and he stepped back.

Finally he turned and slammed the door behind him.

As the lock clicked, Eris's hands curled into fists. "I grew up on Shadow Isle. I know what's waiting for us beneath the water."

As if the sea itself heard her, the ship gave a shuddering shriek, followed by the buckling and breaking of wood. The floor seemed to rise as the boat pitched forward and came to an abrupt stop, throwing Eris and Safire into the wall.

Alarmed shouts echoed above them. Footsteps clomped loudly overhead.

"What in all the skies . . . ?" murmured Safire as water began to creep under the door and across the floor.

"It's called shipwreck alley," said Eris, who, after finding her balance, began to bang both her manacled fists on the door again, "for a reason."

The water seeped to the other side of the room, then slowly started to rise.

Safire joined Eris, making noise along with her.

Soon, the door swung open again. Two pirates came in, and with them, a rush of salt water. Safire was forced out first and shoved down the hall. The moment she hit the deck, she gulped in salty air. The wind whipped her hair across her face and Safire fought it back with her fingers, looking north. Not far from the ship, glistening black rocks rose like jagged pillars out of the mist. Just beyond them, Safire saw the outline of chalky gray cliffs.

The startling beauty of it entranced her.

Much closer, Safire could see other shapes in the gloom. Silhouettes of heads bobbing in the water. Inhuman forms crouched on the rocks.

"Sea spirits," said Eris, suddenly at her side. "Known for breaking ships and eating crews alive."

Safire shivered.

When two pirates forced her to the ship's starboard side, however, she saw that the wind still roared, whipping the waves into a frenzy below. As they crashed against the ship, heaving and receding, she could see the sharp rocks the boat was grounded on.

"In you go," said Rain, reaching for the rowboat secured with rope.

Behind her, Eris was arguing with Kor. But Safire didn't hear a word of what she said. She was looking from the waves crashing against the hull to the sea spirits in the fog.

"Listen, girlie. It's into the rowboat or into the sea. Pick one."

Safire looked to find Rain leveling her with a stare so murderous, she climbed into the boat. Rain climbed in after her.

"It's too dangerous!" Eris said, voice raised at Kor.

Safire looked to where Kor was forcing Eris—hands bound in front of her—toward the rowboats.

Eris's eyes caught Safire's as she reached to pull herself up and into the same boat, sitting down on the bench across from her. Eris must have seen something in Safire's gaze, because her face changed. She glanced down to where Safire's hands gripped the bench so hard, her knuckles were turning white.

"You were right," Safire admitted. "I can't swim."

Eris's gaze lifted in surprise. For a heartbeat, Safire thought Eris looked well and truly afraid for her. As if their boat capsizing was a serious possibility.

But if she thought that, Eris kept it to herself.

The crew still on board undid the rowboat's fastenings and started to lower it down. Safire's stomach lurched as they dropped, then halted, swinging. She stared down at the angry waves, roaring and crashing, wanting to drown her. She looked to the dark and hungry forms beyond, waiting to devour her.

"Hey. Princess. Don't look down there. Look at me."

But Safire couldn't look away.

I wasn't supposed to die this way.

"Safire." Eris reached for her chin with bound hands, tilting Safire's face away from the danger.

Safire started at the sound of her name more than the touch of Eris's fingers. She looked up into Eris's eyes, which were solemn as she said, "I promise I won't let anything happen to you."

Safire glanced to Eris's manacled wrists and knew this was a lie. If their boat capsized, Eris wouldn't even be able to save herself. She wouldn't be able to stop the sea spirits from eating either of them.

But it was kind lie, meant to reassure.

So Safire said, "What good is a promise from a low-life pirate?"

But she smiled as she said it.

Eris smiled slowly back.

Fifteen

Their boat nearly capsized twice.

Kor was an utter fool to attempt it. He knew just as well as Eris what sky-high waves could do to a small, rudderless boat. The only reason for such recklessness was the wrecked ship at their backs.

As Rain and Lila rowed, Eris kept her eyes on the fog. She could smell the stench of the sea spirits—like rotting fish—but could no longer see their dark shapes. If she had any love left for the Skyweaver, she might have sent a prayer skyward.

"If I were you," she said to Rain as the stench got stronger, "I'd row faster."

Rain grunted as she tugged on the oars, but otherwise ignored Eris.

A scream pierced the air behind them, followed by the sound of teeth ripping into flesh. Across from Eris, Safire spun, gripping the sides of the rowboat and staring into the fog. More screams erupted, half-cloaked by the roar of the sea. Rain and

Lila strained on the oars. Eris listened, completely still, as Kor's crew was dragged one by one from their boats and into the water.

They were coming up on the shore. Half a dozen hard pulls on the oars would get them there. Behind Safire, in the back of the boat, Kor screamed for them to row harder. His black hair had come free of its band and now glistened with sea spray as he yanked on his oars.

That was when Eris heard the wave. She heard it a heartbeat before she felt the boat rising end over end. Her heart lurched as the sea spilled her out of the rowboat, sending her headfirst into its waters.

The icy temperature sent a shock through her body. The salt stung her wounded wrists. Her shoulder struck the ground beneath the waves. And as she struggled against the pull of the tide, she felt the world tilt. Heard the islands shift and murmur.

There, in the throes of the sea, the past rose up like a nightmare.

She heard their dying screams. Smelled the scorched timbers and tapestries. Felt the heat of the flames devouring it all.

Suspended in water, trapped in her memories, Eris stopped fighting. Instead, she willed the tide to drag her down to the depths. She begged the sea to drive the air from her lungs.

After the horrors she was responsible for, it was no less than what she deserved.

Before the sea could do her bidding, someone grabbed her. Fingers drove into Eris's arm as their owner yanked her to her feet, dragging her toward the shore, sloshing through the waves and away from the danger. When the ocean receded and the wet sand squished beneath her feet, Eris fell to her knees. When she looked up, Kor stared down at her.

"Get up," he said, shoving her shoulder with the pommel of his dagger. "We need to keep moving."

"Where's Safire?"

Eris looked back over her shoulder to find Rain dragging their rowboat up above the tideline. It was one of only two rowboats that made it. Nearby, Safire spluttered as she, too, was dragged up the shore by Lila.

At the sight of her alive, Eris let out a breath. She looked farther out, over the water. Beyond the mist, she could just make out the shapes of several sea spirits watching from the waves.

She forced herself to get to her feet and started walking.

Jemsin would realize they were gone by now. He would hunt Kor down—or get his summoner to do it for him. But Kor might easily drag Eris to the empress before Jemsin found him. Eris needed to escape, track down the Namsara, and bring her to the captain.

It was the only thing standing between her and freedom. And right now, as Eris looked from the corpse-infested waters to the man about to hand her over to her worst enemy, she wanted freedom more than ever.

But as Kor forced her up the beach and toward the mist-shrouded trees, a stinging pain halted Eris's thoughts. She looked down at her now-enflamed wrists, locked in stardust steel. In just a few days the steel would eat right through her— skin, muscle, and bone.

First, she needed to find a way to get these off. *Then*, she would track down the Namsara.

And if she couldn't get the manacles off, so be it. Kor would not be handing her over to the ones who'd taken everything from her.

Eris would escape and locate the Namsara—with or without her hands.

Shadow Isle was the smallest and most southern of the Star Isles. For the first eleven years of her life, it was the island Eris called home.

She tried not to think about this fact as they trudged through the woods.

Rain, Lila, and a few others hacked at junipers and balsam firs, trying to clear a path through the muddy, silty soil until they found the footpath. Kor and two more pirates walked behind Eris and Safire, watching them like hawks. But Eris could feel the tension in them. Mere moments ago they'd heard their crewmates get eaten alive, and now they were walking through an eldritch forest. Who knew what would come for them next?

Safire hadn't said a word since they left the shore. The whole way from the ship, she'd sat stiff with terror. Now, with her feet back on solid ground, her face softened as she took in her surroundings. Eris watched her study the twisted, silvery trees; the sheer cliff edges; the barren, mossy rock.

Eris knew that look. The Star Isles lured you in with their beauty and mystery. And only when you were good and truly snared did they reveal their true nature. But by then, it was too late.

At that thought, Eris checked the sky for ravens. Part of her hoped Jemsin's summoner—as much as she feared the creature—would come for her. It would be the easiest way out of this. But the only birds flying overhead were gulls.

When she looked back, she found Safire studying a hedge of white berries they were passing.

"Scarp berries," Eris told her, their shoulders brushing. Safire glanced up. "The dart I pricked you with the other night? It was made from a scarp thistle thorn. Their berries can be used the same way."

Safire's brow furrowed and her lips pursed as she stepped toward the scarp plant—earning her a shove from Rain.

Safire threw the girl a dirty look as Eris glanced back, quickly counting the pirates behind them. She winced when she found Kor glaring at her, bringing up the rear of the group. *Four behind and four ahead.* The odds were definitely against her.

But the odds had been against Eris plenty of times before.

They walked for most of the day. When it began to rain lightly, the damp smell of the earth and junipers brought a rush of bittersweet memories. That was when Eris started to recognize the landscape around her. Soon, their pace quickened and Eris realized it was because they'd hit a path. A familiar path. One she'd walked thousands of times as a child.

Suddenly, she knew exactly where they were.

"No," Eris whispered, halting abruptly.

This time when Kor shoved, Eris ground her heels in, refusing to budge.

"Move," Kor growled.

"I'd rather die."

Safire stopped and looked back, studying her.

Kor motioned for two of the other pirates to haul Eris onward. But the moment their grip closed around her arms, Eris dropped to her knees.

They would have to drag her if they wanted her to go any farther.

Suddenly, she felt the press of steel at her back. "I don't have time for this."

Eris wished she knew where her spindle was. But it could be hidden on any of these pirates. And even if she had it, the stardust steel locked around her wrists prevented her from going across.

She was completely powerless.

Eris squeezed her eyes shut. "Kill me, then. Right here. What you're going to do is worse than death anyway."

Kor stepped in front of her, staring down at Eris out of those fierce dark eyes. Eris looked beyond him, to the path between the misty trees. A path that led up through gray shale cliffs and along the sea.

A path that led home.

No, she thought, hardening her heart against it. *Never again will it be my home.*

The whole party came to a halt. Those up ahead circled back to see what the problem was.

"Kor?" said the burly Lila, looking to the gray sky, her hair shiny with rain. It had gotten considerably colder and grayer due to the storm coming in. "We have a day's walk ahead of us, and this weather is only going to worsen. I think we should make camp."

Kor sheathed his dagger, then ground the heels of his palms into his eyes. He looked weary suddenly. And Eris wondered if he felt responsible for the massacre they'd left behind.

"Deal with Eris, will you? Rain. Lila. I want your eyes on her all night."

"And this one?" Lila nodded to Safire.

Kor dropped his hands. His eyes narrowed on the commandant. "Tie them up together. They'll be easier to watch."

They tied them to a balsam tree with rope from the boat, with Safire on one side and Eris on the other. Together, Lila and Rain wound it around their stomachs and across their chests, constricting their arms, before tying it in a complicated knot.

The two girls stood over their captives, admiring their handiwork. Rain wiped her brow, then uncorked the water jug and took a long swig before passing it to Lila, who drank, too.

Knowing Safire had vomited up all her liquids and was likely to be more dehydrated than any of them, Eris said, "You going to offer us some of that?"

Lila looked to Rain, who nodded for her to go ahead. So Lila crouched down, holding the jug to Eris's lips and carefully tipped it back. After Eris took several gulps, Lila rose and brought the jug to Safire.

But the commandant turned her face away. "I'm not thirsty."

Eris frowned. There was no way that could be true.

Lila shrugged and returned to Rain's side.

It was as the two of them turned away that Eris noticed a strange taste in her mouth.

From the water, she realized. A bitter taste. It reminded her of a draft Day used to make her drink as a child whenever she had difficulty sleeping.

A sudden heaviness crept in, flooding Eris's limbs, making her thoughts sluggish and slow. Her eyelids closed against their will.

Eris forced them open, suddenly realizing what the taste was.

Scarp berries.

She blinked. Her vision blurred as she turned her face, looking over her shoulder to where Safire was secured on the other side of the tree.

Clever girl, she thought, just before sleep dragged her under.

Sixteen

A voice hissed in Eris's ears as someone shook her awake.

She opened her eyes. A blurry red–gold glow flickered at the edge of her vision. Blinking, she turned toward it.

A young woman knelt over her in the dark, holding a torch made of kindling wrapped in cloth. At least, it seemed like a woman. The shape of her was fuzzy. Focusing hard, Eris could just make out blue eyes and dark eyebrows knit in a frown.

Eris reached for the girl's name, but it was lost in the murk of her mind.

When the world started to spin, she closed her eyes to stop it. The sleep came, lulling her back into the fog. . . .

A sudden shock of cold brought Eris back. She spluttered and sat up this time, gasping.

The world cleared a little. Looking down, she found her clothes wet. The rope tying her to the balsam was gone. But the stardust cuffs around her wrists were still there. Only now they were attached to a rope. Her gaze followed the rope to find it gripped in one of Safire's hands. In Safire's other hand was the empty water jug. And in the trees beyond her, Rain and Lila lay sleeping.

Safire yanked on a rope, jerking Eris's manacles and making her wince. When Eris didn't immediately move, Safire shot her a venomous look, clearly relaying what she wanted Eris to do: get up and *not* wake the sleeping pirates.

Eris rose to her feet and instantly stumbled, still dizzy from the poisoned water. With the forest spinning around her, she stepped toward the two unconscious pirates. Safire grabbed her arm, stopping her.

"I already have their weapons," Safire hissed.

Eris looked the girl up and down to find a dagger tucked into Safire's belt and a knife hilt protruding from the top of her boot.

Clever *and* efficient.

But it wasn't weapons Eris needed, it was her spindle. She looked to Rain's sleeping form, then to the leather pouch at Lila's hip.

"If it's that spindle you're after," Safire whispered. "I already used it for kindling."

Eris froze, then spun to face her. "You didn't."

Safire held out the torch to show her the flame. Proof of her crime.

Eris wanted to curse this girl to the bottom of the sea. "That spindle is my—"

Lila stirred, halting Eris's words. Both their heads snapped to look. The girl hadn't opened her eyes yet, but she was murmuring anxiously now.

Safire motioned with her chin for Eris to start walking. And, because she'd rather be this girl's captive than Kor's, Eris did as Safire directed.

The lingering effects of the scarp berry draft made the world fuzzy at the edges. For a long time, all Eris knew was the blur of dark green, the dip and sway of the earth. She barely heard the thunder rumble above her or the wind screaming above the trees. Barely felt the rain soaking through her clothes, turning her skin clammy and cold.

"Where are you taking us?" she asked Safire as they walked.

"To the Lumina."

Of course. Had Eris really expected any different? Safire was a soldier. Not just a soldier, a commander of soldiers. She loved the law. And Eris was a lawbreaker. Why *wouldn't* she hand her over to the Lumina? Safire and the Lumina had mutual goals. They were one and the same.

The thought struck Eris to the bone.

"Why not just stay with Kor, then?" Eris said coldly. "He'd have delivered us to the empress in half the time it'll take you to find your way to the capital."

"I'm sure he would have," said Safire. "But I dislike being at the mercy of others."

Eris, who'd been at the mercy of others all her life, felt something snap inside her. "Spoken like a true princess."

Safire cut her with a gaze.

Eris looked away angrily.

They walked on in silence. As the effects of the draft began to wear off, Eris realized that Safire was leading them in the same direction they'd been going yesterday. She was taking the same shortcut Kor had chosen to take. The one that led straight past the place Eris swore she'd never go back to.

At that, Eris halted. The manacles drew taut against her wrists. Eris hissed as the steel dug into her wounds, bringing with it a vicious sting.

"We're going the wrong way," she said, her lie wrestling with the sound of thunder above.

Safire turned to face her. The torch was dying, too wet to burn brightly. The bit of flame struggling to stay alive made Safire's dark hair glow red and in her hand was the rope. All she had to do was yank on it to send that stinging pain through Eris again.

"The boats are in that direction." Eris used her chin to point beyond them, down the cliff path. "One of which you'll need if you hope to get to Axis Isle."

Safire shook her head. "Your friends will be expecting us to go for the boats. We need to get out of this storm." Safire eyed Eris's soaked and shivering form. "Otherwise we'll soon have bigger problems than Kor. We're going up there." Safire pointed with her dying torch to a black, looming shape at the top of this cliff.

At the sight of it, Eris went rigid, her thoughts full of smoke and fire.

She shook her head and planted her feet.

"You go right ahead. I'm staying here."

Safire stared at Eris like she was a small, annoying child.

"How about this," Safire said, tying the end of Eris's rope around her belt loop. "If you cooperate, the first thing I'll do when we get to the capital is find a metalsmith to deal with *these*." She tugged on the rope connected to Eris's steel manacles.

The resulting pain in her wrists made Eris's anger spark. She gritted her teeth. "So at least I'll have my hands when you hand me over to the empress's dogs? I don't think so."

Safire stepped in close, grabbing the wet collar of Eris's shirt and bunching it tight in her fist. "Listen, you petulant piece of sea scum. We are going up there, and if I have to drag you the entire way, I swear to the skies, I will." Her gaze was hot on Eris's skin. "Or I can tie you up here and leave you for Kor to deal with. Your choice."

She let go. Eris fell back, seeing in her eyes that she meant it.

But there was something far worse than Kor waiting for Eris at the scrin.

She felt sick at the thought of it.

Eris could try to overcome Safire, but this girl was the king's commandant. She was armed now, and Eris knew from watching her spar with her soldiers in Firgaard that Safire was strong and skilled in combat. Eris wasn't. Eris had always relied on other abilities to survive. Without her spindle, with her hands cuffed, those abilities were severely constricted.

In her current situation, she was no match for Safire. And Kor would have noticed their absence by now. He would have sent Rain and Lila back to the boats, and pressed on ahead himself—or vice versa. If Eris continued to drag her feet, it would only ensure they were caught.

More important, she needed the location of the Namsara. If Eris wanted to track her down, staying close to the Namsara's cousin was her best option.

"If you cooperate," said Safire, breaking up her thoughts, "I'll tell you where I buried your spindle."

What? Eris glanced up. "I thought you used it for kindling."

Safire shrugged. "I lied."

It was then that Eris saw the hard clench of Safire's jaw— trying to hide the fact that her teeth were chattering. She, too, was soaked to the bone. Wet and cold and shivering.

Eris had a strange, sudden urge to take her somewhere safe, build a fire, and warm her up.

She shook off the ludicrous thought, then looked to the top of the cliff.

If Eris went with Safire now, despite the horror of what lay up there, she would learn where her spindle was buried. At that point, all she'd have to do is get free of this girl and double back to dig it up.

"Fine." Eris glanced down to the hilt peeking out of Safire's boot. "But if you want me to cooperate, you need to give me that knife."

"So you can cut my throat with it?" Safire turned back to the path, tugging Eris after her. "I don't think so."

Worth a try, thought Eris, who winced and gave in.

Not that she really had a choice.

✦✦✦

By the time the trees thinned, the torch had gone out completely. The lightning flickered across the sky, illuminating their way. They followed the dirt path through the darkness and up the cliffs. When the sandy soil turned to crumbling shale steps wet with sea spray, they started to climb.

Eris's legs were soon burning as they rose higher into the cliffs. It had been seven years since she'd walked these steps. As the lightning lit up the black sea below, Eris thought of all the nights she'd sat watching storms surge over this same sea. Letting the thunder silence all the unanswered questions inside her.

The higher they rose, the closer they came. With every familiar sight and sound and smell, Eris's gut twisted. Memories she thought she'd locked away sprung loose, making her nauseous.

I can't do this. . . .

Eris stopped, halting Safire. She pressed her hands to her knees, trying not to throw up.

"What's wrong?"

"Nothing," she whispered, squeezing her eyes shut, trying to keep it all back with the sheer force of her will. "Just . . . an effect of the scarp berries."

When the nausea—which had nothing to do with the scarp berries—settled, Eris avoided that too-keen gaze and stood. Safire watched her in the darkness. Eris ignored her and pressed on.

Soon she was breathing hard. Her legs shook with exertion. It had been so long since she'd made this climb. But when she looked to Safire, no sweat broke across the girl's hairline. No wheezing breaths issued out of her lungs. She was as fresh and alert as when they started.

When they arrived at the top of the slab steps, Eris slowed her pace. A huge black shape now loomed before them. Eris felt its presence like a knife in her ribs.

She forced herself to raise her eyes and look. It wasn't the home of her childhood that stood in front of her now; it was the nightmare she'd run from.

Flashes of lightning illuminated it. Once clay-red and creeping with dark green ivy, the walls were now blackened and scorched. The shattered stained-glass windows gaped like too many mouths of broken teeth. The timbers hadn't been able to support the roof as it burned, and it had long since caved in.

No dogs barked at their approach. No animals brayed.

The silence felt like a weight around Eris's neck.

Sometimes, when she was out at sea, or inland doing a job for Jemsin, she could pretend it had all been a dream. But now, as Eris stared up at this ghost from her past, that horrible night came back to her like a rushing wave, crashing over her.

When Safire stepped up to her side, Eris whispered, "Welcome to the scrin."

Seventeen

Safire gaped at the scorched and soulless wreck before them. It seemed to her like something between a lighthouse and a temple, half burned to the ground.

The scrin.

Had she heard Eris correctly? This was the scrin—the place Asha and Torwin had set out for?

A horrible thought struck her then.

What if they were in there as it burned?

"No . . ."

Suddenly, she was running, dragging Eris behind her. She passed beneath the entrance, where flames had eaten the doors right off their hinges. Her heart pounded in her chest. Her stomach tightened into knots.

Eris halted just inside, forcing her to stop. "Safire."

Safire didn't hear her. Her gaze hastily scanned the dark interior, looking for . . .

Fingers dug into her shoulder. On instinct, Safire spun,

drawing her stolen knife, eyes wild. Eris let go, raising her bound hands, and took a step back. Eris's pale hair was slick against her face and her body shivered uncontrollably. Safire could see the girl's collarbone through her shirt, soaked as she was.

"It happened a long time ago," said Eris.

Lightning crashed above, illuminating the ruin. It was then that Safire saw the leaves, decomposing in the corners. And the fallen timbers, soft and rotted with rain and age.

Asha must have arrived, found the scrin a ruin, and left.

Unless she was still here. . . .

Safire glanced around her. They stood in a wide room with high ceilings, its purpose unclear to her. Piles of ash and rubble gathered along one wall while several archways—their doors long since burned away—stood empty on the other.

The only unbroken window rose high on the north-facing wall. A faceless woman was cast in multiple shades of blue and purple glass while seven stars crowned her forehead. In one hand she held a loom, and in the other a spindle shining like starlight.

Safire recognized her. It was the same image woven into the tapestry on her office wall. The tapestry Eris stole.

"The Skyweaver," Eris explained, looking where she looked. "A god who spins souls into stars and weaves them into the sky."

Eris stepped forward, toward a statue standing beneath the window. At first glance, Safire thought it was a dog. But when she looked closer, she saw chiseled wings and a lion's tail. Talons and a head like an eagle.

The statue was cracked, the head fallen to the floor. Eris

picked up the head in both hands, almost tenderly.

Safire looked at the pile of rubble at her feet. Reaching down, she pulled out a shaft of burned wood.

What happened here?

She turned to ask Eris, but paused when she found the girl picking something else up off the floor. From where Safire stood, it looked like a small gold disk. And from the way Eris stared at it, it seemed to be important.

"What is it?"

Eris looked up, her brows stitched in a frown as she seemed to be piecing something together.

"A button," she said, her thumb tracing its circumference. "Belonging to someone you know."

She flicked it. The button arched toward Safire, who caught it in her free hand. When her fingers uncurled to reveal the object on her palm, Safire's heart skipped.

She remembered that day on the dragon fields with Asha, who'd worn her new flight coat. The one Dax had made uniquely for her, his Namsara. Safire remembered the way the sun glinted off the golden buttons down the front, each one impressed with an image of a namsara flower.

The button lying on her palm was one of those same buttons.

"She's here," said Eris, already turning, her gaze searching the shadows. "Or was here recently."

Safire glanced up to find Eris changed. Standing before her was no longer the drugged, drenched waif of a girl she'd climbed the stone steps with. This girl looked more like the one on Jemsin's ship, that night in the rain. Her hair shone like starlight and she smelled like a storm—surging, *powerful.* Her green eyes lit up as her gaze searched the scrin, hungry to find her prey.

The sight made Safire remember what Kor said.

Let me tell you something about Jemsin's precious Death Dancer. . . .

Safire remembered how Eris had been reluctant to come here. How she seemed weighed down—almost sick—the closer they came.

Seven years ago, she set fire to a temple full of people. Half of them children. Not a single one of them escaped.

"You did this," Safire realized aloud, drawing her stolen dagger. Eris spun. Seeing the blade, she drew back. But the rope was still tied to Safire's belt. She was still a prisoner. "The temple Kor spoke of . . . it was this place." Safire shook her head at the monstrosity of it, imagining the ones locked inside these walls as they burned. Imagining their panic and fear. "*This* is why the Lumina are hunting you. Because you're a monster."

Filled with loathing, Safire backed the Death Dancer up against the wall, keeping the blade pointed at her chest.

"That's right," Eris said bitterly, her back hitting the charred red-clay bricks. "Why not finish the job you prevented Kor from doing? It's what the empress will do as soon as you hand me in anyway. This way, you can save yourself the misery of my company."

Safire heard the resignation in her voice as she said it. As if she truly wanted Safire to plunge the knife in. To end it all.

But a remorseful murderer was still a murderer. This one had killed innocents. Eris wouldn't hesitate to hunt down Asha in exchange for her freedom—especially now that she knew how close the Namsara really was. Right here on these islands.

Eris stared Safire down, a challenge in her eyes. "Go on," she said, pushing back, forcing the steel of Safire's blade to pierce her skin. "Get it over with, princess."

Safire's grip tightened around the dagger. But this crime hadn't been committed against her. Safire wasn't going to take Eris's life. She would deliver her to the empress and let the laws of the Star Isles deal with her.

Seeing her hesitation, Eris whispered, "What happened to the girl who puts knives through the hearts of her enemies?"

Safire narrowed her eyes.

Jarek. She never should have said his name aloud. Not in front of Eris. But it was too late. And Eris's question—the thought of him—threw Safire back to the night of the revolt: the king was dead; Dax had won; Jarek stood surrounded by their rebel army.

Safire had waited her whole life for that moment: to see her tormentor brought to his knees. But Jarek wouldn't kneel. At the very end, he was still standing, still fighting, refusing to bend to the new order.

Safire had never hated him more than in that moment. Hated his defiance and loyalty. Hated it because, just for a moment, it made her understand him.

It made her see herself in him.

So, yes. She put a knife through his heart.

She thought her hatred would go with him. That his death would soothe the ache of a lifetime of loathing. But it didn't.

As Safire stood over Jarek's corpse that night, with the killing blade in her hand, her hate remained swollen inside her. She felt sick with it.

"Safire?"

The voice chased the memory away. Immediately, she was back in that ruined room, and though it was *her* pressing a stolen dagger to Eris's collarbone, she was the one who felt unexpectedly defenseless.

It happened sometimes, when she was alone on her rounds. Or awake in her bed. Or even standing watch over the king in a busy assembly. Suddenly, irrationally, this feeling would come over her: a craving to be held. For someone to tell her it was going to be all right.

That *she* was going to be all right.

It shamed her, that feeling. Because *of course* she was perfectly fine. Safire didn't need someone to take care of her. She took care of herself.

"I'm sorry," Eris said suddenly. "For whatever he did to you."

Safire abruptly became aware of just how close they were standing. Close enough to feel the warmth of Eris against her. Close enough to smell the scent on her skin—like thunder and lightning.

And then, from behind them, someone cleared his throat.

Safire went rigid. Eris glanced up, over her shoulder.

"Am I interrupting something?" came a deep, familiar voice. A voice Safire would know anywhere. Her heart leaped at the sound of it and she whirled to look.

"Dax!"

The dragon king stood before her, dressed in a gold tunic. A saber hung at his hip and four guards flanked him. His dark curls glistened with rain and though exhaustion dulled his brown eyes, the relief at the sight of Safire—*alive*—was clear in his smile.

She hadn't realized she missed him until that moment. How much she missed all of them. Her cousin's presence sent a rush of joy through Safire. She wanted nothing more than to hug him, but Eris's rope was still attached to her belt and Safire's blade was still pointed at the girl's chest, keeping her from trying anything.

So instead, she asked him, "How did you find me?"

Dax opened his mouth to answer. But his eyes fell on Eris and he said, "Who's this?"

Safire looked to the Death Dancer, who'd gone uncharacteristically quiet.

"This . . ." But what could she say?

The girl who'd burned down this temple along with everyone in it?

The thief who intended to hunt down Asha and deliver her to the deadliest pirate on the Silver Sea?

The empress's fugitive?

Safire took a step back, putting space between herself and Eris. Because of course, Eris was all of those things. "Never mind that right now. There are pirates nearby and I'd rather avoid them if we can."

"They've already been dealt with."

Safire tilted her head at Dax. "You caught them?"

He nodded, his gaze flicking from her to Eris and back. "They're being taken to the ship as we speak."

He glanced over his shoulder, motioning for guards Safire couldn't see until they stepped out of the shadows and into the starlight. The four soldats moved in, blades drawn, surrounding Safire's captive. "We can take her from here, commandant."

But Safire shook her head. "This girl is the worst kind of criminal," she told them, grabbing Eris's shoulder and pulling her away from the wall. "She remains with me."

There was no way she was entrusting Eris to anyone else's care. Now that she'd captured the Death Dancer, she couldn't let her escape.

Asha's safety depended on it.

A Breaking

For seven years, Skye had waited for him. Watching the shore, the cliffs, the trees. Wanting her friend and confidant.

How dare he return today—of all days—only to leave her for good.

Skye did not return to her wedding festivities. Instead, she hauled her dory down to the shore and rowed it out to sea. Pulling hard on her oars, she swore to herself she wouldn't come back until she'd rowed out all her fury and grief. Until she was so tired and sore, she no longer cared about the shadow called Crow.

The sky darkened above her.

Skye kept rowing.

The sea swelled around her.

Skye rowed harder.

The wind screamed its warnings. The rain tried to drive her back. But Skye was a fisherman's daughter. She'd spent her whole life on the sea.

She wasn't afraid of a little rain.

And then, far from shore, she felt it: power surging beneath her. Coming up from the depths.

The storm had brought something with it.

Skye stopped rowing.

"Crow?" she whispered.

Had he changed his mind? Had he come back for her?

Suddenly, the waves began to beat their fists against her hull. They spilled their froth over the sides.

The sea was trying to sink her.

Whatever was in the water wasn't Crow.

Skye tried to turn. Tried to row back to shore. But the sea grabbed her oars and pitched them into the storm.

Skye grabbed the sides of her boat, determined to stay in the dory. To keep it upright.

The very next wave turtled her boat.

Salt water surged up, cold and dark as death. It silenced Skye's screams. Wrapped its icy fingers around her ankles. Dragged her down and down and down.

Into the darkness.

A world away, Crow felt it: Skye's life draining away.

He surged over the water, searching the sea. His too-human heart beat a terrified tattoo. Was this his fault? His punishment for leaving her?

By the time he found her, it was too late.

The sea had dashed her on the rocks.

"Skye . . ."

The water was eerily calm as he pulled her to him. The sand glittered against her death-pale skin.

Skye's eyelids fluttered open. Her life was fading fast. "You came back."

He had mere heartbeats now, and a choice to make. It was the nature of mortal things to die. All Crow had to do was say good-bye. To hold her tight as her soul passed into a place he could never follow. It was the last lesson his human girl could teach him.

Except . . .

Make me immortal, she'd asked.

If Crow had never met her, it would have been easy to say no. But Skye had taken the god in him and taught it to be human. Taught him to want and crave and yearn.

In that moment before she slipped away for good, Crow took her strong, skilled hands in his. There, on the rocks, with the sea silent and still around them, he laced his fingers with hers. Fingers that hauled and rowed, mended and wove.

Weaving is what she loved best, *he thought.*

In exchange for all the gifts she'd given him, he gave her one back. He made her Skyweaver and gave her dominion over the souls of the dead, fashioning her into his opposite: a god of hope. One who could light the way through the dark.

When he finished, Crow stepped back and looked at what he'd done.

She was no longer Skye, the fisherman's daughter. With her mortality, he'd taken everything that made her. She did not remember her cove, or the dory she'd spent half her life in, or the husband she'd left pining on the shore.

She did not know Crow. She did not even know herself.

He'd changed her.

She was now deathless. Formidable. A god of hope and light.

And though she was magnificent, she was not his Skye. The human girl he loved was gone. And where his heart had once been—if indeed he ever had one—there was now a roaring, empty void.

Eighteen

The next morning, on the deck of Dax's ship, Safire leaned against the taffrail and into the salt spray of the sea. After last night's storm, the ocean was calm and glittering like a jewel.

With Dax at her side, Safire tilted her head back to watch the dragons above, their massive wings spread wide as they glided beneath the sails and around the stern of Dax and Roa's ship, locked in a game of chase. Dax's slender yellow mount—a gentle creature named Spark—was currently in the lead. The others belonged to various soldats aboard the ship—all except one, which hung back from the group.

This solitary dragon flew farther out, all alone. Safire watched the sunlight ripple across Sorrow's white scales as she and the king filled each other in on everything that had happened since Darmoor.

Dax explained that Sorrow appeared on the horizon shortly after their ship left Darmoor's port, surprising everyone. Roa worried about what they would do with him once they arrived in Axis. But Dax thought it could be good for Sorrow to be in the company of other mounts—dragons who were paired with riders. They might teach Sorrow how to play and fight and, most important, show him that not all humans were things to be feared. They might teach him how to be a dragon again.

Safire, studying the solitary creature, had her doubts.

"I don't understand," said Dax from beside her, watching the shoreline glide by as they followed the coastline of Axis Isle, heading for the harbor. He'd just informed her that it had been an off-duty soldat—one who often worried about his commandant's lack of consideration for her own safety—who'd followed Safire to the Thirsty Craw. When she didn't come out, he reported it to Dax, who'd been tracking her ever since. "What does a pirate like Jemsin want with Asha?"

"It could be a ransom," said Safire, thinking of something Eris said. "Or he could be trying to get at *you.*" She squinted up at him in the sunlight. He wore a golden tunic today, embroidered with the royal crest, and his damp curls were even curlier than usual from the mist rolling off the sea. "Have you harassed any pirates lately?"

Dax tilted his head. "Not that I can think of."

"Maybe it's not Asha he wants," came a voice from behind them.

Both Asha and Dax turned to find the dragon queen approaching. Roa wore a simple wool dress that came to her ankles, the elegant hood pushed back and falling loose around her shoulders. No golden circlet adorned her dark brow, where black curls were cropped close to her head, and there were shadows beneath her eyes. She'd grown so wan and thin since her last visit to the scrublands, like she was wasting away. Her worry and grief over the starvation of her people had sharpened Roa's soft edges. And if it pained Safire to watch, it was certainly excruciating for Dax, who loved his wife more than life itself.

Safire hoped that whatever gift the empress intended to give them truly would alleviate the suffering in the scrublands.

Unconsciously, Roa touched her own shoulder. The one, Safire knew, bearing eight years of claw marks. Essie, Roa's sister, had spent eight years trapped in the form of a hawk and in those eight years, she'd never left her sister's side and could often be found perched on Roa's shoulder. Roa, Safire had noticed in the months of Essie's absence, had a frequent habit of running her fingers across the scars. Almost fondly.

Roa turned her dark brown eyes on Safire. "Asha and Torwin have the Skyweaver's knife."

Safire remembered it—the weapon Roa used to save her sister—in Torwin's hands the day before they left. It was their sole reason for traveling to the scrin.

"It's possible Jemsin wants the knife Asha carries, not Asha herself." In her dark eyes, Safire could see the night Roa set her sister's soul free. She remembered the corrupted thing Essie had become in the end. Roa would never have been able to save her without the Skyweaver's knife.

"But what would Jemsin want with a knife that cuts souls?" Safire murmured.

No one had an answer to that.

"What about the Death Dancer?" Roa asked, hugging her thinning frame now against the chill of the wind. Seeing it, Dax reached for his wife, sliding his arms around Roa's waist and drawing her against him. "What's her part in all this?"

At the thought of Eris, Safire pulled the girl's spindle out of her pocket. She'd lied to her about burying it so that Eris wouldn't try to steal it back. "She seems to be some kind of indentured servant rather than a part of Jemsin's crew. Jemsin gives an order, and she obeys." She ran her thumb over the worn wood, examining the smooth curves, as she remembered something Kor said. "I think Jemsin may be hiding her, and in exchange for his protection, she does whatever he asks."

"Hiding her from what?"

Safire looked up into Dax's worried eyes. "From the empress."

Safire hadn't quite filled him in on this part of the story yet. So she told him and Roa everything she'd learned about Eris. That she wasn't just an uncatchable thief. She was the empress's fugitive.

"Apparently the empress has been hunting the murderer who burned down the scrin for years. She just didn't know that person was also the Death Dancer."

When she finished, Dax's eyes were dark and Roa's lips were pressed into a hard line.

"How did you capture her?" asked Roa from the circle of Dax's arms as she watched Safire's hands run over the spindle. "I thought the Death Dancer was uncatchable."

"I thought so, too," said Safire. Back in Firgaard, the girl seemed to be a ghost. Walking through walls. Disappearing right in front of her. But then Kor captured them and locked Eris's wrists in those horrible manacles, and Eris's strange abilities had just . . . stopped.

Why?

She shook her head. "The important thing is keeping her confined until we deliver her to the empress."

"Well, it won't be long now," said Dax, resting his chin on the top of Roa's head as he looked to the prow. "We're almost in Axis's harbor."

"I'm sure Leandra will want to know that her waters are infested with pirates," said Roa. "We should offer to help her eliminate them."

It wasn't until her thumb's third time around the spindle that Safire noticed the symbols carved into the wood. Seven stars ringed the widest part, almost completely worn away. And there was something else, too.

Safire lifted it to her face, squinting at the carved word.

Skye, it read.

Safire frowned at the name. But why she was surprised, she didn't know. Eris was a thief. Of course the spindle was stolen.

"And then you can fly to the southern tip of Axis Isle and make sure Asha's safe," said Dax.

Safire looked up, startled. "Is that where she is?"

"Torwin sent a message the night you went missing. I'll show you the letter. It should be easy to find."

Those words pricked her. If Asha was easy to find, then if Eris ever got free . . .

At that thought, Safire realized it had been a while since she'd checked on her prisoner.

Gripping the spindle hard in her hand, Safire pushed away from the taffrail. "Then as soon as Eris is safely locked away in the empress's prison, I'll find Asha and warn her about Jemsin."

Safire was still thinking about the spindle as she headed for the cabin Dax had designated as hers. She remembered her first encounter with Eris. She'd bumped into her, disguised as a soldat, and the spindle had fallen to the floor. Safire picked it up and handed it back.

The second time, in Safire's bedroom, the spindle was there again. Safire had seen it in Eris's hand before she disappeared.

Clearly there was some connection between this spindle and Eris's disappearances.

What is it?

As she stepped through the doorway and into her cabin, two soldats greeted her. In the center of the lavish room stood Eris.

Dax wanted to put her in the brig, where Kor and his crew were currently confined. Safire prevented it, remembering the look in Kor's eyes that night on his ship. Criminal or no, she didn't want that man anywhere near Eris.

Now, in an ironic swapping of places, Eris's manacles were chained to one of the beams above her head. But the look of pain on her face made it difficult for Safire to gloat. She quickly glanced to find the girl's wrists raw and bleeding.

Stardust steel would take three days to eat through human flesh, Eris had told her.

How many days had passed?

Almost two.

Safire's stomach twisted at the realization. But they were nearly in Axis. As soon as they made port, she would make sure they found a metalsmith who could take them off. It would be safer and smarter to head straight for the empress, but those cuffs were a perverse kind of cruelty. And Safire didn't abide cruelty. She would just have to keep a close eye on Eris while they made their detour.

"Leave us for a moment," she told the soldats.

As they stepped out, Safire shut the door.

"You royals sure travel in style," Eris said the moment they were gone. Her voice had a lazy, mocking edge as she looked around the room. "The upholstery in here alone could pay to feed a starving village."

Safire looked around her. The cabin was decorated with lavish furniture made of dark wood and upholstered in rich blues and purples. Portraits hung from the walls, and on the table, silver goblets rested beside a decanter of wine.

Eris tilted her chin toward the bed. "And I bet those silk sheets—" The words died on her lips as her gaze fell on the object in Safire's hand. Something desperate flashed across her face.

It was the confirmation Safire needed.

"First you say you burned it," said Eris, her eyes meeting Safire's. "Then you say you buried it. That's twice you lied." Her lips curved in a slow smile. "Looks like I'm starting to rub off on you."

The comment rankled Safire. She didn't respond. Just grabbed the chair from the desk and turned it around, sitting down before her captive.

"I have a theory," she said as she tossed the spindle up and down. Taunting Eris in the same way Kor had. "The rumors say the Death Dancer is uncatchable." Up and down went the spindle. Eris never took her eyes off it. "They say she can escape any cell. That she walks through walls. That she eludes even death."

The next time the spindle landed, Safire's fingers closed around it. She looked up to find Eris's gaze intent on her face. "Not so long ago, I watched you disappear before my own eyes. And now, here you are. *Caught*. What's the difference between that night and this one?"

When Eris didn't answer, Safire lifted the wooden object by its slender end, holding it up.

"It's the spindle," she mused aloud. "It somehow allows you to disappear."

Eris smiled with just one side of her mouth. "Why don't you give it to me, and I'll show you if you're right."

Leaning over the back of the chair, Safire smiled back. "I know I'm right. Without it, you're nothing more than a common thief."

Eris's elegant jaw hardened. "So this is what you do with all your captives, right before you march them to their deaths? Taunt them? Gloat over them?" She shook her head, disgusted. "It's beneath you."

Safire smarted at those words. She sat back, her cheeks reddening with heat.

But what did she care about this lowlife's good opinion?

She did care, though. She cared that Eris was right: taunting and gloating *were* beneath her.

I've been spending too much time in the company of criminals, she thought.

Still, Safire rose from the chair, unsettled, and walked to the small porthole. "I'm not marching you to your death," she said softly, looking out to the harbor in the distance. She could just make out wharves and fishing sheds and boats moored to docks. Beyond it, the city sprawled out and up the mountain at its back. "The empress will give you a fair trial."

Eris snorted. "You're a fool if you think that's true."

Safire turned in surprise to face her. "What do you mean?" In Firgaard, every criminal had a right to a trial. Things hadn't always been this way, but they were now, under Dax and Roa's rule.

"If she puts me on trial, I'll tell the truth. And Leandra doesn't want me telling the truth." Eris's eyes were unnaturally bright. "Trust me, princess. I'll get no trial. She'll take me up to the immortal scarps and dispose of me—like she does with everyone she hates most."

Safire crossed her arms, turning back to the porthole, watching the smoke from Axis's chimneys curl into the distant sky. She needed to be careful here. She knew Eris was perfectly capable of manipulating her.

Hesitant, she asked, "And what's the truth?"

"You've already decided what it is," said Eris in a small voice.

Safire turned to face her. "Try me."

So Eris told her.

Seven Years Previous

"We've hidden her here as long as we can."

Eris hadn't intended to spy. She'd only come to Day's room because the weavers were out of purple dye and had asked her to fetch more scarp thistles. She'd come to tell Day she was going up to the meadow.

Day liked to know where Eris was at all times.

When Eris heard voices inside the room, she immediately turned away, knowing how her guardian felt about eavesdropping. But at the sound of her own name, Eris stopped.

She couldn't help herself; she turned and listened at the door.

"The Lumina are getting stronger." It was the Master Weaver's deep voice. "If she stays any longer, she'll bring sorrow upon us."

"I understand," came Day's soft answer.

"You know how I feel about the girl. How we all feel. But . . . I'm sorry, Day."

The door opened suddenly. Before Eris could hide, the Master Weaver halted, the silver tassels of his robe swishing. His clear black eyes stared down at Eris, full of surprise.

Day stepped out beside him.

"Eris . . ."

The two men exchanged a look above her head.

"I'll see you at dinner," said the weaving master. Before he left, he touched Eris's shoulder in what could only be good-bye.

As his footsteps padded away, the implications of his words unraveled inside her.

He wanted her to leave? But this was her home. Everyone and everything she loved was here. Day. The looms. Her best friend, Yew. The cliffs and the meadows and the sea . . .

"Why?" Her voice sounded strange in her ears. Like a mirror breaking. "Why will I bring sorrow on everyone?"

Day bent toward her until their eyes were level. He wore no tasseled robes, but a knit gray sweater and trousers stained with dirt. He was only a caretaker, after all.

"Listen to me. . . ."

Eris wasn't listening. She was panicking.

She'd always known she was no one important. She was an orphan, taken in out of charity. Because the weavers had made a vow to the Skyweaver: to harbor those who needed harboring.

But she never thought they would send her away.

"I can't leave," she said, her voice cracking. "Where would I go? I have nowhere to go, Day. I'll be all alone!"

"Eris." His strong hands came down on her shoulders. "You are never, ever alone. No matter where you are."

She shook her head. Tears burned in her eyes. He didn't say: Everything will be all right. He didn't say: I won't let them do this.

"You don't want me either," she realized then. She'd always feared it, deep down. But here was the proof. "No one wants me."

"Eris . . ."

She didn't want to hear any more of his empty words.

Pulling out of his grip, Eris turned and ran.

She ran hard down the halls—bumping into apprentices as she escaped the scrin. Beneath the setting sun, she ran up the dirt paths, through the silver boreal forest, along the rocky cliffs facing the sea. Her footsteps pounded the earth, trying to outrun what she'd overheard.

She didn't stop running until she reached the meadow.

It smelled of juniper and sea salt up here. In the distance, far below, the sea roared as it crashed against the rocks.

Eris had just collapsed in the grass, weary from running so fast and so far, when a sound came from across the meadow.

She looked up to see Yew bumbling toward her. Bleating loudly, his stubby white tail bouncing as he ran across the field. He butted Eris's shoulder with his soft white head, then proceeded to nuzzle her.

Eris threw her arms around Yew, breathing in his musky smell and burying her tear-streaked face in the sheep's wool—which was fuzzy from being recently sheared.

"Why does no one want me?" she whispered.

As if in answer, Yew curled up beside her and put his soft white chin in Eris's lap.

When she'd cried herself out, she lay in the golden grass, staring up at the blue sky. Picking up her knife—the one Day gave her for cutting scarp thistles—she ran her fingers over the embossed star pattern in the silver sheath.

"To remind you the Skyweaver is always with you," he'd told her the day he gave it to her. "When you use it, say a prayer to her."

Eris closed her eyes, thinking of the prayer Day recited with her every night before bed:

When the night descends . . .
I look to those who've gone before me
lighting my path through the dark.

When I am deserted and alone . . .
I know your hands hold the threads of my soul
and there is nothing to fear.

When the enemy surrounds me . . .

I remember you are with me.

And though they break my body, they can never take my soul.

They always spoke the last line together. Eris recited the prayer twice now and when she opened her eyes, she felt calmer. Less angry. But still hurt.

I should be grateful that they took me in at all, *she thought.* Me, a worthless orphan.

Using this thought as a shield against the hurt, Eris got to her feet. Spotting a patch of scarp thistles growing in clumps near the cliff edge, she drew the knife out of its sheath and went to cut some.

"As a good-bye gift," she told Yew, who lay in the grass now, watching her with deep brown eyes. "For the weavers."

Eris didn't know when it had gotten so late, only that when Yew bolted upright, staring toward the sea, the sky was dark and the stars were coming out.

Eris let go of the thorny scarp stalk and lowered her knife, looking in the same direction.

Yew bleated, agitated. Eris laid her free hand atop his warm back, peering through the blue twilight. A silhouette came into view. Something—a man?—was walking toward them from the cliffs. Above him, a massive black raven soared through the air.

Eris frowned. There was no path up or down those cliffs. You had to climb the steps on the other side of the scrin.

So where had he come from?

Day's warnings about strangers filled her mind and Eris stepped back.

"Who are you?" she called out.

She could see from where she stood that his gait was clumsy and stiff. As if he were limping.

He stumbled.

Eris sheathed the knife and ran to him. Yew trailed nervously behind her. As she got closer, she saw he was an older man, maybe Day's age. His clothes were soaked and a hideous red gash sliced his forehead just above his right eye. Blood—now dry—had run down his cheek and neck, pooling in the hollow of his throat. That black raven circled above him.

"Are you all right?" Clearly, he was in some kind of trouble. "What's your name?"

"Jemsin," he rasped. "My ship . . ."

His hands shook, and Eris could see his fingers were scraped and bloody.

Had he climbed those cliffs? She looked from his hands to his face as admiration flared within her.

The raven dived suddenly, flapping its massive wings as it landed on Jemsin's shoulder. It stared down at her with bloodred eyes. Growing strangely cold beneath its gaze, Eris stepped back.

"A wicked wind dashed us right up on the rocks," Jemsin said. "Like we were nothing but a leaf. Where am I, girl?"

"Shadow Isle," she said, eying the raven as she stepped carefully beside Jemsin, ready to catch him if he stumbled or fell. "The scrin isn't far. They'll help you. Where's the rest of your crew?"

He shook his head, his shoulders sagging. "Eaten. The sea spirits got each and every one of them before they could swim ashore."

Eris thought of his men, swimming through the cold silver waters as one by one their comrades were pulled under by clawed and scaly hands.

She shivered at the thought.

"Come on," she said, taking his hand in hers as she led him back down the cliff paths, through the boreal forest, forgetting all about the scarp thistles. The raven flew from his shoulder and began to circle the sky above once more. But as they drew nearer to the scrin, something made Jemsin stop.

"Wait," he hissed, grabbing her arm. Yew bleated at him. The man let her go, raising his hands. "Do you smell that?"

Eris sniffed.

The acrid tang of smoke hit her. She turned, looking in the direction of the scrin. Through the darkness, above the tops of the junipers, she could see a multitude of red sparks spitting at the sky.

Cold dread spread through her.

"No . . ."

The man reached for her again, but Eris was already running. Straight toward the fire.

Straight toward home.

Yew bleated somewhere far behind her.

It wasn't long before she saw the flames themselves. Huge, ravenous flames. Orange and red. Devouring the scrin.

Swarming all around it, watching it burn, were men dressed in black, with silver blades strapped across their backs.

But that wasn't what halted Eris's footsteps.

It was the man being forced to his knees. Being forced to watch.

"Day . . . ," she whispered.

A woman stood before him, her pale hair twisted back in a severe bun. The way she held herself—chin high, shoulders back—said she was used to giving orders. She was dressed in black like all the other soldiers, her hand gripping a silver sword as she stared down at her captive.

"Did you think you could hide from me?" Eris heard the commander say, her voice ringing out over the crackling flames.

Day held her gaze from where he knelt in the dirt.

"Where is it?"

Day didn't say a word.

"Shall I tell you how she screamed in the end? How she begged?"

Day's jaw clenched and for a moment, Eris thought he might lunge, but he stayed where he was and did nothing.

"Tell me where it is!"

Day stared past her. Stony and silent. Giving no answer.

The commander hit him in the jaw with the hilt of her sword. Day spat blood, shook his head once as if to clear it, then looked up. Past the woman. To the stars.

Eris saw her guardian's lips move. Watched his mouth form the familiar words.

"'When my enemy surrounds me . . .'"

It was the prayer he'd taught her. The one they recited together at night.

"'I remember'"—his voice seemed to get louder, floating up to Eris—"'you are with me.'"

The commander sneered at Day, drawing back her sword.

Eris knew what was about to happen. Knew she was powerless to stop it.

"No . . ."

"'And though they break my body, they can never take my soul.'"

The commander plunged the silver sword through Day's heart.

Eris felt her body freeze over.

Before she could scream, Jemsin's hand came down hard over her mouth. Pulling her back. She tried to push him off. Day needed her. She had to go to him.

The woman withdrew the blade. As she did, Day looked straight at Eris. As if he'd known she was there all along.

Their gazes locked. Eris saw the blood seeping through his gray sweater. Saw that his eyes were already clouding over. She stopped struggling.

In that moment before death stole him away, he mouthed one word. "Run."

And then Jemsin was hauling her back to the trees, telling her the same thing as Day.

"Day! The scrin!" She sobbed. "My friends are all inside!"

Jemsin grabbed her shoulders and made her face him. "Listen to me, lass. Your friends are dead. There's nothing you can do for them now." He pulled her against his wet, salt-encrusted clothes. "We have to run. It's what he would want: for you to survive." He pulled her away, wiped the tears from her cheeks.

Eris looked up into his brown eyes.

"Are you ready?"

Eris nodded.

They ran.

They needed a way off the islands, but everything Jemsin owned had sunk to the bottom of the sea, and the Across would only shelter them temporarily—the only door within it led straight back to the scrin. So Eris tried to barter her spindle for passage aboard a ship. The shipmaster sneered at her, turning them both away—until he saw the knife at her hip. The one Day gave her. "That," he told her with gleaming eyes as he called her back, "is a fairer trade."

So Eris sold her knife in exchange for passage.

It was only after they sailed out of the harbor, only after the Star Isles disappeared in the distance, that Eris wondered: Why Day? Why had *the commander of the Lumina army forced* him *to watch the scrin burn, and no other? He was only a caretaker.*

And what had they been looking for? What was so important, it warranted burning the scrin with everyone inside it?

But Eris remembered the conversation she'd overheard. The Master Weaver had given her a clue when she eavesdropped on him and Day: If she stays any longer, she'll bring sorrow upon us.

Day hadn't disagreed with him.

Eris didn't know why the Lumina had come, or what they wanted. But she did know this: The destruction of the scrin, the slaughter of all her friends, the death of her guardian . . .

These things were her fault.

Nineteen

Eris had never told that story to anyone. She only told it now because it might earn her Safire's sympathy. If she had Safire's sympathy, she might be able to change the commandant's mind about handing her over to the empress.

But another part of her told the story because ever since Kor told Safire it was *Eris* who burned down the scrin, Eris couldn't stop thinking about the look that had come into Safire's eyes. Horror. Then disgust. And last of all: loathing.

Normally, these things didn't matter to Eris. Who cared what other people thought about her?

But for some stupid reason, it mattered what Safire thought.

In the silence after finishing her story, Safire stood immobile, staring out the porthole. Eris shifted uncomfortably, waiting for her to say something. The pain in her wrists made her jaw clench, and her legs shook from being forced to stand all night.

Finally, Safire turned. "You expect me to believe," she whispered, "that the empress slaughtered a temple full of people devoted to her patron god . . . and blamed it on a *child*?" Her voice had gone strangely hollow. "How stupid do you think I am?"

Swallowing the knot of disappointment in her throat, Eris bit back the first cutting retort that came to mind.

What did you expect? Eris thought. *That she would believe you—a petty thief in the service of a horrible pirate—over the benevolent ruler of a peaceful society?*

Of course Safire would side with the empress. She was royal—just like Leandra.

Eris watched Safire roughly untie the pale blue ribbon keeping her black hair off her face only to retie it around her wrist. She then ran frustrated fingers through the strands, pulling them back, her fingers working an angry knot. "It's in your best interest to win me over," she said, her voice heated now as she slid a slender knife through the knot, pinning it in place while concealing the blade. "You need me to let you go."

Well, yes, that was exactly what Eris needed. But that wasn't the only reason she'd told the story. It also happened to be *true*.

She felt like she'd been tricked into giving away something precious, only to have it spat on.

When did I get so naïve? she thought bitterly.

Safire shook her head in disgust. "I can see why you're invaluable to Jemsin. You're not just an excellent thief. You're a masterful liar."

"You're right," said Eris in defeat. "I made it all up so you'd set me free."

Safire scowled. "Free to hunt down my cousin the moment

you have the chance? Even if I *did* believe you, I wouldn't set you free."

Someone called from above, interrupting. Eris glanced to the door, her body tense.

"We're coming into port," said Safire, looking out the porthole.

Axis Isle. Where Leandra's citadel resided.

"Perfect," she murmured, even as a sick feeling festered in her gut. "The sooner we get this over with, the sooner you're out of my life."

"Can't wait," said Safire.

After the ship dropped anchor, Safire and a handful of others went to find the king and queen's escort, leaving Eris in the charge of two soldats. The dragons were taken away for a brief quarantine. Apparently, they made the empress uneasy.

Eris's guards forced her to sit at the edge of the dock, where her only mode of escape was the sea. With her hands bound, if she tried to jump in and swim, she would drown.

Eris was contemplating such a fate as she stared down at her wrists. Her skin was caked in dry, cracked blood now; and the wounds were getting deeper. By tomorrow she'd be able to see the bones. *If* she lived that long.

What would the empress do once she finally had her precious fugitive?

A sudden splash interrupted her thoughts. The smell of rotten fish wafted over her.

Eris's skin prickled. She knew that smell.

Turning toward it, she found two eyes greeting her. Bulging and fish-like. The thing had pulled itself up out of the water and now sat on the dock, perching there and staring at Eris. Its lithe body sometimes made of scales, sometimes made of starlight.

A sea spirit.

Eris's heart thumped wildly as the rest of her went stone-still. She remembered the sound of teeth tearing the flesh of Kor's crew as they rowed for shore.

"I know you," said the spirit, its voice liquid and lilting.

"I doubt that," said Eris, her lungs freezing in her chest. She didn't dare look back over her shoulder to where her guards stood. Eris didn't want to make any sudden movements. Right now it was being friendly. But that could change in an instant.

She looked past it instead, around the wharf, where the crews of other ships were milling about. Did no one else see it?

"The Shadow God grows stronger." The creature kicked its scaly legs, letting them dangle off the dock. "We thought you'd want to know."

"Why would I want to know?" asked Eris, keeping her eyes on the wharf.

"Because you feel it, too." The sea spirit smiled a sharp-toothed smile. "Once he's free, he'll come for her."

Eris frowned. This thing was talking nonsense. She felt no such thing. "Come for who?"

"You know."

"I really don't," she said.

Suddenly, it leaned closer, reaching scaly fingers toward

Eris's wrists. "Who did this to you?"

Eris pulled her bound hands back. "Please. Just go away."

"I could help. I could soothe."

Eris paused, studying it. The thing had no eyelids, only liquid black eyes. Its feet were slightly webbed, and its teeth were needle sharp. But there was something ethereal—something almost serene—as it pursed its thin lips at the sight of her bound wrists.

"I could . . . remove."

"Yeah?" Eris hissed under her breath. "I know your kind like the taste of flesh. Is that what it would cost me?"

It wrinkled its nose. "Silly thing. Not *you*. It would be a gift . . . from those who want him free."

A sudden chill swept over Eris. She glanced up into gleaming, razor-sharp teeth.

"Want who free?"

It sighed a long sigh. "I just told you. The Shadow God."

A noise interrupted. Footsteps on the dock.

Behind them, a familiar voice said, "Eris, we're—"

The sea spirit's eyes snapped toward the sound. Eris turned to find Safire, frozen at the sight of the monster. When Eris looked back, she realized why. The sea spirit's eyes were now blood red, its face changed from serene to . . .

Hungry.

It lunged for Safire, its white teeth flashing as its jaw yawned open.

Eris grabbed its scaly leg. The creature hit the dock. It kicked, hands scrabbling for a hold on the wood, trying to drag itself toward Safire. Desperate. Crazed.

Safire drew her knife, trembling as she did.

Eris's grip was slipping. Knowing exactly what would happen if it slipped entirely, she dug her fingers in *hard*.

The spirit screamed, then swung back to face Eris. It hissed in her face, angry and wild.

But it didn't bite. It didn't want Eris.

When it hissed again, Eris hissed back.

The spirit blinked, as if startled. "Fool," it spat, then it glanced back once at Safire, eyes ravenous, before turning sharply toward the dark sea. Eris let go as it dived into the water and disappeared with a plop.

Safire's chest heaved. She lowered the knife.

Eris held up her bound hands, signaling for her not to step any closer to the water. But the sea was calm, and all sign of the sea spirit was gone. The only sound remaining was the rubbing of hulls against the wood of the wharf.

Beyond Safire, the soldats had all drawn their blades, their eyes on Eris.

She ignored them, looking Safire over. "Are you all right?"

Safire tore her gaze from the water to stare at Eris. After a long moment, she whispered, "Why did you do that?"

Eris's mouth parted, but she didn't have an answer.

The sea spirit had been offering her freedom. It would have killed Safire—the very person determined to bring Eris to her enemies. It would have even taken the manacles off Eris's wrists.

If Eris hadn't stopped it, she'd be free right now.

She clenched her teeth. *Why are you so stupid today?*

And then the sound of heavy footsteps thudded down the dock. Eris looked to find several men dressed in black. The lamplight pooled around their polished black boots, reflecting off the silver buckles. Blades crisscrossed against their backs.

Lumina soldiers.

The sight of them brought a rush of panic.

She saw Day, suddenly, kneeling before one of those blades. Smelled the scrin burning behind him. Heard the weavers screaming, trapped beyond the doors.

She stumbled backward.

Safire grabbed her, stopping her from falling into the sea.

As the Lumina shoved her up the dock and through the city gate, she said to Safire, "I wish you had let me drown."

Better to drown than be given over to *them*. The ones who took everything from her.

This was Eris's worst nightmare come true.

Twenty

Eris saved my life.

Safire's mind hummed with the realization as she fiddled with the ends of the blue ribbon tied around her wrist.

Why would she do that?

Eris could have easily let that monster kill her. Kill all of them. She'd be free right now if she had.

As they walked the streets of Axis, Dax and Roa rode on horseback up ahead, flanked by their guards. But Safire kept back, watching over Eris. Several Lumina soldiers walked with them, each one bearing a circle of seven stars across their chest.

All around them, the sounds of drunken voices clashed with music and clapping. Everywhere Safire looked, ribbons streamed from ankles and wrists, faces were smeared with silvery paint, and blue forget-me-nots were plaited in the hair of men and women alike—as well as strewn all over the cobble-stones.

Safire, who would normally be memorizing every street

corner and storefront and face right now, kept her attention on Eris—whose hands were now free of their bonds.

Safire had made the girl a promise. So, as soon as they entered the city, she demanded they find a blacksmith to remove Eris's manacles. The Lumina soldiers refused, saying the empress was impatient to meet her guests. Safire insisted, saying she hadn't brought the empress's fugitive all this way for the girl to lose her hands to such a barbaric practice.

This was perhaps the wrong thing to say. Accusing your hosts of being barbarians? Not the best first impression. The soldiers all narrowed their eyes at her, and even Dax threw his cousin a desperate look. One that said, *Please don't ruin this.*

But Roa came to her defense, pointing out a forge across the square.

Now, Eris walked at Safire's side. Her hands were bound with rope now, but even this felt awful. The girl's wrists were brutalized, the cuts deep and bleeding. The rope was clearly irritating them.

Most of all, Safire could feel Eris's energy coiled tight, as if waiting for her chance to run. It was the reason Safire kept the end of the rope firmly in her hand—to keep the thief from escaping.

"We've been trying to catch her for years," said a sudden voice from beside her. Safire looked to find a tall young Lumina soldier at her side. The chest of his uniform bore the Skyweaver's crest like all the others. "How did you manage it?"

"Actually," said Safire, her attention fixing on something in the distance, "she caught me."

Beyond the rooftops lining this square, a black and solitary tower rose up into the gray mist. It seemed to never disappear from view. No matter how many streets they turned down, it was always there. Watching over them.

As Safire told this young man the story, there was a sudden tug on the rope. Safire's gaze shot to Eris, her grip tightening. But the girl had merely tripped over the heel of the Lumina in front of her.

"Don't worry," said the soldier at Safire's side, sensing her unease. "We'll be at the citadel soon. So long as this crowd lets us through." He winked at her. "I'm Raif, by the way."

Eris cast a look their way.

"I'm Safire."

"I know."

Safire looked up into gray eyes framed by blond lashes. Raif smiled down at her.

"You've arrived right in the middle of Skye's Night," he said, stepping closer.

"Oh?" said Safire, feigning interest as she felt another tug on the rope and turned to find Eris scanning the square now. As if looking for something.

"Do you know about Skye?" asked Raif. "The girl who fell in love with a god?"

Skye. She shook her head, despite recognizing the name. It was carved into Eris's spindle.

"She's something of a legend in the Star Isles."

If Skye was a legend, surely there would be lots of girls named after her. That spindle could belong to any number of them.

"Skye's Night is her festival. It's a day of promises and

betrothals"—he smiled mischievously—"and a night of secret unions."

"It's a drunken orgy," Eris muttered from beside her.

Safire looked around her. Ribbons and petals danced through the air. They passed a priest performing a binding, then a circle of couples dancing, their faces smeared in silver. The women wore flower wreaths on their heads as their partners led them in the steps of the song.

Soon the crowd thickened, then thickened again. Safire watched Dax and Roa grow smaller up ahead. But Raif and two other Lumina soldiers remained behind. And all the while Raif smiled at her and told her about the city. How it was built a thousand years ago, after the defeat of the Shadow God. How the empress's crest—which he proudly wore across his chest— was symbolic of the seven Star Isles, as well as the seven stars in the Skyweaver's crown.

Last of all, he told her he knew where the most beautiful beach in the world was, and, if she wanted to see it, he could take her to watch the sunset sometime.

Beside her, Eris smirked. "Trust me, *Raif*, she's not the sunset-watching type."

Safire turned to face her. "Is that so?"

"You're not," said Eris, staring straight ahead.

She was trying to provoke Safire. Messing with her mind again. Safire knew the best thing to do was ignore her. But there was something in her tone. Something almost possessive. Safire couldn't let it go unchecked. "You don't know a thing about me."

Eris's mouth curled to one side as she looked ahead to the

backs of the Lumina marching before them. "You're not that difficult to figure out, princess. Order, routine, control . . . these are the things that excite people like you. Not spontaneity. Not beaches and sunsets."

An angry blush rose to Safire's cheeks. "People like me."

"Aye," said Eris, catching her gaze. "People like you. You're as predictable as a rock."

Safire's anger roiled and churned inside her.

But what did it matter what Eris thought of her? She was a thief and a murderer. She was *nobody*.

Raif turned the corner in front of them.

The moment Safire turned it, too, though, she nearly barreled into him, taking Eris with her. Before she could look to see why he stopped, he put his arm out, pushing her back. Safire glanced up over his shoulder, and found the reason.

Five Lumina soldiers stood some ten strides away, dressed in black, light glinting off their blades. They stood in a circle as one of them beat some kind of club against what looked like a sack of grain.

When Safire looked harder, she realized it was a young woman.

She froze, staring as the club swung down, again and again. The sight sent a memory slicing through her. In an instant, she was back in Firgaard. Barely fourteen years old. Curled up on the mosaicked tiles of the palace floor. . . .

The dark shapes of Jarek and his soldats stood over her, their boots finding their marks in her stomach and back, her shoulders and legs. Places people were less likely to notice the bruises. With every blow, pain burst through her. But she would rather the blows than the names they called her. Horrible, disgusting things. The same things they called her mother.

And then, like she'd stepped right out of an old story, Asha was there, dressed in her hunting gear, splattered with dragon blood. Her black eyes were wild as she gripped her throwing axe in one hand, screaming at them. Screaming things twice as horrible as the things they'd screamed at Safire.

Raif spun on his heel, grabbed Safire, and drew her—and Eris along with her—out of that quiet alley faster than she could draw breath. The crowd hummed around them once more. But the past had Safire in its claws, and it wasn't done with her yet.

Dax stood behind Asha, the storm in his eyes belying his calm demeanor, suggesting he wanted more than anything to draw his weapon and join his sister. Instead, his knuckles tightened around the hilt of his undrawn sword as he stood between the soldats and the two girls at his back, using himself as a shield.

Raif took her arm this time, jolting Safire out of the memory. "Keep walking."

It didn't matter that her cousins came to her rescue, though. The next day, those soldats returned to their stations, waiting for the next moment to strike. And if they didn't return, others just like them did. But that was never the part that stayed with Safire.

The part that stayed was Asha and Dax, coming to her aid, *always.*

Who did that woman have coming to hers?

"She needs our help," said Safire.

"Trust me," said Raif, staring straight ahead. "That woman's beyond our help. Just keep your head down and walk fast."

"I'm with Raif on this." Eris's solemn gaze met hers. "That woman is as good as dead. You will be too if you interfere."

If that's true, thought Safire, *then someone needs to stop them.*

Handing Eris's rope to Raif, she turned back, pushing through the crowd. Someone growled at her to get out of the way. She heard Raif yell for her to stop.

And then she was in the alley again, the market bleeding away as she strode toward the circle of Lumina. The one with the club was so involved in his brutal game he didn't see Safire until she stepped between him and the woman lying bruised and broken on the ground. Safire caught the club in the palm of her hand.

It should have hurt badly. But all Safire felt was her own swelling rage.

The Lumina's pale blue eyes widened in shock. The others stood frozen, staring.

"You dare interfere with the law of the empress?" said the soldier before her, trying to wrench his club from her grip. With a muscular frame and a strong jaw, he was the type of man she would have called handsome in other circumstances. But then, these types often were.

Safire's fingers tightened, holding on. She tried to summon Dax's calmness, even as her whole body shook. "Surely there's no crime that calls for such a wicked punishment."

His gaze raked up and down her. "You're clearly not from these parts. So I'll be generous with you, girl. If you walk away *now*, you'll suffer no consequence." He nodded for her to go.

For the briefest moment, hesitation flickered in Safire. Perhaps she was wrong. Perhaps the woman at her feet was responsible for some truly heinous crime. Safire was a guest in Axis, after all. She shouldn't assume she knew better than the soldiers who lived and worked here. More than this: stirring up trouble would sabotage Dax's visit. It might prevent him from getting the help he needed for the scrublands.

She was about to stand down when a terrified voice cut through her thoughts.

"P-please, miss. . . ."

With her hand still gripping the Lumina's club, Safire glanced to the young woman below her. This close, she looked very young. Perhaps as young as Safire. Her arms trembled as she rose to her knees. Her left eye was swollen shut, and Safire could tell her arm was broken. When her right eye met Safire's, it shone with tears. "Don't leave," she whispered. "They'll kill me."

It was what Eris said: *That woman's as good as dead.*

A shiver rushed across her skin. The day Dax made her his commandant, she swore to defend those in need of defending. No matter what this woman's crime was—if she was indeed guilty of any—the punishment should never be a beating to the death.

And if Dax were here, he would agree.

Safire drew herself up to her full height. Wrenching the club free of the soldier's grip, she said to the young woman at her feet, "Run."

In response to her defiance, several blades were drawn at once.

"Run *now.*"

The woman did. The moment one of the soldiers moved to stop her, Safire swung the club, slamming it down between his shoulder blades. The provocation worked. He turned away from his prey and back to her.

"Stupid girl," said the Lumina whose club she'd stolen, rolling up his sleeves. "That's all right. I'm feeling generous today." He glanced to the others, cracking each of his knuckles. "Let's show her how we treat enemies of the Skyweaver. . . ."

Safire flipped the club, catching the base. Ready for him. Ready for all of them. She'd been here a hundred times before. There was nothing they could do to her that hadn't already been done.

But before he could even throw the first punch, Eris was there. Free of the rope that bound her a moment ago. Her eyes bright, her hair gleaming. She held the spindle in her hand—retrieved from Safire's pocket—and was bending down, drawing a glowing silver line across the sandy cobblestones. . . .

Her hand slid into Safire's as she rose. Silver mist flooded the alley, engulfing the Lumina, who disappeared first. Then the noise of the distant market. Then the street.

Safire couldn't see—not Eris, not anything. But she felt those warm fingers, woven tightly through hers. Pulling her through.

"Don't let go," said Eris.

She didn't.

Twenty-One

When the mist turned to dark gray fog, Safire looked up. For a single fleeting moment, the sky was deep black and littered with stars. So many stars. Brighter and clearer and closer than ever before. So close, Safire lifted her fingers skyward, convinced she might touch one.

And then, quite suddenly, the fog dispersed. In its absence came the sounds of the night market they'd left behind. Warm bodies jostled Safire. The smell of sugar and flowers enveloped her. Music played by multiple stringed instruments beat loud and strong in her ears.

"*Hells,*" Eris cursed, materializing beside her, their fingers still entwined.

"What just happened?" Safire asked, looking around them. Skirts twirled and ribbons fluttered as couple after couple spun or stomped past them, lost in the throes of the music. The girls all wore flower wreaths on their heads and their smiles were brighter than stars.

A tightly packed crowd ringed the dancers, watching and cheering them on.

"I was so desperate to leave that alley . . . ," said Eris, looking around, too, the anguish clear on her face. ". . . I was thinking more about *it* than the place I wanted to go to." She shook her head. "The crossing got muddled. So now we're back here."

None of that made any sense to Safire.

"Where is *here?*" she hissed.

"It's a betrothal dance," Eris said, watching the particular steps of the dancers now. Her grip was getting increasingly tighter by the moment. Safire looked from the rosy-cheeked couples spinning around them to the ring of spectators closing them in. All of them laughing and singing and shouting encouragement.

It was suddenly familiar. They'd passed this way not long before, she realized. But they'd been outside this dancing circle then. Now they were inside it.

One by one, the gazes of the crowd fell on the only couple standing still within the circle: Eris and Safire. Their brows furrowed and their lips moved. Someone held a flower wreath out for Eris to take, misunderstanding their reason for being there.

Safire looked beyond them, farther out in the square, where Lumina soldiers rushed by, stopping revelers to question them, shouting for other soldiers to help in their search for the fugitives.

Eris must have seen it, too. Because suddenly she was sliding the throwing knife from the knot of hair at the back of Safire's neck, making her hair fall loose around her face.

"What are you doing?" she whispered as Eris took the flower wreath, then set the ring of blue forget-me-nots on Safire's head.

Eris's arm slid around her waist. "Pretend you're hopelessly in love with me," she murmured, eyeing the soldiers out in the crowd. "And follow my lead."

Before Safire could protest, Eris was leading her in the steps of the dance—while the Lumina hunted for them just beyond this dancing ring. Normally, Safire's uniform would have given her away. But she was still in the unmarked clothes she'd worn to spy on Jemsin in the Thirsty Craw. There was nothing to distinguish her as the visiting dragon king's commandant.

Someone gave a whoop of encouragement. Safire looked to find the crowd cheering as she and Eris joined the betrothed couples. Most were pairs of men and women—except for one pair of young men on the far side, beaming at each other, both wearing wreaths on their heads. Eris tipped her head at the man who'd handed her their wreath. But Safire could see her eyes searching the square beyond, keeping her attention on the Lumina—none of whom thought to check the dancing circle. Why would they? They were looking for a dangerous fugitive and a disobedient soldier, not a lovestruck couple.

Safire should have stopped Eris. Should have dragged her out of that circle and brought her to the searching Lumina. But she'd seen the look in that man's eyes. He'd wanted to hurt Safire in the same way he'd hurt the one she saved from him.

She remembered Eris's account of the night the scrin burned. *What if she was telling the truth?*

Most of all, though, this wasn't Firgaard. Safire didn't know the punishment for directly challenging—worse, *attacking*—one of the empress's soldiers. Safire might be the commandant of a visiting king, but she didn't know how much that would count for.

Safire had very little power here. And Eris had saved her—how many times now? She'd lost count.

In a strange turn of events, one thing was certain: she trusted Eris. At least for the moment.

So, as Eris counted out the rhythm of the steps for her, Safire followed her direction, helping them blend in. At least until she could figure out what to do.

It was a strange sensation, letting Eris lead. It made her palms sweat and her pulse hum.

Soon, they were breathing as hard as the other dancers. As the caller shouted directions—ones Eris understood but she didn't—Safire's loose hair began to stick to her sweaty skin. Every once in a while, after a rosy-cheeked Eris scanned the perimeter, she would glance back at Safire, catch her gaze, and grin.

Like a shared secret, that grin made Safire's heart beat too fast. It made her duck her eyes, trying to crush whatever warm thing was stirring within her.

Suddenly, the music stopped and Eris caught Safire hard around the waist, keeping her close. Their chests rose and fell with the breaths they took, and for a moment both of them looked beyond the circle. The Lumina were moving on. Only a few soldiers remained behind, speaking quietly with one another near one of the flower stalls.

Safire heard the crowd rumble around them as the caller—
the man who'd handed Eris the wreath—shouted one last
instruction. Eris went rigid, snagging Safire's attention. She
looked away from the Lumina and back to the circle.

Shouts of encouragement rose up around the ring. Safire
looked to find the young man next to them reaching for his
partner, then kissing her hard on the mouth. Safire glanced
to the other pairs of dancers, all of them locked in intimate
embraces.

Soon, the gazes of the spectators fell once more on the only
couple not doing as instructed: Safire and Eris. The crowd
began to chant as the caller repeated his final instruction, this
time just for them.

Safire glanced to Eris, who was staring back at her.

The chanting grew louder. The Lumina soldiers glanced up
from across the square, searching for the source of the increased
noise.

Seeing it, Eris's warm hands slid across Safire's jaw, bringing
her attention back. Safire looked up into her soft eyes.

"Ready?" she whispered.

Safire opened her mouth to say, *You can't be serious.*

But Eris was already tipping Safire's head back.

Already *kissing* her.

Cheering erupted around them.

At the touch of her lips, Safire's nerves sparked. Sensing her
panic, Eris's thumb gently stroked her jaw, her throat. Soothing
her. Coaxing her deeper into the kiss.

"You're okay," she murmured. "Just follow my lead."

So Safire relaxed, doing just that.

Eris tasted like a storm. Like thunder and lightning and rain, all mixed into one. Safire reached for her shirt, needing an anchor against the tempest rising in her.

A tempest woken by Eris.

Eris smiled, her mouth curving against Safire's, her hands sliding to her hips, drawing her closer.

Safire knew right then that if she didn't pull away now, she might never pull away.

The thought frightened her.

She stepped quickly back, breathing hard.

The moment she opened her eyes, a glint of gold caught her attention. She tore her gaze from a startled Eris. She glanced beyond the circle, and found a young man watching her. His golden tunic bore the crest of a dragon twined round a sword, and his brown eyes were full of shock.

Dax.

He'd seen the whole thing.

Safire suddenly remembered herself. Remembered who she was with and what they were capable of. She'd just kissed the Death Dancer—the girl who'd stolen a jewel out of Dax's treasury, one meant to assuage those hit worst by the scrubland blight.

The girl planning to hunt down Asha and deliver her to Jemsin.

Safire turned quickly back, reaching for Eris—to stop her from leaving. To make this right.

But Eris was already gone.

Twenty-Two

This time when Eris stepped through the gray, she focused hard on her destination. As the mists swirled, she no longer walked Axis's festive streets, full of color and laughter and dancing. She strode beneath that star-studded sky, the silence sparkling around her as she took the path across.

When that dark blue door painted with a moon and stars appeared before her, Eris relaxed. She'd successfully escaped. Reaching for its silver knob, she opened it and stepped through, straight into the labyrinth, its stained-glass walls flickering in the eerie floating white lights above.

Shutting the door behind her, Eris let go of her focus. Looking down, she uncurled her fingers to reveal a pale blue ribbon lying across her palm.

Unlike the last few items she'd stolen from Safire—taken only to provoke—she had a purpose in mind for this one.

As Eris strode into the maze, she thought of Safire. Remembering the warmth of her mouth, the softness of her lips . . .

and that look of horror on her face as she abruptly pulled away. While Eris smiled like an idiot.

What an utter fool I am.

She closed her hand around the ribbon, squeezing it tight.

"Good evening, Eris."

The rasping voice behind her made her spine straighten. Eris whirled, stumbling away from the thing stepping out of the shadows she'd just come through. He had blue-black feathers, hooklike talons, and eyes as red as blood.

Kadenze.

Jemsin's summoner.

Half man, half monster, Kadenze was the one thing that could follow her through the mists and across: to this in-between place. It was the reason she had never successfully escaped Jemsin—because it could track her anywhere.

The summoner's hellish gaze burned into her. "I've been waiting for you."

Eris shoved the ribbon behind her back, swallowing hard. "What does he want?"

"Jemsin is very concerned."

Eris narrowed her eyes at the monster before her. "Yeah? Well you can tell Jemsin that his good mate Kor delayed me considerably."

"Jemsin will deal with Kor," said Kadenze, its bloody gaze moving over her. "You do your job."

"I'm on it," Eris growled. "Just give me some time. *Tides.*"

"He wants to remind you," said Kadenze, moving closer, "of the cost of failure."

But Eris had never failed a job, and she wasn't about to start now. Certainly not with so much at stake. If she handed him the Namsara, Jemsin would let her walk free. If she failed, he would deliver her to her enemies.

Of course she wouldn't fail.

A sudden, sweeping cold rushed in, making her shiver. Feeling it, the summoner looked up over Eris's shoulder to the stained-glass panels behind her. Eris didn't look. She knew what it was: the ghost moving in the labyrinth, probably drawn to the sound of their voices.

"Why does Jemsin want her?" It was a question Eris hadn't cared to ask before. She asked it now only because, being forced into Safire's company these past few days, she couldn't help but notice how the girl worried over her cousin. How protective she was of her.

"It's the empress who wants her."

Eris's chin lifted. She hadn't expected that. "What?"

The summoner shifted from foot to foot, its feathers ruffling and talons clacking against the ground. As if something had unnerved it. "Leandra made the captain a deal he couldn't refuse."

Eris narrowed her eyes, thinking of Jemsin's meeting with the empress. It was his sole reason for sending Eris to Firgaard. Leandra must have made her proposition then.

"What did she offer him?"

"Full access to her waters—*if* Jemsin delivers the Namsara."

Eris whistled, wishing Safire could hear this. What kind of benevolent ruler gives a pirate permission to wreak havoc all over the Star Isles? It was a trade much further in Jemsin's favor, and it made Eris wonder: What did Asha have that the empress wanted so badly?

And why not just *invite* her along with her brother—who was currently on his way to the citadel now?

Unless she had and Asha refused the invitation.

Eris shook her head. All of these questions were starting to give her a headache. What did it matter, anyway? It wasn't her business. With the ribbon gripped tight in her hand, Eris turned away from the monster.

"Are we finished?" she asked, walking toward the first turn in the labyrinth.

"For now."

The door creaked open. Eris didn't wait for it to shut before she continued on. Her feet had long since memorized the way to the heart of this maze. The images on the stained-glass walls were so familiar to her, she often dreamed them in her sleep: seascapes and stormy cliffsides and sleepy little coves. When she arrived at the center, the familiar sight of her loom warmed her just a little.

Eris sank down into the soft white carpet on the floor. Staring up at her empty loom, an image flickered through her mind: Safire with her hair down and her head crowned with blossoms. She leaned over her basket full of skeins, running her fingers gently over colors. Looking for something that matched the ribbon she stole.

The door to Kor's burned ship was useless to her now and needed replacing. She'd woven that door from torn strips of the

Sea Mistress's sails and it had opened onto the ship's galley. That was the only way the magic would work—using objects from the place she wanted to go. It was Day who told her this. Who taught her how to turn the weavings into doors.

This place will keep you safe, he'd told her.

But that was before he died. Before Jemsin found her. Before she realized Kadenze could hunt her down no matter where she was—even across.

An old sorrow clumped in her throat. She swallowed it down, pushing the memory of Day far away. Where it couldn't hurt her.

Right now, Eris needed a door that would take her to a person, not a place. She'd never made such a thing before. She didn't know if it would work.

These were the things she did know, though: Asha, the Namsara, was in the Star Isles. And very soon, Safire would make contact with Asha—to warn her about Eris.

So Eris would make a door that led to Safire. She would keep to the shadows, like she had in Firgaard, waiting and watching. And when Safire made contact, she would unknowingly lead Eris straight to the Namsara.

Eris picked up a light brown skein of wool for the warp and started to unwind it. As she did, the air grew colder. Eris paused, sensing something watching her through the glass. She knew what it was.

She kept unwinding the yarn. But the ghost remained. It was common for it to come and go while she was in the labyrinth, but rarely did it linger.

"What do you think?" Eris asked. "Do these colors match?"
She often talked to the ghost. It never talked back.

Except this time, it did.

"Who hurt you?" Its voice was like wind scratching at a door.

Eris's hands fell still. Slowly, she set down the skein and looked up. The ghost loomed over her. Black as the night sky and shaped like a man. But it wasn't a man.

Her heart beat fast.

The ghost stared her down, silent as death. Eris knew that stare. It had watched her for years now, ever since the first time she'd stepped across.

But why talk now when it never had before?

It seemed to be staring at her arms, studying the damage the stardust steel had done. Her wrists were bloody and raw where her flesh had burned away.

"Does it hurt?"

She nodded.

The ghost moved closer. Eris held herself still. It reached for her wrists, and as it touched her, a rush of feelings swept through her, all of them familiar, none of them her own:

The terrible longing for someone you can never have.

The empty ache of forever being alone.

The soul-crushing darkness of despair.

If she'd been standing, she would have fallen to her knees with the overwhelming weight of them all. She shuddered. But as the ghost's feelings flooded her, they expunged the stinging, throbbing pain in her wrists.

The ghost stepped back. And though its sorrow lingered in her, everything else had been taken.

She drew her hands into her lap and stared down at her wrists. They were sore and festering just moments ago. Now the pain was gone and there were ugly red scars where the open wounds used to be.

Scars that would be there, she knew, for the rest of her life.

"Thank you," she whispered.

The ghost said nothing.

"What are you?"

"Nothing good," it said.

She frowned. If it wasn't good, why had it taken her pain away? "What's your name?"

"I'm . . . Crow," it said finally. "Or I was, once."

And then it melted back into the shadows.

Twenty-Three

"What in all the skies was *that*?"

Dax's jaw hardened as he ran his fingers through his curls, staring at Safire like he suddenly didn't recognize her. Which made two of them.

Not only had Safire let the empress's fugitive slip through her fingers—a fugitive who was now free to hunt down Asha—she'd *kissed* her.

Safire shoved the thought out of her head. She was desperately trying not to think about that kiss. How it felt like waking up. Like every day before this one, she'd been asleep and hadn't known it.

She tried to quickly stopper the emotions swirling inside her. Confusion, shame, fear—they were all foreign feelings. She didn't know what to do with them. "She was trying to blend in. To escape detection."

She was just using me.

Safire looked back over her shoulder. New songs started up again as new lovestruck couples moved into the dancing circle.

"And you let her," said Dax, his voice accusatory. But she could see the confusion in him, too. He was trying to make sense of what he'd seen. Trying to come up with a logical reason. One that would allow him to still trust and admire his cousin—who knew just how badly he needed this visit to go well.

But there was no sense to make of it.

A commotion broke out behind her. Dax reacted, stepping to Safire's side. She turned to see a flash of black uniforms and silver stars. Several Lumina soldiers surrounded them.

Safire's stomach knotted at the sight of the man leading them. It was the same soldier from the alley. The one whose club she'd intercepted.

"Kindly move aside," he told Dax, though his eyes were on Safire. "She's under arrest."

Dax's eyes widened. "What?" Safire saw his hand reach for his hilt. She grabbed his wrist to stop him. Their eyes met as he whispered, "For what crime?"

"Impeding the law," the Lumina answered.

Suddenly, Dax and Roa's guards were there, forming a protective ring around their king, queen, and commandant.

This was not good. Roa and Dax hadn't even arrived at the citadel yet, and they were already making enemies of the empress's army.

This was Safire's fault. She needed to fix it.

"He's right," she said, remembering the woman cowering in the alley. "I did impede." She held the gaze of the soldier in command. *But not a just law.*

Safire knew a couple of bad soldiers didn't mean an entire army was corrupt, though. The empress, she was sure, would want to hear her story. And once Safire gave it, the Lumina involved would be punished for their abuse of power.

The captain nodded to the two soldiers at his left. "Restrain her."

Frowning fiercely now, Dax moved to intervene. But Safire gripped his wrist harder and shook her head. She'd ruined enough things for one day. She didn't want to ruin the alliance between Dax and the empress before it even began—especially if Leandra really could help the scrublands.

"What happened?" asked a familiar voice as the two soldiers gripped Safire's arms, their hands pinching like vises. "Where's the fugitive?" A newly arrived Raif stood near her now, his gaze sweeping the scene. In his hand was the rope Safire used to bind Eris's hands. Eris had picked the knot.

"I lost her," said Safire.

On their way to the citadel, the Lumina marched Safire through three checkpoints, with Dax and Roa following closely. At the third and final gate, the checkpoint guards stopped them, taking the Lumina captain aside.

The checkpoint was a thick, wrought iron gate that rose nearly as high as the walls of Firgaard. The steel twisted in a repeating star pattern all the way around, and when Safire glanced up, she found the top fixed with tall, serrated points—to dissuade climbers.

Beyond the gateway was what seemed like a vast, empty courtyard. Only Lumina marched across it. Anyone getting past the gate would have to walk or run to the fortress wall, which was heavily guarded from the top, meaning any runners would be spotted—and likely shot with arrows—long before they reached the wall.

"Take *her* to the holding area," Safire heard the Lumina captain say as she studied the last gate. The iron twisted like frothing waves. "The king and queen you may show to their rooms."

Roa moved through the soldiers, flanked by her personal guards, each of them handpicked by Safire. "We would appreciate it," she said, her dark brown eyes flashing as she tried to join her commandant, "if you took all of us to the holding area until this is sorted out."

The captain grabbed Roa's wrist, halting her. "The holding area is for *criminals*, my lady."

A flame ignited within Safire. Roa's guards all drew their weapons.

The dragon queen was considerably smaller and shorter than the Lumina captain, but her defiant stance and withering gaze made them appear equally matched. Her voice was thunder as she said, "Kindly take your hands off me."

"Step away from the criminal"—the captain glared down at her—"and I'll think about it."

And then Dax arrived.

"First you detain my commandant like a felon"—the dragon king's voice belied just how much restraint he was demonstrating as his gaze pinned the captain—"and now you manhandle my queen?" His hand wasn't on his hilt, but it might as well have been. The look in his eyes was murderous. "Is this what hospitality looks like in the Star Isles?"

Faced with the implacable king and queen, surrounded by their guards, the Lumina captain released Roa. But he didn't stand down. Safire could feel the tension building like a coming storm.

And a storm *was* coming. A storm in the shape of a woman.

"Someone please explain to me why my guests are detained at my gate."

All eyes turned toward the one approaching from beyond the iron bars. She spoke with the authority of someone who was used to being obeyed, completely and immediately, but she didn't look like a queen.

No guards trailed her. She wore no extravagant fabrics or ornaments and nothing but a pale braid crowned her head. In fact, as Safire's eyes trailed her, from her calf-high boots, to her shining belt buckle, to her fitted blue jacket that buttoned down the left side, she thought this woman looked more like a navy captain than a monarch.

She seemed neither young nor old, but something in between.

"Tides, Caspian." The soldiers parted for their frowning empress, who was staring at where two Lumina gripped Safire's arms, keeping her hostage. Her eyes were the color of a raging sea as she turned her gaze on Caspian, the captain. "I hope there's a very good explanation for this."

Caspian gave her a swift account of the events leading up to this one. He tilted his chin toward Safire. "We were punishing a miscreant when this girl interfered."

Safire narrowed her eyes at the word *girl*. In Firgaard, she was commandant. Had they been there now, she would have shown him just how greatly she outranked him.

"In interfering," he continued, "she lost the fugitive we were bringing to your gate."

At the mention of her fugitive, something flashed across the empress's face. Annoyance or disappointment. Maybe both. After all, she'd spent years hunting the criminal who burned the scrin.

The empress turned to Safire, her hands linked behind her back. "And do you wish to give your own account?"

For someone who—according to Eris—despised the truth, this woman seemed deeply interested in it.

"All of what he said is true." Safire threw the captain a look. "I saw six heavily armed men beating a defenseless woman. It didn't occur to me *not* to intervene. But, yes. Unfortunately, I lost your fugitive in the process." She tried not to look at Dax, whose gaze was currently boring a hole in her. And because she needed to fix this mess—and still needed to stop Eris from finding Asha—she said, "I captured her once; I'll capture her again. That's a promise."

The empress went quiet, her lips pressed in a thin line as she studied Safire. Finally, she turned to Caspian. "Release her."

Caspian's jaw twitched, as if he wanted to argue. Instead, he looked to the soldiers detaining Safire. With a swift nod, the pressure on her arms let up as the soldiers stepped back.

"My army has been unable to catch this criminal," the empress said to Safire, who was massaging her upper arms where her captor's fingers had dug in. The skin was tender, already bruising. "I'd like to know how *you* caught her, as well as what you've learned. Perhaps we can find a time to speak more about it while you're here."

Safire nodded. "Of course."

"As for the rest of it"—the empress looked to Caspian, waving her hand dismissively—"an honest mistake, I'm sure."

Safire paused, about to correct her. It was no mistake. Those soldiers had been severely abusing their power. She had seen it.

But when Safire looked to Dax, she saw hopeful relief in his gaze. The empress had invited them here for a purpose. Leandra had heard of the suffering in the scrublands, and she wanted to help alleviate it.

Safire had undermined Leandra's soldiers, then botched things further by losing Eris. She didn't want to sabotage Dax and Roa's visit further.

So she held her tongue.

"You must all be tired," the empress said, leading them forward. "I'll show you to your rooms so you can rest before dinner."

Being inside the citadel felt like being underwater.

Every room and hall was painted a shade of the sea: from velvety blues and cold grays to bright teals and turquoises. The lintels and crown moldings were the pale beige of sea-foam and the sound of trickling water came from nearly every room, due to the fountains at their centers. Each one featured a marble statue of a ship in full sail or a mermaid hiding behind her hair or a breaching whale.

It was why, when the empress led them down the next hall, Safire paused.

This hall was different.

The walls were hung with floor-to-ceiling paintings that

swept from one end to the other. Safire followed Dax and Roa, studying the shining brushstrokes that transformed the paint into a froth of white waves or swirling dark eddies. In the beginning, the pictures inside the frames depicted squalls and tempests and maelstroms.

"Some time ago," the empress said to Roa from several paces ahead, "news of the blight in your homeland reached me."

Safire was only half listening. Because now the paintings depicted monsters, too. Dragons and kraken and sea spirits with their needlelike teeth, crunching the bones of sailors whose ships they'd wrecked.

It made her think of Eris saving her from the creature on the dock—a choice that came at the cost of her freedom.

Unless protecting Safire had been a calculated move, like the dancing and the kiss. Both had been a way for Eris to blend in, unseen by Lumina. What if protecting Safire—just like giving her a contradictory account of the night the scrin burned—was a way to make Safire sympathetic to her cause, ensuring she got what she wanted?

And now Eris was loose in the Star Isles. Hunting down Asha this very moment.

The walls felt too close suddenly. Safire didn't want to be here. She wanted to be out *there*, looking for her cousin.

"I invited you here because I know what's killing your crops in the scrublands," the empress was saying from much farther ahead, making Safire realize she'd fallen behind. "It's the same disease that struck these islands when they were under the Shadow God's dominion."

As Safire's pace quickened down this hall, out of the corner of her eye she noticed a reoccurring image in every painting on the walls: a looming shadow on the horizon.

Slowing again, Safire looked from one painting to the next. The first depicted a ship in the distance. In the next, it was joined by several others. Then a whole fleet. And leading them all, standing at the helm, was a younger empress. Her cheeks red with windburn, her hair tangled by wind and salt.

The paintings showed her mooring on the Star Isles, climbing the rocky gray cliffs, traversing dark boreal forests and mossy meadows, then finally arriving at a tower with a thousand steps. And all the while, the shadow on the horizon grew bigger and more ominous.

"I have a solution to your problem," the empress said.

At the very top of those thousand steps, sitting at a loom, was another woman. A crown of seven stars rested atop her head, and her hand held a spindle.

Skyweaver.

It was a near-identical image from the tapestry hanging in Safire's office. The one Asha gave her. The one Eris stole.

"What is this?" said Roa, at which point, Safire looked to find the empress lifting a silver chain over her head. Instead of a pendant, a small egg-shaped capsule hung down.

"My gift to you," Leandra said, letting it drop into Roa's cupped hand. "The reason I invited you here."

Safire tore herself away from the paintings and came toward them, staring as the empress clicked the capsule open and a tiny seed fell out and onto Roa's palm.

"Salvation for your people." She studied Roa as she said this. "It's impervious to the blight. I have several granaries full of that same seed. Before you leave, I'll have my soldiers fill up your ship."

Roa's fingers trembled as they curled closed around the seed, holding it tight. As she looked up into the empress's face, her eyes glimmered with tears.

"You don't know what this means to us. To *me*."

The empress smiled kindly back. "I think I do."

"There must be something we can give you in exchange," Dax said, his arm curling gently around Roa's waist. To a stranger, he would seem calm and composed. But Safire heard the smallest tremor in his voice. "To show our deep gratitude."

Ever since the news arrived of Roa's father, of Lirabel and her baby, Safire had watched Dax retreat inside himself. He wasn't just failing the scrublands, he was failing his wife—who'd stopped eating due to grief. Before the empress's invitation arrived, Dax could hardly look Roa in the eye.

Now, as Safire watched the horrible weight of the blight lift from her cousin's shoulders, as Roa's face shone with hope, Safire knew whom she believed. And it wasn't Eris.

As the empress refused any kind of payment for her gift, Safire returned to the last portrait hanging in this hall. It showed Skyweaver descending the steps of her tower to meet the young empress. This time her hand gripped not a spindle but a knife, curved like a slivered moon.

As Safire's gazed traced the blade, her thoughts were on Asha, who was carrying a similar-looking knife at this very moment, trying to locate its maker here in the Star Isles.

It's only a matter of time before Eris finds her, thought Safire.

She needed to get to her cousin first, then bring her here to safety. Because if there was anywhere Eris would never set foot, Safire was certain, it was inside the citadel of the enemy she'd spent seven years running from.

Safire didn't go to dinner. The empress had no sooner escorted them to their rooms when Safire knocked on Dax's door and told him she was leaving to find Asha. Still overjoyed with Leandra's generous gift, Dax was eager to put the issue of Eris behind them and forgive Safire's mistake. More than this, he wanted Asha safe as much as Safire did, so he gave her the letter Torwin sent him, along with a map of the Star Isles, showing her the small village on the southern tip of Axis Isle, where the letter said they were heading. Dax told her to take Spark—his golden dragon—with her.

One of the conditions of Dax and Roa traveling with dragons was that they had to be stabled inside the citadel for the duration of the visit, ensuring they wouldn't be flying over the city and scaring the people of Axis, who were not familiar with the massive monsters. Permission therefore needed to be granted from the empress for a rider to fly a dragon into and out of the citadel.

But when Safire arrived at the covered courtyard where the dragons were kept, she found them not stabled, but muzzled and chained to the floor.

She nearly dropped her letter of permission.

Surely Dax didn't agree to this, she thought, looking around her. The five dragons who'd traveled with the king and queen's ship all lifted their heads at the sight of her. Bands of metal encircled each dragon's jaws and hind legs, and the iron chains rooting them to the ground were so short, they could barely stand, never mind walk.

All at once, the dragons stood up, stretching their wings as if to say *Are we leaving now?*

As Safire looked from one to the next, she noticed one dragon was missing.

Sorrow.

He must have panicked at the sight of Axis. Sorrow abhorred cities. He probably flew off long before the others were quarantined. The thought made her glad. Being chained and muzzled like this would have done irrevocable damage to a dragon like Sorrow.

A soldier approached, interrupting her thoughts.

"They're supposed to be stabled," said Safire, handing him the empress's letter.

He arched a dark brow, then motioned to the courtyard around them. "What do you think this is?"

A prison, thought Safire as every slitted pair of eyes followed her and the soldier toward Dax's golden dragon, Spark. She didn't dare say it aloud. She'd already caused enough chaos today. Biting her tongue, Safire pulled on Dax's flight jacket and gloves as she waited for the soldier to unlock the dragon.

As soon as her chains fell off, Spark shook herself out, vibrating with excitement. Safire clicked the commands she'd been taught, and Spark obediently came to her side. Scenting her rider on Safire's jacket, Spark sniffed her for several heartbeats, then nuzzled her hip.

Dax doesn't know, she wanted to tell the dragon, rubbing her scaly forehead. *But you can be sure I'll tell him as soon as we return.*

Asha was going to be livid.

With that thought, she mounted Spark, then waited for the soldiers to open the gate at the north end of this courtyard. As the cranks groaned and the iron bars lifted, Safire saw that the light was disappearing with the sunset.

Spark shifted from foot to foot, anxious to be out of here.

You and me both, she thought.

The moment the gate was up, Spark bolted toward the open gardens beyond. She had a gentle, graceful gait and before Safire could blink, they were out of the courtyard and in the sky.

As the citadel fell away, and the cold air made her shiver, Safire felt lighter. Beneath her, Spark hummed with her new-found freedom as they headed south.

She was tempted to not bring her back.

Their flight took longer than it should have, partly because the sun was gone and partly because Safire was looking for lights. The other villages they passed had been speckled with the glow of oil lamps in windowsills, spilling out onto the street.

They passed the village they sought three times before Safire even realized it was there.

When they landed, she could barely make out the shapes of houses in the moonlight. With a clicked command, she told Spark to wait, then started down the overgrown path between homes. It was so silent, her footsteps seemed to echo in her ears. In the light of the moon, she studied each house. The windows of the first one were all broken. The roof of the second had all but caved in. The door of the third had rotted off its hinges.

Safire stopped.

"No one lives here," she realized aloud.

The frame of the nearest house groaned in the wind, making her jump. When the silence returned, Safire called into the darkness: "Asha?"

No one answered.

Cupping her hands around her mouth, Safire shouted, "Asha!"

She was about to return to Spark when something rustled in the grass behind her.

Asha?

She felt the heat of the newcomer at her back. Felt the massive bulk of it. For some reason, she thought of the shadow in the empress's paintings and quickly spun, her heart thudding hard.

Two slitted eyes stared at her through the darkness.

"Kozu?" Safire immediately relaxed. "Is that you?"

But Kozu only had one eye. As the shadow came closer and the moonlight flickered across its scales, Safire saw they were white, not black.

"Sorrow?"

Sorrow clicked, almost pleasantly. As if happy to be remembered by Safire.

Any hope she had was extinguished. She pressed her palms to her eyes as Sorrow studied her. "She's not here, is she?"

Did that mean Asha found what she needed in this abandoned village and moved on? Or did it mean Eris found her and had taken her to Jemsin?

It was one thing to steal Asha. Safire fully believed Eris capable of that. One prick of a scarp thorn dart when Asha was alone would be enough to overcome her, after which Eris could easily disappear with her—just like she'd disappeared with Safire—only to reappear somewhere else. Like on Jemsin's ship.

But there was still Kozu and Torwin to contend with. If Eris kidnapped Asha, both of them would go after her. The only problem was, as Eris made clear several days back, dragons could be killed with harpoons. And Jemsin had plenty of them aboard his ship.

Even if Eris hadn't found Asha yet, Safire knew she would soon. She was the Death Dancer, after all. There was nothing she couldn't steal.

Sorrow clicked, interrupting her thoughts. Safire looked up. "Where is she, Sorrow?" Safire stepped toward the dragon. "Can you find her for me?"

Sorrow tilted his head. But as Safire took one more step, she came too close. Sorrow panicked. The skittish creature darted away as quickly as he'd come, leaving the space before Safire empty once more.

Safire breathed a weighty sigh.

There was only one course of action she could think of: return to the citadel and seek the empress's help.

The Shadow God

No one knew where he came from, but with him came death, disaster, and disease. Wherever the Shadow God walked, chaos followed. The wind grew cold and cruel, making it harder to grow things. The ocean rose up and gorged itself on cities and villages alike, sweeping their homes and their loved ones out into its depths. The fish disappeared, and in their hunger the spirits of the sea—who once lived peaceably with islanders—began killing and eating them instead.

From her loom, Skyweaver listened. She heard the despair of the Star Isles. She felt their misery and fear. Unable to bear it, she left her weaving room, descended the stairs of her tower, and sought the Shadow God out.

She walked for days until she came to the immortal scarps—the highest point in the Star Isles. There she found him, perched on a dark elder throne: a black, twisted shape with eyes of white fire and a gaping, hungry mouth.

"Why are you doing this?" she cried.

"It is my nature."

"What will make you stop?"

"I can't stop my nature any more than you can yours."

Skyweaver begged and pleaded. When he could bear her beseeching no more, he finally said, "Your weaving. Give up your weaving and I will give up my chaos."

Skyweaver frowned. If she stopped weaving, there would be no one to turn the souls of the dead into stars. No stars to light the way for those left behind. No one to give hope to the living.

She swallowed and shook her head. "I cannot." It was her sacred task.

Something flickered in the Shadow God.

"Then get out of my sight."

Skyweaver fled. But when she returned to her tower, she could not weave. She was too furious. Too heartsick. Too powerless to stop the terrible power of the Shadow God.

Until the day a savior arrived.

She came from the sea with a fleet of golden ships. Leandra, she called herself. From halfway across the world, she'd heard of the chaos tormenting the Star Isles and was here to stop it.

Leandra built a walled city where people could seek refuge from disaster and disease. She sent her soldiers out to hunt down the sea spirits terrorizing the islands. She made treaties with neighboring kingdoms for the things the islanders needed that they could no longer harvest—from land or sea.

Last of all, she climbed the steps of the Skyweaver's tower.

"Join me," Leandra said, standing before her loom.

Skyweaver wanted to help. Wanted to put an end to this horror. But what could she do? All she had was her spindle, her loom, and her skill as a weaver. All she knew was how to take souls and turn them into something else.

Leandra drew a knife, put it in the Skyweaver's hands, and said, "You can kill him."

But could she?

The Skyweaver paced her tower for three days and three nights. Finally, she agreed to Leandra's plan.

Skyweaver didn't spin souls into stars that night. Instead, she called the Shadow God, saying she'd considered his proposition and had decided to accept.

The Shadow God heard her.

The Shadow God came.

The moment he stepped through her door, Skyweaver spun a web made of starlight to catch him. She bound him up tight in her threads.

As she raised the knife to kill him, though, she found before her not a mighty god. Not a bringer of chaos and destruction. But a creature full of sorrow. A thing to be pitied.

"Do it," he hissed.

But she couldn't.

Instead, she hid the Shadow God away, in a place between worlds, where no one would ever find him.

And then she took something precious from him. Something that would ensure he remained ensnared forever.

Something he didn't even know he owned.

She told Leandra it was done. The Shadow God was dead. What did it matter if she lied? He would never get free of her web.

So peace returned to the Star Isles . . . for a time.

Twenty-Four

Eris, whose fingers were cramped from weaving all night, had only meant to rest for a moment. But when she shut her eyes, sleep claimed her. She dreamed she'd failed to do as Jemsin asked, and now the summoner was walking the labyrinth, coming for her.

Eris woke with a start, sweat soaked. Heart hammering.

For a moment, she lay quiet and still, listening for the clicking of talons.

But all was silent.

Just a dream.

She remembered her half-finished weaving and sat up. The sooner she finished, the sooner she could find the Namsara and trade her in for freedom. So Eris rose from the bed of woven blankets.

It wasn't her bed, just like the clothes in the wooden chest weren't her clothes. They'd been left by whoever came here before she did. This place had never felt like hers, but rather like she was borrowing it until its true owner decided to come back.

Unlike the rest of the labyrinth, the bedroom had a natural warmth. The floorboards were well worn. Candles were lit on top of the dressers and bedside tables. And the embers of a forever-dying fire glowed in the fireplace. She'd never seen that fire go out, only burn. Same with the candles. She had no idea who kept them lit.

Maybe the ghost.

Now, as Eris passed the blue gown hanging over the chair in front of the vanity, she paused to study it. The weaving was so fine—expertly done—and no dust soiled it. No dust soiled anything inside the labyrinth.

The weaving, she reminded herself. *The door.*

Eris withdrew her hand and returned to the loom.

As she sat down before her half-finished tapestry and her fingers picked up the threads once more, she thought of what the summoner said: that Jemsin only wanted the Namsara because the empress wanted her.

Whatever she wants her for, thought Eris, sinking down on the soft rug and staring up at her progress, *it can't be good.*

She should probably warn Safire.

Except no. Why would she? Safire and the rest of them had intended to hand her over to monsters today. Safire would do it again in a heartbeat.

She couldn't care what the empress wanted with Asha. She *didn't* care.

Eris thought of her goal. Of what Jemsin promised her: *Freedom.* Freedom to leave, to run, to never be hunted ever again.

Her gaze followed the dark blue threads of the weft. Reaching for Safire's ribbon, she tied it on, then started weaving it in.

She had just fallen into a rhythm when that familiar soul-chilling cold swept through the room.

"Couldn't sleep either, hmm?" she said as she worked.

Silence answered her.

When Eris looked up, the ghost was back. It was no longer quite so formless. If she looked hard enough, she could almost make out edges, like a silhouette. It even seemed more . . .

Human.

Eris thought of the bed that didn't belong to her and the chest of clothes she'd never worn.

"Did they belong to *you*?" she murmured, wondering about this ghost's story. Who it was, how it came to be here, how long it had wandered this lonely labyrinth.

It didn't answer her. So Eris went back to weaving.

"Are you trapped here?" she guessed as she worked.

"Yes," it said.

Her fingers fumbled the thread. Recovering, she thought of something Day used to tell her: that sometimes spirits with unfinished business didn't cross from one world to the next but got stuck in between instead.

"Did you forget to finish something before you died?"

"I'm not dead," said the ghost.

Sure, thought Eris. *You probably all think that.*

"I'm imprisoned."

"Oh?" She paused again. "Who imprisoned you, then?"

When it didn't answer her, she glanced back. For a moment,

Eris could swear the ghost had fingers now. And those fingers were turning into claws. But the next moment, they were fingers again. So maybe she'd imagined it.

"Someone I loved," said the ghost. "She'll pay dearly for it."

Eris turned to look more fully, to ask *who* would pay, and *who* it had loved, but by the time she turned around, the ghost was gone.

Sighing heavily, she shook her head. It didn't matter. Only one thing mattered.

She returned to the loom.

Eris finished her weaving just before dawn. Cutting it free, she lifted it up to study the brown and blue threads and to run her fingers along the bits of Safire's ribbon showing through.

She'd never done it before—made a door connected to a person. Normally, a door took her to the same place every time. She didn't know if it would work the same way with a person.

Time to find out, she thought, moving through the labyrinth now, her candle illuminating the images depicted in colored glass. Mossy green meadows and bright orange bogs. Grassy headland and rocky shorelines. Brightly colored fishing huts. Hooks and nets and boats.

Eris was so used to the images trapped in the glass, she hardly saw them anymore.

Finally, she arrived at the yellow door. The one leading to Kor's now destroyed ship. Setting down her new weaving, she opened the door. Silver-gray mist poured in. But she didn't step through. Instead, she slid the pins out of the hinges, and pulled the whole thing off.

The moment it came free, the door dissolved into thread. Now her hands held a weaving made of yellow and gold threads, tied with pieces of the *Sea Mistress*'s sails. She'd made it years ago, when Kor was first given a ship and became the one Eris reported to.

Good riddance, she thought, dropping it on the floor. Lifting up the new tapestry, she hesitated a moment before sucking in a breath and setting it into the empty doorframe. The moment she did, the blue and brown threads faded and hardened, transforming into wood. Eris slipped the pins back into the hinges.

A door the color of Safire's eyes stood before her now. Waiting to be opened.

Pulling it open, Eris stepped through and into the silver-white mist.

Twenty-Five

Safire strode across the uncovered walkway leading to the empress's receiving room. She could see the grid-like streets of Axis below her—so unlike the twisting roads and alleys of Firgaard. Another difference between Axis and Firgaard: the sun didn't beat relentlessly down on her here. Instead, the afternoon was cool and damp; and even from this high up in the citadel, she could taste and smell the sea.

As soon as she and Spark returned, Safire requested an urgent meeting with Leandra. The empress, she'd been informed, would receive her midafternoon.

It was midafternoon now as Safire followed her armed Lumina escorts through the citadel and its many walkways. As they approached a set of massive teak doors, carved with seascapes—waves and sails and scaly-finned creatures—Safire's skin prickled with a familiar sensation.

Someone was watching her.

It was the same sensation she'd felt back in Firgaard, while trying to catch the Death Dancer. Her footsteps slowed. But when she turned to look, there were only her escorts and a handful of guards standing at attention down this hall, each of them ignoring her.

As the Lumina soldiers announced themselves, Safire shook off the feeling.

The doors opened and an attendant looked out—a young woman with auburn hair pulled tight in a bun. She took the folded summons from Safire's escorts and, after scanning its contents, wordlessly let Safire in.

The room beyond was perfectly round and brightly lit by shafts of sunlight coming through the windows that climbed to the ceiling. At the center of the room, bathed in light, sat the empress at her desk, her hand moving furiously as she inked something on the parchment before her.

For such a sterile room, it smelled strangely like brine.

Safire's gaze lingered on the large sword hanging on the wall behind the empress's desk. The steel was thick, the edge thin and razor-sharp. The plaque beneath it read: *The Severer.*

The severer of what? she wondered.

"Good day, Safire," said Leandra without looking up. "Please take a seat." She motioned to the chair on the other side of her desk. It seemed to be fashioned from the vertebrae of a very large mammal—a whale, Safire thought—and cushioned with velvet. Hesitantly, Safire sat.

She waited for the empress to finish, looking from window to window. In the west, the sea shone silver. To the north, looming above Axis, a white mist was collecting in the scarps high above the city. It made Safire think of something Eris said, back on Dax's ship: *She'll take me up to the immortal scarps and dispose of me—like she does with everyone she hates most.*

Were those the scarps Eris spoke of?

"I apologize for not being able to see you immediately." The empress sprinkled sand across what she'd written, then gently blew on the ink. "As I'm sure you can imagine, I have a great many questions for you."

Safire nodded. It was why she was here—to tell the empress what she knew and hopefully get some answers in return. Answers that might help her track down Eris.

But there was something she wanted to address first. "I wonder, Empress, if it's necessary to keep our dragons muzzled and chained."

Setting aside her letter, the empress leaned back in her chair, crossing her arms as she studied Safire. "You're displeased with the arrangement?"

The empress's cool tone made Safire's skin prickle with warning. "It . . . surprised me. In Firgaard, we let our dragons roam freely. They fly where they want and come when we call. We don't lock them up."

The empress was silent a moment before responding. "I must apologize, then. The people of the Star Isles are not well acquainted with dragons. The stories we've heard have made me cautious. Tell me: is it true that a dragon burned down half of Firgaard not so very long ago?"

Safire sat up straighter. "Well, yes, that's true. But—"

"Didn't that same dragon nearly kill your cousin?"

Safire blinked. "Um. Yes, but Asha—"

"I have a responsibility to the Star Isles, Safire. Your people have a contentious history with dragons. That, combined with my own inexperience, leads me to err on the side of caution. Surely you can understand my position."

Safire didn't know what to say. Seeing it, the empress continued.

"While you and your dragons are guests in my home, I would ask that you accept the precautions I take. They are for the safety of the people of the Star Isles." She tapped her lip with a single finger, then looked to the windows. "I can tell my soldiers to loosen the chains, however. Would that make you feel better?"

Safire swallowed. "I . . . suppose that's fair."

"And now can we move on to more pressing matters?"

Feeling scolded, Safire nodded.

"Good." Leandra folded her hands on her desk. "Your king tells me that you're . . . well acquainted with my fugitive."

Safire blushed. *Well acquainted?* It was an interesting choice of words. *What, exactly, did you tell her, Dax?*

"As you know, my soldiers have been hunting this criminal for several years. Up until yesterday, we knew nothing other than her age. We didn't even know what she looked like." When she looked up, her gray eyes were calm as the sea. "How did you find her?"

Safire explained about the thefts in Firgaard. "I almost caught her. I was *so close.* But . . ." She paused. "This is going to sound strange, but she *disappeared.* Right in front of me."

The empress's eyes narrowed a little. But she nodded for Safire to continue. Safire told her the rest of it—being kidnapped by Eris and brought aboard Jemsin's ship.

"The pirate Jemsin?" the empress interrupted suddenly. "Are you sure?"

Safire nodded. "She works for him."

Suddenly, the mist coming down from the scarps blocked out the sunlight coming through the windows. The room grew cold.

"I see" was all the empress said.

Safire told her about the deal Jemsin made with Eris: her freedom in exchange for bringing the Namsara to him. She told her about being intercepted by Kor, then escaping him with Eris in tow.

"And that's when you lost her."

Safire nodded. She left out the parts where Eris saved her life—twice—as well as Eris's account of the night the scrin burned. And also the part where Eris kissed her.

Heat bloomed in her at the memory.

"Do you have any idea where she might be now? Perhaps back on Jemsin's ship?" She looked hopeful about this.

Safire shook her head. "I don't think so. She knows the Namsara is in the Star Isles, and intends to hunt her down. It's why—"

"*Is* the Namsara in the Star Isles?" the empress asked, leaning forward in her chair.

Safire glanced up, remembering suddenly that Asha had declined the empress's invitation. She might see it as a slight,

Asha visiting her islands but not visiting *her*. It might do more than offend her; it might sabotage the alliance forming between her and Dax—an alliance that meant salvation for the scrublands.

"Asha is"—Safire struggled to think of an explanation that wouldn't offend her—"searching for someone. It's of the utmost importance that she finds them, and only recently has her search taken her here, to these islands." The next thing she said was a lie. "Dax only got word in Darmoor."

Maybe Eris really is rubbing off on me. . . .

Leandra's gray eyes remained fixed on her face. "Perhaps I can be of assistance in this search. Who is she looking for?"

That was the problem. They didn't know who this maker was, only that a clue might be found at the scrin.

Which no longer existed.

"She's looking for the owner of an artifact," Safire explained. "A weapon called the Skyweaver's knife."

Abruptly, Leandra rose from her desk, walking toward one of the windows. The silence built, glistening around Safire. "The weapon your queen used to save her sister," she finally murmured, as if suddenly a world away.

"Yes." Safire frowned. "How did you know that?"

"I heard . . . rumors," said the empress. "Roa confirmed them over dinner yesterday." She glanced over her shoulder at Safire. "I confess: it was part of the reason for my invitation. I wanted to know if the rumors were true."

"I went to warn Asha," Safire went on. "But she wasn't where she was supposed to be." Safire stood. "This is why I need your help. Eris escaped me only yesterday, and—"

"Eris?" Still turned toward Safire, the empress's mouth twisted, as if she'd tasted something sour. "Is *that* the fugitive's name?"

Safire nodded.

Leandra said nothing for a moment, then turned back to the window. She stared hard into the distant hills, then nodded for Safire to go on. "Eris," she murmured, as if testing the name on her tongue.

"She doesn't know Asha's precise location. I don't think it's possible she's found her yet, but I'm certain she *will* find her— and soon."

"You don't want her getting to the Namsara before you do." Leandra fisted her hand, pressing it to her lips. "Well. Neither do I." Dropping her hand, she said, "I'll send out soldiers to every village in the Star Isles. Starting today. If the Namsara is here, we'll find her."

Safire felt a weight lift from her. "Thank you. She has a dragon with her—a massive black dragon with a scar through one eye. He's difficult to miss."

Leandra nodded. "I'll pass that information along. Now, if you could do *me* a favor and recatch my fugitive . . ."

Safire bowed her head. "Of course."

"And if you think of anything else I should know, report it directly to me." She motioned to her attendant—the young girl Safire had all but forgotten. "Will you please see King Dax's commander out?"

The girl nodded, motioning for Safire to follow her.

"If there's anything else I can do for you," said Leandra, returning to the window, watching the mist from the scarps slowly descend on the city below, "please let my staff know."

"Actually," said Safire, halting halfway to the doors, then turning back, "there is one thing. I was hoping you could tell me anything *you* know about her that could help me track her down. Perhaps the village she grew up in, or if she has any—"

"I've already told you all I know about the fugitive," said Leandra, looking south—the direction of the ruined scrin.

Safire could tell she was overstepping her bounds now. But if she was going to find Eris in these islands, she needed as much help as she could get.

"Then I wonder if I could speak to one of the pirates Dax captured?" she pressed. "Kor seems to know Eris fairly well. He might be able to give us more information. Is there someone who could show me to the prison where he's being kept?"

"Kor and his crew have already been executed," said Leandra, her voice cold. "We got the information we needed from them."

Safire froze. Had she heard that correctly?

"Executed?" She breathed the word. "Without a trial?"

The empress didn't turn as she said, "They're pirates, Safire. They don't get trials."

Twenty-Six

Two Lumina soldiers escorted Safire back to her rooms. The whole way there, the empress's last words rang through her mind.

Executing pirates wasn't a choice Safire would have made. But as she thought of the hungry rage in Kor's eyes when he looked at Eris, she shivered. Could she really blame the empress for not giving him a trial? After she herself had given Jarek no trial before she put a knife through his heart?

Still, she needed to find Dax and tell him—about this, and the dragons, and Asha not being where she should be.

He'll know what to do.

A note was waiting on her dresser when she arrived, however. Written in Dax's shaky script, it said he and Roa were visiting the granaries, where their seeds were being packed for the journey home, and they would see her at the banquet this evening—one being held in honor of their newfound alliance.

Safire lowered the note, looking to the window. The mist coming down the mountains hadn't cloaked the city yet. She could still see the sun's position in the sky.

It was late afternoon. She wouldn't need to wait long.

Glancing up into the mirror, Safire found a small horror looking back. Her hair hung down in wind-blown chunks. Deep crevices under her eyes said she hadn't slept in . . . she couldn't remember how long. And her clothes were coated in salt and grime.

Safire stared at herself. *What must the empress think of me?*

She shook off the thought. If she were going to this banquet—and since the banquet seemed her only opportunity to confer with Dax and Roa, she *was* going—then she desperately needed to wash.

So, after running the bath, she stripped out of her clothes and sank into the hot, soapy water. Setting immediately to work, she rigorously scrubbed the salt and grime from her hair.

Gross. Safire scrunched her nose, soaping her hair as she wondered how Eris could have borne kissing her like *this*.

The thought brought a rush of embarrassment.

Maybe that's why she left so quickly.

At the thought of Eris, Safire remembered something the Death Dancer said just before they anchored in Axis's harbor.

I'll get no trial.

Safire stopped scrubbing.

She hadn't believed her at the time. But now, as she thought of Kor and the other dead pirates, she wondered if Eris was right.

If Safire managed to capture her for the empress—as she'd promised to do—would Leandra execute Eris as easily as she'd executed Kor?

And if so, she thought, sinking down into the water to wash the suds from her hair, *could I really deliver her to her death?*

Despite the warm water she soaked in, Safire shivered.

She lay still, considering the dilemma over and over, trying to find a solution. The bath was so warm, and Safire was so tired, that after a short while, she fell asleep.

She woke to a sound in the bedroom. Bolting upright in the now-cold water, it sloshed over the tub. Safire sat perfectly still, listening as she gripped the cool ceramic sides. But no sound came from the room beyond this one.

Slowly, she lifted herself from the bath and wrapped herself in a towel, peering through the doorway.

At first, she saw nothing unusual or out of place. It was only as she began toweling her hair, scanning the room for a second time, that she saw the dress hanging over the chair in front of the vanity. A dress that hadn't been there before she got in the bath.

Safire approached, all her senses on high alert. The dress was sky blue and she ran her fingers across the tightly woven wool threads. She looked for the weaver's mark, but all she could find was a tiny silver star embroidered into the sleeve of the left wrist.

Lifting the fabric, she pressed it to her face and breathed in.

It smelled like the sea.

Like Eris.

Her skin prickled at the thought.

Safire lowered the dress, looking slowly around. But there was no other sign of the Death Dancer walking her rooms while she bathed.

Maybe she was wrong. Maybe the dress was a gift from the empress, as a thank-you for the information she'd given. After all, Eris would never venture inside the citadel of the enemy she'd been running from for seven years.

Whoever gave her the dress, it was the only thing Safire had to wear, seeing as her only other clothes were in a grimy, salt-encrusted pile on the floor.

She had only just pulled the dress over her head when a knock came on the door.

"Commandant?"

Safire recognized the voice. It belonged to one of Roa's personal guards. A young woman named Saba.

"Yes?" Safire called as the dress cascaded down her.

"The dragon queen is wondering where you are."

Safire frowned as she reached to fasten the button at the back of the neck. "Clearly I'm right here," she said, swinging open the door.

Saba stood before her, dressed in her soldat uniform with the dragon queen's emblem proudly displayed across her chest: a white hawk in a circle of jacaranda flowers. "The banquet started a little while ago," Saba said, her dark brown curls circling her head like a cloud.

A little while ago? thought Safire. *How long was I asleep?*

"Shall I tell her you're on your way?" Saba offered.

Safire touched her damp hair, then nodded. "I'll be right there."

As soon as Saba left, Safire twisted her hair into a knot, then pinned it quickly into place. Before leaving for the banquet, she did another scan of the room, even going so far as to look under the bed and inside the chest full of blankets.

But she was alone.

At the bottom of a spiraling staircase in the heart of the citadel, the noise of wind instruments playing a reel wafted down to her as a glass chandelier hung from the ceiling four stories above. Its blue and white glass threw glittering light all down the wide staircase.

Safire paused on the bottommost step. Ever since Dax promoted her to commandant, Safire attended official events in uniform. As Safire smoothed the woolen dress over her hips now, she felt exposed and vulnerable.

Sucking in a breath, she started upward, needing to find Dax and tell him everything she'd learned. She climbed the steps until she reached the uppermost floor, where two Lumina stood guard at the entrance to the grand ballroom.

Safire stepped into the biggest room she'd ever seen. Bigger than any of Firgaard's courts. Rows of columns ran from end to end, holding up the glass roof. The archway depicted monsterlike creatures cast in gold, and the white walls were broken up by floor-to-ceiling windows where guests stood talking and drinking as the moon rose over the city below.

It was times like this when Safire most felt like an imposter. All around her, people were dressed in silks and furs and glittering baubles, in rich purples and yellows and blues. Yes, she was a princess, related by blood to the dragon king. Yes, she'd been born in a palace. But those things didn't tell the whole story— one of a girl who'd been kept out of sight of the court, kept away from her own cousins. Ashamed of and despised because of the choice her father made. Because of who her mother was.

She might be a princess, but she hadn't been raised as one. And she'd never belonged in places like this.

Safire spotted Roa and Dax across the room, within view of their guards, speaking with the empress. Between them and Safire, however, stood Raif. The young soldier who'd escorted her through Axis last night. He was speaking with his captain, Caspian, and Safire thought she heard him say her name, then cast his gaze out over the room, looking hopeful.

Safire was not in the mood to deal with Raif. Before his eyes fell on her, she turned on her heel . . . and walked straight into a starry crest.

"Draw attention," came a familiar voice, "and you'll never hear what I've come to warn you about."

Safire's gaze lifted.

Eris stood before her wearing a stolen Lumina uniform that hugged her curves: black shirt, black leggings, gray calf-high boots. Her blond hair was knotted loosely at her nape, and a soldier's cap shielded the upper part of her face.

The sight of her unearthed a storm of feelings in Safire.

She knew what she should do: grab Eris and yell for reinforcements. But if she did that, what would happen? If a petty pirate like Kor had gotten no trial, neither would Eris. The empress would certainly execute her.

Safire glanced around the room full of Eris's worst enemies and whispered, "Are you out of your damned mind?"

Twenty-Seven

Eris hadn't meant to walk out into that crowd of people. She'd meant to only stand in the shadows, waiting for the perfect moment to get Safire alone. But as Eris watched Safire step into the room, she'd seen the change come over her.

In an instant, Safire was no longer the cousin to a king. No longer the commander of his army. Somehow, that room transformed her into someone small and lost and alone.

Eris couldn't stand it.

So, fool that she was, she went to her.

Her whole body buzzed with unease. Her hands were slick with sweat. But at those words from Safire—*Are you out of your damned mind?*—the fear drained out of her.

Safire wasn't going to alert them to her presence.

Why? What had changed?

She shook off the question. Pressing her free hand firmly against the small of Safire's back, Eris led her to the far end of this uselessly large room, then pushed her out between lush gold curtains and onto one of the balconies.

Eris pulled the curtain closed, concealing them both from view. The mist was thick around them.

Safire spun to face her. The sight of her made Eris's heart beat twice as fast.

Her black hair was twisted up in its usual knot, held in place by one of her throwing knives, and she wore the blue dress Eris left in her bedroom. The hue complemented her eyes perfectly.

"She killed them," Safire blurted out.

Eris frowned. That was not what she'd expected her to say. "Killed who?"

"Kor. Rain. Lila." Safire's hands fisted at her sides, as if she were only just now considering the words she was saying. "She executed all of them."

It didn't sink in at first. The idea of Kor and the others being dead, when they'd been alive just yesterday . . . she couldn't make sense of it. And then, when it *did* make sense, Eris didn't know how to feel. She hated Kor, that was certain. She'd stabbed him and set his ship ablaze, after all. But she'd done those things because she was angry and tired of being abused; not because she'd wanted to kill him. If she'd wanted to kill Kor, she would have locked him inside that burning room.

Eris didn't want him dead. Nor any of the others.

"Are you sure?"

Safire turned away, looking out over the balustrade, into the mist-cloaked city. "I didn't see it with my own eyes," she said, hugging herself. "But it's what she told me: *Pirates don't get trials.*"

Eris watched her, unsure of what to say. She wasn't surprised by this. But Safire clearly was.

"Why are you here?" Safire whispered, her voice sounding small.

Eris stepped up to the balustrade. "I know what Jemsin wants your cousin for."

Safire turned, her blue eyes hard as jewels. "And?"

Tides, this would be so much easier if you weren't so pretty. Eris shoved the thought away, needing to focus. She was deep in enemy territory right now. She needed to keep her head about her.

"The empress made him a deal: she'll give him free rein over her territorial waters if he delivers Asha to her."

Safire's dark brows knit in a skeptical frown. "You have proof of this?"

"Not . . . exactly." Eris looked down to her stolen boots. "No."

"So I'm supposed to take you at your word."

"Yes?"

"It doesn't make any sense." Safire murmured, staring out into the mist. "What does she want my cousin *for*?"

"I have no idea. But if she's making deals with pirates in order to obtain her, my guess is: nothing good."

Safire studied Eris for several heartbeats. "Does this mean you won't hunt Asha down?"

Eris glanced up. "What?"

"If the empress wants my cousin," Safire said, crossing her arms tightly against her chest, "and you believe the empress is a monster, then it should follow that you've decided *not* to uphold your bargain with Jemsin."

Eris stepped closer, keeping her voice low. "If I *don't* deliver your precious cousin to Jemsin, he'll hand me over to that monster instead." Eris shook her head. "Don't you understand?

Leandra won't show me any more leniency than she showed Kor. If she doesn't execute me . . ." She touched the spindle tucked into her stolen belt, suddenly thinking of Day. Of the blade driven through his chest. "She'll make me wish she had."

"I see," said Safire stiffly. "So you came here to say that a villain wants my cousin, for reasons unknown to you, but you think those reasons sinister enough to warrant warning me." Safire's eyes were like bright flames as they bore into Eris. "But it's not going to stop you from hunting Asha down like prey and delivering her to that *same villain*." Her voice was rising now. The air seemed to grow hot with her anger. "Did I get that right?"

Eris stared at her. "Did you not hear what I said? If I don't do what Jemsin wants, I'm as good as dead."

Safire's mouth curled in disgust. "Maybe you deserve to be."

Eris stepped back, stung.

"You're a criminal, Eris. A thief. A pirate. A *murderer*." Her voice was hardening. Where before there had been hesitation, there was now resolve. "The world needs to be protected from people like you."

Eris stared at her. "I never murdered anyone."

"So you say." Safire lifted her chin, eyes flashing. "Where's your proof?"

What hurt the most wasn't that Safire didn't believe Eris. It was that she didn't care what happened to her.

Of course she doesn't care, thought Eris, setting Safire's stolen knife down on the balustrade before turning to leave.

No one had cared what happened to Eris. Because she didn't matter.

Twenty-Eight

Safire picked up her knife from where it rested on the cold, hard marble. Normally she could see a clear path and take it with decisive action. But ever since she'd met the thief known as the Death Dancer, the path had disappeared and she was stumbling through the murk.

No more.

Safire knew that to sound the alarm—alerting every soldier in the ballroom to Eris's presence—was to bring a death sentence down on her.

She also knew that to *not* sound the alarm was to let a dangerous criminal go free—one who cared more for her own hide than the lives of others.

When Dax promoted her to commandant, Safire took a vow to bring order where there was chaos. To protect innocents from those who wished to do them harm. She was a soldier, first and foremost, and her soldier instincts told her to detain Eris. To stop her from walking away and call for the Lumina soldiers in the ballroom.

So that's exactly what she did.

Safire turned to find Eris now thrusting aside the curtain, about to step back inside. "The enemy of the Skyweaver is here!" Safire shouted, pointing her knife at the girl in a stolen Lumina uniform. "Arrest her!"

Silence fell over the grand ballroom. Eris froze in place as several soldiers turned toward them, the sound of their blades ringing free of their sheaths.

"If you so much as reach for that spindle in your belt," whispered Safire, stepping close enough to smell the sea on Eris's skin, "I won't hesitate to put this knife in your back."

"You've already put a knife in my back," said Eris, keeping her gaze on the Lumina—swarming now, running for the balcony they stood on. "What's one more?"

She let go of the curtain and stepped backward, closer to Safire and the balustrade, as if to put space between her and the enemies coming for her. But there was no escape. Nowhere for her to go.

Raif arrived well ahead of the others, his sword drawn, his mouth curling in a vicious scowl as he pushed back the curtain. He pointed his blade at Eris, his eyes cold and hard as she stepped slowly forward. "Palms up, *fiend*," he barked. "Move away from the commandant."

Several more Lumina arrived, halting behind Raif.

"Lock the doors!" he shouted as they all drew their swords. "The fugitive is on the balcony!"

But Eris couldn't be confined by things like doors and locks.

She was the Death Dancer.

As the room beyond them exploded in panicked murmurs and shouts, Safire fixed her gaze on the spindle at Eris's hip, keeping her knife trained on her. The moment Eris reached for it, Safire would have no choice but to . . .

"Maybe it's time you took a good, hard look at your allies," said Eris. She looked up, her gaze catching Safire's. "Are they heroes or villains? And what does that make you?"

Safire narrowed her eyes. *Manipulative until the very end.* If Eris thought she could drive a wedge between her and those who'd come to Safire's aid, she was dead wrong.

"At least I have allies. Who do you have, Eris? No one."

She expected the thief to smirk. To say something sarcastic and cutting.

Instead, Eris said so softly, only Safire heard: "To think I fancied myself in love with you."

Those words were like a blow, knocking her backward.

"*What?*" Safire whispered, lowering her knife.

With Raif screaming commands several paces away, with the soldiers at his back pressing onto the balcony, Eris shot Safire one last look. It was the Death Dancer stripped bare of her confidence and cockiness. It was longing and hurt and regret, all woven together.

And then, before Safire could stop her, before she even knew what was happening, Eris leaped onto the balustrade and dropped into the mist below.

Twenty-Nine

Safire stared into the gray fog, her heart in her throat.

"No one could survive that fall," Raif said from beside her, the frown on his brow deepening. "We're five stories up."

Eris can, she thought. Or maybe it was more like *hoped*.

Because suddenly, in Eris's absence, things seemed murkier than ever.

As Raif told one of the other soldiers to go check the gardens below, the empress herself arrived. Her naval uniform had been replaced by a gown of the same shade that was fitted to her torso, then fell in shimmering waves from her waist to the floor, revealing a silver underlayer at the bottom that frothed like waves.

"What happened here?" Her voice was cold and commanding.

Raif looked to Safire, clearly wondering the same thing.

"Your fugitive was here," she said. "Disguised as one of your soldiers."

Every pair of eyes was on her now. Safire burned beneath their gazes.

"She jumped off that balcony just a moment ago," added Raif.

Leandra's eyes narrowed on Safire.

"She was here—on this balcony—with *you*?" Her voice was edged with accusation. "How long were you two alone for?"

Safire swallowed, trying to stave off the heat sweeping through her at those words.

"Perhaps she was under threat," said Dax, moving their attention to himself. Safire didn't know how long he'd been there, but his eyes remained fixed on her.

He was giving her a way out.

"She had a knife to my back," Safire told him. "If I'd called for help, she would have thrust it in."

She didn't really believe that. She only said it because it might curb the skepticism in the empress's eyes.

"So she forced you out here," said Leandra. Her lips thinned and her jaw stiffened. "She came, she singled you out, she *isolated* you. For what purpose?"

Safire forced herself to meet the empress's gaze. "She came to turn me against you." This was pure truth. "She said you're the one who made the deal with Captain Jemsin. That it's you who wants the Namsara."

Leandra tilted her head, her gaze locked on Safire's. "And what, exactly, would I want her *for*?"

Safire shook her head. "She didn't say. But it's nonsensical. He's a vicious pirate. And seeing as you just executed Kor and his crew, you don't seem fond of pirates."

From the corner of her eye, Safire saw Dax turn his head, puzzled by this news.

"And," Safire went on, "why would you make a deal with a pirate when you could just invite Asha to your citadel?"

But you did invite her, thought Safire. *And Asha declined the invitation.*

And in their conversation earlier, Leandra seemed eager to send her soldiers out searching for Asha—but that was because she was in danger of being hunted by Eris.

Neither fact was proof of anything, though. All Safire had was Eris's word. And that, she knew, was useless.

There was movement from behind the empress as Caspian stepped up beside her. "There's no body," he informed her. "She must have survived."

Safire felt the hard knots inside her—knots she hadn't even known were there—loosen at this news.

"That's impossible," said Raif, shaking his head, staring down into the mist below once more.

Before Safire could join Dax, the empress stopped her.

"If she comes to you again, don't detain her. Don't call for help." Leandra's gaze bore into Safire, as if it was just the two of them alone on that balcony. As if the others didn't exist. "The next time she seeks you out, I want you to kill her. Is that understood?"

Safire held that stormy gaze. "Understood."

The word was like ash in her mouth.

Thirty

To cancel the banquet—one held in honor of her esteemed visitors—would be seen as weakness, so Leandra insisted they continue on as if no interruption had taken place. As a result, Safire now sat at a long table, staring down into the glazed eyes of the mackerel on her plate. While those around her had all but eaten the bones of their meals, their plates now cold, Safire hadn't so much as touched hers. She kept thinking of the way her heart stopped as she watched Eris jump from the balcony. Of the last words she'd said, and the look in her eyes.

To think I fancied myself in love with you.

"Are you all right?"

Dax's voice jolted Safire out of her thoughts. She looked up into her cousin's brown eyes.

"I . . ." The thought of the empress's kill order turned her stomach.

He glanced around them. To his right sat Roa, and beside Roa, the empress. To Safire's left sat Raif. Leaning in, Dax lowered his voice as he said, "You did the right thing."

Had she? Then why did she feel so wretched?

Safire kept her voice down as she said, "Is killing her the right thing, too?"

Normally upholding the law made Safire feel good and right and *worthy*. This time, it made her one of them: the Lumina who beat women in the street; the empress who executed people without a trial.

Safire quickly glanced around the table. Raif was deep in conversation with Caspian. Roa had the empress talking about the blight.

"What if she's right?" Safire thought of Eris's question on the balcony. "What if I'm not one of the good soldiers?" She swallowed, suddenly seeing herself through different eyes. *What if I'm one of the bad ones?*

"Safire . . ."

"Leandra executed those pirates you brought her without a trial, Dax."

He nodded. "I know."

She frowned up at him. "You know?"

"It's not a decision you or I would have made." He looked down to his plate, the line of his jaw hardening a little. "But we can't go around imposing our ways of doing things on everyone else. The laws of the Star Isles are the laws of the Star Isles. And while we're guests here, we need to abide by them. It's not our place to interfere."

Safire stared at her king. "And if those laws are unjust?"

He glanced at her. "What if they *are* just? You and I have

never had to deal with pirates, Saf. Leandra has to. There may be good reason for not giving them trials."

Safire felt like her body was turning to stone. "Are you listening to yourself?" she whispered.

Dax had never cared if Safire challenged him. In fact, he welcomed it. He always wanted her opinion—most especially when it was contrary to his—because he respected and admired Safire. Because in arguing with her, in talking through the issue, Dax came out the other side better prepared to make whatever decision needed making.

Now, though, instead of arguing back like he usually did, his eyes darkened and he looked away from her.

"What would you have me do?" He kept his voice so low, it was almost a whisper. "Challenge her? Condemn her laws? Tell her you won't catch the criminal you promised to catch for her?"

Safire opened her mouth to respond, only to find she didn't have an answer.

"We need her, Safire. The *scrublands* need her. Without those seeds she's promised us, hundreds of thousands will die. Tell me those lives matter to you."

Safire's throat burned. Of course they mattered to her. How could he ask her that?

Because if they mattered, she realized, *I would put them first. Above Eris.*

People were starving to death. Roa's *family* was starving to death. And here Safire was, compromising the very alliance that would save their lives.

She suddenly wanted to rise from the table and leave. Not just the grand ballroom. Not just the citadel. But Axis itself. This city, these islands, they were was twisting her into someone she wasn't.

Sensing her agitation, Dax said, "What is really going on here?"

Safire couldn't look at him. She couldn't look at any of them. So she stared down at the dead fish on her plate and said, "I killed a man I hated once. That decision haunts me. I won't kill a girl I—" She stopped herself, afraid to say the words aloud.

Dax turned to her a little more, casually resting his elbow on the top of his chair as he reached for his goblet—but he didn't drink. He was trying very hard not to draw attention to their conversation. But his gaze was sword sharp.

"Saf," he said gently. "This is the same thief who ran you ragged back in Firgaard. All you wanted was to lock her up."

Safire studied the fish's blackened scales and limp fins as she thought, *Things have changed since then.*

"She tortured you on Jemsin's ship."

"Actually," Safire said, knowing she was grasping, "she had other people do the torturing."

She thought of Eris watching as Jemsin's men dunked her head again and again into the water. Trying to break her. To force information out of her.

Dax threw her a strange look. *"Safire."*

She was losing him. She could hear it in his voice. And the awful thing was, he was right. Eris wasn't some innocent; she was a criminal.

But she was also the one who held back Safire's hair while she was seasick. The one who stopped that sea monster from eating her alive. Eris had saved her from Caspian and the other Lumina soldiers in that alley.

They would have beaten that woman to death, she thought. But that didn't prove anything. Every barrel had a few bad apples. And not so long ago, a few of Safire's own soldats had plotted against Roa—their queen. There were always going to be a few corrupt soldiers in a sea full of loyal ones.

"You yourself believe she's planning to hand Asha over to a deadly pirate," Dax reminded her.

Safire sagged under the weight of those words.

All these things were true.

And yet.

"She saved my life," Safire whispered. "More than once."

Dax roughly rubbed his stubbled cheeks. "And if she's manipulating you?"

Safire looked away, across the room, to the balcony. The curtains were thrown back and the mist from earlier had receded, leaving a clear sky full of stars.

"I've heard of things like this before," said Dax.

Safire glanced back. "What things?"

"A kind of . . . illness," he said, almost gently. "An illness of the mind."

Safire frowned. What was he talking about?

"Sometimes, when a person is kidnapped and abused, the mind becomes warped—to protect itself. The person becomes convinced that she and her kidnapper are . . . in love. That her kidnapper isn't a villain, but rather, a kind of hero."

The words chilled Safire. She searched Dax's face. "You're accusing me of such a thing?"

He said nothing. Only watched her.

"You are," she whispered, feeling the table full of guests blur around them.

But then, hadn't she let Eris kiss her? The very girl who kidnapped her, then ordered Jemsin's men to torture her?

More important: Hadn't she *liked* kissing Eris?

If she were honest with herself, as she stood on that balcony with Eris wearing that stolen soldier's uniform, she'd wanted to kiss her again.

Maybe Dax was right. Maybe there was something wrong with her.

Safire upheld the law; Eris flouted it. Safire hated pirates; Eris worked for them. Safire loved her cousin; Eris was currently hunting her cousin down.

She thought of that moment in the rowboat, when Eris learned Safire couldn't swim.

I won't let anything happen to you.

And that moment in the alley, surrounded by men who wanted to hurt her. It was Eris who'd come for her.

Don't let go.

But how much did it matter?

And who was Eris, really?

Safire didn't know. No one knew.

But Dax was her cousin. And not just that, her friend and her king. As children, he'd taken the brunt of Jarek's abuse when he could. Not so long ago, he'd fought a war at her side, then made her his commandant.

Safire couldn't—wouldn't—go against him. They were supposed to be on the same side. They'd always been on the same side.

"Where are you going?" Dax asked as she rose from the table.

"I need some air."

Thirty-One

Eris walked the lamplit streets of Axis feeling like she'd swallowed a prickle fish.

After jumping from that balustrade, she'd landed on the balcony one story below. Hurt by Safire's betrayal, she wanted nothing more than to step across. But as she'd slashed the spindle over the balcony tiles, the silver line shimmering before her, the voices above made her pause.

Hidden by the fog, Eris listened.

The next time she seeks you out, I want you to kill her. Is that understood?

The memory of Leandra's icy voice made Eris shiver now. But it was nothing like the gaping wound that opened in the wake of Safire's answer.

Understood.

Eris's hand had shaken as she finished drawing the silver line. Her vision blurred with hot tears. She should have been focused on the labyrinth as she stepped into the mists. But the hurt and loneliness and utter *lostness* overwhelmed her, and all she could think about was Safire's answer to Leandra's question. All she could see was the horrified look in those blue eyes as Eris stupidly blurted out her true feelings.

Which was how she'd stumbled out into the grid of Axis's streets instead of Across. And now that she was here, free from the empress and her soldiers and most of all, Safire, Eris had changed her mind. She didn't want to go back to that haunted lonely labyrinth, with nothing but a ghost to keep her company.

Safire was right. Eris had no one.

Her footsteps echoed on the cobblestoned streets now, which were empty and quiet as midnight crept closer. After years of running from these islands, after swearing she'd never set foot here again, Eris stood in the heart of the Star Isles. Surrounded by her bitterest enemies.

One of them bitterest of all.

Past the fountains and the lit lanterns and the storefronts, through the boughs of the scattered trees, Eris's eyes were drawn upward to the highest structure in Axis—even higher than its twin, the empress's citadel.

It tapered like a needle as it pierced the sky, black like onyx. So black it stood out against the night, which was bright with starlight.

The Skyweaver's throne.

Like a magnet, it both attracted and repelled Eris. Reminding her of the night she'd been running from for half her life. How the god of souls did nothing as her servants were burned in their beds. As Day sent a prayer skyward. As Eris watched them take everyone she'd ever loved away from her.

She'd never hated anyone as much as she hated the god of souls.

That coal-red rage ignited within her, just like the night she'd watched the *Sea Mistress* burn. Her teeth clenched with it. She wanted to walk the tower's thousand steps, smashing every window on the way. Wanted to bang on the door at the top and break it down. Wanted to spit at the Skyweaver's feet and ask her how she could stand by and do *nothing* as the scrin burned. As Day died with her name on his lips.

Day.

The memories of him flooded her. Eris fell to her knees. Tears pricked her eyes as she thought of him carrying her to bed when she fell asleep at the looms. She thought of him holding her hand up near the cliff edge—ensuring she couldn't run off while he taught her which plants were best for dyeing. Thought of him telling her stories of the god he loved best.

The tower blurred before her, fading into the dark sky.

When the night descends—Day's prayer filled her mind—*I look to those who've gone before me, lighting my path through the dark.*

Eris looked beyond the tower to the thousands of stars shining above it. The thousands of souls who'd been put there by Skyweaver's hand.

She hated that prayer, because it was for *her.*

But she loved it, too, because it was Day's favorite.

I remember, she thought, reciting the words near the end, *you are with me.*

As the stars glittered above her, with Day's memory in her heart, the rage in her fled.

And though Eris was still alone, she no longer felt so lonely.

Thirty-Two

Safire walked the blue halls of the citadel, longing for home and the comforts of routine. Back in Firgaard, there was nothing a good sparring session or a long hard run couldn't fix.

She missed her soldats. Missed the hot sun on her face. Missed the way things were before a certain thief walked into the king's treasury and threw her life into chaos.

As Safire stepped out onto one of the uncovered walkways, a sheet of cool fog enveloped her. It made her uneasy, that fog. She didn't like not being able to see what was several paces in front of her. Anything could be hiding in the gray.

As if summoned by her thought, Safire felt a presence. Lurking. Watching.

Her footsteps slowed as she listened.

She could see the dim glow of torchlight in the distance. She was almost at the end of the walkway. But the closer she came to the archway leading into the next citadel hall, the presence got stronger.

Finally, Safire stopped. Ready to reach for the knife—tucked back in the knot of her hair—she called out: "Who's there?"

At first, only silence answered her. But then, through the gray, she heard a familiar sound: rapid clicking. Safire looked up to the spiral rooftop where it came from.

Two slitted eyes stared down at her through the mist.

"Sorrow?" she whispered.

The eyes disappeared. Safire heard the soft scraping of scales against stone as the dragon slithered down from the roof. A heartbeat later, a gleaming white head with two horns—one of them broken—came out of the fog.

Safire glanced from Sorrow's dark eyes back over her shoulder, checking for guards. But the fog was too thick to see. "What are you doing here?" she whispered.

Sorrow clicked back at her, urgent this time. And then he did something he'd never done before: he pressed his snout into Safire's palm, nudging it firmly. Almost as if he wanted something from her.

Safire remembered the last words she spoke to the white dragon—last night in the abandoned village, searching for Asha.

"Did you find her?"

In answer, Sorrow crouched down, lowering himself against the stone walkway, all the while keeping his eyes on Safire. As if to say, *Get on.*

Carefully, Safire climbed atop him, knowing that at any moment she might make the wrong movement, trigger the poor creature, and be dumped. Or trampled. Or worse.

Sorrow did none of these things. He tensed a few times,

looking back over his shoulder as Safire adjusted the blue dress—which needed to be hiked to her knees if she were to ride properly—but he didn't panic. At least, not until voices came out of the mist behind them.

"Do you see that?"

Safire looked back just in time to see two shapes materialize out of the fog.

"See what?"

"Something's out there. . . ."

Sorrow's tail began to lash, his muscles bunching in fear. Safire pressed her palm to the creature's scales, willing him to keep calm.

"It's a . . ."

Sorrow swung around to face them. To keep from falling, Safire threw her arms around the creature's neck, locking her hands.

"Dragon!"

The Lumina soldiers drew their swords in unison, their eyes lifted from the dragon to its rider just as Safire clicked the command for *flight*.

Sorrow spread his wings, hissing as he did.

The two men drew back in fear. Safire could see the whites of their eyes and the tightening of their hands on their hilts.

"Sorrow, now!" Safire whispered, clicking the command again, fearing the dragon didn't know it. Fearing these men would charge and kill him.

Before they could, Sorrow turned and leaped from the walkway. The fog instantly covered them as his wings caught a wind current. Safire clung on, hearing the shouts of alarm increase behind them. But the fog kept them concealed as Sorrow glided through it, rising ever upward.

The voices behind them faded into the night.

Good boy, thought Safire, pressing her cheek to the dragon's neck and relaxing into him.

As the city of Axis fell away beneath them, Safire felt for the bond she knew was supposed to form in first flight. Asha described it as a lock, clicking into place. But no matter how hard Safire concentrated as they soared through the air, she felt no clicking lock. No forming link.

Maybe it was true that Sorrow would never link with a rider.

Maybe that's okay, she thought.

Eventually the fog cleared and beneath the silver light of a waxing moon, the sea gleamed below them, its waves crashing softly on the shores of a small cove nestled beneath a massive headland. From up here, she could see a smattering of tiny houses out on the point, their windows shining with lamplight.

At the crest of the headland, Safire could see a silhouette. No, *several* silhouettes. Three people and a dragon. One of them held a glowing lantern in their fist.

Sorrow was heading straight for them.

They circled once. Kozu looked up first. Safire could see his one yellow eye burning in the night. Sorrow started to descend too quickly, then remembered he was carrying the weight of a rider. They were headed straight into the tuckamore forest.

Safire felt him panic. Panicked, too, she forced herself to be calm and ran her hands smoothly over the creature's scales, murmuring encouragement even as the night screamed in her ears and the trees rose up too fast.

At the last moment, Sorrow banked, catching a current, then slowed his descent. The tuckamores faded. Mossy rock appeared beneath them. And finally, Sorrow landed—a little clumsily—in the moss.

"Perfect boy," Safire murmured into his neck, then patted him gently as she dismounted.

Sorrow seemed to brighten, watching her.

"Safire!" came Asha's voice at her back. Safire turned to find her cousin standing in the knee-high grass. "How . . . ?"

The orange glow of the lantern flame illuminated the Namsara's black eyes and scarred face. At her side stood Torwin and a bearded, bowlegged man. His windswept dark hair was peppered with gray. Behind them, Kozu tilted his curious head at Sorrow.

At the sight of them, Safire felt a weight lift from her. She ran, the grass hushing against her legs, and threw her arms around Asha, squeezing her tight, breathing in her smoky scent.

"Are you all right?" Asha murmured, squeezing her back.

Safire swallowed. "I missed you."

"Are you *linked*?" Torwin interrupted. When Safire pulled away, she found him studying Sorrow. His hair was mussed and his cheeks were pink from the cold.

As they watched the white dragon, who was already shying away, moving to more barren ground, Safire said, "I would feel it, wouldn't I? If we were?"

Asha nodded.

"That's all right," Torwin said, his smile sliding away.

"Safire, this is Dagan." Asha gestured to the man with them. He tipped his head to her. "He was just in the middle of showing us something. Come, I want you to see. . . ." Asha reached for her arm, already turning.

Safire braced herself. "Asha, no, we need to leave. You're in grave danger."

All of them turned to look at her.

"What?" said Torwin.

Asha frowned. "What danger?"

Safire quickly told them everything. Starting with being kidnapped by the Death Dancer—the very thief she tried to catch in Firgaard—to losing that same thief in Axis. She made it clear that Asha was next on the Death Dancer's list of things to steal.

Asha frowned. "Even if she could *steal* me, she doesn't know where I am. And Kozu would be here in a heartbeat if I called him. And I have *this*." She tapped the hilt of the Skyweaver's knife where it hung from her belt. More like a dagger than a knife, the blade was hidden in a silver sheath embossed with strange symbols.

But none of those things would stop Eris. Eris and her poisonous scarp thistles that could make a person sleep with a single prick. Eris, who could disappear and reappear somewhere else, taking someone with her.

Asha could be drugged and dragged halfway across the world before she even realized the Death Dancer was in the room with her.

Safire told her as much.

"You need to come with me."

Asha's dark eyes narrowed and her mouth turned down. "And where would I go?"

Safire was about to say *the citadel* because that's where Eris wouldn't set foot. Except Eris had disproved that theory tonight when she walked straight into the middle of the empress's ballroom.

"If she's so formidable, why would I be any safer anywhere else?"

Safire opened her mouth to respond, only to realize Asha had a point. Was there anywhere safe from a girl who moved like wind and walked through walls?

"You've warned me, and I'll be vigilant. Now come. I want to show you something."

Safire went to protest, but Asha grabbed her arm and pulled her.

"Dagan has been telling us about a girl who used to live in this cove, centuries ago." As she talked, her eager pace quickened and Torwin and Dagan fell behind. "She's become a kind of myth in these islands, and there seem to be different versions of the story. All of them begin with her falling in love with a god. But some end with the god killing her, while others end with him giving her immortality. In all the stories, though, she disappears and her body is never found."

Safire slowed. This sounded familiar. "Skye," she murmured.

Asha stared at her. "Yes. How did you know?"

Raif had told her something similar when they arrived in Axis yesterday.

But it was also the name carved into Eris's spindle.

At the thought of Eris, Safire's body buzzed with anxiety. She needed to make Asha realize just how dangerous the Death Dancer was, along with the pirate captain who commanded her. If Asha didn't come with Safire, then the only way to ensure her protection was to hunt Eris down and . . .

Safire remembered the look in Leandra's eyes as she gave her order.

I want you to kill her.

A chill swept through her.

"Asha." Safire halted again. "What if we returned home to Firgaard? I could keep you under armed guard at all hours. If the Death Dancer—"

"There's a story here," said Asha, not really listening. "I intend to find it." Tired of being held back, she let go of Safire's arm and drew the Skyweaver's knife from its sheath, revealing the silver-white blade. It glowed faintly—like starlight—and Safire could feel a faint hum emanating from it.

"It's been doing that ever since we set foot on these islands." Asha held it up, her face shining in its eerie light. Safire could see the fierce determination in her jaw. It was the same look she used to get when she was still the king's Iskari, and a dragon was reported near the city. "I can't be sure, but I have the strangest feeling Skye's story and this knife are connected."

She continued on.

With no other choice, Safire followed her down the dirt path through the tuckamore forest, with Torwin and Dagan trailing quietly behind them. As they walked, Safire debated telling Asha more—about the empress's kill order and her conversation with Dax and also, maybe, her feelings for Eris. Before she could, they stumbled out of the tuckamore forest and into a grassy meadow.

Around her, nine gray stones the size of big men rose up in a wide circle around her.

"Aren't they incredible?" said Asha, her eyes shining as she walked the circumference of the circle.

Safire stared at the shapes. *They look like . . . rocks.*

"They're from older times," said Dagan, who drew up beside her. Safire glanced up into his face to find it sun darkened and weathered from years of grappling with the wind and sea. "When people still worshipped the Shadow God."

Safire frowned at that. "I didn't know people worshipped him."

"Neither did we," said Torwin, watching Asha set down the lantern and walk out past the circle, toward the edge of the head. Beyond Asha, the moon rose over the sea, its white reflection rippling on the black water below.

Lured like a dragon to a story, Torwin walked out to meet her.

As he did, Safire breathed in the smell of this place: salt and juniper and moss. Just for a moment, despite her chattering fears and conflicted feelings, Safire felt a presence. Not like Sorrow waiting in the mist, or Eris following her through the halls. This was something else. Something far older and deeper. It was as if the spirit of these islands had come to brush up against her.

Safire lifted her palm to one of the giant stones.

From beside her, Dagan said very quietly, "I thought I recognized that dress."

It wasn't the words he said so much as the way he said them

that made Safire turn. The fisherman stared at the left wrist of her raised hand, to the silver star embroidered there. At the sight of it, his dark brown eyes shone with sorrow.

"That's the mark of the scrin."

Safire lifted the embroidered sleeve closer, squinting through the lantern light.

"I used to trade with them for fish," he whispered, his eyes seeing something else. "They'd give me garments in exchange." He blinked, then peered down to Safire's wrist once more, staring at the mark. "They sold for a near fortune in Axis's market. People would come from all over to buy them, just because of that star."

He looked up, suddenly. "Where did you get it?"

"It . . . was a gift," she said.

He nodded once, and she could see in his eyes that he was finished talking about this, that there was pain here and he was ready to change the subject.

Safire couldn't let him do that. Here before her stood someone who might know things: about the scrin, about the night it burned. She couldn't let this chance to find out the truth escape her.

"Actually," she said, knowing the risk and taking it anyway, "it was a gift from the empress's fugitive. A girl named Eris."

His face jerked back to hers. "What did you say?"

"Eris." Safire touched the silver star. "She left it in my room tonight."

He swallowed and when she looked up, his eyes were staring at her the way a hungry man stared into a bowl of rice.

"Is that true?" he whispered, looking into the darkness around him, as if fearing he might be overheard. "Is she alive?"

Safire felt her pulse speed up. She nodded, wanting to keep him talking, needing to know what he knew. "Did you know her?"

He reached for the stone next to him, then missed it, losing his balance and stumbling. Safire caught him before he fell.

"I need to sit."

She found him a low stone and helped him down onto it, then sank into the grass next to him. The lantern burned between them, lighting up their faces.

"No one beyond the scrin knew of her existence—not even I," he murmured, looking out to sea. "But there was an accident one day. I'd made a delivery and was preparing my boat to leave, when this little girl with a nest of white hair came tearing down to the scrin's wharf, demanding my help. She and another weaver had been gathering scarp thistles for dyeing when her friend fell from one of the cliffs. Her friend was stuck on an outcropping, his leg broken. Grabbing a coil of rope, I went with her, and together we pulled him up. I helped her get him safely back to the scrin, and the moment we stepped through the door, the Weaving Master took me aside. He begged me not to speak of what I'd seen. To never tell a soul about Eris."

Safire rested her chin on her knees, frowning hard. "Why?"

Dagan shook his head. "They were giving her sanctuary. Someone wanted to harm her, he said, and if her existence was made known beyond the scrin, it would put her in grave danger."

"But who would want to harm a child?"

"I don't know." Dagan shook his head. "We quickly became friends, Eris and I. She'd help me unload the fish, talking all the while. She never stopped talking, that child. It's how I found out that whenever there were visitors, she was confined to her room—an old cellar behind the kitchens—or sent up into the cliffs to collect plants for dyeing.

"I was happy to keep her secret. I swore an oath to never speak of her beyond the scrin. It's an oath I've kept all these years." He looked to the star on the wrist of Safire's dress. "Until now."

Safire felt hungry for more. She wanted to learn everything she could about Eris from someone who had truly cared about her. But Dagan had fallen silent again, staring into his weathered hands.

"Do you think she burned it?"

His face darkened like a storm. "What?" he hissed.

Safire drew back. "The scrin, I mean. They say she burned it down."

"A child who loved nothing more than to weave and run wild and help the groundskeeper in the dye room? Do I think she burned down a temple with the only family she'd ever known inside?" He scowled as he said it, balling his hands into fists. "The Lumina came and questioned all of us. Everyone who'd ever supplied the scrin with goods. They were looking for the one who started the fire—a dangerous criminal who escaped in the night. An enemy of the Skyweaver, they called her." He glanced at Safire. "That's the highest form of treason in the Star Isles."

Safire leaned over the lantern, needing more. "If it wasn't Eris, then who did it?"

He shook his head and kept his voice low. "All I know is if that girl is the Skyweaver's enemy, so am I. Skyweaver is supposed to be a god of hope, lighting our way through the dark. But I have no use for a god who does nothing while her servants are slaughtered."

Dagan turned his face up to the dark sky, as if to scowl at the stars—which were hidden now behind the clouds that had gathered.

"Some say the Shadow God is coming," he whispered. "I say: let him come."

Safire felt a drop of rain on her face, then lifted a hand to find several more. Soon the sound of hundreds of thousands of raindrops echoed all around them, clinking on the rocks.

"Who says the Shadow God is coming?" asked Asha.

They both started at the sound of her voice. Asha stepped into the light of the lantern, her black hair wet with rain, her fingers laced with Torwin's. Safire wondered how long they'd been there.

"The islands," said Dagan. "The wind and the sea and rock all whisper his name. Just listen and you'll hear it."

As the others fell silent, listening, Safire's thoughts were loud in her mind.

Just who *was* Eris? More important, if Eris was telling the truth, was there a way to prove her innocence?

Safire rose to her feet and stepped toward Asha.

"If I leave you here," she said, not liking the words at all, only saying them because she knew she would not be convincing her cousin tonight, "will you promise to watch your back?"

Asha smiled. "I always watch my back." Eight years of hunting dragons would do that to a girl. "Dagan lives in the yellow house on the point. You can find us there."

"Don't do anything reckless," Safire said, reaching for the Namsara and pulling her into a hug.

"When have I ever?" Asha whispered, holding her tight.

"Every day of your life," Safire whispered back.

Mounting Sorrow, Safire said good-bye, then flew through the rain to the scrin, taking Asha's lantern with her.

She arrived just before dawn. The rain had stopped and the twilight soaked everything in blue. As Safire stepped inside, Sorrow waited at the charred entrance, watching the cavernous doorway swallow her rider.

Safire's footsteps echoed off the walls of the empty ruin as she thought of what Dagan told her.

Whenever there were visitors, she was confined to her room—an old cellar behind the kitchens. . . .

Safire searched the main floor of the scrin, but what the flames hadn't eaten, years of rot and decay had destroyed, making it hard to decipher what each room was. She found a stairway leading down into the dark, though, and took it.

The floor below was damp, and it was clear the fire hadn't burned quite so savagely here. Beneath the blackened soot, she could still see the star patterns in the tiles beneath her feet.

She opened the first door she came to and found the room inside almost completely preserved. There was a rusted wood stove to her right and a rotting wooden table before it. Copper pots and pans hung from the ceiling, and on the far side, in the corner, stood a door with peeling green paint.

Safire crossed the room and opened the door.

The inside was cool and small and smelled like old vegetables. Lifting the lantern Asha leant her, Safire saw that in the corner lay a musty pallet. It was too small for an adult but just large enough for a child. The small wooden frame of a loom leaned against the wall and on the floor beside it lay several baskets, each of them piled with dusty skeins of yarn.

Safire stepped into the room. A jar full of dried scarp thistles sat beside the pallet, and on the mattress lay a ragged cloth doll, with beads for eyes and thick yarn for hair.

Safire crouched down and picked up the doll.

"This was your room," she whispered, pulling the doll to her chest.

From behind her, a soft voice answered, "Aye, princess."

Thirty-Three

The sight of Safire standing in her childhood bedroom, clutching her doll to her chest, made Eris go silent and still.

"I'm so sorry," Safire burst out.

Eris heard the words, but she no longer saw the girl before her, only the room she'd left behind. It was exactly as she'd left it, untouched by the fire. Her bed. Her loom. The wool she'd dyed and spun herself.

The smell of it made her think of happier times. Of when she had a place to call home and people to call family.

"I should have believed you." The words trembled, as if Safire was about to cry.

Safire came back into sharp focus. She was drenched from the storm. Her long black lashes clustered like stars and the blue dress clung to her frame.

"I never should have called the guards." Her forehead crinkled in a severe frown. "And those things I said . . ."

"Like telling the empress you'd kill me on sight?"

Safire looked sharply away, her shoulders sagging with shame. She looked wretched and small and not at all like the proud, brave girl Eris so admired.

Eris couldn't help but go to her.

"Hey," she said softly, watching a warm tear spill down Safire's cheek, wanting to brush it away but not quite daring to. Why was she crying over this? Over *Eris*? "I wouldn't have believed me either."

She reached for the doll in Safire's hand—a doll Day had brought back from the market one summer. A doll she'd simply called *Doll*, because she thought it was clever. She pressed her face into the doll's dress, breathing in. But it smelled only of dust and damp, and nothing of her life before this one. So she set it back down where Safire found it.

"I want to show you something," she said, looking up into bright blue eyes. "Will you come?"

Safire nodded, swiping at her tears.

Taking her hand, Eris pulled her from the room.

She led Safire back through the scrin, then down a pine path through the woods, away from the cliffs. As she did, she ran her thumb along Safire's skin, gentle and slow, wondering if it had the same heart-skittering effect as it did on her.

She didn't look to find out. Because the sky was lightening now, and dawn would be here soon. She wanted to get there before sunrise.

Finally, the trees broke and the path ended. All that lay before them was a creamy ribbon of sand encircling a small, shallow bay. Letting go of Safire's hand, Eris grinned as she said, "So you see, Raif isn't the only one with a secret beach."

Bending over, she tugged off her boots. After rolling her trousers up to her knees, she headed in. The sea rushed up her ankles, smelling of brine, welcoming her back. Eris closed her eyes and breathed it in.

A heartbeat later, she heard splashing behind her and looked to find the hem of the blue dress knotted up over Safire's hips.

Side by side, they watched the red sun rise.

"Well?" Eris glanced over, wanting to know if she'd pleased her, and found Safire staring back in a way that made her breath catch. "*Are* you the kind of girl who likes sunrises?"

A blush of color rose in Safire's cheeks, and she ducked her eyes.

"Eris?" she asked, dodging the question. "Did you mean what you said on the empress's balcony?"

Eris remembered the shock in Safire's eyes when she'd carelessly made her confession. *To think I fancied myself in love with you.* She should deny it. Or better yet: make a joke of it. Save herself the humiliation.

"I . . ." It was Eris's turn to look away. "The first time I ever saw you, I wanted to despise you." She kept her eyes on the sea frothing around them. "A commander who'd been given her position simply because her cousin was king? A princess who lived a privileged, comfortable life without ever knowing a day of hardship? You represented everything I hated . . . or so I thought." Eris bit her lip. Was she really admitting this out loud? "I saw what I wanted to see. Mostly because the first time we met, you injured my pride."

Safire glanced up. "What?" Her brow knit in confusion. "How?"

"I had just stolen a tapestry from your office. You ran straight into me, looked me over, and dismissed me in a single glance."

Safire jaw dropped in surprise. "I was responding to a security breach," she said, a little defensively. "And you were dressed as a soldat. I make a point of *not* noticing my soldats—not like that. It's unprofessional."

"Ah." Eris smiled a little. "I see. Well, it irked me. More than irked me. Afterward, I made it my mission to ensure you not only noticed me, but couldn't stop thinking about me." More softly, she said, "I wanted to drive you as mad as you were driving me."

Safire looked away then, the color rushing back into her cheeks. "Well, you certainly succeeded."

"Did I?" asked Eris, studying her. Safire's gaze lifted, catching hers. "I meant what I said on the balcony," Eris whispered, stepping in close. "You are brave and noble and good." She lifted hesitant fingers to gently trace Safire's jaw, then her throat. "How could I not fall in love with you?"

Safire sucked in a breath, blue eyes sparkling, letting Eris touch her. "I thought you didn't go in for spoiled princess types."

Eris reached for the knife keeping Safire's hair up. "I only said that to save your ass." She tugged it out, spilling Safire's hair down her neck, then buried her hands in it. "You are exactly my type." She pressed her lips to the arch of Safire's throat, feeling her pulse pound like tempest rain. "Soft and strong and oh so pretty," she murmured. "When I'm with you, I want to be *better*. I want to be worthy of you."

This seemed to get through to Safire, whose hands slid up under Eris's shirt and over her skin, skidding up her back. Eris's hands trembled as they cupped Safire's neck. Wanting this—wanting *her*—more than she'd ever wanted anything.

When she captured Safire's mouth with her own, Safire kissed her hungrily back.

The tide came in, rushing against their legs. Safire and Eris ignored it. The waves came in faster and harder, until one of them nearly knocked them both over, dousing them in cold water.

Safire sucked in a breath at the shock of it. Eris laughed. "Come on," she said, tugging Safire's arm.

Was this what happiness felt like?

They stumbled back to the beach, where Eris dropped into the sand, bringing Safire down with her, both of them yearning to finish what they started as the sun rose over the sea.

Thirty-Four

Safire woke nestled beneath the blankets of a warm bed, with the memory of Eris on her skin. Candles burned in sconces around her, illuminating this room. If she could call it a room. The walls were made of brightly colored glass and the only thing within was a bed and a chest.

Where am I?

It felt like neither night nor day here, but something in between.

Am I dreaming? she wondered.

Somewhere in the distance, a noise made her turn her head and listen: *clack, clack, clack.*

It drew her from the bed.

Safire followed the soft and steady sound through this strange maze of stained-glass walls, the glow of the candle illuminating her path, which twisted and turned as she followed the clacking sound. Twice she was greeted by dead ends. A third time she took a turn only to end up back where she started.

Finally, she found the source of the noise and stepped into a room lit by dozens of candles.

Eris sat cross-legged on a white carpet. Before her was a loom.

Safire knew she should announce herself instead of standing here spying, but she found herself immobilized by the haunting elegance of the girl at the loom. Eris's sleeves were rolled to the elbows. Her hands were steady and sure as they moved the shuttle back and forth, back and forth, in a gentle rhythm that mesmerized Safire. The glow from the candles clustered all around Eris, catching in her pale hair, making it gleam.

Safire thought of the beach. Of her fingers tangled in that hair. Of those hands and how they knew exactly what to do.

Who are you? The question had been living inside her ever since the mysterious Death Dancer turned up in Firgaard.

Eris's voice broke through her thoughts. "Are you going to stand there all day?"

Safire froze, caught.

Eris didn't turn around, just kept weaving. So Safire came to the carpet and sat down beside her.

"Where are we?" she said, glancing around them.

"Across" was all Eris said.

From here Safire could see the color of the threads: sunrise red and creamy beige and sea blue. It was nearly finished, making Safire wonder how long she'd been at this.

"What are you making?" Safire asked.

"You'll see."

When Safire looked closer, she saw things were woven

among the threads: beach grass, seaweed, and a small white stone with a hole worn through it, looped with yarn and tied in.

"Who taught you how to do this?" Safire asked, studying the weaving.

"The weavers at the scrin," Eris said softly. "It was their job to preserve things. Stories, mainly. They kept the stories of Skyweaver alive by weaving them into tapestries."

"Tapestries that burned with the scrin," murmured Safire.

Eris nodded. "They say Skyweaver walks among us, here on the islands."

Safire listened, mesmerized by the movement of her hands.

"The black tower that looms over Axis? It's her tower. They say she spends all night up there, spinning souls into stars and weaving them into the sky."

Safire could hear the bitterness in Eris's tone as she said this. It reminded her of Dagan's words: *I have no use for a god who does nothing while her servants are slaughtered.*

They both fell silent. Eris weaving; Safire watching.

"Why would she burn it?" Safire asked suddenly. "What threat could a temple full of craftsmen possibly pose to an empress?"

The loom fell silent as Eris's hands fell still. "It's a question I ask myself every day."

Safire thought of what Dagan said—how he wasn't allowed to speak of the child who'd been given sanctuary by the scrin. None of the weavers were. As if she was some kind of dangerous secret.

Safire looked from Eris's hands to her face. The line of her jaw was hard, her teeth clenched, and her eyes were strangely blank.

What if, thought Safire, *you're the threat?*

But what damage could Eris possibly do to the empress?

It didn't make any sense.

One thing was certain in Safire's mind: she needed to return to the citadel and tell Dax everything. He needed to know who exactly he was allying himself with. But then what? Dax and Roa needed the seeds the empress had offered them.

Maybe the only thing to do was wait. Soon their visit would be over and the seeds would be loaded aboard their ship. Once that happened, Dax and Roa and Safire could go collect Asha and Torwin, and together they could all return home, putting the empress and her islands behind them.

Before she rose to her feet, Safire said, "I think you should come with us."

Whatever dark thoughts Eris was lost in, Safire's voice shattered them. She glanced up. "What?"

"To Firgaard, I mean. I can protect you there." Speaking the words aloud strengthened the conviction inside Safire, until it was hard and strong as steel. "No one will touch you. Not the empress. Not Jemsin. Not anyone."

Eris set down the shuttle, keeping her gaze away from Safire.

"Jemsin's summoner will come," she whispered, staring at the loose threads before her. "It always does."

Safire didn't know who Jemsin's summoner was, but it didn't matter. "Then I'll be ready for it."

"Even if you could . . ." Eris shook her head and looked up, her gaze cutting into Safire. "You'll harbor the criminal who stole a jewel from your king's treasury? A criminal who's done far worse things than that?" Eris's pale brows pinched together as she tilted her head. "You're the commander of the king's army, Safire. How do you think that will go?"

Safire, who'd forgotten all about the jewel Eris stole, suddenly realized exactly how that would go. If she brought the Death Dancer to Firgaard, she'd have to imprison her for her crimes.

"I'll tell Dax everything," Safire continued on, determined. "That the empress burned the scrin. That Jemsin forces you to steal for him."

"He doesn't always force me," Eris looked back to the loom. "But none of that matters. Your king hates me." Eris said the next part so softly, it was as if she didn't want to hear herself speak the words. "I'm the girl who plans to hunt down his Namsara and exchange her for my freedom, remember?"

Safire grew suddenly cold. After everything that had happened between them, after this morning on the beach . . .

Things had changed.

Hadn't they?

"Surely you're not still planning to uphold your bargain with Jemsin." Safire shook her head. "I don't believe you'd put an innocent person in the hands of a monster."

"Believe what you want." Eris moved to stand up.

Safire grabbed her wrist, keeping her down. Her heart beat hard and fast as she held that piercing gaze, feeling like she was about to lose something she'd only just found. "You won't endanger the life of someone I love. That's not who you are."

Eris scowled. Twisting free, she staggered to her feet. "And what about my life? You'll do anything to keep your cousin safe. Of course you will. I understand it, and I admire you for it. Even though I know that when it comes down to it—and it will come down to it, Safire—you'll choose her over me. Her life over mine."

"What are you talking about?" Safire rose to her feet. "I just told you I'll protect you. From the empress. From Jemsin. From anyone who ever tries to harm you. I swear it."

Eris shook her head, almost mournfully. "This was a mistake," she said, backing away now, her eyes strangely hollow in the candlelight. "You have no idea what it's like. How could you?"

Turning, she stepped into the stained-glass maze, as if desperate to escape.

"You live in a different world than I do."

Thirty-Five

Eris's thoughts were wild and out of control as she moved swiftly through the labyrinth. She could feel the cold shadow of the ghost beyond the twisting stained glass walls, hiding just out of sight. It suddenly felt too small and cramped here. Like a prison.

Eris needed air and sea and open sky.

Fool. *Fool.*

She'd made a mistake, bringing Safire here. Taking her to that beach. She never should have kissed her. Never should have laid her down in the sand. The smell of her was everywhere now—like sunrises and juniper berries. The taste of her, too.

Safire tasted like the sea. Like someone Eris wanted to kiss every day. First thing in the morning. Last thing before bed.

Which was why she needed to leave. To finish this job and get as far away as she could from the girl standing before her loom. A girl who came from a different world. One she could never belong to.

Eris was so focused on getting to a door—any door—and stepping through it that she didn't see what was before her until she almost walked into his feathered chest.

Eris stumbled back.

The summoner stood in front of her, its red eyes peering into hers.

"Jemsin wants you."

A dark dread crept over her.

"I nearly have her," said Eris, about to shoulder around the creature. "Tell Jemsin I just need one more day."

"It's not about the job," said the summoner, blocking her way.

Eris's stomach twisted at those words. She was about to double back, to head for a different door.

"It's about the girl."

The words stopped her feet. "W-what?" she whispered. "What . . . girl?"

"The one I can smell all over you."

Eris felt suddenly small and exposed.

"No . . . ," said the summoner, looking up, over her shoulder. "I can smell her *here*."

Like the sea spirit on the dock who'd transformed into a bloodthirsty monster at the sight of Safire, the summoner shifted, shedding its black feathers to reveal a sickly-looking creature with fanged jaws.

In that moment, Eris knew what it would do. She'd seen it do it a hundred times before—tear a person limb from limb. On Jemsin's command.

Unlike the sea spirit, there was nothing Eris could do. The summoner was something far older and more lethal. She'd seen it break men like twigs. Seen it pull out their livers and gorge on their hearts.

"You're wrong," she said, blocking his way. "She isn't here."

But just as she said it, Safire stepped into view, drawn to the sound of Eris's panicked voice. Eris could see the reflection of her in those bloodred eyes.

The summoner's black lips pulled away from its teeth.

"No!" Eris screamed.

It shoved her against the glass. Eris heard a crack before she felt the bloom of pain in the back of her head. She tried to get up. If she didn't, Safire was as good as dead.

But before it could devour Safire, before it even reached her . . . something stepped between.

Eris's vision blurred, but she recognized that icy chill seeping through the air. Knew the presence that came with it. When her vision cleared, it wasn't a shadow that stood between Safire and the summoner, but a man. Raven haired and gray eyed. Handsome and stiff jawed.

Crow. The ghost in the labyrinth.

The summoner reared back in surprise, snapping its sharp jaws and shaking its head.

"Kadenze," said Crow's melodic voice. "Pirate's pet now, are you?"

The summoner's claws clenched and unclenched. It looked from Crow to the labyrinth around him, sneering through its teeth. "So this is where she caged you."

Crow's eyes flashed silver at those words. "Leave," he told the summoner, the look on his face inhuman. "Or when I'm free, I'll hunt you down and rip you into as many pieces as there are drops in the sea."

"You'll never be free," Kadenze hissed. But it stepped back. As if it wasn't quite sure of the words it spoke. And then, looking over its shoulder, it said to Eris, "You have two days to bring Jemsin what he wants. You know what happens if you fail."

"I've never failed him before," said Eris.

Gathering its cloak of feathers around it, the summoner's monstrous shape dissolved into the form of a blue-black raven. Eris ducked as it soared past her, its wings shuffling air, and disappeared into the darkness beyond.

Crow, too, was losing his form. No longer a man but a hunching shadow.

So this is where she caged you.

What did that mean?

"Wait!" Eris rose to her feet, her head throbbing.

But the ghost in the labyrinth was already gone, leaving Safire and Eris alone.

Safire gripped her throwing knife in her hand. "What was that?" Her voice shook as she stared into the empty space where two ancient creatures stood mere heartbeats before.

"*That* was Jemsin's summoner." Eris got to her feet and moved quickly past her. The other creature, though—the ghost called Crow? She didn't know. Back at the scrin, Day used to tell her a story every night before bed. His favorite was the

Skyweaver's defeat of the Shadow God. She thought of it now as she returned to the loom, her hands moving quickly as she cut the new tapestry from the wooden frame, half afraid the summoner would return.

Skyweaver spun a web made of starlight to catch him. She bound him up tight in her threads. . . .

She knew the story by heart. Everyone in the Star Isles knew it. Skyweaver kills the Shadow God and in doing so, saves the islands from his reign of terror. But as Eris rolled up the tapestry, she remembered her conversation with the sea spirit.

The Shadow God grows stronger, it said. *Once he's free, he'll come for her.*

Eris paused, thinking of the night the scrin burned. Of the god of souls who never came down from her tower.

We thought you'd want to know.

"But why would *I* want to know?" she whispered, unable to make sense of it.

"Know what?"

Eris spun to face Safire, who was watching her from the doorway, her arms crossed against her chest.

Eris needed to get her out of here. The sooner she did, the sooner she could find the Namsara.

They're just stories, she told herself. *And you have a bargain to uphold.*

Tucking the tapestry beneath her arm, she grabbed Safire's arm and pulled her through the twisting maze and toward a purple door. One that led to Firgaard.

Halting before it, her hands worked quickly, taking the pins from the hinges and pulling off the door that led to Safire's home. Safire sucked in a breath as it transformed back into a tapestry, one tied with items Eris had stolen from the palace so she could return, again and again: a piece of the queen's curtains, a key to one of the king's rooms, a sliver of painted wood chipped from the chair in Safire's office.

Eris set it aside and lifted the new tapestry into the frame, where it, too, shifted and changed—this time into a door the color of last night's sunset. Grabbing hold of Safire's hand, she reached for the crystal doorknob, opened the new door, and stepped through, dragging the commandant with her.

They stepped out onto that same creamy sand beach. The sun was setting over the boreal forest at their backs, and from the long shadows it cast, Eris knew it was late afternoon. That skittish white dragon was waiting. At their sudden appearance, he rose up from the sand, black eyes on them, his spiked tail thrashing warily. Eris let go of Safire's hand and drew out her spindle.

Disoriented, Safire turned. "No, wait. . . ." She reached for Eris. But Eris had already drawn a silver line in the sand. Was already stepping through the mist and back across.

She didn't want to know what Safire had to say. She couldn't let whatever was between them get in the way of the job. Because succeed or fail, it would be her last job, and she only had two more days.

Eris left Safire on the sand and didn't look back.

Thirty-Six

I've never failed him before.

Eris's words rang through Safire's mind as she and Sorrow flew through the cloudless sky.

She'd been naïve to think the Death Dancer would give up her hunt for Asha. Jemsin had made Eris a deal, and Safire now knew what would happen if Eris didn't come through on it. She'd thought she could protect Eris. But in the face of that creature, his bloodred eyes and snapping jaws, she suddenly realized what Eris was up against.

She should have returned to the citadel and reported to Dax. Instead she and Sorrow flew straight to the cove where Asha was hidden.

Dagan lives in the yellow house on the point, Asha had told her. *You can find us there.*

But when she walked through the door of the house, it wasn't Asha who stood within it. It was the king.

He stood at the window facing the sea with his hands linked behind his back.

"Dax . . ." She shut the door behind her. "I'm so glad you're here. Where's—"

"You were seen," he said without looking at her.

Safire's footsteps paused, heart skipping. "What?"

"This morning," he said. "On the beach."

Safire frowned, confused. *The beach?*

Finally, Dax turned to her. It was then that she knew something was wrong. Her cousin was staring at her as if she were a stranger. "The empress had soldiers watching the scrin. In case the Death Dancer returned." His normally warm brown eyes were full of anguish. "They saw you with her on the beach."

Safire swallowed, realizing what he was saying.

"The empress has postponed the warrant for your arrest." He looked away from her, as if it were difficult to get the words out. Like it wasn't Dax, her cousin and her friend, who was speaking them. But someone else entirely. Someone who needed to distance himself from her.

"I've asked her for leniency," he said. "If I can convince you to hand over the fugitive"—*Why was he calling Eris that? He knew her name*—"Leandra will overlook this transgression."

Safire stared at him. This was the king she helped put on the throne. The friend she sought first when she needed advice. Dax was the person in her life whose good opinion mattered most. And he hadn't even asked her *why*. He didn't trust her enough to have a good reason for being on that beach. Because he thought she was being manipulated. That she was too weak to see Eris for what she really was.

She forced the words out: "And if I refuse you?"

Dax jerked his gaze back to her. "Are you considering such a thing?"

Safire said nothing, waiting for his answer.

"You'll be arrested, Safire. The empress will consider it a breach of our alliance." He turned fully toward her, his voice pleading. "If you don't turn the fugitive in, Leandra won't give us the seeds she promised us. Scrublanders will die. Roa's family will starve to death. Don't you understand?"

Safire's heart squeezed inside her chest. *The seeds.* She understood perfectly.

"Either I deliver Eris to a death she doesn't deserve," she said, "or I deny the scrublands the seeds they need to keep from starving. That's the choice you're giving me."

"It's a choice you've given yourself," he said, eyes dark.

Safire stepped toward him, defiant. "Eris might be a thief, but she's not a murderer. She was only a child when the scrin burned. The people inside those walls were *protecting* her. It's the empress who killed them all."

"Is that what she told you?" said Dax, keeping his distance. Seeing the answer in her eyes, his fists clenched. "It doesn't make any sense, Saf. Why would the empress want to burn down a temple full of weavers?"

"I don't know," said Safire. But she intended to find out.

"Can't you see what's happening here? You're in league with a criminal. She's *using* you."

Safire studied her king, standing at the window, illuminated by the afternoon sunlight. *He has to believe her,* she realized. The scrubland's salvation was in those seeds. If Dax didn't believe

297

Leandra, he would fail the scrublands. He would let the blight push Roa's people into further starvation and poverty and death.

Most of all, though: he would fail Roa. And that was unacceptable.

It broke Safire's heart—because she understood it. She didn't want him to fail the scrublanders. She wanted him to *save* them. And in order to do that, he couldn't side with her. He had to side with Leandra.

"Dax," she said softly. "When you made me your commandant, you made it my duty to uphold the law. You made it my mission to always choose what is right and good and just." She held his gaze. "I'm sorry I can't prove it to you; I wish I could. But I know in my heart that to hand Eris over to the empress is to deliver an innocent into the hands of a fiend. And if that means I have to go against you, and Roa, and even the kingdom, then that is what I must do."

Dax stared at her, his hands clenching and unclenching, as if facing down a terrible choice. "I can't stand against her without proof," he said, as if to himself. "But if I return to the citadel with this news, she'll send her soldiers to arrest you. You'll be imprisoned for aiding an enemy of the Skyweaver. There's nothing I can do to stop it." She could see in his eyes that his heart was breaking. "There's only one way I can save both you *and* the scrublands."

Safire frowned. "What do you mean?"

"I'm sorry, Safire," he whispered. "But seeing as I can no longer trust you, I hereby strip you of your title."

She fell back, the breath rushing out of her. "What?"

"You're no longer my commandant."

Those words hollowed her out. "But . . . my place is by your side."

Dax wasn't just her dearest friend. He was her *family.* She and Dax defended each other, always.

He shook his head. "I won't sabotage the alliance—Roa's people need it too much. But nor will I watch them put you in a prison cell."

"Dax, please." Safire stepped toward him, wondering if it was too late to take it all back. To change her mind and do as he requested. But to do so was to go against her own conscience. "Where am I supposed to go?"

More important: what if he needed her? He would be walking into that citadel alone, delivering news the empress didn't want to hear. What if she punished *him* instead of Safire?

"Dax, it's too dangerous . . ."

Ignoring her, he grabbed his flight jacket from where it hung on the back of a chair, then swung it on.

"Get as far away from here as you can," he said, heading for the door. "Leave these islands, Safire. That's a command from your king."

Thirty-Seven

When Eris stepped back across, silence greeted her. The ghost was gone. The summoner, she assumed, had reported to Jemsin.

In the dim light of the labyrinth, Eris leaned against one of its stained-glass walls and sank down to the floor. She pressed her palms to her eyes, willing herself to go numb. To not think about the choice ahead of her.

Because it wasn't a choice. It was what she must do if she wanted to survive: wait for Safire to return to the citadel, then follow her there. She was sure, now that Safire knew Eris wouldn't give up hunting her cousin, that she would go to warn Asha. In doing so, Safire would lead Eris straight to the Namsara.

But as Eris waited, the emotions swirling within her grew into a maelstrom. She thought of the look in Safire's eyes when she realized nothing had changed. That Eris was still the same petty thief she'd always been—one who would endanger the life of someone she loved by delivering her into the hands of the enemy.

Eris steeled herself against this. *Who cares what she thinks of me?*

But from the day she first set foot in Firgaard and ran straight into the king's commandant, Eris cared.

She pushed the thought from her mind. If she stayed here, there was a chance she would talk herself out of this. She couldn't afford that. She needed to act *now*. Needed to get this over with.

Forcing herself to her feet, Eris went to fetch her scarp thistle darts and her dart shooter, then stood facing down a door the same shade of blue as Safire's eyes. The one that reminded Eris of the sand on her skin and Safire's legs tangled up with hers and that moment when she remembered—for the first time in seven years—what happiness felt like.

Don't think about it. Just do your job.

Reaching for the knob, she pulled the door open and stepped through.

When the mist cleared and the world came back into view, it wasn't the grand halls of the citadel around her, but worn clapboard walls that smelled strongly of fish. The air here was different, too. Dry and warm and slightly smoky.

Eris looked up to find an open window letting in the salt air. In the distance, beyond a garden full of red and yellow poppies, she could see the sea.

The sound of raised voices in the room at the end of this hall made her go quiet and still.

She heard heavy footsteps, then the shutting of a door, followed by silence. Careful not to make a sound, Eris crept to where the hall ended, then peered around the corner just in time to see Safire—still wearing the blue dress—collapse into a wooden chair. Eris watched as she pressed her face into her hands and began to shake with silent sobs.

The effect on Eris was instantaneous. She immediately forgot about Jemsin. And Kadenze. And the empress. The sound of Safire weeping made Eris want to step into that room and make whatever had broken her heart better.

Before she could, the door opened . . . and in stepped the key to Eris's freedom.

The *Namsara*.

The first thing Eris noticed was the burn scar that took up nearly half of Asha's face and neck. Her dark hair was woven into a braid down her back and a knife glinted at her hip. The moment she entered the house, Asha's black eyes found her cousin and she crossed the room in three steps, dropping to her knees before Safire. "What happened?"

Eris ducked back down the hall, waiting for her chance as Safire told Asha everything: how soldiers had seen her and Eris on the beach. How Dax had come to offer her clemency *if* she handed Eris in. How she'd refused to do it, forcing Dax to strip her of her title. He'd told her to leave the islands, because Lumina soldiers would be coming to arrest her.

Eris listened to all of it, her heart pounding in her chest, as she kept her cheek pressed against the clapboard facing the open window.

Safire had chosen Eris—chosen to protect her—over everything she held dear: her family, her loyalty, her kingdom.

"What if I've ruined everything?" Safire asked her cousin.

Suddenly, a blue-black raven flew to the windowsill, stretching its wings as it perched there, its bloodred eyes fixing Eris with a stare.

She would know those eyes anywhere.

Kadenze. Come to ensure she did her job.

Eris grew cold, remembering the way it lunged at Safire in the labyrinth. There was no ghost to intervene and protect Safire this time. Eris knew the price she'd pay if she didn't see this through.

"Stay here," Asha said from the room beyond. "I'll fetch Torwin. We'll figure out what to do."

Eris heard the floorboards creak.

"Everything will be all right."

When the door clicked closed, Eris knew this was her chance. Gripping her dart, she listened as Asha's footsteps led away from the house.

But her thoughts weren't on the Namsara. They were on the girl in the room beyond this hall. Safire had protected Eris and was suffering as a result.

Why?

You won't endanger the life of someone I love, Safire had told her in the labyrinth. *That's not who you are.*

Kadenze stared from the windowsill, watching her. If Eris didn't act, she not only wouldn't be free, she would be dead. And, from the look in the summoner's eyes, Safire along with her.

Eris forced her feet to take her to the window. The blue-black raven flew from the sill to the roof. Eris climbed out.

Dropping into the bed of poppies, she turned in the direction of the Namsara, who was already disappearing down the path through the tuckamores.

With the summoner circling above, Eris forced Safire from her thoughts. Gripping her scarp dart, she followed the girl into the woods.

Because Safire was wrong. *This* was what Eris was: someone who would do anything to survive, to escape those who hunted her. She wasn't noble and soft and respectable like Safire.

The sooner you get this over with, she thought, her heart heavy as a stone in her chest, *the sooner you'll be free.*

Eris caught up to the Namsara, her footsteps silent as the wind. She could see Asha was alone and unarmed, except for the knife at her hip.

But despite her efforts to remain unheard and unseen, Asha felt her.

When the path widened, the girl stopped. Turning her face slightly, she called out: "Who's there?"

It was now or never.

Eris lifted her dart shooter to her lips. She sucked in a breath, about to blow a scarp dart into the soft part of Asha's shoulder, when the trees rustled up ahead and a man stepped out.

"Dagan," Asha breathed his name. "You scared me."

At the sight of the newcomer, Eris froze.

The man on the other side of Asha was older than she remembered. His face was lined by years at sea and his hair was almost entirely white with age. But she knew him. A sudden memory struck her, of running down the scrin's wharf at the sight of his boat's sails. Of the smile that greeted her when he'd cast anchor. Of the weathered hands that passed her baskets of fish.

Dagan.

A lump formed in her throat at the sight of her old friend. And in that moment, she forgot to keep herself concealed.

The old fisherman looked up, over Asha's shoulder, and saw her.

His forehead folded in a frown. And then his eyes shone with recognition as he whispered her name.

"Eris?"

It was the way he said it that undid her. He was speaking to the girl she used to be. Not the girl she was. He was seeing the child she'd been before everyone and everything she loved was torn away from her.

Eris stepped back, not wanting him to get close. Not wanting him to realize what she was about to do.

Because above them, Kadenze flew in slow circles. Watching her.

"Is that really you?" Dagan said, taking a step toward her.

Asha had turned around now. Her eyes narrowed on the dart shooter in Eris's hand.

A *caw!* broke the moment—a warning about the cost of not coming through on her deal.

If she didn't act now, she would lose everything all over again.

Eris faced down the Namsara—the cousin Safire loved, and who loved her back. Eris had known that kind of love once. Lifting the shooter once more to her lips, Eris sucked in a breath. Only this time, as she blew with all the force in her, she tilted it skyward.

The dart flew.

Straight at Kadenze.

The raven writhed as it hit, then quickly regained its balance. She could almost feel its shock . . . which quickly turned to rage as it swooped back, its red eyes on her.

Eris stepped back. It hadn't worked and now Kadenze was coming for her.

It must be immune. . . .

Kadenze stumbled, dipping, then recovering.

Eris stopped her retreat.

It dipped again, losing control, then dropped into the forest.

Eris looked back to Asha and Dagan, then exchanged her dart shooter for her spindle.

"Wait," said Asha, stepping closer.

"The empress made Jemsin a deal," said Eris, already crouching down. "I don't know why Leandra wants you, but I suggest you stay far away from her."

Her hands trembled as she drew a silver line in the earth. It glowed faintly as the mist poured out.

What have I done? The question beat in her brain. She needed to run. Needed to head for the furthest port from here and stow away aboard a ship. . . .

Once the poison wears off, Kadenze will come for me. It always does.

She shook off the thought.

I have to try. . . .

"Eris," said Asha, taking another step.

"That raven," she interrupted. "It's not a raven. I don't know how long you'll have before it wakes, but once it does, if Safire's nearby . . ." She shook her head, her heart aching at the thought. "Please, get her away from here. As quickly as you can."

The mist was rising. Eris glanced up once more, to Dagan this time.

"I'm not the girl you knew," she said. "I'm sorry."

Just before she stepped across, the knife at Asha's hip gleamed in the setting sun, catching her eye. Those designs etched into the hilt . . . she'd seen them before.

Eris didn't have time to figure it out, because once the scarp poison wore off, Kadenze would wake. She needed to go—*now*.

So Eris stepped into the mist, leaving them all behind. Praying that Asha would do as she said and get Safire somewhere safe. Praying that Dagan would remember the girl she'd once been instead of seeing the one she was.

It was only after she walked the path through the mist and stars, only after the walls of the labyrinth solidified around her, that she remembered.

The knife Asha carried at her hip . . . it was Day's knife. The one she'd sold on the night the scrin burned, buying her and Jemsin passage aboard a ship. A knife Day had given her for cutting scarp thistles.

What was the Namsara doing with it?

A Dangerous Liaison

After the defeat of the Shadow God, the people of the Star Isles took Leandra as their sovereign. Under her reign, the Star Isles prospered and, with peace returned, Skyweaver turned back to her weaving.

Centuries passed. The Star Isles forgot the Shadow God and the misery he'd caused.

But Skyweaver didn't.

Sometimes, on the darkest nights, she heard him calling. In the beginning, she ignored it. But he was insistent, summoning her until his voice became a haunting.

Unable to bear it, Skyweaver rose from her loom one night, banished her servants, and went to him.

"What do you want?" she asked, careful to keep her distance from the web she'd ensnared him in.

"Someone to talk to," he said, never taking those burning eyes off her.

"You're a horror," she told him. "I have nothing to say to you."

"I wasn't always a horror."

Skyweaver doubted that. But she listened.

He spoke of a little cove beneath the cliffs, where he used to walk, long ago. He told her about the dirt paths through the junipers, the howl of the north wind, the taste of the salt of the sea.

Skyweaver might be merciful, but she wasn't a fool. The Shadow God could tell her all the tender tales he wanted. She knew what he *was. She'd seen the terrible things he was capable of. If he hoped to gain her sympathy and trick her into freeing him, he was deluding himself.*

When he finished his stories, she excused herself and left.

He didn't call again until several years later. Skyweaver ignored him this time, too. But he was her responsibility. She had lied to Leandra. She had kept him alive instead of killing him.

So Skyweaver rose from her loom, once again banished her servants, and went to him.

This time, he didn't tell her of his beloved cove but of the girl who lived there. A fisherman's daughter. A girl who'd been born too early, and as a result, was too small. So small and so mortal and yet she had tamed the god of shadows. Had taught him to be human.

"I didn't know how lonely I was until I met her," he said.

After that, Skyweaver sat at her loom, night after night, century after century. Waiting for the rest of the story. But the Shadow God didn't call for her again.

Lonely, she thought as she wove. Is that what I am?

This time, he didn't summon her. But Skyweaver went.

"Tell me what it feels like," she said.

So he told her all of it: the ache of hunger, the glow of joy, the bitterness of grief, the swell of rage. This time, when he looked at her, his eyes weren't ravenous flames. This time, they were soft as the morning dew.

"You remind me of her."

Those words unraveled the last of her resolve. Skyweaver heard the longing in his voice. She felt it echoed in her own heart. She might know who he was and what he'd done, but her curiosity outweighed her caution. She wanted more.

So when the monster reached to touch her, she let him. More than let him.

Night after night, she went to him. Over and over, he showed her. He was kind and gentle and tender—all of the things that monsters weren't.

And then one day, Skyweaver felt herself changed. Surprised, she looked down to find her belly swollen and something growing within her.

His child.

Thirty-Eight

The first thing she did when she got across was destroy Safire's door.

Just in case she was tempted.

The second thing she did was pack: her spindle, her dart shooter, and some dried scarp thistles in a jar by the bed. She kept a small stash of coins in the chest full of clothes and just as she was lifting the lid to take them, the ghost arrived.

"I can help you."

Eris dug below the layers of woven cloth and found the leather purse.

"Trust me," she said, pulling it out and shoving it in her pack. Out of the corner of her eye, she could see the shadowy shape of him. "No one can help me."

The ghost moved closer, closing the gap.

"You will never be safe, no matter how fast or far you run. You know this."

Eris's eyes prickled. "I have to try," she whispered. She was out of options. Shouldering the pack, she turned and found the dark shadow before her, its chilling gaze on her face. "Please. Move out of my way."

He was shifting again, from shadow to man. "They took something from both of us."

Eris frowned at him. "What did they take from you?"

"Something precious."

It was no longer the ghost standing before her now, but Crow. Human again: strong jaw, black hair, gray eyes staring down into hers.

"Your enemies are my enemies," he said. "Help me, and I will destroy the one you call *empress*, then hunt down those who do her bidding. They will never hurt you again, Eris."

Eris glanced up. He'd never spoken her name before. She didn't think he knew it.

"Help me," he said, his eyes shifting from gray to silver and back, "and you will never have to run again."

As she studied the man before her, Eris thought of the way Kadenze drew back in fear of him. She'd never seen Kadenze afraid of anything before.

"What are you?" she asked him.

"Nothing good," he said simply.

If Eris ran, Kadenze would find her. But if Crow was telling the truth, if he really could help her, she wouldn't just ensure her own safety. She would ensure that the one who'd burned the scrin and taken the lives of everyone she loved was stopped from doing the same thing again.

"What do you need me to do?" she asked.

"Climb the Skyweaver's tower. Take back my soul. Then bring it here, to me."

"Your soul?" Eris shivered. *Is that what they took from you?*

"I cannot escape this prison without it." He looked around him at the labyrinth walls. "It's the condition of the curse she placed on me."

"But how do I find such a thing?"

He seemed to flicker before her, as if straining to keep his solid form. Very softly, he said, "Skye was an expert weaver."

Eris frowned. *Skye?* It was the name on the spindle Day gave her. She'd asked about it once, but all Day would say was that it belonged to someone he loved.

"She was good at taking things and turning them into something else." His silver eyes flashed as they met Eris's. "Just like you."

Like me?

He meant the tapestries, she realized. The ones she turned into doors.

But I just weave them. The labyrinth changes them . . . doesn't it?

"She will have disguised it," said Crow. "And she will have kept it close." Turning, he headed deeper into the maze. "Come. We must act quickly."

Eris followed, gripping the straps of her pack. Crow seemed to glide rather than walk as he led her down a hallway Eris had trained herself never to go down—because it always turned her about, sending her back to the beginning. She followed him now into a part of the labyrinth where she'd never been before, to a door she'd never seen. It was the blue-black of midnight, its handle carved of ivory, and there were familiar words inscribed into the wood.

When the night descends . . .
I look to those who've gone before me
lighting my path through the dark.

It was part of Day's prayer. She could almost hear him speaking the words over her bed every night.

What would she find on the other side?

She forced herself to reach for the knob. Her skin sparked at the contact. Despite the chill of the labyrinth's air, the smooth curve of it was warm against her palm. Almost comforting.

"Where does it lead?"

"To *her*," said Crow. "You'll need to hurry."

Nodding, she turned the knob. The moment she pulled it open, silvery mist flooded in.

Eris didn't look back. Just stepped across the threshold and into the mist beyond.

Remembered

Dreams are for mortals, not gods. And yet, as the child grew within her, Skyweaver dreamed.

They were insubstantial, fleeting things at first. Like flashes of fish underwater. But the bigger the baby grew, the clearer they became. Dreams of a blustery cove. Of a father's weathered hands and nets of flickering fish. Of a boy who stood at the edge of things. A boy made of shadows.

Why did it feel so familiar?

As her belly swelled, Skyweaver struggled to weave. Souls slipped through her fingers. The night sky refused to bend to her will.

What's happening to me?

Fearful of being found out, she dismissed all but one loyal servant: a devout man named Day, who swore to keep her secrets.

The dreams began to come in the daytime. Vivid, insistent. Until Skyweaver could smell the piney scent of juniper berries and taste the tender flesh of cod and feel the sting of the northeast wind on her cheeks.

The more she dreamed, the more the baby grew, and the more she changed. Until one day she looked to find that her hands were not those of a god but of a human. Callused and coarse.

Skyweaver locked herself in her tower until Skye's Night. On that night, Skyweaver had no choice but to descend the steps and join the empress of the Star Isles for Leandra's yearly celebration of her defeat of the Shadow God.

Skyweaver wove herself a flowing gray gown for the occasion. One that would hide the bump of her belly.

The Shadow God was supposed to be dead. She wasn't supposed to be carrying his child.

Skyweaver descended her tower and entered the citadel. She sat at the queen's table and smiled when they toasted her. She clapped when they reenacted her defeat of the Shadow God. But on the inside, she wondered: Can they see my lie?

It started when they brought out the wine: a sharp pain in her belly that came like the tide. Ebbing and flowing. Contracting, releasing.

She knew what it meant.

The baby was coming.

Pain stabbed her like knife. She reached for the table to steady herself, gripping it hard, waiting for the ache to subside.

It didn't. Instead, it gave her one last dream.

Leandra's citadel disappeared. Skyweaver could taste the salt of the sea on her lips. Could feel the wet wooden oars blistering her palms. Could hear the crack of thunder.

You remind me of her, *the Shadow God's voice rang through her mind.*

They weren't dreams, she realized, clutching the bump of her belly. They were memories.

I am the fisherman's daughter.

And this was a memory of the day she died.

Skyweaver saw the wave crash down on the boat—her boat—turning it over, pushing her out. She felt the shock of the ice-cold sea, the force with which it sucked her under. Chest burning. Lungs filling.

And dragging her down were the hands of the one who'd come for her.

Just before she drowned, Skye opened her eyes. And there in the water's dark depths, staring back at her, was the face of her murderer.

Leandra, god of tides.

Thirty-Nine

When the mist cleared, Eris stood before a black tower rising high enough to pierce the sky.

The Skyweaver's tower.

Its base was a raised platform where a locked door barred the citizens of Axis from entering. Not that anyone ever dared. The platform was guarded by Lumina, who were currently doing their rounds.

All Eris had to do was elude the guards, climb the tower, and steal Crow's soul from under the Skyweaver's nose.

Easy, she thought with a confidence she didn't feel, studying the steps from the ground to a wide platform. Bits of grass and moss were pushing up through the cracks, gently reclaiming the stairs for themselves. *Stealing is what I do best.*

She watched the guards circle it twice, counting heartbeats each time they disappeared until they reemerged from the other side. When they disappeared a third time, Eris bolted for the steps, took them quickly to the top, then tugged the pin from

her hair and used it to pick the door's lock—all the while keeping count in her head.

Her hands were so slick with sweat, she nearly dropped the
pin.

Finally, the lock clicked and the door swung in.

The moment it did, the guards came into view.

"Hey!" said the first, spotting her. "You there!"

"Halt!" called the second. "What are you doing?"

With her heart drumming in her chest, Eris stepped into the
tower, shut the door behind her, and jammed the lock with her
pin. It wasn't a matter of whether or not it would hold—she
knew it wouldn't. It was whether it would hold long enough for
her to climb the steps, steal back Crow's soul, and step across.

There was only one way to find out.

The only light here came from the stars, flooding through
the windows. Before her stood a black spiral stairway that disappeared out of sight. Behind the door at her back, she heard
the rushing footsteps and shouting voices of the guards.

Eris darted for the steps.

She climbed fast. Every ten stairs, a narrow window showed
the view of Axis below. Soon, she could see the citadel. Then
the harbor. Then the cliffs to the east beyond the city.

The higher she rose and the farther the city fell beneath her,
the heavier her legs grew. Soon her breath came in quick, burning gasps. By the time she neared the top, her heart pumped
hard and the air felt thick in her lungs. Looking out the next
window, the lights of the city seemed as far away as the stars.

When the stairs abruptly stopped, a door stood before her.

A steel one this time. For a moment, Eris wondered if it, too, would be locked, but it wasn't even shut. The door stood a little ajar, letting pale light spill onto the stair where she stood.

She heard shouts from below.

Peering down through the window, she saw several black shapes swarming at the base of the tower. Lumina soldiers.

Eris's pulse pounded in her ears.

They hadn't broken in yet. She still had time.

When she pressed her palm to the door, it stung like a jelly-fish bite. She flinched away, hissing through her teeth.

Stardust steel, she realized, recognizing the pale silvery sheen.

So, using the sole of her boot, she kicked the door open. It was only when she stepped inside that she realized something was wrong.

The room was . . . deserted.

A broken loom stood directly across from Eris. Smashed in three places, it caved in on itself like a wounded spider. She could see the cobwebs that had formed over it, glittering in the starlight.

The weaving bench was toppled. The windows were cracked. And Eris saw spots of blood where the glass webbed.

There's no one here.

Everything was coated in a thin layer of dust, as if there hadn't been anyone here in years. Perhaps decades.

It smelled like wood and dust and something else. *Juniper berries,* she thought. The scent brought a strange and sudden dizziness.

More shouts broke out from far below. Eris ignored them.

She had her spindle. Even if they broke into the tower right now, she would be gone long before they climbed the stairs.

Eris walked quickly over to the smashed loom, her footsteps sending up dust clouds. Standing before the massive wooden frame, she reached to touch the broken pieces, and as she did, an image from the past rose up in her mind.

For her entire life at the scrin, a tapestry hung at the foot of her bed in that small, dark room behind the kitchens. Woven by Day, it depicted a small, knobby woman with meadow-green eyes set a little too far apart. The woman hunched at her loom, pausing in her work to look down at the tools in her hands, as if forgetting why she'd picked them up in the first place. Eris fell asleep every night wondering why she looked so sad.

She knew the woman was *supposed* to be Skyweaver. But all the other scrin tapestries depicted her as a faceless god crowned with stars. This was a mortal woman.

Eris stepped quickly away from the loom. Shaking off the memory, she looked to the wreckage around her.

What happened here?

Some kind of struggle, that was certain. One that happened a long time ago. But if Skyweaver wasn't here—hadn't been here in years—where was she?

Sudden shouts echoed up the stairs, breaking her concentration.

Eris strode to the narrow window, looking down. The black shapes of the Lumina were swarming *into* the tower now.

They were inside, and they were coming.

Eris wanted to take out her spindle and cross, *now*, but there was something she'd come for. She'd made Crow a promise, and if she didn't come through on it, he couldn't help her.

She was good at taking things and turning them into something else, he'd said.

Quickly, Eris moved through the room, scanning the floor in the starlight, turning overturned furniture upright. Forcing herself to be calm.

She will have disguised it. And she will have kept it close.

But if that were true—if Skyweaver kept it on her—then Crow's soul wasn't here. Because the god of souls wasn't here.

The voices got louder. Nearer. Soon Eris could hear their sprinting footsteps. She went to the door she'd come through and shut it. But there was no lock on this door. So she dragged the only unsmashed piece of furniture in the room—a heavy dyeing table—against it, needing to buy herself time.

There was a shelf full of empty jars and she searched this, too. She checked the floor beneath the loom. She checked everywhere. But there was no sign of anything harboring a soul.

Thud, thud, thud!

Fists rained down on the door, making Eris jump.

"Who's in there?"

Eris stared at the door, watching it shake with each pound of a fist. The table wouldn't hold it shut for long.

She was out of time.

Eris drew out her spindle and crouched down. Drawing a line across the floor, she waited for it to flare silver. Waited for the mists to rise.

Nothing happened.

The door inched open.

Eris drew a second line, and then a third. The mists didn't come. The way across didn't open for her.

She looked to the walls around her. They shone silvery in the starlight. Like steel.

Stardust steel, she realized, her panicked thoughts humming like bees.

She remembered the cuffs Kor had locked around her wrists. Stardust steel prevented her from crossing.

I'm trapped. Trapped a thousand steps into the sky, with nothing but a door between her and a pack of soldiers. Soldiers who were throwing all their weight into it now.

The door shuddered, and held—but only barely. A loud *crack* was followed by several voices counting in unison. The next time they threw their weight against that door, it would not hold.

Eris looked to the only other possible exit: the narrow window. She pushed her way through broken, toppled furniture until she stood before the cracked glass, looking out. The walls of the tower were perfectly smooth. There were no handholds to climb, and the fall would kill her.

But even if she could somehow survive it: the window frame was too narrow. She couldn't fit through it.

Behind her, the door heaved with the weight of the soldiers throwing themselves against it, forcing the table to move enough to let them through.

The Lumina crawled into the room.

Before Eris could turn and face her enemies, they had her by the shoulders.

This can't be happening, she thought, staring at the broken loom, thinking of the dying words on Day's lips.

When the enemy surrounds me . . .

They forced Eris to her knees, checking her for weapons. She felt the cold kiss of stardust steel as they locked her wrists in manacles.

. . . I know your hands hold the threads of my soul . . .

They growled an order. But Eris didn't hear them.

. . . and there is nothing to fear.

Except the goddess of souls wasn't here. She wasn't where she should be: at her loom, spinning souls into stars.

Day's prayer was a lie.

The Skyweaver had forsaken them all.

Forty

They dragged Eris down the citadel halls and up several sets of stairs, stopping sharply before a cylindrical room where two teak doors carved with frothing waves were thrown wide open.

"Wait," hissed the soldier who held Eris's arm in his meaty grip, halting her before the doors.

The walls of the room beyond them were deepest blue, like the depths of the sea, and painted with all manner of creatures: from crabs and spiny urchins to schools of shimmering fish to majestic humpback whales. In the center of the room, the slender white steps of a throne twisted upward like a conch shell, to where the empress sat on a cushion the color of seafoam.

At the base of the throne stood a young man in a golden tunic, his back to Eris.

". . . I told her if she insisted on keeping company with fugitives, I couldn't have her commanding my soldiers."

"And?" came the empress's voice, cold as the sea. "Where is she, then?"

"She fled," he said. "I'm here to take her place. I accept full responsibility for Safire's actions."

Eris's heart thumped at that name. She knew who this was, suddenly recognizing his tall stature, broad shoulders, and dark curls. It was King Dax before the empress's throne.

"You're here to take her *place*?" The empress's voice trembled with barely restrained anger. "You had time to speak with her, demote her, but not detain her?"

"My cousin doesn't make errors in judgment, Empress. She has impeccable instincts. It's why I made her my commandant. So perhaps you can help me understand why she would believe in Eris's innocence so resolutely." Dax's voice was perfectly calm, belying the rising tension in the room. "Is it true that Eris was only a child when the scrin burned?"

"That *child* was a danger to us all." Leandra's voice trembled through the room. "If you knew what she was, you would fear her. You would dread the thing she can unleash on the world."

"You didn't answer my question," he said softly.

The empress rose to her feet, then slowly descended the steps of her white throne. A hush fell over the room as the sound of her boots echoed eerily through the silence.

"I'm disappointed in you, King Dax," she said, standing before the dragon king now. "I invite you into my home. I promise to help your people. I look the other way when your cousin flouts my laws and opposes my soldiers . . ."

"Your soldiers were beating a civilian to death in an alley," said Dax, his voice tightening with restraint. "If I had been there, I would have opposed them alongside her."

"I see," she whispered, studying him. There was a sparkling

silence. To her captain, she said: "Caspian? Arrest this man."

All of Dax's guards drew their weapons in unison.

"Detain them," the empress ordered without looking away from the king, who said nothing. He made no move to fight her. Eris watched the Lumina descend on Dax's soldiers, who were outnumbered and easily overpowered.

"You have no idea what I am," the empress told Dax. "Nor the things I'm capable of."

"I'm beginning to see that." Dax's gaze locked with hers. "And I'm suddenly glad I made Safire run."

As if in answer, the wind howled from beyond the citadel, beating its fists against the walls. The room smelled like the sea in a storm, and Eris's skin prickled like it often did before a lightning strike.

"Caspian." The empress turned to her captain. "Take the king away. He will take his cousin's place until she can be hunted down and made to pay for her crimes."

"And the dragon queen?" Caspian asked, already binding Dax's wrists.

Dax went rigid at the mention of his wife.

"Leave his queen to me," she said.

They turned the dragon king toward the doors and marched him—along with his captured guards—out into the hall, where Eris stood. At the sight of her, Dax looked, then looked again. As if not believing his eyes.

"Eris . . ." His voice was no longer so controlled. "What are you doing here?"

She raised her own bound wrists in answer.

He opened his mouth to say something more, but the

Lumina forced him past her. Eris glanced back over her shoulder, only to be shoved forward and into the room beyond the doors. There they threw her at the foot of the throne. When she tried to rise, the soldier behind her pressed his stardust steel blade to the back of her neck.

"Stay down, dog."

So Eris looked up instead. Several paces away stood the empress. Leandra wore a gray fitted jacket, fastened down the left. Its silver buttons caught the flames burning in the sconces and threw them back into the darkness. Her ash-blond hair was pulled tightly back.

Eris had spent seven years running from this woman. She'd never seen her up close before. Had never looked upon her face.

The moment their gazes met, the room began to tilt. The ground seemed to crumble away beneath her.

"You."

The stormy eyes peering down into hers were the same eyes she'd met that night the scrin burned. They were the eyes belonging to Day's murderer.

She'd thought it was a Lumina commander who killed him. She hadn't known it was the empress.

Eris moved then, not caring that her hands were bound behind her back. She would destroy this woman.

The soldier behind her grabbed her hair, yanking her head back so hard, tears filled her eyes.

"Be still!"

If she ever got out of these stardust cuffs, Eris would destroy every last one of them.

How had the Skyweaver let this woman rule over the Star Isles for so long?

But as her hatred grew within her, Eris remembered the deserted room at the top of the tower. The broken loom. The overturned furniture.

Something was horribly wrong.

The empress's boots echoed through the room as she walked toward Eris.

That's right, come closer, she thought, *so I can tear out your throat with my teeth.*

As Leandra halted directly in front of Eris, her mouth curved into a thin smile. "Are you the one they call the Death Dancer?"

Eris glared up at her, wishing she had the strength to throw off her guards. "Isn't that why you arrested me?"

"I've arrested you for breaking into the Skyweaver's tower." The empress began to circle Eris, her gaze trailing up and down, stopping at brief intervals to study Eris's hair, her eyes, her mouth. It made Eris's skin itch. "Did you find what you were looking for up there?"

The empress stopped circling, waiting for an answer.

Eris was too busy thinking of ways to choke this woman to death with her hands bound behind her back. When she didn't answer, the empress crouched down, face-to-face with Eris now. Studying her captive as if searching for the answer to a burning question.

"Why did you kill them?" Eris demanded.

"Who? That pack of traitors in the scrin?"

"They were no threat to you."

The empress's eyes gleamed with a terrifying mirth. "No," she murmured. "No, I did that for fun."

Eris's anger glowed like embers within her.

She spat in the empress's face.

There was a long, cold silence. And then the empress brought her hand swiftly across Eris's cheek. The sharp sting was immediately followed by the coppery taste of warm blood. She'd bitten her cheek.

Eris spat the blood out, too.

The empress rose to her feet, stepping back. Her voice hardened around her next words: "I've spent the last seven years searching for two things, Death Dancer: you and that knife."

Eris frowned. *What knife?*

"I know she gave it to that sniveling servant of hers. I thought for sure he would have given it to you. But it seems I was wrong." She glanced up, over Eris's head, to the Lumina soldiers guarding her. "No matter. I have one of you now and am quickly closing in on the other."

And then, like a picked lock springing open, Eris understood: she wanted Day's knife. The one Eris sold seven years ago to buy her and Jemsin's escape from these islands.

That's why you want the Namsara, she realized, remembering the sight of the knife at Asha's hip.

"Captain Caspian?" the empress said softly, as if to herself. "Lock her up with the other one."

The other one? thought Eris, her cheek stinging as the soldier behind her grabbed her beneath her armpits and hauled her painfully to her feet. *What other one?*

They turned her away from the throne. Eris looked back once over her shoulder to find the empress clutching the hilt of a saber at her hip with long, thin fingers. After climbing the steps back up to her throne, she spun and sank down onto the white stone, leaning forward, as if deep in thought.

The soldier at Eris's side forced her onward. As he did, she thought back to the knife Day gave her. One for cutting scarp thistles. It seemed ridiculous now that he would give her a big, beautiful, ethereal knife to perform such a mundane task.

He gave me a spindle, too, she realized. They'd taken it from her in the tower. *A spindle that isn't really meant for spinning wool.*

What if the knife wasn't really meant for cutting scarp thistles?

God of Tides

The god of tides was a creature of tempests and terror. Revered by pirates and fishermen alike, she called herself Leandra and was loyal to no man but one: her brother, god of shadows.

Together, they were wild and fierce and free.

Together, they struck fear into the hearts of men and monsters alike.

Until the day Leandra raised a tempest and her brother didn't come to help her. Only stood and watched with something cold and dead in his eyes. When she dashed ship after ship against the rocks and roared for him to join her, she turned and found he was not at her side.

She called; he didn't answer. She searched the shallows and depths of all the waters. Of all the seas. But he was neither in the shallows nor the depths.

Leandra began to worry. The waves churned. The winds swirled. And by the time she finally found him, all the powers of the sea boiled in her wake.

"Brother!" she called, moving to embrace him. "I thought I'd lost you. I've come to take you home."

The god of shadows did not return her embrace. Nor did he wish to come home.

Leandra lashed out, angry and confused.

Her brother lashed back, striking her down.

Her. His own sister.

How dare he?

Sensing she'd lost him for good, Leandra waged a war against her brother. But with each blow she dealt, he hit back faster and harder until the day she found herself on her knees before him, defeated.

Leandra waited for the killing strike. When the blow didn't come, she looked up into her brother's eyes.

What she found there revolted her.

Mercy? Was this some kind of joke?

He wasn't going to kill her. He was going to let her go.

Who had done this to him? Who had tamed her brother's untamable soul?

Sneering, Leandra took the chance he gave her, swearing to find the culprit. Determined to make this right.

She did not go back to the sea. Instead, she waited and watched. She tracked the god of shadows through the darkness, stalked him all the way to a tiny house at the edge of the water. It was there that she found the source of her brother's weakness: a mortal girl.

A human had turned him against his sister and away from his purpose?

As she stared down at the weak and fragile creature rowing her boat out to sea, the god of tides called the wind and waves around her. She would deal with this mortal. She would remind her brother of his true nature. And when she finished, all would be right again. He would remember himself and rejoin her.

Together, they would be terror and chaos once more.

Forty-One

When the door to Dagan's cottage burst open and the wind howled in, Safire looked up, expecting Asha.

It was Roa who stood in the frame. Rain drenched her lavender dress and her dark eyes were wide with something like fear.

"They took him."

The dragon queen stumbled into the room. Safire rose to catch her, gripping Roa's ice-cold arms as the words rushed out of her. "I told her I would bring a war to her door . . . but she took him anyway." She didn't need to say his name. It was clear on her face that she was speaking about Dax. "She imprisoned him."

Safire's stomach dropped. "On what grounds?"

The door creaked on its hinges, hanging open and letting the rain in. Safire was about to leave Roa in front of the fire and shut it when two more figures entered.

"Roa?"

Torwin and Asha stepped into the cottage, just as wet as the queen. Rain rolled down their faces. As Torwin shut the door, Asha joined Roa and Safire on the carpet, her brow furrowing. "What's happened?"

Roa explained that as soon as Dax gave Safire's refusal to the empress, she accused him of being in league with dangerous fugitives and took him and their guards into custody.

Roa, however, was left untouched.

"I told her this would incite a war between our two nations. I reminded her that we not only had a formidable army but dragons at our disposal." She looked from Asha to Safire. "She was unyielding."

"But she didn't take *you* into custody," said Asha, her thoughts churning in her eyes as she stared down at the Sky-weaver's knife, now lying across her palms.

Roa shook her head. "I believe she wanted me to find you."

"You mean she wants us to come for him," said Safire. She had refused to hand Eris over, and now Dax was being punished for it. "This is my fault."

"No." Roa reached for her wrist, squeezing tight. "It's mine." She let go, looking down to her lap. "We so badly need those seeds. I let Dax convince himself—I let him convince both of us—that Eris deceived you. I'm so sorry, Safire." Roa shook her head, holding Safire's gaze once more. "You should know that he defended you in the end. It's why she's punishing him."

Safire swallowed the lump in her throat, thinking of Kor and the others. Pirates who hadn't been given a trial. Would the empress give Dax a trial? Would she dare execute a king?

"I need to go," she said, rising from the wood floor. "Before the worst happens."

"Wait," said Asha, stepping between Safire and the door leading outside. "There's something else. Something you both should know."

Torwin seemed to anticipate what she was about to say, because he emerged from the room beyond this one with a scroll, handing it to Asha. She unrolled it across the table beneath the window, revealing three pieces of parchment. She laid them out side by side.

Roa rose from the carpet and joined them.

"The stones I showed you?" Asha said to Safire. "There are stories carved into them, worn away by time and the harsh elements here. Dagan says they've been there since before his great-grandfather lived."

She touched the words scribbled across the parchment, many scratched out and rewritten.

"From what I've managed to decipher, they tell the story of three gods: the god of souls, the god of shadows, and the god of tides." Picking up the parchment, Asha handed it to Safire. "The god of tides disguised herself as a human woman and convinced Skyweaver to kill the Shadow God. Only Skyweaver couldn't do it. She imprisoned him instead—in a world between worlds. Somewhere no one would ever find him."

Safire handed back the parchment, every inch of her body wanting to go. To mount Sorrow and fly to the citadel. "I don't understand what this has to do with Dax."

"It has to do with the empress." Asha looked out the window

in the direction of the sea. "According to the stories, Leandra *is* the god of tides."

The room fell silent.

Safire thought of the paintings in the citadel. Ones that told the story of Leandra coming to save the Star Isles and petitioning the Skyweaver for help. She shook off the strangeness of it. Mortal or immortal, it didn't matter what Leandra was. Dax was imprisoned. She needed to get him out of there.

Roa must have seen it in her eyes, because she said, "I'm coming with you."

"Me, too," said Torwin.

Safire thought of Kor and the other pirates, executed without a trial. She thought of the scrin burned to the ground with all the weavers inside it.

The likelihood of any of them—of *all* of them—getting hurt . . .

Safire shoved the thought away. She hated to think about it.

"It has to be me. Alone." She looked from one friend to the next. "It's my job to protect you."

Asha reached for her hand, lacing their fingers together. Those black eyes met hers. "No, Saf. We protect each other." She squeezed hard and didn't let go. "I'm in no danger so long as Kozu's with me. We'll follow at a close distance and keep to the sky. Just in case you need us."

"I'll return to Firgaard," said Torwin, looking from Safire to Roa. "If she refuses to release Dax, we'll want the army on its way."

Roa nodded her agreement. "And I'll propose a truce. If she's willing to hand Dax over, we'll leave these islands immediately, quietly and peacefully. If she refuses"—her eyes darkened at the thought—"then we go to war."

But there were four of them and only three dragons.

It took some coaxing, but Sorrow seemed to understand he was needed, that their friend was in danger. Despite his fear, the skittish dragon seemed willing enough to do his part. So Torwin and Sorrow headed across the sea while the rest of them flew for Axis. Once the grid-like city streets came into view, Asha and Kozu stayed in the sky, keeping their distance from the citadel. Roa and Safire continued on, landing Spark in the empress's courtyard while the rain lashed the earth around them.

They were swarmed by Lumina soldiers immediately. Spark hissed and spread her wings while Roa tried to soothe her.

"Go," she whispered against Spark's scaly throat, pushing gently. "Find Asha and Kozu."

Spark looked conflicted as the soldiers dragged Roa away from her. She seemed to understand, though. And before the soldiers came for her, too, Spark flung herself into the sky.

Safire watched the dragon's golden form disappear into the mist as they shoved her inside.

They marched Safire into a familiar, circular room with rain-streaked windows on every wall. As the doors slammed shut behind her, she turned to find herself alone with four soldiers at her back, guarding the entrance.

Roa wasn't behind her.

"Where have you taken the dragon queen?" she demanded.

"My business is with you, Safire. Not your queen."

Safire looked to find Leandra standing at the widest window, looking out into the storm.

"If it's me you want," said Safire, "then release Dax. You're already treading on dangerous ground by imprisoning him without just cause. If you don't let him go, you'll have an army at your gate and a horde of dragons burning your city to the ground."

Leandra sighed, staring out toward the water. "What are armies and dragons compared to the power of the *sea*?" Not for the first time, Safire noticed how she seemed neither young nor old, but both at once. *Ageless.*

Asha's story clanged in Safire's mind.

"I think I'll keep your precious king *and* his wife," said Leandra. "At least long enough to coax your cousin down from the sky."

Safire narrowed her eyes. "Asha is the Namsara. Kozu will eat you alive before he lets you anywhere near her."

"We'll see," said Leandra, clasping her hands behind her back. "She has something that doesn't belong to her. Something I've been hunting for a very long time. In the wrong hands, it could unleash a monster. One I thought I put to rest a long time ago."

The Skyweaver's knife? Safire wondered, thinking of the blade sheathed at Asha's hip.

"Now." Leandra turned toward Safire. "*You* have been a thorn in my side since you first walked through my gate uninvited. You will need to be disposed of." In the window at her back, thunder cracked, followed by a flicker of lightning. "Before you leave us, though, you should know: I did what you failed to do. I captured your precious Death Dancer."

An uneasy feeling twisted in Safire's stomach.

"Liar," she said, her hands bunching at her sides.

The empress continued, as if she hadn't heard her. "Tomorrow I'll give her the same punishment I give every enemy of the Skyweaver. Do you know what that is?"

Safire heard the breath of the soldier behind her. Felt the shadow of them fall across her back. Her spine straightened and she reached for her throwing knife—but they'd taken it from her.

"No," said Leandra. "Of course you don't. Let me tell you."

A cloth sack came down over her head. Safire gasped for breath as something tightened around her neck and a familiar bitter smell filled her nostrils.

Scarp berries.

Safire held her breath, trying to resist their poison.

"First," the empress said as Safire struggled to fight the soldiers off, "I'll take Eris to the immortal scarps."

Safire couldn't hold her breath forever. Soon enough, she felt her arms growing heavy and slack. Felt her legs giving out beneath her.

"There, I will cut off her hands."

At those words, Safire struggled harder, even as that dull fog crept over her mind, lulling her, insisting that she close her eyes and sleep.

"And then," the empress said as the world began to fade, "I'll watch the daughter of my enemy die a slow and agonizing death."

Forty-Two

Eris watched as one of the soldiers took out a ring of keys, slid one into the lock, and turned it. The door swung open. The room beyond was much smaller and darker than the throne room, but just as high. It was also empty—or so Eris first thought.

When they nudged her inside, she found herself at the edge of a marble platform, its surface damp and slick. Below her, water surged and Eris could just make out shadows moving beneath the dark surface. Things with spines and jagged teeth.

She looked up.

High above, a dozen cages swung from the ceiling like hideous ornaments, their chains secured to huge iron hooks in the walls. Eris watched as one of the soldiers unhooked one. A heartbeat later, a swift rattling sound filled the room as it plummeted downward, halting just before it hit the water. Bouncing on its chain, the cage swung in frantic circles.

Using what looked like a long shepherd's hook to grab it,

a second soldier pulled it to the platform they stood on and swung the door open.

That was when Eris realized she was meant to get in it.

There was no point in fighting them. Her hands were bound in stardust steel, and she wasn't a fighter. But she fought anyway, digging her heels in, and when that didn't work, dropped to her knees. They threw her inside easily, and locked the cage behind her.

Safire would have lasted longer, thought Eris miserably, staring out at them between the bars. *Safire would have taken a few of them down before they overcame her.*

But Safire wasn't here. Safire was long gone—or so she hoped.

Most of all: she needed to stop thinking about Safire.

The cage lifted off the floor as the soldiers heaved on the chain, pulling it up toward the ceiling. It swung back and forth as it rose, spinning and spinning, making her dizzy. Between the spinning and the increasing distance to the churning water below, Eris had to shut her eyes, feeling nauseous.

It was only when the cage stopped rising that she opened them. Other cages—all of them empty—hung aloft around her. Beyond them, slender shafts of light sifted in through narrow windows high up on the walls.

Looking out between her bars, Eris found the platform impossibly far below and the soldiers filing out—all except two, who now stood guard. As if they expected her to make an escape attempt.

The door slammed.

Sitting now, Eris slumped forward, letting her forehead rest against the bars of this cage, waiting for it to stop spinning. An eternity seemed to pass before it slowed. When it finally did, she opened her eyes . . .

And found herself staring into a woman's face.

Eris shot upright.

The other prisoner sat across from her, locked inside her own cage, bathed in a beam of silvery light. Into the silence, the woman said, "Dear child. Why have they brought you here?"

"I . . ." Eris looked around them, but all of the other cages were empty. "Who are you?"

She looked back to the prisoner, and her gaze caught on the woman's hands. Or rather, the place her hands would have been, if she'd had any. The fact that she didn't, that her slender arms stopped just above her wrists, told Eris what she needed to know.

This woman was a traitor. An enemy of the Skyweaver.

Eris looked from the stumps of her arms up to the woman's face.

And that was when her breath caught.

The woman's eyes were pale green, like a meadow in late summer, and set too far apart—one of them looking in the wrong direction. Her body was knobby in places, as if she'd been assembled differently than other people.

Her presence wasn't the startling thing, though. The startling thing was that Eris knew her.

This was the woman from the tapestry at the foot of her bed. The one Day made her.

"My name is Skye," said the woman, studying Eris back. "What's yours?"

Sacrifice

Another contraction made Skyweaver cry out. Pushing away from the empress's table, she rose to her feet, stumbling. Leandra turned to look and saw what Skyweaver had worked so hard to keep hidden: a belly swollen with child.

Accusation darkened her eyes.

Skyweaver fled, needing to escape her true enemy.

Needing to set the Shadow God free.

Her servant, Day, helped her climb the steps of her tower. But half-way to her weaving room, Skyweaver collapsed in the pains of labor. She could go no farther. So Day lifted her into his arms and carried her.

Inside the weaving room, he set her down and barred the door, trapping them both inside.

The baby came, wailing and beating its fists. As it did, Skyweaver gave it what was left of her immortality.

In the world beyond, the wind rose. The rain pummeled the panes. The sea raged.

The god of tides was coming.

Day looked below to find Leandra approaching the tower with an army at her back.

"I know a place you can hide her," he said, taking the baby and swaddling it in a blanket. "But we must go now."

He held the child out to Skyweaver. But the god of souls only gazed at her newborn with sorrow in her eyes.

She did not take her baby. Instead, she lifted her weaving knife and held it out to Day. "Keep Eris safe. Until I find you."

Far below, Leandra's soldiers broke down the tower door. Their footsteps echoed up the stairs.

Skyweaver went to her weaving bench and picked up the spindle there.

"The key to your escape," she whispered. Taking her servant out into the hall, she drew the spindle across the floor. In its wake, a silver line shimmered delicately on the floorboards. On one side stood the door to her weaving room. On the other . . . a world of mist and starlight.

Day looked from the mist to the god he served.

Skyweaver looked to her daughter, seeing a life she might have had. I could still have it, she thought. She would fight for that life—and for her daughter. She would defeat Leandra just as she defeated the Shadow God.

The soldiers' footsteps were close now. As their shouts got louder, the baby started to wail.

Skyweaver kissed her daughter's brow. She tucked the spindle into the blanket swaddling her, then turned to face the enemy on the stairs.

"Come with us," Day begged.

Skyweaver shook her head. "I must end this," she said as Leandra appeared before her, as cold and ruthless as the sea. "I will find you when it's done. Now go!"

With no other choice before him, Day obeyed. Clutching the child in one hand and Skyweaver's knife in the other, he stepped across the shimmering line and into the mist.

Leaving his god behind.

Forty-Three

Safire woke to a bitter taste in her mouth. She lay on her side, her wrists and ankles bound, her mouth gagged, and her body aching from the constant bumping of a cart's wheels on rough terrain.

It smelled like fish and brine here. And though the cloth sack over her head blocked out the world, Safire could hear the clop of horse hooves and the softer hush of waves lapping against a wharf.

Axis Harbor, she thought.

Suddenly, the cart jerked to a stop. Someone stood over her. Safire flinched, waiting for whatever was coming. But whoever it was simply untied the rope around her ankles. A heartbeat later, they dragged her from the cart by her armpits and set her on her feet.

Safire would have tried to run, except she couldn't see. The effect of the scarp berries hadn't completely worn off yet, making her sluggish and dizzy. She tried to listen, taking in every sensory detail she could.

She heard the clink of money and the murmur of voices as they shoved her up a slope of some kind. As soon as the ground leveled, her boots thumped against wooden planks, and she knew she was on a ship.

The pressure around her throat let up as they untied the sack, then pulled it off her head. Several faces swam into view, none of which were familiar, and then, quite suddenly, she was being shoved down through a hatch and into a dark, dank hold where several people huddled against each other.

Safire rose, shakily, to her feet. Her hands were bound behind her back. She looked up just as the hatch slammed shut, plummeting her into darkness once more.

"Where am I?" she asked.

From the darkness, the deep-throated voice of a man answered, "In the belly of the *Angelica*."

That meant nothing to her. "The *Angelica*?"

"A ship that trades in human cargo."

"Where is it headed?"

"A far distance from here, lass."

Safire turned toward the voice. "What do you mean?"

"He means," said a woman's voice from farther away, "you've been sold by the empress. It's what she does with petty criminals. Selling them is more profitable than imprisoning them. Or killing them."

Safire was starting to lose feeling in her hands. The rope binding her wrists was too tight. She breathed in deep, trying to focus. Needing to take stock of the situation.

These were the things she knew: Eris was in terrible danger. Dax and Roa were in the clutches of the empress. Asha would soon be forced to hand over the Skyweaver's knife. And she herself was trapped on a ship bound for some godsforsaken place she'd never heard of, where her friends would never find her.

A cranking sound thundered around them, and Safire knew from the limited time she'd spent on ships that they were hauling up the anchor. As soon as it was fully raised, they'd head out to sea.

First things first, she thought.

"There's a knife in my boot," she spoke into the darkness. "Could someone cut me free?"

Forty-Four

Skye. It was the name carved into her spindle.

"How long have you been in here?" Eris gripped her bars as she stared at the woman in the cage across from her own. Her face and clothes were streaked with dirt and grime.

"Oh, child." Skye's tiny frame heaved with a sorrowful sigh. "Years and years." She tilted her head then, carefully pushing herself to the edge of her cage—so as not to set it spinning. "You look so familiar"—her gaze gently traced Eris—"almost as if—"

"But why did they put you here?"

"Because I defied her." Skye's jaw tightened. "She declared me an enemy of the Star Isles and accused me of colluding with the Shadow God. Of creating an abomination—one she would never stop hunting." Her green eyes narrowed, as if remembering. "They took my hands to punish me." She lifted the two stumps of her arms. "But they couldn't take my child. My servant, Day, hid her away."

Eris's heart constricted at that name.

"Day?" she whispered. It was Day who made her stay in her room when visitors came to the scrin or sent her up to the scarps to cut plants for dyeing. As if he didn't want her seen. Swallowing hard, she said, "Day was the name of the man who raised me."

Skye lowered her arms, staring fiercely now. "What did you say?"

Eris swallowed. "I . . . was abandoned. Day found me on the steps of the scrin and convinced the weavers to take me in." If the Lumina hadn't taken the spindle Day gave her, she would have reached into her pocket and shown it to Skye.

Skye leaned closer to the bars of her cage. Her green eyes flickering back and forth as she studied Eris. "The night Leandra turned against me, I gave Day three things to guard with his life."

Eris ached with a sudden, hungry need. "What did you give him?"

"The knife I used to betray the man I love."

Eris thought of the knife she'd sold to buy passage aboard a ship.

"A key disguised as a spindle."

Eris squeezed the bars, thinking of the spindle the soldiers took from her.

"And"—Skye looked up, her gaze sharp as a needle—"my baby girl."

Eris swallowed.

"Her name was Eris," whispered Skye. In the stunned silence

that followed these words, she said, "It's also your name, isn't it?"

Eris stared, frozen, as the pieces locked into place.

She'd been no more than a baby when Day found her on the steps of the scrin, swaddled in a woven blue blanket. Or so he'd told her, years later, when he gave her a knife for cutting scarp thistles and a spindle for spinning wool into thread.

"I knew it the moment they brought you in here," Skye whispered, her gaze turning tender as it moved over Eris. "I see him when I look at you." She shook her head. "Day didn't find you on the steps of the scrin. He *brought* you there—to hide you from my enemy. To keep you safe. He knew they were searching for you."

That was why Leandra killed Day.

Eris remembered the night the scrin burned. How right before Leandra murdered him, Day looked to the stars and whispered a prayer to the god of souls.

"You're her." Eris swallowed. "*Skyweaver.*"

Skye's silence confirmed it.

My mother.

Eris's heart squeezed at the thought.

She hadn't been abandoned. She'd been hidden and protected.

But if Skyweaver was here, locked in a cage, who was spinning souls into stars?

Who would save the Star Isles from the empress?

"Day's dead," she whispered. "Leandra killed him."

"I know," Skye whispered back, her eyes shining with the grief of it. "Eris, listen to me." Her voice gleamed like a polished blade. "You were Day's greatest hope. I failed to stop Leandra. But you—you are a daughter of stars and shadows. You will not fail. Day knew this, as I know it."

Eris lifted her head. Even if she weren't locked inside a cage, how could she possibly stop Leandra?

Skye leaned forward, looking toward the door far below them. Lowering her voice, she said, "A long time ago, before you were born, I stole something of your father's and hid it in plain sight. It must be returned to him."

Eris frowned, thinking of the ghost in the labyrinth. Of what he told her when she asked what he wanted.

Climb the Skyweaver's tower. Take back my soul. Then bring it here, to me.

"You took Crow's soul," she realized aloud.

"He wasn't Crow then," said Skye, glancing down into her lap. "He was . . . something else."

But that means . . .

"He's the Shadow God," Eris realized at the same time Skye said, "He's your father."

They were one and the same.

Suddenly, the world was spinning too fast, and it wasn't from the rotating cages.

I know him, she realized, thinking of the man with raven-black hair and gray eyes. *I've known him all this time.*

But if her parents were gods, what did that make her?

"Leandra knows what will happen if the Shadow God gets free of his prison. She'll do everything in her power to stop it from happening. It's why she's been hunting you all your life."

"The knife," said Eris, thinking of the weapon the Namsara was carrying. "You hid his soul in your knife."

The Skyweaver nodded. "Do you have it?"

Eris shook her head. "And they took the spindle. So even if I had the knife, I wouldn't be able to bring it across." She looked away. "I can't free him."

The Skyweaver shook her head. "The spindle isn't important. It's a key your father made me, when I was mortal. One that led to the place he built for me. I gave the spindle to Day because it was the only way for him—for a mortal—to cross and escape with you. But *you* are the daughter of the Shadow God. And the Shadow God walks where he wills. Day needed the spindle and the doors, just like I needed them. But you don't. You can walk where you wish—just like your father."

"Even with these?" asked Eris, raising the stardust steel manacles.

The Skyweaver's mouth turned down at the sight of them. "No. Not with those. You'll have to find a way to get them off."

A loud noise echoed up through the room, making both Eris and Skye lean toward their bars, looking down. The empress stood below, looking up. Her gray eyes fixed on Eris, completely ignoring the Skyweaver.

Eris's cage shook suddenly, then swung as one of the Lumina soldiers unhooked the chain fastening her cage to the wall. As they started to lower her, Eris gripped the bars, glancing back to the Skyweaver.

"There's something else," said Skye, her gaze fixed on Eris.

"Your father turned me into a god to save me; and in saving me, he destroyed the girl I once was. But you . . . you gave her back to me—my memories, my mortality."

Eris frowned, not understanding.

"I'm human," she said, speaking quickly now. "I can't spin souls into stars. Only a god can do that."

And then, just as she disappeared from view, Eris heard her whisper: "You *could* do that."

Me?

But Eris wasn't a god.

Was she?

Forty-Five

Safire had difficulty determining how long they'd been out at sea. There was no light in the hold except for the occasional flash of lightning that managed to squeeze through the cracks in the deck above.

She'd cut the other captives out of their rope bonds long ago and they now crawled through the darkness, looking for any object that might prove useful against those above deck. In their search, they'd found barrels of water, bottles of spirits, sacks of potatoes, and a variety of salt fish and pickled goods. The closest approximation of a weapon was a broken broom, which Safire gave to a girl several years younger than her. Some of the men were currently smashing bottles and handing them out—their broken halves would be able to slice a man as easily as any knife.

"Once we're up on deck, we'll need to use the element of surprise to our advantage. The point isn't to fight them. The point is to lessen their numbers as quickly as possible. As soon as your feet hit that deck, don't think. Just do whatever you can to get them over the side of the ship and into the sea."

There was a mumble of assent.

"Don't be afraid of them," said the man who'd broken the bottles, now standing at Safire's side in the dark. His name, she'd learned, was Atlas. "Damaged goods fetch less of a price—or no price at all. And that's what we are to them: goods. They'll do everything they can not to damage us."

Surprised by this, Safire looked to Atlas, but could make out nothing but the rough shape of him. "I hadn't thought of that," she said.

"I wasn't so different from them once," he said. "I know how they think."

Now for their most pressing problem: getting out of this hold.

The ship's crew had pulled up the ladder leading down into the hatch, and the space between it and the floor was now too high for a single person to reach.

To solve this problem, they rolled barrels full of salt fish and set now-empty boxes of spirits below, creating makeshift steps up to the hatch. Safire selected five others to go with her as the first line of defense, while the next five would ensure everyone escaped from the hold.

Once everyone was on deck, they would do whatever was necessary to thin the crew and take the ship.

When they were all in position, Safire pressed both her palms to the door of the hatch. She was just about to push, when someone screamed from above, "Monster!"

Safire froze.

"Sea monster!"

A shout of alarm rose up, echoing across the deck over Safire's head. The thud of running boots filled her ears.

"A sea monster will sink us," came a voice near Safire.

Panicked murmurs filled the room around her.

"We'll be drowned in here," said someone else.

"Hush!" Safire ordered. "Stay calm."

But it was too late. The unity of their common purpose broke. So Safire calmed herself, ignoring the fear bleeding through the captives around her, and listened.

She felt the ship rock, its wooden frame creaking beneath a massive weight, and the little bit of lamplight trickling into this room disappeared. As if a great shadow blocked it out.

She heard the sound of bodies being hurled through the air. Of men and women screaming as they were sent overboard and into the sea.

And then, drowning it all out, came a ferocious roar.

The sound sent chills through everyone in the hold—everyone except for Safire. She knew that sound. It made hope spark within her.

"It's not a sea monster," she realized. "It's a dragon."

This did nothing to calm the panic.

Suddenly, the hatch clicked from the other side. The room hushed as it swung open and the rain gushed in. With it came the light from a lantern.

"Found you."

Safire looked up into her cousin's scarred face. Asha's dark hair was a damp, windblown mess and her eyes were fierce as they scanned Safire first, then the crowd of captives below her. Behind Asha, one big yellow eye came into view as Kozu looked down into the hatch, fixing on the people huddled there. Several of them stepped back. The girl with the broom stood staring though, awed by the sight of the First Dragon, his scales slick with rain.

"It's all right," said Safire. "They're here to help."

Beyond Kozu, the sky was dark with storm clouds as Spark flew in lazy loops around the ship's ocher sails.

Asha grabbed Safire's arm and pulled her onto the deck, then wrapped her in a tight hug. Her clothes were soaked through.

"How did you find me?" Safire whispered into her shoulder.

Asha let go, then turned toward the young man at the helm. Torwin gripped the wheel looking like he had no idea what he was doing.

Beside him gleamed a white dragon with a broken horn.

"It was Sorrow," Asha explained. "Torwin was on his way to Firgaard when Sorrow suddenly turned back. There was nothing Torwin could do to sway him. Sorrow found us in the air and started flying in circles, clicking furiously at Kozu and Spark. When he headed out to sea, they followed him. He led us straight to you."

Safire frowned, glancing up into Sorrow's black eyes, which were now peering curiously at the captives huddled in the shadows.

"You're linked," said Asha. "It's the only way he could have known where you were."

"But wouldn't I feel it?" Safire watched the white dragon

hop down from the upper deck and cautiously make his way to where the captives were climbing out of the hatch.

"He might not bond like other dragons," said Asha, watching, too. "Maybe you'll never sense it. Or maybe it's the kind of link that grows stronger over time." Suddenly, she turned away from Sorrow. "I take it things didn't go well at the citadel. Where's Roa?"

"Leandra has her."

Safire's conversation with the empress came flooding back. She thought of the hood coming down. Of Leandra's last words.

I'll watch the daughter of my enemy die a slow and agonizing death.

"She has Eris, too. She's going to kill her, Asha. I need to find her. She said she was taking her somewhere called the immortal scarps?"

Asha's gaze snapped to Safire's face. "The immortal scarps . . . According to the stories, the Shadow God turned Skye into Skyweaver at the bottom of the immortal scarps. They're the highest point in the Star Isles. Atop the red-clay cliffs on the northern side of Axis Isle. But I doubt a ship will get to them in time." She looked up at Kozu's massive black form coiled on the deck. "A dragon, on the other hand . . ."

"Asha!" Torwin called through the wind and rain. "Trouble's headed our way."

They all turned to find Torwin frowning into the distance.

A boom of thunder made them all flinch. Safire joined Torwin as lightning flickered across the sky, illuminating the silhouette of another ship sailing rapidly toward them. When lightning flashed again, Safire saw a man at its helm. The lantern in his hand illuminated a scar over his right eye.

"Jemsin," Safire scowled.

As if hearing his name, the pirate captain looked directly at her. Their eyes met across the water.

"We can assist," said a voice at her side. Safire looked to find Atlas, the burly man who'd broken bottles of spirits and helped her roll barrels of salt fish in the hold. His clothes were dripping now, and his face was slick with rain. At his side stood a handful of other prisoners. Nodding to the helm, he said, "I've sailed ships almost as big as this."

Safire looked from them back out to sea. There was something familiar about the cliffs in the distance. If she squinted and waited for the lightning, she could see the familiar shapes bobbing in the water.

Sea spirits.

"The ship wrecking grounds," she murmured, remembering Eris's name for them. Remembering the advice Kor didn't take.

"See there?" said Safire, pointing to the dark silhouettes in the waves. "There are rocks just beneath the surface. They'll put a hole in your hull and you'll be easy prey for sea spirits." She looked back to the masts of Jemsin's ship, getting closer by the heartbeat. "If you can get around to the other side of them, you might be able to lure those pirates straight into the wrecking grounds."

When she turned back, the wheel had already been taken from Torwin, who was watching Asha mount Kozu.

Sorrow stared at Safire across the rain-slick deck, wings

spread, ready to fly. Safire crossed to him in five easy strides, then mounted up.

A heartbeat later, she nodded to Asha.

Together, their dragons leaped into the storm.

Forty-Six

The soldier jerked Eris to a hard stop. Looking back over her shoulder, she found the empress staring up at the only occupied cage above them.

"Lower her down."

One of the Lumina unhooked the chain of Skye's cage, then slowly lowered it. The chain creaked and groaned until the bottom of the cage hit the platform with a clang.

"I should force you to watch." The empress looked Skye up and down, taking in her filthy dress and knotted hair. As if Eris's mother was beneath her. "I should show you the consequence of your crime firsthand."

Skye stared back from behind the bars. For someone who'd been imprisoned eighteen long years, who'd had her very hands taken by the enemy before her, there was no trace of hatred or contempt in her eyes. Only pity.

She said not a word to the empress. Instead, Skye turned her face to Eris.

"Remember who you are," she said, her green eyes intense.

"My daughter. Day's hope. Your father's heir—an heir of shadows and stars."

The empress growled an order. In an instant, they were forcing Eris out of the room, away from Skye. She looked back just as the door slammed shut, separating her from her mother.

As they marched her through the citadel and out into the daylight, Eris thought of everything her mother said. About the Shadow God's soul, hidden in a knife, and how it needed to be returned, to free him of his prison. But Eris didn't have the knife. And even if she did, the stardust steel cuffs on her wrists prevented her from going across and delivering it to him.

There was nothing she could do.

They put Eris on horseback and marched her through the streets of Axis. At the sight of the newly captured Death Dancer, more and more people came to look, curious about this dangerous fugitive who'd eluded their empress for so long. The manacles around Eris's wrists were linked to chains held by four Lumina soldiers, two before and behind her, to keep her from running.

"Where are you taking me?" she asked the one closest when they passed through the final checkpoint at the edge of Axis's border, leaving the city—and its citizens—behind.

The soldier didn't answer, just pointed up the dirt road before them. Eris's gaze followed it as it rose, higher and higher, up to the scarps.

Eris knew what was at the top of those scarps and what happened to the criminals they took there.

She knew what they were going to do.

✦✦✦

When the city of Axis lay far behind them, it started to rain. Not long after that, a storm rolled in, darkening the sky.

As they reached the highest point, where the steady incline of gray rock leveled out into wet meadow, Eris saw the sea. As she stood facing that vast expanse of water, Eris realized just how alone she was. Her mother was locked in a cage. Her father— the god of shadows—was imprisoned in a place she couldn't get to. Safire was long gone—she hoped—and far away from here.

There was just Eris now.

But that was nothing new. There had always been just Eris. It was what she was best at: being alone.

Now, though, as the ground leveled out, as they marched her through the meadow and toward the cliffs, Eris found herself wondering how things might have been different. What would her life be like if the scrin had never burned? If she'd never had to run?

Who would she be?

Who did she *want* to be?

Thunder shook the earth as they marched her across the meadow, closer to the cliff edge. While lightning slithered across the sky, Eris tried to estimate the distance from the top of the scarps to the water below. Unlike the chalky white cliffs near the scrin, these were red clay and considerably higher. No jagged-tooth rocks lay below. Or if they did, they were hidden beneath the sea.

If there weren't any rocks below those crashing waves, it *might* be possible to survive a fall from this height. The likelihood was certainly higher than what the empress had in store for her.

But Eris didn't have time to contemplate the idea. The soldiers swung her around, so her back faced the sea, and forced her two hands onto a long stone slab, slick with rain. In the light of their spluttering torches, she saw that the ground beneath the slab was dirt, as if nothing had grown there for years. And straight in front of Eris, some kind of steel bar had been curved and fitted into the slab, though for what purpose, she couldn't say.

Leandra stood opposite Eris, a wicked-looking sword sheathed across her back. More soldiers stood behind their empress—some of them watching Eris, the others watching the perimeter.

The thunder bellowed and the lightning flickered. As the rain lashed down, Eris thought about that drop from the cliffs to the waves.

Possible, thought Eris. *But not probable.*

A Lumina soldier stood across from her, holding the chain fastened to her stardust steel cuffs, keeping her hands squarely on the stone slab. Another Lumina stood behind her, keeping himself between her and the cliffs.

Leandra drew the Severer from its sheath at her back. Eris had never seen it before, but she knew the stories. A stardust steel blade so sharp and lethal, it could cleave through bone in one fell swoop.

The empress's hair dripped with rain, her gray jacket clinging to her frame. And as she stepped up to the slab of rock, Eris knew what came next.

They couldn't afford to keep her alive. She was the only one who could set the Shadow God free. The only one who could save the Star Isles from the liar on its throne.

It was why they'd brought no medic. Nothing to cauterize a wound.

They were going to sever her hands and leave her to die.

Eris couldn't let that happen. Contemplating that thousand-foot drop at her back, she calculated what it would take to get there. Before the Severer came down, if she could create some sort of distraction, she might be able to pull her chain free, then fling herself off that cliff and pray she survived.

As the empress readied herself, Eris's eyes met the soldier before her—the one who held the chains of her manacles. When his mouth stretched into a wicked grin, it was the motivation she needed. She launched herself over the altar—straight into him. He grunted as her small body knocked the air out of his lungs. In his shock, he released her chains. Recovering her balance, Eris looked to the cliff and the sea and the sky beyond it.

Freedom.

She flew for it. Ready to jump. Ready to fall. Ready to be dashed upon the rocks if it came to that—because at least it would be a death on *her* terms, not the empress's.

Someone grabbed the back of her shirt before she reached the edge. The collar choked her hard, halting her momentum. They swung her back and threw her violently down, holding her cheek against the cold altar stone with their weight pressing down. Crushing her.

"Hold her still," Eris heard the empress say as she gasped for air. "We'll do this one at a time. . . ."

At the empress's icy touch her left manacle fell open. For one delusional moment, she thought the empress had changed her mind. Was setting her free.

But when the pressure on her back disappeared and Eris tried to move, to rise, to run again, she found she couldn't. The manacle that had enclosed her left wrist a moment ago was now locked around the curved bar fitted into the altar. Keeping her prisoner. Preventing her from running.

No, no, no . . .

Panicked, Eris tugged and twisted and strained against it, her eyes filling with tears as she realized there was no escape.

Forty-Seven

The storm worsened.

As Safire and Asha flew through the rain, the clouds darkened to black. Soon the thunder was over them and lightning seemed to strike wherever they'd just been. Any moment now, it would strike Sorrow and Kozu, too.

"We're not going to make it!" Asha shouted above the rain. "The dragons can't fly up there without risking all of us."

Safire kept her gaze fixed on the smooth red cliffs in the distance. The rain stung Safire's face and hands. She was losing feeling in her fingers.

"Get me as close as you can," she whispered, clicking to Sorrow, who propelled her forward through the storm.

Kozu followed close behind.

As the cliffs drew nearer, Sorrow started upward, as if making a dash for the summit, when a flash of light and heat temporarily blinded Safire. She cried out at the same time Kozu roared, and then they were half falling, half banking away from the lightning strike.

Safire wrapped her arms hard around Sorrow's neck, closing her eyes as she clung on.

Suddenly, she was thrown forward. There was a crash of showering rocks and red sand as Sorrow tried to land on a precipice that was proving to be too fragile to hold him. Kozu landed farther up, on even less stable ground.

In a moment, they'd have to dive back toward the sea. But Safire could see the top of the cliffs from here, shrouded in mist. She knew the dragons wouldn't get her any closer than this.

Letting go of Sorrow, she swung her legs over and slid down the dragon's scaly hide.

"Saf!" Asha cried out.

Her feet hit the ground, which trembled and shook beneath her as more rock slid out from under her.

"Find somewhere safer to land!" Safire called back, ducking beneath Sorrow's flapping wings and carefully beginning to scale this crumbling precipice, heading for higher and more solid ground. "I'm going up there!"

She contemplated the gap between this quickly dissolving outcropping and the large solid-looking rock beyond it. As more stones fell to the water below, she didn't look down. Just threw all her weight into a jump.

Her feet landed firmly. Turning, she saw Sorrow leaping into the rain, while Kozu remained behind, massive wings beating.

"You need a weapon!" Asha called into the rain, unbuckling something at her belt. "Take this!"

The silver sheath of the Skyweaver's knife winked as Asha tossed it through the air. Safire caught the cold, eerie blade in both hands, then secured it to her belt. When she looked back, Asha glanced over her shoulder as Kozu dived into the mist below.

Safire turned and ran for the summit. As the lightning flashed around her, she carved her way through the trees. When the woods opened up and the ground leveled out, she saw them. Or rather: saw the shining silver blade, gripped in the hands of the empress.

Eris knelt before a stone slab, chained to the rock like some kind of sacrifice.

A whole meadow stood between them. And into that meadow, stepping between Safire and Eris, were a dozen Lumina soldiers, all drawing their weapons.

Her heart beat fast and hard in her lungs. She knew she couldn't get to Eris in time. Knew she couldn't get to Eris at all.

"Eris!" Her voice battled the wind and rain as she drew the Skyweaver's knife. It wasn't a throwing knife, but that didn't matter.

Despite the wind and rain, despite the distance across that meadow, Eris looked up.

She saw her.

The empress saw her, too. Safire heard Leandra give a command. Saw the soldiers start toward her. But Safire's eyes were on Eris. She squeezed the hilt of the Skyweaver's knife hard in her hand.

And then she threw it.

Forty-Eight

The Skyweaver's knife landed right next to Eris, the blade stuck halfway into the dirt.

The moment before Safire called her name, she'd already succumbed to despair. No matter what she did, they were going to take her hands. Going to watch her die here, at the top of the scarps. Why bother fighting anymore?

But then Safire called her name. And Eris looked up.

And everything changed.

With the knife in the dirt beside her, Eris now had what she needed to set the Shadow God free.

She just had no way to get to him.

The spindle is unnecessary, her mother had told her.

But even if Eris could manage to cross without it, there was the stardust steel manacle locked around her right wrist, keeping her trapped on this side of the mists.

The empress turned away from the sight of Safire, smiling victoriously. She'd already won.

As the Severer rose, gleaming in the rain, Eris looked to the girl across the meadow. A girl who stood weaponless in the face of the armed and swarming Lumina, staring back at her.

Safire had come for her.

And though it terrified her, Eris suddenly realized there *was* one way to go *Across*. But only one.

Which was why, when the Severer came down, whistling through the air, she didn't scream. Didn't despair.

Eris watched it happen—*let* it happen—before she ever felt it: the steel splitting her flesh, then tendons, then bone. She saw it split her right hand from her wrist. The hand she used to steal and spin and weave.

The stardust cuff went with it, falling to the stone. Into the blood that was already pooling.

Eris stared, stunned into paralysis, just for a moment.

And then her mother's voice echoed in her mind.

Remember who you are.

Eris looked from her severed hand to the knife stuck in the dirt.

My daughter. Day's hope. Your father's heir.

Eris wasn't alone.

She'd never been alone.

Leaning down, she grabbed the knife with her left hand— her free hand—then reached *Across* with her will alone. To her surprise, the mists rose around her, silver and shining, beckoning her away from the horrors of this place.

Eris walked straight into them.

Forty-Nine

The pain came all at once, bringing with it the full truth of what Eris had done. Of what she'd *lost*. As she stepped through the mists and into the labyrinth, she stumbled and fell. Crying out at the overwhelming shock of it, dropping the knife to the floor.

Her right hand was gone.

Gone.

It was only when someone grabbed her shoulders that Eris came back to herself. To the pain and the blood and the knife on the ground. And then: to the man standing over her.

"What have you done?" said Crow, his face white as the scrin's chalky cliffs.

"I brought you the knife." Eris stared at him, cradling the bleeding stump of her arm in her lap. "It was the only way."

Crow fell to his knees, his eyes filling with tears. "Oh, my child." And for the first time, Eris let herself hear those words. *My child.* She belonged to someone. She was wanted. Crow cupped her face in his hands, staring into her eyes. "This was not your burden to bear."

I choose to bear it, she thought, remembering her mother staring down the empress with pity in her eyes, in spite of everything that had been taken from her. Remembering Day and all the others who'd borne the burden of something far bigger than themselves.

The labyrinth blurred around her. Eris felt suddenly dizzy. She tried to focus on Crow, tried to find herself in his face the way Skye found him in hers. But he was slipping away from her. Everything was slipping away from her.

She'd lost too much blood. She was going to bleed out here, far away from the world, without a chance to say good-bye. . . .

Crow pulled her against him, holding her gently. And as she slipped a little farther, Eris thought: *How nice it is to be held.*

"I can't restore it," he whispered. "But I can give you this. . . ."

He changed then, back into that shadow she'd first known him as. The darkness engulfed her and as it did, the pain trickled away. She was ready to let go, to walk alone to Death's gate, when suddenly the shadows turned back into a man, and Eris found herself still on her knees, in her father's arms.

Eris looked down to find her severed wrist healed into a rounded stump. As if years had passed. She lifted it, staring. And while it was still a grievous shock to find her hand gone, there was no more pain. No more blood.

She was alive.

Crow kissed the crown of her head and let her go. He stood, picking up the knife. For several heartbeats, he stared at it, his eyes bleeding to black. And then, with a deafening cry, he smashed it at his feet.

Fifty

Safire heard the blade come down. Heard the horrifying sound of splitting flesh and bone, and felt her heart split with it.

"Eris . . . ," she whispered, and suddenly it didn't matter that eight Lumina had her surrounded, or that they were closing in.

She needed to get to Eris.

Safire scanned the rain-drenched soldiers, her blood humming, ready to fight. All she had to do was disarm *one* of them. She did a quick scan and chose the youngest one—likely to be the most inexperienced—and had just lunged for him, fists swinging, when the storm took a sudden turn.

The ground shook. Lightning struck the meadow in several places at once, blinding her for the second time, the charge raising the hair on her arms. When her vision cleared, all eight Lumina soldiers were dead on the ground. And someone stood beside her.

Safire looked up to find Eris, her pale hair twisting about her face in the storm, her green eyes glowing. "But you . . ." Safire looked down, her heart stopping. Not only did Eris have a missing right hand, the wrist had already healed.

Safire started to reach for her when a sudden scream shattered everything. Both of them turned toward the sound. A shadow blacker than Kozu now stood across the meadow, growing bigger, gathering the dark around it, absorbing the power of the storm. Lightning flickered through the shadow, illuminating the silhouette of a man.

Unsure and afraid, Safire reached for Eris's left hand, holding on tight.

"The Shadow God is free," murmured Eris. "He's come to make things right."

Leandra fell to her knees before him, begging. Her scream was followed by another sound—the horrifying crush of several bones at once.

The lightning and thunder stopped.

The darkness broke.

When Safire looked again, someone was walking up the path and into the meadow. She stared determinedly toward the god of shadows, like he was the only thing she saw.

"That's my mother," whispered Eris, more to herself than to Safire.

At the sight of her, the Shadow God seemed to remember himself. He turned away from the empress, lying broken in the dirt, and began to walk toward the woman.

He halted suddenly, trembling. As if he—a god of chaos and destruction—was about to weep.

The woman didn't stop. Her pace quickened as she called his name.

He took a step toward her. Then another. With every step he took, he became less of a shadow and more of a man. Finally, the woman closed the space between them. They stood there, staring at each other for a long time. And then, slowly, the Shadow God reached to touch her, taking her face in his hands.

Fifty-One

SIX WEEKS LATER

Safire ducked as the waster swung straight for her head, whistling as it did. It was twilight, and the rooftop was lit by the glow of several lanterns.

"I'm going to the training grounds today," Asha said, stepping back, almost to the edge of the roof. She flicked her wrist, spinning her wooden training weapon. "We're starting to build soon. I want you to look at the plans for the new school and tell me what you think."

"I'll try," said Safire, thinking of all the things she needed to do before she and Roa left for the scrublands tomorrow.

It had been several weeks since the Shadow God defeated Leandra. After witnessing the demise of the god of tides, Safire had flown straight to Axis, only to discover that Roa had already broken herself and Dax out of the empress's prison.

Because Roa was brilliant like that.

"Sorrow misses you," Asha pressed.

Safire nodded, only half listening. Thinking instead of Eris.

She'd invited the former Death Dancer back to Firgaard, but Eris refused. With the Lumina scattered and the empress dead, there was so much work to do, and her place was in the Star Isles.

Safire understood. After all, she had a place, too—here in Firgaard.

That didn't mean it didn't sting, though.

Back when Eris was just an uncatchable thief stealing precious objects from under Safire's nose, she'd loathed the girl. Now, she longed for that familiar presence trailing her through the palace halls. But no pirate thief watched her from the shadows anymore. She hadn't heard a word from Eris since the day they'd said good-bye.

Now candidates for a new government were in the process of being chosen in the Star Isles and while Dax returned tomorrow to help oversee the vote, Safire and Roa were traveling to the scrublands with more rations. Dagan and other fishermen from the Star Isles had sent a second supply of salt fish, along with sacks of wheat and boxes of vegetables to tide the scrublanders over until the new seeds yielded their first harvest. Due to the fisherfolk's generosity, Roa's father was almost fully recovered, and the physician had reported that Lirabel and her baby were healthy again.

Asha swung her waster, scattering Safire's thoughts.

In the golden light of the lanterns, Safire lunged for her cousin, who quickly and easily darted out from under her.

Though they were the same height and build, Safire had always been stronger, faster, and lighter on her feet. Asha was good at hunting and taking down prey. Safire was good at hand-to-hand combat. Today, though, Asha caught Safire's blows easily.

She stepped back, frustrated. Normally she'd have broken through all of Asha's defenses by now.

"You should take him with you," Asha said as she stepped out of range of Safire's next swing, deflecting it easily.

"Who?"

"Sorrow." Asha shook her head, lowering her waster. "Haven't you been listening?"

Safire stepped back, wiping sweat from her brow as Asha frowned. Beyond them, Firgaard's copper domes and filigreed towers glowed warmly in the light of the rising sun.

"Ever since we returned from the Star Isles," Asha continued, "you haven't been yourself."

This, Safire told herself, was due to the fact that she was no longer the king's commandant. She had no duties, and therefore no routines. She felt adrift.

"Saf." Asha knocked Safire's waster out of her hand. It landed with a soft thud among the stones, bringing her out of her thoughts.

Safire glanced around the palace courtyard below, to see if anyone had seen her easy defeat, but it was dawn. The palace staff were only now rising from their beds.

It was just Safire and Asha here.

And then, suddenly, her legs were kicked out from under her. Her back hit the ground. Safire winced at the pain, then looked up to find Asha crouching over her, the tip of her waster pressed hard against Safire's collarbone.

Safire stared up at her cousin, stunned by the trouncing.

Asha met her gaze, equally stunned.

In all their years of training, Asha had never beaten her.

"New move," Asha explained. "I've been practicing with Torwin."

Safire frowned up at her. "Wonderful. You can tell Torwin it worked. Now get off." She was about to shove her cousin, when something at the roof edge made both of them look up.

The dragon king was climbing the steps to the terrace. His shirtsleeves were rolled to his elbows and his curls were a mess, catching the sunlight. He looked as if their fighting had woken him, and he'd come to chase them back to bed.

"Perfect. An eyewitness." Asha smiled at Safire. "Now you can't deny it when I tell everyone I beat you into the dirt."

This time, Safire did shove her.

"Asha?" said Dax. "Can you give Safire and me a moment alone?"

Asha's smile disappeared. She glanced at Safire, who looked quickly away, toward the Rift mountains.

"It won't take long."

Grabbing both wasters, Asha dismissed herself. As she passed Safire, she said, "Come to the training grounds before you leave for the scrublands."

Safire nodded.

In the quiet that followed her departure, Dax came to join his former commandant at the edge of the roof.

Safire looked down at her feet.

She and the king had barely exchanged five words since the day of their argument, when Dax stripped her of her title. Whenever they were alone together now, a stilted silence seemed to wedge itself between them. Safire had been keeping her distance, trying to escape it.

"I think we should talk about what happened in the Star Isles."

Safire hugged herself, staring out over the city. "Really, Dax, there's no need. I'd rather put it behind us."

"I owe you an apology," he said.

Safire glanced up, studying him. "What?"

It was Dax who looked away this time. "I should have trusted you. If I had . . ."

"You were in a horrible position, Dax. You did what you thought was necessary. I understand."

"No. It's more than that." He caught her gaze with his own. "Let me explain myself."

Safire nodded for him to go on.

"That first day in Axis, I saw the hope in Roa's eyes when Leandra gave her that seed. In that moment, I swore to do whatever was necessary to ensure those seeds were delivered to the scrublands. I couldn't fail them again. I couldn't fail *Roa* again. But my determination to not fail . . . it came with a cost. And that cost was you." He swallowed hard. "I've never been more ashamed of myself than when I didn't believe you. I should have trusted Eris because *you* trusted Eris. I've been trying to think of a way to make it up to you, but I'm not sure there is one. I failed you, and I'm sorry."

Safire stood there, speechless and staring.

"I'd like to restore you to your former position of commandant," he said. "If you still want it, that is."

Safire was about to say yes, of course she wanted it. Commanding the king's army, training his soldats, protecting him and the queen . . . it was what she was meant for.

She opened her mouth to say so, but something stopped her.

You haven't been yourself, Asha had said.

Was it because she was no longer Dax's commandant? Or was it something else? After all, Asha had proven she didn't need Safire anymore. She had Kozu, the First Dragon, to protect her. She had Torwin to stand at her back.

And Roa and Dax didn't really need Safire, either. They had each other, not to mention their loyal guards, as well as the full support of the kingdom.

Safire looked past Dax, out over the city below them.

Once, this was all she wanted: a life free from fear in the place she called home, and the ability to protect the ones she loved. Safire had spent her whole life wanting to belong in Firgaard, in the palace, with Asha and Dax. And while she knew she would always have a place here, would always be bound to her cousins by blood and friendship and love, she wondered, for the first time, if it was enough.

Or if her path lay elsewhere.

Because these past six weeks, Safire found herself longing for islands shrouded in mist. Found herself missing the sound of the sea. Found herself aching for a girl who'd once trailed her like a shadow through the palace halls.

"I do want it," said Safire, looking up at Dax. "But I think there's something else I want more. And the only way to know for sure is to go find it."

Dax's lips parted, but he must have seen in her eyes what she meant, because he smiled.

"Well then," he looked past her, toward the Rift. "Here's your chance."

Safire looked where he looked. An ivory-scaled dragon flew through the sky, coming down from the training grounds, his pale wings outstretched.

"Sorrow," murmured Safire, stepping closer to the edge of the roof.

It wasn't long before Sorrow flew overhead. Seeing Safire, the dragon dived for the roof she stood on. Safire and Dax ducked, getting out of his way as he hit, sending stones skittering as he batted his panicked wings. Sorrow nearly went straight over the edge of the rooftop terrace, found his balance, then turned back, his talons gripping that same edge.

Cities made him nervous, and he trembled ever so slightly as he stared at Safire through intense black eyes.

"You didn't go to him," said Dax. "So it seems he's come to you."

Safire stepped toward the dragon, pressing her palm to Sorrow's warm, scaly throat. At Safire's touch, Sorrow stopped trembling.

"I think," said Dax softly from behind them, "that maybe he's not the only one who's waiting for you."

Safire glanced to her cousin.

"Go," he said, smiling. "We'll be here when you need us."

Fifty-Two
SIX WEEKS LATER

In the weeks since she'd set the Shadow God free, Eris had learned that while it was difficult to weave without a hand, it was far from impossible.

She had acquired a hook that could be fastened to her wrist, and though it had taken some getting used to at first, and it sometimes hurt to wear, it was proving to be useful. She still needed help with things like getting dressed and cutting up her food, but she was getting used to this, too: depending on others.

In the beginning, her mother stayed with her, showing her what to do. Eris quickly learned that spinning souls was not so different from spinning wool, and once she felt confident to do the work on her own, her mother started rebuilding the scrin, then recruiting weavers and spinners and dyers to fill it. So there were always apprentices around to help Eris if she needed it.

Her life was so full of people now that she sometimes missed being alone.

◆◆◆

One morning, after a long and frustrating night of weaving, Eris threw down the shuttle and growled through her teeth. It had been a bad day. One in which she'd kept forgetting her right hand was gone.

It happened often, and the sensation was so strong, Eris could feel every finger and thumb as if they were still there. Like ghosts, they haunted her. And every time it happened, she'd have to realize all over again everything she'd lost.

Eris pushed the sorrow away and set down her threads. Leaning back from her loom, she stretched. Her back ached and her hand cramped and her vision was starting to blur from the dim light of the oil lamp. Looking out the windows of the scrin, she found the sun rising over the Star Isles, its golden light catching in the mist. But it was what lay beyond the mist that she wanted.

For eighteen years, while her mother sat in Leandra's prison, there was no one spinning souls into stars. As a result, there was a lot of catching up to do.

But the work would still be here come sundown. And Eris would be too—because she'd chosen this. She *wanted* this.

Right now, though, the sea was calling.

So, getting up from her bench, Eris descended the steps of the scrin's newly constructed mezzanine, where they'd rebuilt the Skyweaver's loom. Tiptoeing past the young apprentices, who were just beginning to rise from their beds and head down to breakfast, Eris escaped out the garden door. She walked through the meadow glistening with dew, watching the mist evaporate with the heat of the rising sun, then headed down to the scrin's wharf, tucked away in a quiet cove. A sailboat, used for deliveries, bobbed gently on the surf. When it wasn't in use, it belonged to Eris.

Just before stepping aboard, Eris felt a familiar prickle at the back of her neck. A gust of cold rushed down her spine, and she spun to find she wasn't alone.

Bloodred eyes burned into hers.

Eris's heart beat fast and hard. She stepped quickly back to find the summoner looming before her, its blue-black wings hiding its true form. She hid her hook behind her back—a habit she'd fallen into lately.

"What could Jemsin possibly want from me?" Eris growled, trying to sound fiercer than she felt.

"Jemsin's bones are at the bottom of the sea, Skyweaver."

"What?" she whispered, shocked by this news.

"That girl of yours, her friends lured him into the wrecking grounds," the summoner rasped. "His crew were eaten. His ship sank. Jemsin—nor I—will never bother you again."

Eris's hook fell back to her side.

"I thought you should know."

Eris swallowed, nodding. "Thank you," she said as the summoner melted into the shadows.

Alone, Eris paused, thinking of Jemsin. The man had been both rescuer and captor, and now he was dead. Had she already spun his soul into a star? The thought made her realize she bore him no hatred. Only wished him rest.

That girl of yours . . .

Just for a moment, Eris let herself look south across the Silver
Sea, thinking of Safire. She'd thought, weeks ago, that perhaps
Safire would stay. Instead, she said good-bye, boarded Dax's
ship, and returned to Firgaard.

Eris understood, of course. Safire's whole life was in Firgaard.

She'd thought about visiting her. She didn't need the doors
anymore. Eris could call up the mists herself and step right from
her tower into Safire's bedroom if she wanted. But every time
she longed to, she would look at the hook where her right hand
used to be and talk herself out of it.

Eris tried to put the girl with sapphire eyes out of mind as
she climbed into her boat. Unfurling the sails, she untied the
ropes from the wharf, then steered herself out into open waters.

Eris listened to the rise and fall of the sea's hushed breath. The
water was calm today. It would make for easy sailing from here
to the scrin.

With her hook curved around the wheel, Eris closed her
eyes. No more Jemsin. No more empress. No more hiding or
running away. With the wind in her hair and the salt on her
lips, her newfound freedom glowed within her. Making her
blood hum.

And then: a shadow passed overhead.

Eris opened her eyes. Looking up, she found a dragon flying
directly above her.

Suddenly, the beast dived, swooping lower to the water, falling in line with Eris's boat. On its back rode a girl whose face
was half-hidden in a scarf. The wind whipped her raven-black

hair and above the scarf, her eyes shone blue as sapphires.

"Where are you headed, sailor?"

Eris stared, not wanting to believe it. In case this was a dream.

Finally, she shook off her shock and shouted back: "I guess that depends on who's asking."

Eris thought she saw those blue eyes crinkle. And then, tired of keeping pace with such a slow craft, the dragon sped up, swooping in lazy circles around the ship.

"I'm wondering," the rider called out, "if you're still fond of princesses, or if you've changed your mind."

Eris bit down on a smile. "Princesses are fine." As the dragon swooped, Eris turned another circle, keeping it and its rider in her sight. "Though I prefer soldiers."

"What about a *former* soldier?"

Eris's heart skipped at that. "Why don't you come down here and we'll talk about it face-to-face?"

A moment later, the dragon was keeping pace with the boat again, soaring low, mindful of the sails. His rider patted his neck, saying something softly. As the dragon kept himself steady and close, Safire swung her leg over and jumped.

Her boots hit the deck and she rocked, throwing out her arms for balance. When she found it, she rose to her full height and pulled the sandskarf down from her face.

Her gaze went straight to the hook where Eris's hand used to be. Eris fought the urge to hide it behind her back.

Wanting to divert Safire's attention away from her missing hand, Eris nodded toward the wheel. "Want to try?"

Safire looked up, arching a brow. "Me? Steer a boat?"

"It might come in useful someday," said Eris, feeling strangely nervous. "When you turn pirate."

Safire shook her head, smiling, then stepped toward the wheel.

"All right," said Safire, her eyes guarded but bright. As if she were just as nervous as Eris. "Show me."

Carefully, Eris touched Safire's hip with the curve of her hook, guiding her in front, then showed her where to grip the smooth wood of the wheel.

Safire reached for it, but kept her hands too close together. So, very gently, Eris nudged them apart, pushing them into proper position.

"Like that," Eris said, standing close.

It was quiet for several heartbeats. After a long while, with her heart thudding against her ribs, Eris said, "What are you doing here?"

Safire turned then, abandoning the wheel, clearly not interested in sailing. Her eyes never wavered from Eris's face as she said, "I left something behind."

Above them, the dragon rose skyward, keeping watch. Around them, the sea had gone silent and still.

"Oh?" Eris swallowed. "And what's that?"

Safire stepped in close. Reaching for Eris's hook, she pressed it to her chest.

"My heart," she whispered, touching her forehead to Eris's.

And Eris thought: *This is home.*

No more running and hiding. This was where she belonged.

Acknowledgments

Heather Flaherty, for believing in these four fierce girls from the beginning.

Kristen Pettit, for always knowing what my stories need to level up. You are brilliant and kind and I'm forever indebted to you for turning me into an author. Thank you from the depths of my heart.

The team at HarperTeen, especially Elizabeth Lynch, Renée Cafiero, Allison Brown, Michelle Taormina, Audrey Diestelkamp, Bess Braswell, Olivia Russo, Martha Schwartz, and Vincent Cusenza.

Rachel Winterbottom, who saved one of Eris's hands *and* Dax's tender heart. Thank you for your ever wise and thoughtful feedback.

The whole team at Gollancz, but especially Stevie Finegan, Paul Stark, Cait Davies, Amy Davies, and Brendan Durkin.

Gemma Cooper—my lovely, savvy agent across the pond.

The team at HarperCollins Canada, especially Ashley

Posluns, Shamin Alli, and Maeve O'Regan.

Myrthe Spiteri and the crew at Blossom Books (with an extra special shout-out to Maria Postema).

Jenny Bent and the Bent Agency team.

My foreign agents, publishers, translators, and cover designers.

The good folks at Café Nymph (where so much of this book got written) for letting me sit and write for hours on end.

Hay Cove: for your kindness, generosity, and warm welcome (and for looking in on me when I was snowed in and alone . . . and then shoveling me out!). I wish everyone had neighbors as wonderful as you.

Words Worth Books, for being so supportive of me.

E. K. Johnston, who cried for two hours after finishing this book (or so she tells me). Kate: thank you for your friendship, your publishing advice, but most of all your bighearted and beautiful stories.

Alice Maguire, for reading this book all night while you rocked Charlie to sleep. (And for loving it the best of the three.) I admire you more than you know.

Asnake Dabala, for driving across the country, getting lost in Quebec, making maji maji, and helping renovate the house. I would never have gotten this book written without you, my brother.

The women who raised me: Shirley Cesar, Emily Cesar, Mary Dejonge, Nancy McLauchlin, and Sylvia Cesar. If my fierce girls ring true, it's because I was raised by the fiercest of women. You were (and are) the greatest role models a girl could ever hope for.

Mum, Dad, Jolene, and my entire family—for loving me, supporting me, and always being there for me.

Joe, for being the one I long to come home to every day, always. Thank you for fighting so hard for me this year.

Last of all: my readers, for your love and support. Seeing your smiling faces in my signing lines and reading your heartfelt messages is one of the best parts of this whole adventure. In so many ways these books are about finding your strength, and I wrote them because I believe this with my whole heart: that you, dear reader, are so much stronger than you think. I hope you find that strength within you. I hope you hone it, wield it, and use it for good.

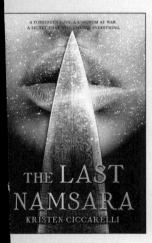

JOIN THE

Epic Reads
COMMUNITY

THE ULTIMATE YA DESTINATION

◀ **DISCOVER** ▶

your next favorite read

◀ **MEET** ▶

new authors to love

◀ **WIN** ▶

free books

◀ **SHARE** ▶

infographics, playlists, quizzes, and more

◀ **WATCH** ▶

the latest videos